THE MASSACRE OF INNOCENTS

The continuing voyages of HMS SURPRISE

ALAN LAWRENCE

'Amidst the rolling waves of oceans comes the lovely thought of you,
Through the soughing of the breezes and the sparkle of the dew,
In the shining light of morning and the blackness of the night,
Come wondrous recollections and dreams of past delight;
In the horror of bitter struggle when my heart is gripped with fear,
When my soul seems lost in darkness, blind and frantic, you are near;
Giving faith and courage to carry me o'er the steepe roaring sea,
In the bleakest of moments you shine bright in my memory,
Bringing rays of sunshine, my tired hopes restored anew,
I cast aside the darkness, and cherish the lovely thought of you.'

Caroline Byron

THE MASSACRE OF INNOCENTS
The continuing voyages of HMS SURPRISE

The isles of Greece, the Isles of Greece!
Where burning Sappho loved and sung,
Where grew the arts of war and peace,
Where Delos rose, and Phoebus sprung!
Eternal summer gilds them yet,
But all, except their sun, is set.

Lord Byron

A tale of the struggle for Greek independence by
ALAN LAWRENCE

Mainsail Voyages Press Ltd, Publishers,
Bideford, Devonshire

www.mainsailvoyagespress.com

THE MASSACRE OF INNOCENTS
The continuing voyages of HMS SURPRISE

This first edition is copyright (c) 2013 by Alan Lawrence.

Published by Mainsail Voyages Press Ltd, Hartland Forest Golf Club, Bideford, Devon, EX39 5RA. Alan Lawrence asserts the right to be identified as the author of this work in accordance with the Copyright, Designs and Patents Act 1988. The reader may note that this book is written by Alan Lawrence. It is not authorised, licensed or endorsed by Patrick O'Brian's family, agent, or publishers. There is no association with any of those parties.

ISBN 978-0-9576698-0-2

Typeset in Palatino Linotype 11 point.

Printed and bound by CPI Group (UK) Ltd, Croydon, CR0 4YY and Edwards Brothers Malloy, Ann Arbor, Michigan, 48104 (US).

Cover painting by Ivan Aivazovsky
'The Battle of Chesme at night'
Photograph courtesy of www.russianpaintings.net

The Reef Knot graphic in this book is courtesy of and copyright (c) United States Power Squadrons 2006

Huzza! Hodgson, we are going,
Our embargo's off at last
Favourable breezes blowing
Bend the canvass oer the mast,
From aloft the signal's streaming
Hark! the farewell gun is fired,
Women screeching, tars blaspheming,
Tell us that our time's expired
Here's a rascal
Come to task all
Prying from the custom-house;
Trunks unpacking
Cases cracking
Not a corner for a mouse
Scapes unsearched amid the racket,
Ere we sail on board the Packet.

Lord Byron: on leaving Falmouth in 1809.
Published posthumously in 1830.

THE MASSACRE OF INNOCENTS
The continuing voyages of HMS SURPRISE

A FOREWORD BY THE AUTHOR

This historical novel is founded upon the continuing voyages of *HMS Surprise* – not, please note, the 28-gun ship of 1796 in Patrick O'Brian's marvellous, fictional series (a ship design based on the captured French ship *Unité*), but the later 38-gun, Leda-class frigate of 1812 (also a design based on another captured French frigate, *Hebé*), as will be explained below. This latter *Surprise*, though a relatively young ship, lay at Plymouth Dock in 1822 about to be reduced to a prison hulk. In this story her fate takes its fictional turn for the better. Her sister ships, *Trincomalee* and *Unicorn,* to our good fortune, remain preserved in Hartlepool and Dundee respectively.

I fondly imagined for years that the many fans of Patrick O'Brian's seafaring tales of Jack Aubrey and Stephen Maturin sorely lamented, as did I, the end of his wonderful, utterly exceptional stories, and hugely missed those two warm and intensely fascinating individuals; characters always of the most engaging interest while possessed of the most human of personalities; for that surely was O'Brian's gift: Jack Aubrey and Stephen Maturin never resembled superheroes, rather in their warmth and fallibility they endeared themselves to us as any current personality might well do, and the gulf of two hundred years between their (fictional) lives and ours simply faded away. With no prospect (sadly) of any further historical novels from Patrick O'Brian, and missing his characters so much myself, I decided I must write a sequel, so as to bring them back, to enjoy their company all over again. After writing the first draft and by then in a dialogue with his estate, I was made aware of Patrick O'Brian's wish that no sequel to his series should be published, and hence a different course was subsequently plotted; the finished result being no longer a faithful reproduction of his ingredients but a book with different characters, though one which still draws its inspiration of colourful form and rich flavour from his genius.

For any novelist the writing of historical seafaring tales set in the early 19th century is to follow in the footsteps of and to strive for the literary heights reached by the author so appropriately described as *"the greatest historical novelist of all time"*. It most certainly represents a challenge of the very first order. Who would honestly conceive that there could be two writers of his ilk? Certainly not I, and so this book could never have become one that reads as if written by the master himself, and I make no claim of attaining his glorious pinnacle: it would plainly be an unrealistic aspiration. Consequently, the reader must be content with an historically detailed, seafaring tale of adventure; a story of battle and fascinating exchanges between all aboard ship; a tale which chronologically follows the enthralling Aubrey & Maturin novels, and hence a story which might well have been conceived by O'Brian had he been blessed with more time to continue his superb series.

The officers of the early nineteenth-century Royal Navy were drawn from every part of England, Scotland, Wales and Ireland (including the present Republic). It has been estimated that one in eight officers were Irish (though Catholics were not accepted) and that Scots represented a higher per capita ratio of officers to population origin than the Irish. The author therefore feels perfectly justified in enlisting a Scot as first lieutenant to serve alongside his Irish captain. Similarly, Scots were well represented as ships' surgeons in those times, and another has come aboard for this story.

This tale, a detailed and interwoven fabric of history and fiction, is set in the early nineteenth-century war of Greek independence. From the factual detail herein I hope that the reader may find his or her own interest in the history of that period stimulated to find out more, as I did. The subject matter of this novel, generally the war fought for the independence of Greece and the story of the Philhellenes, is seldom taught (except in Greece), and hence appears to be little known in any great detail outside the most narrow of academic interest. Yet it presents a most suitable subject for a work of historical naval fiction.

The conflict was a long one, but this story must necessarily restrict itself to a very few of the significant and the minor naval engagements, detailed references to many of which are singularly few and hard to find even in these days of the facility of the web. Conversely, there are numerous contemporary books and reports from the Philhellenes themselves, the ones by Gordon and by Finlay being remarkably detailed. Two more modern accounts are well worth reading: *That Greece Might be Free* (1972) by William St. Clair, an excellent book, and one which recounts the exploits of the Philhellenes of all nationalities; and the more general 2011 book by David Brewer, *The Greek War of Independence*. For an authentic description of life at sea in the early nineteenth century and battle in all its gruesome detail, it would be hard to surpass Roy Adkins' superb book, *Trafalgar*.

Adding to the treasure trove of actual events that the historical novelist is blessed with are the real people of those times, many of whom grace this book. It is particularly pleasing to develop this rich *mother lode* into brief but colourful appearances within the story, the places and timing of which, if not the actualité, accord with the known detail of their lives. Lord Byron is one such person, and the author has taken the liberty of including a few words (in Chapter 5, for 22nd November 1823) of simple yet sublime prose which Byron himself wrote within his journal for the 17th October 1823, describing his quietude in Cephalonia some weeks before he departed for his destiny in Missolonghi.

A selected verse of Byron's famous poem (within a poem) *The Isles of Greece* (within Canto III of *Don Juan)* precedes each chapter, the first verse being on the front title page. Lord Milton's stirring address to the formative London Greek Committee on 3rd May 1823 is similarly reproduced verbatim. The reader may also perceive the influence of that engaging wit Mark Twain gracing a few of these pages.

Notwithstanding that this is a work of fiction the author has strived for the inclusion of many real historical events throughout the story. It is little realised, for example, that the phrase *'truth is stranger than fiction'*, now in commonplace use, actually originated from Lord Byron. The capture of Byron's companion, Count Gamba, by the Turks, which is described in Chapter Six of this book, was a real event, and there surely cannot be anything stranger in fiction than the true tale of the Turk captain recognising his Greek captive counterpart, his own former rescuer, after an interval of fully fifteen years.

The historical researcher's task is made more difficult by the many and varied names which almost all the Greek, Turkish, and other locations referred to within this story have possessed: not only since the early nineteenth century when these events occurred, but from centuries beforehand as these lands and islands were within the grasp of a succession of colonial overlords, including Genoese, Venetians and Ottomans. For contemporary veracity many Greek places are referred to in this story principally by their then still widely used Venetian names, their Greek names generally only being used when mentioned by Greeks. These include, with today's name following:

Candia / Crete
Cape San Maria / Cape Mycale (Turkey)
Cerigo / Cythera
Cephalonia / Kefalonia
Colones / Pythagoras (Samos)
Leghorn / Livorno (Italy)
Modon / Methoni
The Morea / The Peloponnese
Nauplia / Nafplio
Scala Nova / Kusadasi (Turkey)
Thira / Santorini

The author would like to thank the following people, all experts of the first rate on their subjects, for their courteous and helpful assistance: Hugh Ferguson on Paganini, Peter Cochran on Lord Byron, and the immensely helpful and enthusiastic Elaine Vallianou on Kefalonia. Thanks are also due to: Edward Gaskell for encouragement in the early days, Don Fiander for consent to use the Reef Knot graphic, Ivan Gorshkov for the cover photograph, Paul Jones for help with the cover graphic design, Geoff Fisher at CPI for persevering throughout my many queries during the long gestation of this book, Jackie Taft for editing help; Anna Ravano, Anthony Gary Brown, and Larry Finch for valuable comments on the emerging book; Don Seltzer and Mark Myers - both invaluable - for considerable ship- and sail-handling guidance; a very helpful David Lilley, HMS Trincomalee shipwright; Kerry Webb for proof-reading and thought-provoking comment; Howard Piekarz at Edwards Brothers Malloy, my brother Geoff who long ago introduced me to the inspiring O'Brian novels; and my son Alastair in particular, who managed to prise me away from prevarication disguised as continuing research for this book with a wholly appropriate *'Just get on with it!'* Last, but far from least, heartfelt thanks are due to my love and greatest supporter, Sally.

Mr Mower's beautiful poem, at the beginning of this book, the recitation of which begins in Chapter Three and the complete poem in Chapter Four, was written by Sally's mother; the late, much loved and missed Caroline Byron: bless her. With just a very little of artist's license, the first and third verses of the song in Chapter Four are the author's modest adaptation of the traditional song *Mary of Dungloe*, an Irish song originally penned in 1936 by a Donegal stonemason, Pádraig Mac Cumhaill. The second verse is from *The Setting*, a marvellous song from Ralph McTell. The two songs are customarily performed melded together by that musical treasure of the south-west of England, *Show of Hands*.

At the end of the book there is a glossary of contemporary words occuring within the story with which the reader new to the naval historical world may be unfamiliar.

This book is dedicated to all those who have served in the Royal Navy, past and present: to whom, lest we forget, our debt is immeasurable.

Give you joy, shipmate! Come aboard: voyage with HMS Surprise; share her crew's reminiscences in familiar old haunts, and revel too in their exciting new adventures. Come aboard, swiftly now; there is not a moment to be lost!'

Alan Lawrence   April 2014

THE MASSACRE OF INNOCENTS
The continuing voyages of HMS SURPRISE

HISTORICAL NOTE

On the 24th of February 1582, Pope Gregory, by decree, determined that the Catholic world would abandon the Julian Calendar, introduced by Julius Caesar in 45BC, and change to the Gregorian Calendar after October 4th (of the Julian) when the date next day would be October 15th (of the Gregorian), ten days therefore being lost from that year's calendar. The two calendars differ only in the rule for leap years. The Julian has a leap year every fourth year while the Gregorian also has a leap year every fourth year except in century years not exactly divisible by 400. The Julian year therefore averages (over four years) 365 and one quarter days in length while the Gregorian year (averaged over 128 years) is 365 days exactly, and so after every 128 years (after 45BC) the date in the Julian calendar lags one further day behind the Gregorian.

Those regions of the early Americas, including lands now part of the United States and influenced by the colonising Catholic states of France and Spain, changed over in 1582 as per the Pope's edict, but the originally-British colonised States changed over when Britain did herself, in 1752, losing eleven days from that year's calendar. Greece however, not independent until 1829, did not make the change until as late as 1923. The reader of Greek history may therefore be presented with Julian dates differing from dates referred to by other sources using the Gregorian calendar, the same day having two dates twelve days apart. The sea battle off the Greek island of Samos, for example, is sometimes quoted as having happened on 5th/17th August 1824. The battle did not take thirteen days! The Julian (Greek history) date being 5th August and the Gregorian (British history) date being 17th August, which was the date on which the climax of the six-day battle was fought, it having started on the 12th.

Alan Lawrence   December 2013

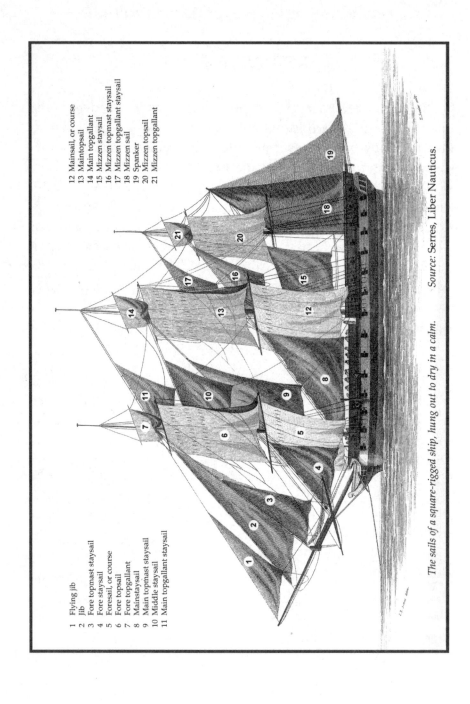

1   Flying jib
2   Jib
3   Fore topmast staysail
4   Fore staysail
5   Foresail, or course
6   Fore topsail
7   Fore topgallant
8   Mainsail
9   Main topmast staysail
10 Middle staysail
11 Main topgallant staysail

12 Mainsail, or course
13 Maintopsail
14 Main topgallant
15 Mizzen staysail
16 Mizzen topmast staysail
17 Mizzen topgallant staysail
18 Mizzen sail
19 Spanker
20 Mizzen topsail
21 Mizzen topgallant

The sails of a square-rigged ship, hung out to dry in a calm.   Source: Serres, Liber Nauticus.

Chapter One

The Scian and the Teian muse,
The hero's harp, the lover's lute,
Have found the fame your shores refuse;
Their place of birth alone is mute
To sounds which echo further west
Than your sires' 'Islands of the Blest'

Thursday 1ˢᵗ May 1823   Westminster, London

The public saloon of the Feathers tavern, off the Strand and within the Liberty of Westminster, a very dimly illuminated room even approaching the top of the day, was filled with the drifting smoke from Mrs O'Donnell's faltering efforts to rejuvenate the smouldering logs on the stone flags of the hearth; near to which, in a much creased, green leather armchair, sat a nondescript man of large stature and indeterminate age, dressed in even less determinate and somewhat crumpled attire, slumbering fitfully, coughing occasionally, but resisting persistently any inclination to fully wake or shift despite the rising clamour and bustle of the growing preparations for the customary midday clientele.

The Feathers tavern, being a particularly convenient and welcoming hostelry for visitors to the nearby grand offices of State, was also oft frequented by actors and publishers, as well as politicians of several inclinations and generally fewer principles, but the man between sleeping and waking states in the chair was not of that ilk. Lieutenant Duncan Macleod - albeit a relatively seldom visitor, having been in near all the past twenty years more often than not to be found on board one or other of His Majesty's ships – was almost a member of that extended family of genial hosts, headed by Mrs O'Donnell, who served the Feathers clientele so personally, and he was directly responsible for the presence at the Feathers of the two attractive young ladies, Sandra and Emma, his twin nieces from the isle of Lewis, now busily serving the food

1

the aroma of which appetisingly permeated the room. It was, however, the matronly presence of Mrs O'Donnell that tipped the scales in favour of waking; her optimistic if none too careful crashing deposit of a very large log sending the consequent explosion of sparks and crackling embers cascading out from the hearth towards the fireside armchair and its occupant.

'Ah, Mr Macleod: to be sure 'tis yourself, sir. A pleasure to see you this fine morning, indeed it is. Would you care at all for coffee?'

The nondescript figure looked up. 'Thank ye kindly, Mrs O'Donnell. A more welcome an' roborative beverage ah cannae think o' at present. The stronger the better, if ye will, an' perhaps a toasted muffin might be forthcomin'?'

'Yes, sir: which the pot and butter have been a'waitin' these five minutes past.'

'Here you are, sir, and why ain't you a'sleepin' in our best room?' from Mrs O'Donnell with the coffee pot and a huge plate of hot, buttered muffins a few minutes later, whilst fending off the keen interest of Sandra and Emma, neither of whom had previously realised it had been Macleod slumbering in the chair.

'Bless ye, Mrs O'Donnell. It was a long an' most exhaustin' journey these past foor days. An uncomfortable crossin' on the packet from Stornoway, a horse through the Hielands, a tirin' coach journey from Edinburgh, another post doon from Nottingham yesterday, an' so ah am brought here long past midnight. Being so very cold an' damp ah partook o' just a wee supper, grateful fer this fire, wi' a wee dram o' the malt, an' then ah fell asleep until just noo.'

Mrs O'Donnell, who knew the lieutenant well of old, had the shrewd conviction that he had eaten nothing at all for his supper, certainly no breakfast since, and that he had simply fallen asleep in his clothes whilst warming in front of the fire, and likely very soon after his arrival. 'I will send Sandra to air you a room, sir, d'reckly. Come along you two, leave the gentleman to his coffee, and see now to your duties. You can attend him later.'

'Thankee again, but ah must away at three o'clock fer a most important assignation. Ah will return this evenin', an' 'tis to be hoped Captain O'Connor will be here to join ma. Please prepare supper fer eight o'clock, Mrs O'Donnell: His Majesty's captains dinnae care to eat later.' The man in the chair yawned wide, smiled at Mrs O'Donnell, and relapsed into a contented doze.

In that awakening state between indistinct haze and sharp focus, his thoughts of hunger banished with some difficulty, a tired Lieutenant Duncan Macleod contemplated the events of the recent few days and the brief letter he had received with uncomprehending astonishment from no less illustrious a person than Lord Melville, First Lord of the Admiralty. It was exceedingly fortunate that the letter had reached him since for almost two weeks beforehand he had been contemplating leaving his Lewis croft, his half-pay of eighteen pounds fifteen shillings per quarter proving woefully inadequate to eke out even the most parsimonious existence on the windswept, bleak four acres of moor that represented his home on that northernmost Hebridean island. He had previously determined to accept the offer he had long held in abeyance – command of the tiniest of merchant vessels, a Buckie-built scaffie, plying her trade, fishing, around the outlying Hebridean islands - a position to which was attached the princely pay of seven pounds a month. Her retiring master had long ago submitted his retirement resignation to MacDonald of Stornoway, her long-time owner, and Macleod's departure so abruptly and unexpectedly presented after his initial and grateful acceptance of employment had met with the stony faces of men who held long memories in small places. Macleod's interests were, he had discovered, more than life on Lewis could offer him. He had concluded during his ruminations through a cold, wet winter, huddled and often shivering in front of a smoky hearth fire for its meagre warmth – his peat stocks being so damp – that his interests lay in a much broader spectrum. Although a keen participant in, and a proponent of, the traditional folk music of the Western Isles and of Scotland generally, and a Gaelic speaker, he held a passionate interest too in the sketching and painting of landscapes, a pastime he had been able to indulge himself in during many voyages throughout the Mediterranean and across all the oceans.

He now longed so dearly for the company of his shipmates of those long years serving in the Royal Navy during the testing times of struggle against the Corsican tyrant, his very good friends Captain Patrick O'Connor, a Galwayman; and Doctor Simon Ferguson, ship's surgeon, a fellow Scot who hailed from Mull.

For the four years from September 1815, after the end of the interminable strife to counter Napoleon, O'Connor had commanded, and the three friends had served aboard, *Tenedos*, a Chatham-built, 38-gun frigate of the Leda class. Post-war the Admiralty had designated Falmouth as her home port. After a summer in the Mediterranean in the year sixteen, she had patrolled on the South Atlantic station until the year nineteen when she had paid off from active service for the final time and went into ordinary at Chatham. The next two years Duncan Macleod had spent at O'Connor's fifteen-acre farm on the Atlantic coast near the village of Claddaghduff in Connemara, County Galway. After that first two years ashore the captain and lieutenant, the closest of companions, had gone their different ways: Macleod had returned to Lewis with his wife, O'Connor's sister-in-law, and his daughter to pick up the pieces of his neglected Hebridean croft; to draw and to paint, the wild and rugged landscapes of Harris and the Uists being his particular fascination. Pat O'Connor had remained on his small farm to try to scratch out a living on half-pay. Their other firm companion, Doctor Simon Ferguson, formerly surgeon aboard *Tenedos*, and also a Gaelic speaker, had returned to his adopted Plymouth Dock where employment was assured with a local doctor and fellow of the Royal College of Surgeons, Cornelius Tripe. The two medical men served the seafaring community founded on the Royal Navy base. Very little seafaring was now called for by their Lordships as post-war Admiralty budgets were severely trimmed, numerous ships decommissioned, experienced crews laid off, and many captains and even admirals pensioned off.

It was therefore with rising joy and great expectation that Macleod looked forward to meeting again with his close friend and captain of the Napoleonic war years, Melville hinting in his unexpected and mysterious letter that O'Connor would also be

4

summoned by the First Lord. Why, he asked himself, had he a lowly lieutenant received such a letter from Lord Melville, requesting his earliest attendance in London, and at Melville's home rather than at his office in the Admiralty? He had not the slightest clue to the purpose of the request. Though he had, in parallel with his duties as *Tenedos's* first lieutenant, sent periodic written reports on political developments and sentiments from some of the South Atlantic ports that *Tenedos* had visited to a longstanding friend at the Admiralty, never before had he received a communication from such exalted heights. The message had fortunately reached him by messenger on the final day of his preparation for departure from his tiny croft. His interest piqued, he had switched his journey to London rather than, as he had planned, to assume command of the forty-two feet, larch on oak-built, herring lugger, *Monica*; long past her prime, but sound enough at least to ply her trade, fishing, during the summer months around the waters of the Hebrides.

The fire in the hearth now blazed vigorously, the smoke had cleared, and the hubbub in the room had risen considerably as the number of patrons swelled. It was 3 p.m. and Macleod savoured the last of his coffee and determined to stroll slowly to Melville's house, to gainfully use the blessing of a warm and sunny spring day to contemplate his unexpected summons from professional Royal Navy retirement – as life on half-pay had long seemed. His old uniform had been in his sea-chest in his damp croft for four years, and so had been lost long ago to the mould: he consoled himself that, as his invitation was seemingly of an unofficial nature to Lord Melville's private residence and the First Lord not being a commissioned Royal Navy officer, he might be forgiven its absence. Throwing on his old, still damp cape and donning a nondescript and very weather-beaten even older hat Macleod left the Feathers and stepped out purposefully along the Strand towards his mysterious appointment.

What Macleod did not know was that his friend Captain Patrick O'Connor was strolling down the Strand a bare two hundred yards behind him. O'Connor, a man of modest height and stature with flame-red hair, had arrived in London early that morning, and had all the time in the world before his own appointment. He was immersed in pondering his recall from Connemara; summoned by his third cousin, George Canning, the Foreign Secretary; his presence in person also requested by Melville on the morrow. He walked west down the Strand, along the Mall, turned right into Constitution Hill, and thence along Brompton Road, down Cromwell Road, and so to Gloucester Lodge, a brisk walk of a pleasant hour and a half in the clement Spring weather.

'What's afoot?' O'Connor mused as he knocked twice and waited for the door to open.

The formally attired porter responded immediately, and forewarned of his arrival escorted him into the drawing room.

'Ah, O'Connor: how wonderful to see you again,' beamed Canning, a distinguished looking, immaculately attired gentleman in his early fifties, offering his outstretched hand.

'And yourself indeed it is too, sir,' rejoined O'Connor, smiling.

The distant relatives warmly shook hands and gazed for a few moments at each other. Their long-deceased fathers had been the firmest of friends for many years and second cousins. In but an instant, with just that hint of warm inflection in their voices, they achieved that cordiality customarily requiring of years of friendship – the Irishman from remote Connemara and the respected statesman who considered himself to be an Irishman born in London, his family hailing from County Londonderry.

'Come in, come in,' enthused Canning, and closed the door. 'Come upstairs to the library. Allow me to take your cape and hat. It is a rare day that I find I am here near alone. Mrs Malone is away to her sick daughter, and so there is only George the porter to attend us.' Settling into an armchair in front of the coal fire O'Connor was presented with a generous measure of fine old brandy before Canning sat in the other chair, gazing as if in inspection of his cousin, the sight so pleasurable after the long absence. Several minutes passed, both sipping their brandies, until finally he spoke, the warmth in his voice so very evident. 'Welcome, welcome, dear cousin. It is so good to see you again. When was the

6

last time? So long ago, it escapes me. Was it five years, perhaps six or even seven? I hope that you are keeping well.'

'Tolerably so, sir: and yourself? How is Mrs Canning?' O'Connor suppressed his curiosity whilst he keenly awaited Canning's expected revelations.

'Myself; alas, whilst the mind is as vigorous as ever, one laments that the body is less so with advancing years. But I am still in relatively fine fettle. Mrs Canning is well, thank you.'

'And my cousins?'

'You doubtless collect that George died but three years ago of the consumption: I grieve so much for him still. William is a lieutenant himself now; in His Majesty's service, aboard a frigate, *Venus*. Charles and Harriet are well, thank you. How are Sinéad and the children?'

Thursday 1ˢᵗ May 1823, 5 p.m.   *Arlington Street, Westminster*

In his office at home, an uncomfortable Lord Melville and a nervous Lieutenant Macleod had made their formal greetings and sat sipping tea, a grandfather clock ticking loudly in the background, each contemplating the other and passing a few moments in that expectant pause that frequently precedes the subject at hand. Eventually, the moment now pressing upon them, Melville, his considerations apparently satisfied, set down his own cup. 'Lieutenant Macleod, how do you do? My apologies for asking your presence here at such short notice; it is exceedingly good of you to come up from the Isles so swiftly. It is a matter of some urgency, and my letter was prompted by the Board, their Lordships making it plain that immediacy was to be the prime consideration. In fact, Macleod,' he said in a low, significant voice, 'this is also a matter of interest to the Foreign Secretary, who particularly desires that I tell him the results of this interview when we dine tonight.'

Macleod felt overwhelmed by the importance that Melville seemingly attached to his attendance, and could say nothing. He began to perspire, just a very little. His back itched unbearably, but he did not dare scratch it, and his heartbeat seemed to pulse through his every thought. The First Lord, sensing his visitor's

7

discomfort or perhaps his intimidation, continued in a more conversational, re-assuring tone. 'Doubtless you are wondering my purpose in requesting your presence. I thank you again for your swift attendance; most courteous of you, and such a long journey in but a very few days. You will collect it was your most commendable report to their Lordships in respect of the Tucumán declaration of the United Provinces in the year sixteen which engaged my personal interest in your, will I say, *irregular* services. May I say that your subsequent reports from the South Atlantic on the Falkland Islands developments were of the greatest of interest to me?' He looked closely at his visitor, 'Would you care for more tea?'

Macleod simply nodded; trying hard to avoid the appearance of simply staring at Melville, his mind whirring at he strived to think what conceivable further interest in him Melville might reveal.

'Perhaps, Macleod, we now have need of you again in a similar capacity. I will explain my letter. A most intriguing matter was recently expounded to me, one which only most slowly has His Majesty's Government come to consider as worthy of the wholehearted endeavours of the Royal Navy, and one for which I can perceive but two individuals suited to such aspirations: the first is Lord Cochrane, who has exhibited the most exemplary success in similar endeavours in the service of Chile; but any decision as to his present suitability must rest in the delicate deliberations of the highest political circles. I can say no more. You will be acquainted with the second, an individual well known to yourself. I am meeting with him tomorrow afternoon, yet I find myself uncomfortably reticent to postulate said matter to the officer in question in my capacity as First Lord, having only the slightest of personal acquaintance with the gentleman, and that many years ago. I find myself most uncomfortable indeed, and so my letter to you was ...' Melville paused briefly in his halting preamble as the servant entered with the teapot. He leafed through the file of papers on his desk for some minutes. After pouring the tea he pressed on in a somewhat uncertain tone whilst continuing to peruse the file. 'Perhaps I am grasping at straws, but no better person than you

8

yourself could guide me towards how best to broach a somewhat unusual proposition to your friend and brother officer. Yet, perhaps it may not be suited at the present time? He is a young man still. It may be too early in the career of ... of your friend, to merit consideration; but I am talking in irritating riddles, Macleod.'

'Not at all, sir: celerity is, ah find, nae always the friend o' discourse. Pray, take yer time,' said Macleod, cautiously; finding his tongue, and successfully concealing his growing curiosity.

Melville looked up from studying the file on his desk, his tone firming, 'Macleod, I understand from your official service record that you have served for many years with Captain Patrick O'Connor?'

'Why, aye indeed, sir: he is an officer ah have been most pleased to serve wi', indeed the very finest ah have e'er found, an' in so doin' we are noo become the firmest o' friends. Ah wid most dearly wish to depart to sea wi' him on the first tide o' the morrow, an' ah believe O'Connor himself wid share ma feelings aboot a ship agin, ma Lord,' Macleod nodded, as if in reinforcement of his affirmation, his mind striving to find the significance in Melville's words.

'Lieutenant Macleod; that is indeed warm testimony to your captain, and your service with Captain O'Connor was for fifteen years I note. Your own Royal Navy service record is quite unblemished, your conduct unassailable, your occasional... *covert* service to their Lordships of inestimable value; and I note too that with Captain O'Connor you have represented well their Lordships on more than one occasion when called upon for - will I say - matters more requiring of diplomacy, in some of our more far-flung outposts on the Imperial periphery. Indeed, Captain O'Connor has recommended and requested of their Lordships that your step be granted. I note that *Tenedos,* Captain O'Connor in command, with your good self, peaceably resolved that aggravating little spat five or so years ago with the American sealers on Saunders Island. There's many as have received their promotion for much less, Macleod. I will therefore add my own recommendation for your step, late as you may consider it to be.'

9

'Why, thankee... thankee sir; that is most gracious o' yer Lordship,' a pleased and surprised Macleod exclaimed his thanks, the meeting taking the most unexpected but welcome turn.

'Macleod, I will confide in you in this matter,' Melville lowered his voice to a whisper and pushed the file on his desk to one side, 'one on which I have recently been asked my opinion by the Foreign Secretary. Your colleague, it has been mooted, may be suited to a role which is but recently emerging. You will be familiar with the ... the quite *independent* service of Lord Cochrane, several years ago, in Chile, with the frigate *O'Higgins*. Their Lordships are considering whether such a similar scenario might arise in the near future, *the very near future*, and whether another officer suited to a venture of that nature, a suitable ship too, might be forthcoming. His Majesty's Government has observed the developing deterioration in the Ottoman provinces of Greece: that is our area of interest. Political interest is rising in all the states of Europe, most particularly *directly across the Channel*. Contingency planning it is, Macleod. Naturally His Majesty's Government cannot condone serving officers entering into such a venture, which would be quite contrary to the Foreign Enlistment Act, but retired officers and others quite outside His Majesty's Service would be perfectly and properly entitled to serve. It is plain that their Lordships cannot order any serving officer to such a post were they minded to do so, and hence I find this a most uncomfortable task indeed, and you are therefore to consider our discussion is not of an official nature. Hence, before my interview with Captain O'Connor on the morrow, when I intend to ask of his interest, I have asked you here to invite your opinion of his likely inclinations about such a proposal; entirely in confidence of course, and our private conversation, most unorthodox as it is, must never be revealed to any person.'

The First Lord now staring pointedly at him, self-evidently awaiting his reponse, Macleod, striving to grasp the complex extent of what Melville had asked him, and feeling well out of his depth, was sparked to reply. 'Sir, what ye say is of such import an' substance that ah cannae conceivably offer ma oon opinion o' the likely interest o' such a venture to O'Connor,' he replied cautiously, somewhat taken aback by the gravity of what he had just heard. 'From O'Connor's recent letters, which are o' course confidential, an' from which ah cannae quote exceptin' in only the most innocuous o' generalities, ah might conclude that life in Connemara with nae sea-going commission these past few years has nae sat well wi' him. He is a sailor through an' through, certainly nae farmer, an' so the economies o' the fleet lie hard wi' him. He is surely the most temperate o' men in his considerations, none more so, an' ah have nae doot that such a proposal wid receive the most patient reception.'

'It is pleasing to hear that O'Connor holds you in his confidence, and perhaps therein lies the opportunity to ascertain any likelihood of his interest in a scheme such as this,' said Melville, with less than complete conviction, though with his purpose now blindingly clear and his voice now as close to plaintive as ever it might be he pressed on. 'Would it not be too great an imposition, Macleod, to ask you to moot the idea, perhaps in the most cautious of terms; perhaps too to express the search, the requirement, for a senior naval officer, in terms of the third person. Would this allow O'Connor to avoid any answer which might be embarrassing to either of you?' His somewhat awkward request made, Melville relapsed into thoughtful silence, leaning back in his chair; he sipped the last of his tea, now cold; allowed his head to droop, as if to leave Macleod a moment to ponder, to collect his thoughts, the mood of the meeting seeming to slip into uncertainty as he glanced, surreptitiously, towards his visitor, awaiting his response, the significance of his request so very important.

Macleod, having gazed at his hands for several minutes, the clock ticking so slowly but loudly in the background even as his mind raced, looked directly at the First Lord. He so much did not wish to disappoint with his answer. 'Ah am, fortuitously, takin' supper wi' O'Connor this evenin', sir. Perhaps it might be a timely moment to expound upon the subject?' This said in a tone of some uncertainty, of caution, with as much commitment as he could summon.

Melville brightened. 'Capital, capital, Macleod: that would be most obliging of you. Then there is but one other matter to speak of, and I will be brief if you are to be at your abode ere dusk; it is near seven o'clock now. A new body of political interest has been formed: this Greek Committee is meeting on Saturday at noon at an inn in the Liberty of the Savoy, the Crown and Anchor, on the Strand. Should your discussion spark any interest with O'Connor, and failing any immediate arrangement with him, whilst you are both here in London it would seem to be an ideal moment to attend the Committee and gain a grasp of what these gentlemen are about: whether it be practical in substance or mere wind and hot air. Were you also to accompany O'Connor to Greece, reports from that place, with the proven veracity we came to expect of you from the South Atlantic, would be of the utmost value to their Lordships. It would serve them well were you to associate yourself with the emerging Greek authorities, to gain and report some cognisance of their naval officers and capabilities.'

'Sir, ah thank ye fer yer kind words an' yer pledge to support ma step. Ah will do all ah can to help ye. Ah find myself likely late fer supper already, sir, an' must away speedily ere the footpads an' ne'er do well loiterers in the vicinity are emboldened by the dusk. Ah thank ye fer sharin' yer confidences wi' me, and,' after a thoughtful pause, 'whilst ah cannae speak fer O'Connor, ah hope ah may see him supportin' yer proposal, an' ah believe ah may assure ye that we shall both attend the Committee,' Macleod volunteered, taking his cape and hat from the porter, a degree of normality returning to his thoughts, to the timbre of his voice, the interview coming to its close, his spirits bouyant, indeed soaring; his step assured - well, almost. In his wildest of dreams he could never have conceived the day this was proving to be.

'I bid you good day and please accept my thanks for your time and your earnest considerations,' said Melville, in the most cordial of tone, before the porter closed the door.

Macleod set off with a brisk step in order to overtake the approaching gloaming and in hope of reaching the Feathers in the last fading vestiges of daylight, his mind whirling in the most vivid maelstrom of thoughts and emotions.

12

At Gloucester Court George Canning continued his somewhat rambling briefing. 'It seems only yesterday that we were rid of Bonaparte and the prospects for more peaceable times were brightening: yet once again the French have crossed the Bidassoa and the Pyrenees into Spain – have they no shame? But even that, cousin, is not the reason for my murmurings as I will seek to reveal. No, much further away than Spain another spark has ignited and appears to be poised to burst into a flame which could have untold consequences for the interests of His Majesty's Government. Such consequences remain unpredictable, the magnitude of them uncertain, the likely celerity of the changes unknown, and yet it might have been reasonably foreseen that these changes have been long in coming and were surely destined to come about, notwithstanding the very substantial forces aligned to resist them.'

O'Connor, knowing his cousin well of old, and aware that any interjection would likely not be well received simply sat and listened as Canning continued in full flow. 'The Ottoman Empire, O'Connor, is creaking like an old and rusty hinge in need of oil. The Turks are under pressure from the Russians in respect of the Black Sea. Their Egyptian fiefdom is subservient in title but increasingly less so in practical matters of control, and their Greek subjects are revolting against the Turk yoke. The Turk economy has not been a success for some years and the Sultan has had recourse to print new money to fund his military apparatus, with the consequent debasement of the piastre, and so his credit is no longer considered sound in London. He can consequently ill afford to lose his Greek provinces. Even the Janissaries have revolted and been put down. As the frictions between Greek and Turk have been rising the Greeks have resorted to outright piracy in the Aegean; brigands abound in the mountainous terrain of all their territories, and only last year the most severe massacres of substantial island populations were perpetrated on behalf of the Sultan on the Greek island of Chios: reportedly tens of thousands of Christian women and children being taken away to slavery. Subsequently I have received reports of plague and pestilence arising from the unburied

13

bodies of countless victims of both sides. It was not, however, an event that stirred His Majesty's Government to interest, let alone action, until recently. The Treasury is, as ever, urging restraint in case of the slightest thing arising which might call upon the most severely depleted coffers. Since Bonaparte drained us so very nearly dry the government debt is in consequence now large, very large indeed. No, the government will not be stirred to remonstrate with the Porte, let alone move to anything more - will I say - *militaristic*,' Canning paused, as if in expectation of comment or question.

O'Connor simply nodded to his cousin, had no conceivable comment to offer, the subject so far removed from his interests, his purpose in coming to London, that he assumed it was simply his cousin's political conversation, and so he sipped his brandy in silence as Canning resumed. 'Castlereagh, Metternich and even the Tsar have been resolutely opposed to any support for the Greeks. The official French position is unclear and whilst they do favour some form of intervention this is concurrent with their stated belief in the inviolability of the Sultan's territorial integrity.'

'Sure 'tis a pity they don't have the same opinions about Spain,' murmured O'Connor quietly under his breath, recollecting the long years of blockade in the war, many months on station, tossed about at sea in leaking ships, in all weathers, and no prospect of leave.

Canning blinked, and continued in full flow. 'Unofficially, it is clear that France aspires to greater influence in any independent Greece as may come about and is covertly behind the scheme promoted by the Knights of Malta, who have offered a loan of ten millions of francs in return for the permanent sovereignty of Rhodes. His Majesty's Government has recently blocked their loan promotion in London. France is backing both horses in this race and has trained a modern army in Egypt for the Pasha; the Tsar, however, steadfastly ignores the injustices perpetrated against his co-religionists. Yet since the Sultan hanged the Patriarch of Constantinople from his cathedral gates, poor fellow, and the shocking massacre on Chios there is a deal of public opinion fomenting against the Turks, with a growing number demanding support of some nature for the Greeks, both here and in many

14

European populaces. Since August last year I have succeeded Castlereagh ...'

'A blackguard that none will miss, may he rot in hell,' thought O'Connor, his concentration drifting; his Irish republican sympathies now dim but never wholly forgotten, and Castlereagh a brutal suppressor of the United Irishmen. His attention returned to Canning's briefing.

'... as Foreign Secretary, and it is no secret now that I am sympathetic to the Greek cause. As I declared but three weeks ago, "when a whole nation revolts against its conqueror, the nation cannot be considered as piratical, but as a nation in a state of war". His Majesty's Government has since made our friendly relations with the Porte conditional upon a respect for their Christian subjects. Further, I have instructed Maitland, colonial governor in the Ionians, to deprive the Turks of resupply from those islands.'

O'Connor sipped again from his brandy, and wisely refrained from comment, perceiving his cousin not likely to welcome any interruption.

'Lately, as well as the Spanish Committee, there has been formed a self-styled London *Greek* Committee with a goodly leavening of Members of the House, perhaps a score or more of them. For the main comprising of Whigs, Radicals and Liberals but even some Tories: all postulating strong commitment and support for the Greek rebels; seeking supporters; proposing even to raise a loan for a provisional Greek government, though no doubt the more keenly mercenary proponents will have a vested pecuniary interest, as we will doubtless see in time. This committee also comprises military men and persons of some financial stature; there is even talk of enlisting Lord Byron to promote its interests.'

Canning paused once more as if to gather breath, to compose his further thoughts, and O'Connor interjected at last, his brandy exhausted, his patience ebbing like a tide as he politely endured his cousin's blather, for so it seemed, and his curiosity now insistent. 'It seems a near lifetime that I have spent fighting Boney's tyranny; for the most part afloat upon all the oceans and in His Majesty's ships and service. I abhor tyranny in all its guises, most particularly the

15

slavery which is practised by the most odious of regimes; the Ottoman empire is surely one, oppressing Greece, that precious font of civilisation, but pray, may I enquire why this has brought about your direct approach to myself, sir?'

'Yes, yes, cousin, I will return to that subject in but a moment; forgive my loquacious ramblings,' Canning, for the first time, sensing his cousin's impatience, 'which no doubt seem interminable and grow longer as I grow older, but as you will readily grasp, and as I will seek to explain, the essence of the matter is twofold: in the first part the Greeks are perceived by many of His Majesty's Government as brigands and pirates, and therefore unlikely to long forestall the Sultan's territorial recovery and consequent unpleasant retribution, at least without the assistance of more professional military officers to the Greeks being readily forthcoming. As to the second part, His Majesty's Government cannot and does not wish to be remarked assisting the Greek rebels.' Canning reached the crux of the official British dilemma.

'In what form then, may I ask, does His Majesty's Government envisage matters developing?' asked a puzzled O'Connor, in a low voice, staring at his cousin, his mind dimly beginning to perceive the possibility but groping to establish the nature of some indistinct connection with himself.

'There are already a number of – will I use that rather indelicate term for want of another – *mercenaries* assisting the Greeks, including reputable former British officers. Latterly the Committee has enlisted a veteran fellow officer of yours from the war against Boney, a very able officer, Abney-Hastings, a proponent of some new kind of naval vessel. This *modus operandi* appears to offer the opportunity to His Majesty's Government to encourage limited and yet wholly deniable support; *covert* support. This has found favour with certain members of His Majesty's Government who are also aware – thanks to our Post Office friends in Abchurch Lane, who have intercepted and deciphered the letters from several consulates to their governments – that there is an emerging European sympathy for the cause of Greek independence. Old Mr Willes, a capital man, has never been defeated by their ciphers, and his son is an expert *par excellence* with the repair of broken seals. But I digress; I now find myself sympathetic to such aspirations, but this is far from the Government's official position, which is one of friendship with our ally the Ottomans. It has been discreetly mooted to myself very recently the possibility of a loan of an able British captain with appropriate experience, were I able to identify such a candidate officer. There is of course Lord Cochrane. The First Lord, when I pressed him, opined that: 'There could be no finer fighting officer for such a venture than Lord Cochrane.' However, their Lordships at the Admiralty have expressed certain reservations about his candidacy, which we need not go into.'

'I can only concur with his Lordship in that respect, sir, though I am no more than an occasional acquaintance of Lord Cochrane. Sure, we have met in passing when our ships shared the same port. I collect once enjoying dinner with him in Portsmouth, long after *Tenedos* had paid off, and later we exchanged the odd letter, one unemployed captain to another. Well, of course, he is in the Brazil now.' Curiosity now shrieked loud in Pat's mind.

'I believe that you are meeting Melville tomorrow to discuss your prospects of a ship, and that he expects you to attend him in his private house in the afternoon?' Canning resumed, his voice lifting.

'Why, yes, sir, that is the case. I hope that we may discuss my prospects for another command, however trifling they may be. I have long held hopes of a frigate, one of the new twenty-four pounder ships would suit. In my dreams I conceive of a ship-of-the-line, *ha ha*,' Pat joked. 'However, I must refrain from these fanciful notions until I speak with the First Lord on the morrow. Conceivably he may be more minded to speak of the Fencibles, or some receiving hulk. Either would be a bitter blow, to be sure.'

'O'Connor, dear cousin; some moments ago I mentioned Cochrane as suited to such an unusual venture. However, it would seem to me that there is a further candidate, another fine officer, one whose career I have followed at some distance – when time has permitted – whose occasional letters I have much appreciated, and so I conceive that he is perfectly suited to such a task.'

'Sir?' Pat's heart began to thump as he sensed the very purpose of the meeting was upon him, so loud he felt even his cousin must hear it.

'Why, Captain Patrick O'Connor himself.'

'I am most gratified, most honoured, honoured indeed by your opinion of me, sir,' Pat replied, his voice barely a whisper, and rising to his feet in some small state of shock, his brandy glass rattling as it settled on the table.

***

It was fast approaching nine o'clock and the sun beginning to fade when O'Connor reached the Feathers, his mind in turmoil. Macleod had arrived a half hour previously, and his mind too was spinning with the momentous matters which Melville had revealed.

'How best to raise such a delicate subject wi' O'Connor? Mercenary indeed! Yet perhaps Lord Cochrane's past Chilean venture was nae so very different?' pondered Macleod, the significance of the First Lord's request still pressing upon his mind.

No such hesitation subdued Pat's warm greeting for his friend. Upon entering the public bar of the Feathers he immediately encountered a pacing Duncan, who, smiling broadly, offered his hand even as Pat, with the same delight, disregarded it and seized Duncan in a fierce bear hug. 'Duncan! Is it you? Give you joy, dear friend. How are you? I hope Kathleen and Brodie are keeping well,' the questions poured from Pat's mind and lips as if in a swift stream whilst Duncan gasped for breath within his friend's firm embrace.

'Och, ah am glad to see ye too, Pat. Ah am well, very well, thankee. Kathleen an' Brodie are in fine fettle, though Brodie has been unwell this past winter. What o' Sinéad, what o' the bairns?'

Pat could hardly contain his enthusiasm for his old friend and his curiosity for news, 'All are well, thankee, and lamenting still your and Kathleen's departure, Brodie's too. What are you doing here, tell?'

Duncan hesitated for a moment, put his thoughts aside of his meeting with Melville for later before replying, 'Let us proceed

18

directly to supper an' wet the swab, there is plenty to talk aboot. Mrs O'Donnell has been a'fussin' this past half-hoor, an' we are to settle in the snug. Come, let us share a bottle or twae wi' oor news; so much to catch up. How long, pray, are ye here?'

'Why, 'tis but a brief visit; I am summoned by the First Lord. Likely I will be off to Ireland within a day or two. What of you?'

'Och, ah have spoken wi' Melville masel' this afternun. Ah will dootless be off to ma wee croft on Monday, if nae before.' Duncan spoke as casually as he could, not wishing to raise the burning matter of his meeting with Melville so immediately.

Pat was greatly taken aback, indeed astonished that Duncan, a mere lieutenant, would be meeting the First Lord; the day was proving to be the strangest ever he could recall, but he did not press his momentarily burning curiosity. He forced his thoughts back to the joyous reunion. 'Oh for you to come back to Connemara, to Claddaghduff with me; at least for a short spell. Sinéad would dearly love to see you, and we so much would enjoy walking the Twelve Bens together; it has been long in the planning,' said Pat, in hearty good spirits.

A little later, in the privacy and quietude of the snug Pat and Duncan sat together enjoying supper with several of the best bottles from Mrs O'Donnell's cellar, exchanging fond and memorable recollections of their time together aboard *Tenedos* and other vessels in His Majesty's Service: times and adventures which recounted for several hours, neither seemingly willing to let the slightest tidbit of bad news cloud their enjoyment of renewing a friendship built so solidly since a first meeting in Portsmouth in the year three. Subsequently, whilst serving on the brig-sloop *Starling* together, they had discovered their mutual interest in playing musical instruments – the cello and playing of Irish traditional music was a passion of Pat's, and the flageolet or pennywhistle, that delightful feature of Gaelic music, in Duncan's case. It was a pastime which had proved so valuable in cementing their comradeship during many difficult voyages and hardships across all the oceans.

Time passed until, food all consumed, wine near gone, and reminiscences temporarily exhausted, they remained silent for a few minutes, each contemplating the other. It was Duncan who broke the silence. 'Ye seem happy, brother. Dootless contented an' settled ashore after all oor long years at sea, ah fancy,' he observed, with great satisfaction.

'Oh, a landsman's life is not for me, Duncan: such tedium, to be sure. These days I oft collect our time serving together at sea, sixteen long years it was. Oh how I ache for a ship again. 'Tis a long time now since we fetched home to Chatham, and *Tenedos* paid off,' sighed Pat, his voice dropping, a shard of melancholy coming to his mind as he recalled his own pressing objective for his visit and the perhaps doubtful prospects for it, notwithstanding what his cousin had said, for in truth the significance remained unclear to him.

'An' is there nae some wee silver linin' in that dismal grey cloud, Pat: time ashore wi' Sinéad? Time wi' the bairns perhaps? Have ye nae enjoyed these past foor years?' said Duncan, striving for encouragement in his voice.

'Eh? Oh, most certainly, and I would never look into the mouth of a gift horse, even if it be long in the tooth. That is, no, that ain't what I meant, Duncan. These four years past with Sinéad have been the greatest of pleasures, though with the swabs less so; but of late my dreams shift to standing astride a deck; nor even a seventy-four, a tight little frigate with a crack crew would make me the happiest sailor that ever served. Lord, Duncan, I would be content with one of the horrible, leaky *Forty Thieves*, even the smallest brig. To be at sea again is now my dearest wish.' Pat stopped, his thoughts shifting from his own aspirations. He poured out the last of the wine and gazed at Duncan, the warmth of long years of firm friendship lighting his face, his deep affection exuded in his voice, 'And you, old friend; have you been happy in the Western Isles since you took your leave of us? You know you will always be welcome back. Sinéad misses you all so much.'

Duncan smiled and nodded. 'Ah grant ye Connemara is splendid an' nae so very different from the Isles, but Lewis is ma hame, Pat.'

'What news of Kathleen and Brodie? What report do you have for Sinéad who is anxious of her sister and niece, 'tis some months since the last letter?' Pat waved to a distant but attentive Mrs O'Donnell.

'Both are well, Pat, an' reside wi' me in ma wee croft since leaving Claddaghduff. 'Tis in some disrepair, ah grant, as a dwellin', an' lackin' a wee tad o' comfort, but we have spent there many happy days together. Kathleen, bein' another o' your Irish ilk, near fresh off the bog,' Macleod joked, 'she does nae find ma ascetic tastes too disagreeable, an' so 'tis a marriage that works tolerably well. We oft stride together o'er the Harris hills in companionable fashion, an' spend hoors at the hearth in the most cordial o' discourse. We have grown very much closer these past twae years, and ken each other noo so well. Brodie oft accompanies us on oor walks, an' we have a brace o' Shetlands to carry oor dunnage, the easel an' paints – in the main a pleasantly docile breed, as ye ken. Brodie is noo a much more confident wench. She speaks the Gaelic, a wee French too; even she is learnin' the Latin, such a cannie lassie she is. We have passed many occasions in Edinburgh too: such a splendid city, Pat, but noo all is up. Ah nae longer possess o' twenty puns, an' ah must return to sea wi' what employment that ah might find; ah had been near acceptin' MacDonald's offer o' his scaffie.'

'There you are, Mrs O'Donnell; a bottle of port if you will,' said Pat, pleasantly, beaming at his hostess, his attention swiftly returning to his friend. 'But you will all be most welcome again in Connemara, old friend. The twins have repented their objectionable treatment of Brodie, and now lament her leaving. Sinéad so dearly misses Kathleen, Murphy being no companion at all, and hardly ever to be found when needed, always frittering away his wages in beer. Like myself, this landsman's life sits ill with him, and I have had occasion to speak sharp these past months about his slacking off. The man is like a fish out of his depth, Duncan, quite unmanageable for Sinéad; yet the twins adore him. He can be both a pearl and a swine, and at the same time. Fergal and Caitlin, the swabs, become ever more a tribulation; sixteen going on twenty-six, spending all their time with the village lads, no efforts made for the household chores, daily routines hold no interest for them. They can cook neither a simple potato, nor even burgoo, and what am I to do about it? I can't fathom it at all: 'tis impossible to choose the proper course to steer?' This said with a sigh of deep resignation, Pat's spirits dropping momentarily.

'Och, ah am sure o' it, dear soul, yet persevere ye must. Kathleen an' Brodie are in Minorca at present, in Port Mahon: have been these past three weeks. Kathleen is an accomplished artist, as ye ken, an' Brodie has been unwell fer much o' the past winter; so terribly damp it is in the Isles; ah greatly fear that it may be the onset o' consumption, an' so they are enjoyin' the Mediterranean warmth, Kathleen paintin' whilst Brodie recuperates: fer the next few months at least; but what news o' Simon these past twae years?'

'Oh, he is still in Plymouth I believe, though I receive but scarce news from him: perhaps an occasional letter oft lamenting his long absence from his beloved Mull.'

After more enjoyable reminiscences had been shared, the port all consumed, and the relatively recent events of the past two years recounted again they settled to enjoy a pot of coffee, being their particular favourite, brought without bidding by Emma.

Pat's mood began to sink a little. 'The fleet is much reduced, Duncan, my cousin in Portsmouth reports: even those ships that remain are, in many cases, in such poor shape as could hardly put to sea in a breeze, let alone a storm. Many are unfit to sail, much of their timbers devoured by the worm; there is a want of crew, the Press now long gone; all ship's supplies are short, stores of foodstuffs rotten – if they have not been stolen by some dishonest quartermaster, capperbar is rife you know. Powder is lacking and often damp, anyways always insufficient for practice; ship's officers are frequently away, captains at Westminster more often than aboard ship; shipyards merely feign their restorations; port admirals fail on their promises; and over all this debacle their Lordships claim lack of funds to do more. 'Tis a pretty state of affairs: God help us were Boney to come back.'

Pat's reference in passing to the deceased Bonaparte had provided the opening for Duncan to introduce the subject still burning within his mind, Melville's request persisting though the wine and the convivial reminiscing of the long evening. 'Och; ah am fully persuaded of it. Ah dare say 'tis dismayin' to ye, an' but wee consolation that Boney will ne'er come back. But perhaps there is wan matter on which ah might seek yer opinion?' Duncan had been pondering for some time how best to broach such a delicate subject. 'Dootless ye collect oor times in the Aegean watters, pursuing French ships amongst the many isles.'

''Tis certain they will never be forgotten, Duncan, never in life,' rejoined Pat, staring across the table, a gleam rekindled in his eye despite the fatigue now beginning to settle upon him.

'It seems that troubles are afoot there once again, Pat. The Greeks are in rebellion agin their Turk masters, an' great bloodshed is being inflicted throughout the isles an' in the Morea; as ah imagine ye will have read in the press, an' nae doot heard o' even in the wilds' o' Connemara?'

'I have scarcely visited Dublin these past two years, and returned to London not at all since we dropped our anchor in Chatham. Save for a very occasional visit to Galway town I have never left Connemara, paid no attention to anything in London, or elsewhere, save my correspondence with their Lordships, and the farm of course,' replied Pat. 'Now that you mention of it, I do recall some talk about a new form of warship for Greece. Yes, it comes back to me now; a steam-driven vessel, by God, and we have one too: *Comet*, in service, and a second, *Lightning*, on the stocks. 'Tis sure they are the coming thing: I collect *Savannah* steamed across the Atlantic in the year nineteen in but twenty-four days, most assuredly a signal for what is yet to come.'

'Och, ah am nae engineer, Pat: little do ah ken aboot this emergin' form o' motion or the construction o' ships – such things are wholly outside ma experience – but o' wan thing ah am certain, progress is surely relentless in all o' oor activities an' certainly therefore as sure fer the propulsion o' ships.' Duncan was thinking now rather more nimbly as to the line that he might take with this particular subject. 'In fact, noo that ye mention such a device, ah do collect it was spoken o' only this afternun in a discussion ah had wi'

Lord Melville.' Duncan began to feel his way to surer ground, continuing 'His Lordship referred to a most interestin' dilemma which had arisen followin' the succession o' Castlereagh by Canning as Foreign Secretary, an' the emerging interest amongst the Whigs as well as the Radicals fer the cause o' an independent Greece, free o' Turk suzerainty, and wi' a generally Christian society, albeit o' the Orthodox persuasion. Apparently, a committee has recently been established to further this cause, to procure supplies an' funds, military provisions too, so as to aid the Greek liberation. That is where ah recall mention o' this new form o' ship; steam-driven, as ye say, and 'tis propounded by a former naval colleague, Abney-Hastings, an officer whom ah believe served wi' Lord Nelson at Trafalgar.'

Pat began to feel an emerging interest in Duncan's explanation and sloughed off his fatigue; his encyclopaedic mind in all matters naval recalled the name after but a moment. 'Abney-Hastings was a youngster, a volunteer, aboard *Neptune* at Trafalgar, aged but eleven; he later became a lieutenant and master of the survey vessel *Kangaroo* in Jamaica. I collect that he left the service after some disagreement with the flag-captain at Port Royal, who bawled him out publicly, for he had overlaid his cable; Captain Parker shouting from his deck that his ship handling was not seamanlike. Did not Abney-Hastings offer him out, and so was dismissed the service; Melville refusing to hear his case? A thoroughly shabby affair, it was.'

Duncan, sensing firmer ground for Melville's proposal, continued, 'Ah am sure ye are right, Pat, but we digress. Those Members of Parliament, an' others who have declared support fer the Greek cause, meet in committee at the Crown an' Anchor on the Strand this Saturday to procure able military an' naval officers to further the prospects fer the formative Greek government. Ah have heard mention o' Abney-Hastings in tha' respect, an' indeed also Cochrane.'

'Cochrane! Cochrane, the Sea Wolf, the Old Dog!' exclaimed Pat, his voice rising. 'Well I never; his name was mentioned to me only today: this Greek committee too. My cousin, Canning, was

24

sounding out my interest in some rum venture to Greek waters. I cannot fathom it, Duncan. Certainly Cochrane would be an excellent prize for the committee and the Greeks, but, as I collect, he was still in service for the Brazil when we quit the South Atlantic, and if my memory serves me well I believe that he continues in service there?'

Duncan was taken aback to find that Pat had already been introduced, to some degree, to the very same subject which he had been manouevring to broach for some hours, and he gazed with astonishment at Pat. A silent minute or more passed as he summoned, with difficulty, near-forgotten comments from a patchy recollection of a conversation with the Earl of Dundonald himself during dinner in South America several years previously. 'Dootless ye are well informed an' correct as to his whereabouts, as well as his continuing responsibilities, an' there can surely be nae certitude that the Earl would return in response to any call from their Lordships at the Admiralty; indeed, ah imagine that the friction wi' which the Earl engages still wi' ministers might well be prejudicial to just such a proposal.'

Pat nodded. 'Of course the Earl has lobbied hard these past years to secure his pardon and his knighthood restored in the face of the King's unwillingness to entertain his case. 'Tis surely unlikely that he could be persuaded by any pleas originating from anyone associated with His Majesty's Government. No, Cochrane will not do. And a further matter to be minded, Duncan, any serving British officer, myself included, is forbidden from engagement by the foreigner, surely narrowing the field considerably.'

This latter comment from Pat, being a fresh element in Duncan's exceedingly thin knowledge of the restrictions of the British state for its officers in foreign military servitude, stopped his tentative thoughts dead in their tracks until he recalled that any officer acting for the Greeks could not be a serving British officer in any event, as Melville had explained. The Foreign Secretary would only commit to participate in such an undertaking in support of Greece were the arrangement to have absolutely no overt link to His Majesty's Government whatsoever. Of what arrangement was

Melville possibly thinking when he referred to O'Connor? How could he suggest Pat become a participant when Pat was a serving captain of the Royal Navy? Deep fatigue began to overtake Duncan, and the continuation of a subject in which he was clearly foundering on the very limit of his experience was rapidly proving beyond him. Time to leave matters until the morrow, he thought.

'Ah cannae linger wi' ye longer, Pat. Ma bed beckons.'

Pat too, despite the more intriguing elements of their conversation, was flagging, and mindful of his appointment the next day with Lord Melville he resigned himself to his bed. Their eyes met as they rose from the table, and Pat reached for Duncan's hand. 'Good night, brother; 'tis so good to see you. I will surely sleep well tonight.'

'Guid nicht, auld friend,' Duncan nodded, returning Pat's unwavering grip.

Friday 2nd May 1823 Westminster, London

At nine o'clock in the morning, both had slept exceedingly well; Duncan and Pat were back in the parlour enjoying Mrs O'Donnell's breakfast. It was a meal that Pat particularly favoured over all others, whether ashore or at sea. In Connemara his breakfasts were prepared by his steward, Freeman, and were often just the simple sea-going dishes of burgoo or skillygalee, which meals were at the very limit of his steward's culinary abilities. Pat employed two men to serve him: Freeman, an ebony-black, former slave from West Africa, who was his butler and cook for Pat's simplest of meals; and Murphy, who had been Pat's servant and valet for as long as he could remember. Hailing from Galway Town, he had been serving on Pat's first command in Portsmouth in the year three, and had miraculously ingrained himself into Pat's life, the Galway connection perhaps one of the doubtful reasons he had persisted. Freeman had been liberated some six years previously when *Tenedos*, passing through the Caribbean, had stopped and impounded a Bristol slaver, running her cargo of misery long after the prohibition. Freeman and scores of others had been thrown over her side by her captain. Freeman had swum to *Tenedos* and hidden

26

away in the for'ard locker until the slave ship had departed, in fear of being shackled once again. The *Tenedos* crew, and later the officers, had all warmed to his gentle nature and good humour, Pat bestowing his new name upon him, and the crew teaching him his limited English. A reluctant Murphy had been ordered by Pat to take Freeman under his wing as assistant steward, and in this capacity he had excelled - to the point where Murphy, one of life's inveterate grumblers, had long ago become anxious about his own position. Freeman could not come close to Mrs O'Donnell's finest cooking except for his toad in a hole, the meal that Pat and Duncan generally shared for supper when at sea, the cooking of which had been taught him by Wilkins, Jack's personal cook aboard *Tenedos*.

Duncan; still wondering precisely what Canning might have said to his friend on the matter of service for Greece, determined upon a cautious exploration as he returned to the previous night's subject. 'Pat, ye will fergive me fer expoundin' last nicht upon political matters o' which ah ken noot, or at the most just a wee tait, but it crossed ma mind that perhaps Melville may have somethin' worthwhile to add to oor considerations. Indeed, his Lordship might conceivably offer some suggestions, which could be delivered to the Greek Committee on Saturday. Melville suggested ye may care to accompany ma, and we will find oot what these gentlemen are aboot?'

'Certainly: it is a matter of some interest to me, and I would be pleased to do so; though to be sure nothing worth tuppence e'er came out of any committee. Doubtless it will be stuffed with self-important, conceited windbags: parsimonious, niggardly, full of ignorance and hot air; with precious little sense, yet pressing all to endure their ill-considered, pompous blather. I will speak with Melville of the specific difficulty we identified. I am meeting him at his private house at two o'clock,' Pat replied, agreeably, pouring the coffee, the welcome smell of which was so invigorating.

Conversation passed by pleasantly enough for some hours, much of it a return to the subjects of the prior evening, no conclusions being reached in the prevailing background of fundamental uncertainty in the matter in hand - the potential for a

27

return to sea, until at one o'clock Pat O'Connor departed for his appointment with the First Lord. For Macleod it was his first opportunity to speak with his twin nieces, Sandra and Emma. Their mother, Macleod's sister, had died giving birth, and their father, a fisherman, had been lost at sea several years ago. Consequently, Duncan had brought them to London where they were assured of a warm abode and a friendly upbringing. The twins had become, during Duncan's absence at sea, quite beautiful, and also the most wonderful of cooks, turning out meals of a quality renowned throughout the Liberties of Westminster and the Savoy.

'Are ye happy ma bonnies?' ventured Macleod.

'Yes sir,' chorused the twins.

'Learnin' well yer writin'?'

'Yes sir,' trilled their reply.

'An' yer Gaelic?'

At that only a few giggles came back.

'Bless ye, weans,' said Macleod, delighted to see them happy.

* * *

As the St. James's clock struck 2 p.m. Pat O'Connor knocked on Lord Melville's door in Arlington Street. The servant led him into Melville's study where the First Lord, a man in his early fifties, but looking older in his rather dour tweed attire was seated behind his desk.

'Welcome, Captain O'Connor,' said Melville in a loud but cordial voice, rising and extending his hand to Pat with a genuine air of welcome. 'I am most pleased to see you. I hope I see you well. It has been some years, some long years indeed, since we last met.'

'Thank you kindly, my Lord,' Pat murmured; his throat dry in anticipation, he could say no more.

'Captain O'Connor, please be seated. May I offer you tea?' Lord Melville was indeed particularly pleased to greet his guest, and as his porter disappeared for the tea he bestowed his warmest smile, 'Thank you for your swift passage from far Galway; I am in your debt.'

'Not at all, my Lord,' Pat gathered his thoughts, swallowed

28

hard, and launched directly into his plea. 'I have been ashore these four years past, and am most solicitous of your interest in myself. To be sure I had begun to despair of ever going to sea again in His Majesty's service...' his mind began to race but the words would not come.

Pat's nervousness was plainly apparent to Melville, scores of officers had become tongue-tied in similar circumstances in every prior year in this office; his eyes widened as he immediately smiled and interjected to preclude any embarrassing pause developing, his voice maintaining a low, encouraging tone. 'O'Connor, pray take your time.' The servant returned with a tray. 'Will I pour you some tea?' asked the First Lord.

Pat, encouraged, looked Melville squarely in the face, nodded, and resumed, his voice rising with his confidence returning. 'Sir, my only sea time these past four years has been fishing aboard a Galway hooker. The smallest sloop would appeal greatly. I would happily return to the tedium of a blockade, were one in the offing, and even, dare I say it, a Revenue cutter begins to exhibit an appeal. I cannot stay longer on my farm without I forget which is the bow and which the stern. My Lord, if I may? Since I have been recalled from the South Atlantic I have sat cooling my heels in Connemara: my cousin in Portsmouth writes often of ships in fine fettle reduced to store hulks, and new ships off the stocks going straight into ordinary. Nine hundred dockyard men were laid off last year, my Lord; five hundred and fifty the year before: all very dismaying. I have sat like a stone these past four years and certainly gathered a great deal of moss. And when is it to end? Have I any prospect of ever returning to sea?'

Melville looked sternly at Pat for a few moments before replying. 'O'Connor, I wish to speak with you about a prospective command. I do not say that it is one which will suit your interests: that is for your consideration. You speak very plainly, and I understand you well, but you must collect the public purse has been exhausted these past ten years or more. Boney did more damage to the Treasury than ever he did to the Fleet; our resources are much down and tax is higher than ever before, yet we still lack for money; and now ministers are minded to reduce the naval estimates, and postulate that the navy will be adequately served with but forty-four ships: a quite preposterous notion, O'Connor, when one hundred might conceivably be no more than adequate. Many ships of the fleet are old and rotten with the worm, as I dare say you know; such ships cannot endure longer, and are fit only for scrapping, but new ships are also on the stocks. There is, for example, *Asia*, in build now at Bombay. Plentiful timber supplies there, and shipbuilders who do not charge an arm and a leg, and, furthermore, do not put back rotten timbers; there is *Hastings*, was built in Calcutta back in the year nineteen; there is *Unicorn*, in build now at Chatham; there's *Prince Regent* and *Britannia,* launched at Plymouth Dock, both first rates. I venture that these new vessels may not all be known in Galway, or indeed even in Portsmouth, but I do assure you that sound ships we have aplenty. Assuredly and regrettably many fewer ships than previously, and the economies forced upon us by the Treasury have no end in prospect.'

'No doubt, sir. May I beg you to speak of the particulars so far as they relate to me?' Pat asked, quietly, his curiosity overcoming his natural reticence in the presence of the First Lord, and he not greatly following Melville's train of explanation.

Melville frowned and stared closely at Pat's face, as if considering how best to continue, before resuming. 'I was speaking of economies, sir; economies. It is most unlikely that we will see the fleets of Boney's era afloat this year or next, nor for quite some time for that matter.' Pat did not dare to interrupt again, gratefully he sipped his tea. The First Lord rose from his chair and paced towards the window: he looked out for a long minute, as if gathering his thoughts, before turning around to contemplate his visitor. He gazed at Pat for a moment before his stern face at last broke into a slow smile as he resumed. 'O'Connor, I have the conviction that you do prize fortitude, and that you will not be shaken by disagreeable news, however bitter it may come.'

'I hope I can bear it, my Lord.'

'You may not know that when I became First Lord, there were one hundred and eighty-eight officers appointed admiral, though but few were serving with any squadron. Whilst there still remain nine officers appointed to fleet commands, these appointments have become, in the present lamentable diminution of the fleet, somewhat - will I say - hypothetical. It is far worse for captains. And as for lieutenants, well, I will say no more. You are to remember that whilst you are made post, you are – will I say – with little influence, and so can expect to be ashore these next few years, pending perhaps the unfortunate death of several or even a score or more of your fellow captains.'

'Most dismaying, my Lord, bitter news indeed,' was all a shocked Pat could mutter; his discomfit starkly plain, his voice and confidence draining away with the contemplation of unpleasant prospects, an ebb tide leaving exposed all its hidden detritus.

'There is one but one prospect for you, O'Connor,' Melville continued, his voice rising, its tone now more positive, 'I have been in discussion with the Foreign Secretary on a matter requiring of the utmost discretion. Canning has pressed me to expedite matters, and so I will speak candidly with you. Doubtless you are familiar with the events occurring in the Ottoman Greek provinces, which His Majesty's Government deeply laments: particularly as it represents an opportunity for the advancement of Russian – their Orthodox brethren – or even *French* interests in the region; interests which one might easily conceive as being not necessarily wholly coincidental with our own. O'Connor, a great number of Philhellenes, adventurers for the most part, have left for Greece these two years past, from many countries on the continent. These men have been ineffective, fighting and dying on land, and the survivors are now reportedly starving, bereft of any commissary. The Greeks have no regular forces, no artillery, and hence no prospect of reducing the Turk fortresses, which are all resupplied by sea. It has become plain to all professional military men, therefore, that thwarting Turk resupply by sea presents the most propitious means of assisting the Greeks. Substantial funds are being raised in certain circles to purchase proper ships of war for the provisional Greek government. Their Lordships are aware of intentions to procure a small fleet of steam-driven sloops or corvettes, and even heavy

31

frigates: ships which would not disgrace a post-captain, nor any admiral for that matter. For the moment the Greeks have only ships of such small size which can hardly stand against the Turks, were it not for the considerable ineptitude of the Turk officers and crew, yet stand the Greeks do, and they have achieved surprising victories. I am reliably informed that were the Greeks to be assisted by even the most modest of warships with competent officers then substantial success could well be achieved. In fact, even the smallest frigate, well founded and competently manned, would be perfectly capable of dealing heavy blows to the Turk fleet. Captain O'Connor, the Foreign Secretary has pressed me to find one or more officers of the measure and experience of such as yourself to join such a venture. However, such officers cannot be serving Royal Navy officers. Whilst some subterfuge may be necessary at the present time because of that, any officers on such a secondment, if I might use that term, would be highly regarded by their Lordships, by many Members of the House, and indeed by the country at large. Need I say more?'

'My Lord, pray tell me: am I to believe that you wish me to resign the Service? Sir ...' Pat, his mind in greater turmoil than he had ever experienced before, his blood pumping, his curiosity searing his every thought, tried vainly to interject, but the First Lord was once more in full flow.

'The Foreign Secretary did, as you doubtless collect, strive to preclude any French interest developing in the new South American states. He is similarly minded to do the same for any new Greek state. Canning is therefore inclined to do everything within his power to ensure His Majesty's amity for any emerging Greek government is recognised there by their nascent leaders. But assuredly, at this indeterminate stage of potential developments, we cannot be known to be a participant in the current turmoil. However, His Majesty's Government is not averse to the activities of Members of the House seeking to promote independence for Greece, and notes the emerging activities of the so-called London Greek Committee, and its efforts to procure competent military officers in the service of the provisional Greek government. Do you follow my drift O'Connor?' Melville, feeling Pat's self-evident exasperation, paused.

'My Lord, I have not been to sea these four years since fetching home to Chatham,' Pat seized his moment, his voice loud, all care cast aside, his indignation exploding. 'I had thought I am come here to discuss my next ship, or lack of one. Since arriving in town I find I hear little else but constant mention of the Greek war – Greece, the piddling periphery of the Porte's realm, and from all corners – and I confess I am astonished that I find it at the forefront of your own interest too. If I deduce rightly what your Lordship is suggesting, am I now to choose between my rank, with few prospects of active command, or resignation and serving with a country with no navy to speak of – save perhaps for a few fishing smacks? Am I next to command a sardine boat?' Pat spluttered, almost in disbelief that it was himself uttering such words to the First Lord, a being considered by Royal Navy officers to be higher than God in the celestial firmament.

Melville was taken aback, irked by Pat's candour, 'O'Connor, that is coming it a trifle high.'

'I beg your pardon, my Lord.' Pat's outburst exhausted, he sat back, his hand reaching to scratch his head, now drooping with some little embarrassment as his fervour cooled.

The First Lord continued in haste so as not to brook any further interruption, 'You will forgive me for perhaps not explaining matters as best I might. No, O'Connor, it is not suggested that you irrevocably discard your well-earned rank, far from it, and even your worst enemy would hardly deny what a well-earned rank it is, indeed. No, the Foreign Secretary has proposed a rather similar scheme to Cochrane's Chilean adventure, albeit different; actually *rather* different, on consideration; if I might explain?' Pat was speechless, and quite unable to interject as the First Lord continued. 'Certain senior persons in the Foreign Office have devised a scheme which, so they believe, would allow His Majesty's Government to deny any - will I say - *unorthodox* participation in such a venture, as I will seek to describe. You will be aware that we have far more post-captains than ships, and so for the majority of them a life

33

ashore on half-pay is all that they may reasonably contemplate. Some of them are politically well-connected; they have expressed their grievances most candidly: several resigning to take up *foreign* service. The Earl of Dundonald is a perfect example of such a process, O'Connor; well perhaps not a *perfect* example, but you will grasp the general notion. Indeed, in your own case, your service in the South Atlantic was considered somewhat unorthodox in certain circles. Yet in such unconventional arrangements, when notable success is achieved, at a convenient later time it would be churlish indeed to refuse reinstatement to post. In similar circumstances to this Greek venture one might easily conceive of such a possibility.'

At this last point of Melville's, Pat, recovering himself and suddenly realising the attractive prospect of a ship again, thawed very slightly. 'My Lord, I am sorry. I expressed myself badly. I see now that there is something in what you say. If I do not mistake you, your Lordship is suggesting having two bites of the cake and eating the cherry.'

'Exactly, O'Connor, quite so,' replied the First Lord after a momentary pause, and concealing well his inability to grasp the precise provenance of O'Connor's phrase. 'I am heartily sorry for your embarrassment. It would be extraordinary, indeed downright incredible, were a serving captain of the Royal Navy to enter service with a provisional government, and serve in command of no more of a fleet than a frigate and a collection of Greek brigs. His Majesty's Government could hardly expect to credibly deny any allegations of the Porte that such an arrangement was merely a convenient subterfuge to conceal their interest in such a venture. No, such an obvious provocation most certainly cannot be countenanced. Resignation, O'Connor, is plainly a necessity. I venture that this is all highly irregular, and quite beyond any scheme that their Lordships could conceive of, and could only come from a branch of service more familiar with subterfuge and deception, if you catch my drift. I will add that His Majesty's Government can suffer no record of any such arrangement to be made, were such a scheme to find favour with you. Of course, I will assure you of restoration to the List, and with no seniority lost upon your return.'

34

At last, Pat found a moment to speak, but he floundered as the words were still formulating in his mind. 'My Lord, you put the matter very well, and perhaps I was in haste earlier: the scheme has merit, no doubt. Sir, I am most sensible of this mark of confidence: it is most certainly an honour to be described in such terms, and to receive this opportunity; and it is such a welcome and unexpected prospect. To be sure, I find myself taken aback, with no wind in my sails, so to speak. You spoke of a frigate: what ship, sir, will you have me command?'

'Our requirement is for imminence, O'Connor, and so I find I have few choices left to me, the fleet now so much reduced. A frigate would suit our purpose tolerably well. I have considered of *Unicorn*: she is but recently launched at Chatham; though to equip and ready her for service will take several months at best, perhaps a year before she will swim... no, she will not do. Also at Chatham is *Shannon*. I collect you served on her if my memory serves me well. The yard believes it would require of at least four months to bring her out of ordinary, though I am minded she will follow you later. In similar condition at Portsmouth there is *Trincomalee:* she too would require of several more months to bring her to readiness. No, there is but one ship which appears to be eminently suitable, particularly in view of your former command, and which can be spared. Admiral Sir Alexander Cochrane from Plymouth Dock has informed me this past hour by messenger that down there in the south-west, within his province, he has this past month completed the refitting of a fifth rate, a frigate of 38 guns: much the same ship as your former *Tenedos,* eleven hundred tons; she is now fully seaworthy, and awaiting her crew. He tells me that she had been sent there from Milford Dockyard for hulking to a prison ship, but on inspection the shipwrights were amazed at her condition. She was one of the original class of Leda's, and built with the very best of oak, and so has survived both Boney and the worm. She is presently about to come out of ordinary and back to service. Ain't that the most amazing thing?'

'And what ship is she, sir?' Pat racked his brain to recall the names and whereabouts of the frigates in service and in ordinary.

'She is *HMS Surprise*, sister of your former *Tenedos*,' Melville pronounced, the gratification plain in his voice, as if announcing some naval victory to his premier.

'My Lord, at the first, I am greatly pleased to hear such a proposal,' Pat replied, the mystery resolved, deep satisfaction expressed in his own tone, his relief overflowing his every thought, 'and thankfully she is not one of her rotten, fir-built sisters. A fine ship she is, to be sure. I doubt I can further endure the tedium of life ashore, sitting idle on my Connemara farm – these past three years have not been kind for the potato crop – and a return to sea, and on a ship such as her, is the most welcome of prospects.'

'O'Connor, I have this on the most impeccable authority, I will not enlarge on that: you will be purchasing *HMS Surprise*, for she cannot credibly remain a Royal Navy ship.'

Pat had, thus far in the afternoon's interview, experienced a veritable assault on his mind, though he had since rebuilt his equilibrium, yet he reeled with this latest shock, leaving him speechless for a few moments until he spoke, his disbelief plain in his tone. 'It is a delightful thought, my Lord, though I could scarcely buy an Inishturk curragh. *A frigate...* it is far more than I could ever afford.'

Melville smiled in the realisation that he had not explained himself at all well. 'I beg your pardon, O'Connor; I have not made things plain. Whatever may be the cost of this venture, sufficient will be pledged from the secret fund for you to ostensibly pay for her and to bring all restorations about, and at best speed. Should you find my proposal of interest I will be most grateful if you could put in hand immediately such arrangements as you think necessary to bring *Surprise* to readiness, and in any yard that you care to choose. If you will be so kind as to do so then I will look forward to hearing from you with such progress reports as you can offer as her readying proceeds. I will await your decision.'

It had been some considerable minutes in which O'Connor had been striving to grasp the totality of Melville's incredible briefing, and he could not shake off his state of utter astonishment, amazement – nothing like it had he ever heard before. He could barely whisper his reply. 'Perhaps my Lord would allow me to contemplate your proposal for the very briefest of delay before reaching any decision? I find myself, unexpectedly, attending that same Greek Committee on Saturday, with Lieutenant Macleod. With your permission, sir, I intend to discuss this with Macleod after the committee meeting, and before reaching any conclusion. If your Lordship would graciously allow me a little more than twenty-four hours I will deliver my decision to you in person.'

'O'Connor, that is perfectly proper. I will be at the Admiralty tomorrow, and I will expect you at 5 p.m.,' pronounced the First Lord with some degree of relief, rather vaguely indicating the door. 'Thank you kindly and good day, I look forward to seeing you on the morrow,' Melville concluded, rising, and shaking Pat's hand as the porter entered to escort Pat out.

'Good day, my Lord,' was all that a stunned O'Connor could mutter, exiting the study.

The servant showed him out to the street. The walk back to the Feathers was slow, and Pat, wholly engrossed in his ruminations, was almost run over by a carriage and four on the Strand, leaping aside only at the shrill shout of the enraged driver.

* * *

It was approaching seven o'clock when a hungry Pat O'Connor arrived back at the Feathers, long after his customary supper time when at sea, although the thought had not crossed his pre-occupied mind in the slightest until the aromas of the public room restored his attention.

'Duncan, there you are! A glass with you, and perhaps then a bite of mutton,' to Macleod, seated again in his favourite armchair by the fire.

'Pat, will ye tell me aboot yer meetin'?' asked Duncan, setting his cup down and staring intently at his friend.

'I am all at sea. Yes, I must tell you of my meeting with the First Lord. I am dismasted, rudderless, quite brought by the lee. Where will I begin?' A clearly consternated Pat began to recount his meeting. 'It started well enough, Melville welcoming me; he was

37

pleased to see me, and that ain't happened afore, cordiality generally being in pretty short supply from all the First Lords I ever served. The pleasantries did not linger, and I began to see my prospects swiftly foundering until Melville offered me some rum command... *a privateer, indeed it was*. I could not believe my ears... and in *foreign* service! My heart churned over. The devil to that. Pray ask Mrs O'Donnell for a jug of ale, Duncan, a man could pass out in here, it is so damn hot. I had hoped, prayed, he would give me a frigate again, even were it to be in the West Indies, that festering, vile station of yellow pestilence. I would have snatched his hand off, I would have departed on the morning tide, but no, I am asked to resign... *resign*. I have been offered a letter-of-marque, a privateer. Brother, tell, have I ever laid myself athwart his hawse, fouled his cable? What have I done to deserve that? My mind is all ahoo since that moment.'

'Did ye decline his proposal?' The blunt question was asked in some trepidation, Duncan most anxious for the answer.

'Eh? I may seem a whit slow, Duncan, alongside you learned types, but it would never do to turn down the First Lord... to bite the mouth that feeds you; no, no, no, that ain't likely to ever secure you another command. That is a sure way to remain on the beach, half-pay forever, your card marked, there is no doubt... no doubt at all, and I could not countenance that. I said I would consider of his proposal. I am not committed, though to be sure a bird in the hand is surely worth two sitting on the fence. I am to meet with him again on Saturday.'

Long before Pat's return to the Feathers a grasp of the likely well-developed and close association between Canning and Melville had dawned on Duncan, as Canning's careful scheme had become clear. Much of what Pat had recounted therefore came as little surprise. 'A privateer, ye say; in whose service? Wid ah be far astray, Pat, in thinkin' o' Greece? They are in revolt agin the Turk.'

'Greece... yes. It has been a long time since we were in those waters, Duncan. Later, he mentioned a frigate, the sister of our old *Tenedos. HMS Surprise;* a fine ship she is, there is no doubt. It seems that she is now near restored... to be sold... *sold to me...* am I

38

dreaming, tell?' Pat shook his head, his dolorous face exhibiting his confusion.

'Pat, ah see noo that Melville is the instrument o' Canning, an' the scheme has been some time in the making. Ah consider that, Lord Cochrane aside, there cudnae ha' been many worthy candidates fer such a venture. Yet Cochrane is noo servin' in the Brazil, is still in bad odour wi' many at the Admiralty, and so ah cannae conceivably imagine why they would consider him undertakin' such a scheme? Ye are surely... there cannae be any doot... the man they seek.'

'Why, to be sure 'tis back to sea, Duncan. Admittedly in foreign service and in command of some disparate flotilla of small vessels, brigs most likely; anyways likely scarcely bigger than fishing smacks for the most part, and Greeks too. But I will be restored to post and seniority at the end. How long is this enterprise likely to last? God's my life; will I be too old on my return to hoist Royal Navy colours ever again? Forgive me Duncan; I have yet to hear your considerations on this rum proposal: will you tell me your thoughts?'

'Och, ah will nae. Ah beg yer pardon, Pat, ma capacity in service wi' ye was as yer first. Little understandin' o' the Admiralty an' its workings do ah have, let alone the high political circles such that ye noo appear to find yoursel' in. There are days when ah flounder wi' a particular difficulty, a curious predicament perhaps, and ah feel as if ah am fresh from ma dear Lewis, just off the peat bog, but to be sure ma grasp o' the politic in this Greek business falls far, far short o' offerin' any opinion worthy o' more than a Brummagem farthin'. Let us, ah venture, attend tomorrow this Greek Committee, an' ponder further as we assemble oor thoughts,' suggested Duncan.

'Mrs O'Donnell!' Pat hailed, 'Can you find us a leg o' mutton and perhaps a brace o' ducks? 'Tis far past time for my supper.'

'The mutton, to be sure, yes sir, but we have no ducks. We do have a lovely side of venison, slow roasted with fresh herbs, and we have fresh soda bread, baked this past half hour,' volunteered Mrs O'Donnell.

'Capital, Mrs O'Donnell, the venison if you will; and please bring a pair of red, *first rate* bottles of red, burgundy perhaps,' urged Pat, as an emerging inkling of his customary good cheer ebbed back, 'and a fine plum pudding to finish if you will.'

'Yes, sir: d'reckly.'

Mrs O'Donnell hastened away.

The boiled leg of mutton was sublime; with hot buttered mashed turnips and carrots, served with caper sauce; the venison came roasted with young red onions, and was served with steaming bright yellow rice; and the supper finished with the sweetest, fruitiest, richest plum pudding Pat had ever eaten, with liberal sprinklings of cinnamon, and served with custard.

'A magnificent supper, Mrs O'Donnell, thank you kindly, and please be sure to pass these two shillings, one each, to Emma and Sandra,' insisted a now very happy Pat 'and a bottle of Port, Mrs O'Donnell, if you will.'

At 10 p.m., another bottle having followed the way of its fellow, and two pots of coffee having been finished, Pat peered at Duncan for a while, with an uncertain gaze and a furrowed brow, and rose to retire to his room.

'Duncan, a ship and a command again is a powerful sauce for a gander,' Pat steadied himself. 'Yet were I to return from Greek service and their Lordships not recall me to post, my goose would be quite roasted to a crisp.'

'Ne'er in life, dear soul, the public clamour fer the Greek cause will make a hero o' ye, and on yer return ah have nae doot that ye wid be restored to post,' Duncan ventured, a little more optimistically than he felt. 'Yer position wid be unassailable.'

Pat, standing now, paused, supporting himself upon the table edge, before speaking very softly to his old friend. 'Duncan, 'tis the long road we have trod together these past years since Portsmouth. All the world's oceans we have crossed, ships sunk under us, and good comrades lost aplenty. I oft think of many of them: in my dreams I speak with some of them still. Through all these years, in those black moments, I have been most sensible of your enduring friendship, most precious it be. Thank you kindly for what you have told me these two days past. I find I must now go directly to my bed.'

'Aye, pray sleep well Pat, an' guid nicht,' said Duncan, his own head drooping.

Schooner of 10 guns, firing at pursuer.　　　　*J.J. Baugean*

Chapter Two

The mountains look on Marathon —
And Marathon looks on the sea;
And musing there an hour alone,
I dream'd that Greece might still be free;
For standing on the Persians' grave,
I could not deem myself a slave.

Saturday 3ʳᵈ May 1823   *Westminster, London*

'Guid mornin', ma dear,' said Duncan to a still obviously tired Pat, as they settled for a late breakfast. 'Ye will forgive ma curiosity: a deplorable vice fer sure, but have ye considered further Lord Melville's proposal?'

'All night, Duncan; I have scarcely slept a wink considering the pros and cons. No prospects of hoisting any colours, no ship; Melville making it plain this tedious and thankless time ashore could endure for years. Should I enter into this Greek scheme indefinitely? If I do not, will I miss my tide? Should I leave Sinéad in Connemara alone for some years longer? And, were I to accept, what would she think? I don't speak the Greek. And are good men still to be found for a crew, officers too, to join me on such an enterprise? All my life I have been at sea, since I first put on long trousers. The sea is all I know. Four long years now with no ship: I had always thought of Fergal at sea with me, beginning the long road to become made post. I despair, Duncan, I do. I collect you are away directly to Stornoway; you will fly off, abandon me? Will you see me depart for Greece without you?'

'Ne'er in life, soul,' said Duncan, reaching for the bacon. 'Am ah nae tellin' ye fer ever tha' ah am always wi' ye?'

'I am heartily pleased to hear it,' Pat looked at his friend with glowing affection in his gaze.

'There is, to be sure, a tide in the affairs o' men, as the bard said, brother, and will ah deduce that ye conceive that yours has been at its ebb these twae years past, yet such a decision must be taken in the roond, wi' an honest acknowledgment o' all your circumstances: ah allude to yer family in that respect, Pat. Another egg, if ye wid pass that pan please. Is there a wee tint o' coffee left?'

'What a capital shipmate you are, Duncan,' Pat smiled, 'More than anything I have a hankering to return to sea, master of my own ship and with a crack crew serving. But, in Greek service? Is it the sensible thing to stay on the beach these years to come, awaiting a ship and my squadron? I wonder... am I beating about the wrong tree... ' Pat adding after a moment's hesitation, 'barking up the wrong bush?'

'Dinnae suppose ah am unaware o' yer eagerness to set foot aboard ship at the earliest possible moment, Pat. As yer friend ah must also be concerned wi' Sinéad's happiness. Ye will be a great way off, near twae thousand miles or more, and she is nae longer a young lassie. Yer presence at the hearth will dootless weigh more wi' the lass than some escapade in foreign service, fer that is how she will see things. Ye may therefore consider how to reconcile the twae. D'ye suppose Sinéad might be persuaded, were she to accompany ye to some nearer place, some safe haven, oot o' peril, but wi' the prospect o' your company more frequently than she has previously found in these past years at sea?'

'You are very good, Duncan, and I am most sensible of your advice,' replied Pat, grasping at the straw.

'Ah collect that after the tyrant had finally been defeated the Congress o' Vienna established yet more o' His Majesty's far realm in that very location. A protectorate o' wee isles, if ma memory serves me, though precisely where they are ah cannae say. Perhaps an abode fer yer family might be established there, facilitatin' contact wi' a frequency we ne'er afore enjoyed?'

'I catch your drift, old friend; the Ionian isles - *a capital notion*, quite splendid, thankee. I will speak of it with Sinéad.'

As the twins cleared away after breakfast Mrs O'Donnell announced, in a whispering voice plainly filled with awe, 'Mr Canning is here to see you, sirs, if you are at leisure.'

George Canning had arrived, in evident good humour, beaming at Duncan and Pat. 'Macleod, it is a great pleasure to see you after all these years. It has been an age since, since ...'

'Indeed: since ten years at least. Captain O'Connor's visit to ye in the year twelve or perhaps it was thirteen. Och, thirteen it was, after *Shannon* took *Chesapeake*. How could ah forget? 'Tis a pleasure to see ye again, sir,' Duncan proffered his hand with undisguised warmth and cordiality, shaking Canning's hand vigorously.

'And you too,' Canning graciously replied before turning to his cousin. 'There is one thing, O'Connor: I have decided I will accompany Lieutenant Macleod to the Greek Committee this morning, and I will look upon it as a most particular favour were you to join us: it will surely prove most interesting.'

'You are very good, sir, I would like it of all things. Macleod has already suggested I might come along, and I will be most happy to join you. I am particularly interested in hearing of the prospects for new ships of war for the Greeks, which only yesterday were mentioned to me by the First Lord, and also the opportunity, perchance, to meet with one of the proponents of the new steam-driven ships. Not vessels with which I have been acquainted at all. One Abney-Hastings has been mentioned: a veteran of Lord Nelson's victory at Trafalgar, and it would be a particular pleasure were I to meet with him today.'

'Very good, O'Connor, let us be away; 'tis but a short walk,' said Canning, collecting his stick and hat.

In the growing warmth of another fine spring day, walking east through the bustle that was the Strand, it was just a few minutes to reach the Crown and Anchor, located on the corner of Arundel Street and almost opposite the church of St Clement Danes. At the door the meeting was signed 'along the corridor and up the stairs' to the first floor committee room. A hubbub of conversation filled the room from approaching thirty gentlemen including many MPs, largely Whigs, many of whom were known vaguely in passing to Pat from his occasional attendances as an Irish Member in the House.

'Ah, O'Connor, welcome to our small gathering,' from a not entirely unfamiliar person, hand proferred to Pat.

The uncharacteristically friendly greeting from Sir Francis Burdett, an outspoken Whig MP, surprised Pat. 'Ah, thank you kindly. Burdett, is it? Allow me to introduce Lieutenant Duncan Macleod, my particular friend,' Pat replied.

'Macleod: my pleasure, sir. Are you a Philhellene?' asked Burdett in a conversational tone.

'Ah am, sir, a friend o' freedom in every sphere,' Duncan replied cautiously.

'O'Connor, Burdett is a supporter of the Papists you may know, a particular friend of Cochrane too,' Canning volunteered, sensing Pat and Duncan's confusion, 'though he is also one of those promoters of wild ideas, like Tom Paine; revolutionary ideas, democracy and benevolence for all. Bah! Such puerile notions would doubtless lead us to a pretty state of affairs.'

'Och, he has sound qualities then,' remarked Duncan, the remark prompting raised eyebrows all round.

'What have we come to here, Whigs a'plenty and ne'er a Tory can I see? 'Tis a hotbed of Radicals,' said Canning, smiling.

'I am reliably informed that the Committee has at least one Tory, sir; the Reverend Thomas Hughes. Are you acquainted with the gentleman?' asked Burdett, pursing his lips.

'No sir,' Canning scowled.

'A thoroughly ghastly man: doubtless he has missed his true calling. I understand that he advocates the extermination of all the Turks in Greece: hardly the tolerably benevolent approach which we have come to expect from our - will I say - more enlightened clergy. Let us hope the Radicals might serve Greece better,' the hint of triumph plain in Burdett's voice.

'Macleod! What brings you here, how do you find yourself? Tolerably spry, I hope; so good to see you,' came a familiar voice from the nearby throng, a timely and welcome distraction to all. 'You remember of me?'

45

'Why to be sure, ma dear, ne'er forgotten. Pat, allow me to introduce John Lempriere, scholar an' long an acquaintance o' mine. Lempriere, Captain Patrick O'Connor,' Duncan brightened.

'Your servant, sir,' nodded Pat, respectfully.

Duncan was plainly relieved to find an attendee at the meeting who was not a politician, and gladly entered into a discussion with Lempriere about the classical ancient history of Greece. Meanwhile, Canning had disappeared into the far corner of the room and was engrossed in conversation with a trio of distinguished looking gentlemen. Pat had begun to feel a little detached from the gathering, political matters never holding great interest for him, and so he looked around rather hesitantly, as if to search for a fellow military man. Although his gaze fell upon one or two of conceivably military bearing he could not identify any.

Shortly after, nearing 1 p.m., there came a strident shout from the corner: 'Gentlemen, gentlemen: may I bid you all heartily welcome, and the meeting is about to convene. Please be seated, thank you.' The hubbub of conversation died as the assembly sat down, and the announcer resumed: 'Thank you for coming today to this meeting of the London Greek Committee. My name is Bowring and I am Secretary of this new body, which was formed only in March, so we are young in our standing and young in our achievements. However, our aspirations are strong, our support is growing, and we are determined to effect everything we can to support the worthy cause of freedom for the valiant Greeks, striving to shake off their Turk oppressors.' He paused to assess the murmured reception of his words before continuing. 'Today I have great pleasure in welcoming our esteemed new Chairman, and distinguished Member of the House who will give the address. Please welcome, gentlemen, Lord Milton.'

There was a polite ripple of applause, and Lord Milton stood up and began to speak, his voice a little stiff and formal: 'Thank you kindly, gentlemen. I am exceedingly honoured and pleased to be here today as Chairman of this most admirable cause: one which is truly worthy of the support of all parties of the House and all outside, as can be vouched today from your attendance.' While

46

looking round the room, he continued, his voice very low and serious. 'Through our efforts and those of our valiant soldiers and sailors we have seen off one tyrant, Bonaparte, and it is surely within our collective desire to help liberate Greece from another, the Porte.' There was a general murmur of assent from the room. 'Under the most disheartening circumstances the Greeks strive to achieve the independence they have long aspired to, but they are failing. To all friends of humanity and civilisation this insufferable Turk yoke presents intolerable anxiety. Throughout Europe societies have raised considerable sums to support our holy Christian brethren, yet in England little money thus far has been raised. And so it is to this committee and to all friends of the Greeks – formerly a free and enlightened people – that the obligation falls to make public appeal to provide support and funds for the Greeks to throw off the Ottoman tyranny. The Turks have signally failed to put down the early insurrection, and it is clear that the struggle can now end only with independence. It will doubtless be beneficial to England and the world that the Greeks establish a government in the Morea, and in that we will assist. We must also strive to help prevent further Turk butchery, as has taken place on Chios. This committee will henceforth seek the most effective means to do so. We will be seeking donations. We will be seeking also the assistance of military officers of Christian principle to help the Greeks. Gentlemen: your support is sorely needed. These endeavours will be communicated to the provisional Greek government after our next public meeting on the fifteenth of May. Thank you.'

There was warm, vigorous applause for the speech and many shouts of 'hear, hear him' as the formal meeting dissolved into numerous informal and voluble discussions which filled the room, the babble vibrant, busy, enthusiastic.

Canning reappeared at Pat's side. 'O'Connor, I regret I am unable to introduce you to Abney-Hastings. I am informed that he is at present in Hydra, in Greece, and in the service of the provisional government there. However, may I introduce, from the shipbuilder's company, Mr Daniel Brent, who will describe his proposed new ship?'

'Very pleased, sir: I have heard but little of this new steam propulsion and greatly aspire to know more,' said Pat, turning, and with a hearty handshake to Brent, a warm pleasure in his voice.

'If you please, Captain O'Connor, let us repair to the quietude of the saloon downstairs where we can speak further of it.'

'Most happy,' Pat replied.

They left together, engaged already in animated conversation.

'Will he support the idea, Macleod?' Canning asked, the tinge of nervousness, the apprehension and his uncertainty plain in his voice.

'Ah dare say he is turnin' o'er the situation in his mind. We have spoken of it at some length,' Duncan replied, striving to place confidence in his reply, 'and we will probably ken on the morrow, sir.'

'Macleod, how did you receive the address?' Burdett had returned and was standing alongside Duncan, leaning on his stick.

'Admirable words an' worthy sentiments, sir; 'tis to be hoped that such a campaign can be concluded rather more quickly than it took to put Bonaparte doon,' Duncan replied.

'Yes, indeed so,' said Burdett sharply, concealing well a sympathy for the early republican aspirations of Bonaparte's regime.

By now, it being after 4 p.m., Pat had cause to make haste in order to fulfil his promise to the First Lord, and he double-timed down the Strand, no carriage for hire to be had at all. His lack of fitness let him down after fifteen minutes, but he struggled on even as he gazed about him for a coach. It was fortunate that he was able to hail a Hackney carriage, and he urged the driver to haste. Pat was growing anxious as twenty minutes later, as 5 p.m. pealed from the church bells of St. Martin-in-the-Fields, the coach arrived at the Admiralty, to Pat's great relief. He gratefully pressed a half-crown, hastily retrieved from his pocket, into the coachman's hand, and hastened over the cobblestones into the Admiralty courtyard, and thence to the main waiting-room, at that time quite deserted save for a solitary porter. With a nod he passed through to the tiny room adjacent, termed by visiting captains immemorial 'the Bosun's Chair' and reserved for appointments solely with the First Lord. The room was warm despite the high ceiling. Though it was the height of summer the customary fire was lit and exhibited a warming cheer in a room in which generally the occupants sat nervously, awaiting their moment with their ultimate superior; moments which for many had been the make or break of their career. Pat did not sit down, rather he paced slowly up and down the room whilst glancing through the little window from which could be seen the Whitehall Arch. Anxiously he inspected his uniform coat, and brushed off two or three specks which caught his roving eye. He smoothed imaginary creases in his sleeves, his gaze then falling upon his shoes, which he briefly considered buffing with his handkerchief. He dismissed the thought, and gazed through the window, passers-by under the Arch catching his gaze though not his attention. He mused that he recognised one or two of the officers, though at that distance he could not be sure. His nerves were on edge. Had he come to the right decision? He could not waver with the First Lord. He was staring again through the window and started when the summons came; the porter's tone quiet, neutral, but not unfriendly.

'Captain O'Connor, sir, you are expected, and the First Lord will see you now.'

'Thankee, Tom, much obliged,' said Pat, his pulse raised instantly, smiling weakly to a familiar old face of many years service at the Admiralty, and a man who had known Pat since his days as a young lieutenant. With some anxiety he paced the corridor, following the porter, constraining his step behind Old Tom on the stairs, and so to Melville's office.

'Good evening, O'Connor, be seated if you please. Can I offer you tea? How has your day been? Did you find the Greek Committee of interest?' said the First Lord, coming straight to the point, a thin smile offered as he shook Pat's hand.

'I thank you most heartily, my Lord, tea would be most welcome.' The clerk disappeared. 'As to the Committee; they were all more in the political line than anyone I could be comfortable with; not a one a military man at all. I was but a bystander: no, I could never move in political circles, to be sure.'

'Pray, did you consider of my proposal?' Melville pressed, raising an eyebrow as Pat's hesitation, fleetingly passing through a mind flailing in some turmoil, showed plain in his face.

'My Lord,' said Pat, suppressing the nervous anxiety he felt, and speaking with as much authority as he could summon, 'I would give my hearth and home away today for a plum ship, one on any station of His Majesty's realm. It would give me joy to consider of anything which will float; even a receiving hulk begins to exhibit an attraction which I never would have conceived of. I have served their Lordships o'er all the oceans, and so to consider of a ship in some... some *foreign* service is something I have never been accustomed to. I have been quite despairing of ever going to sea again. My Lord, I have found these past three days particularly stirring; I have encountered my dearest friend, Lieutenant Macleod, after an absence of near two years; I have attended a committee formulating proposals for a fledgling new fleet; I have heard explained the mechanicals of the new steam propulsion, for ships only just now coming of age; I have reflected on the likelihood of several more years on the beach, which, my Lord, is not something I am sensible of; far from it, as you are aware. My absence from command, I reflect, gives me great concern; I have only this past day considered your Lordship's proposal for a return to sea... in foreign service... and giving up my cherished post.' Pat searched for the best way to explain his thoughts.

'Yes, yes, O'Connor, but does this, pray, lead you to any conclusion?' prompted Lord Melville with a hint of impatience in his smooth Scotch tone.

Pat stared, unblinking, at Melville for a moment, swallowed to clear his throat, uncommon dry it seemed, and made his commitment. 'Your Lordship will be pleased to know that I will be most happy and I have decided to accept your proposal,' the reply stated with a firm voice, the words coming as if from afar, even to Pat's own ears. He exhaled deeply with the release of tension, the pledge made.

50

'Well done, O'Connor. Excellent! Capital! I am most heartily pleased to hear it,' beamed Melville, rising to offer his hand.

'I have one question of the first significance, my Lord,' said Pat, quickly, sensing that the interview would be short.

'Please to continue, O'Connor.'

'I must necessarily require officers of the very first rate for this enterprise, and so I must be assured of your Lordship's commitment – your personal commitment, sir – to restore any that join me to the List when this venture is concluded.'

'Of course: on that you have my word, O'Connor,' Melville replied, unhesitatingly, and with some relief, shifting quickly to conclude the interview. 'Weel, I have an eight o'clock appointment with the Foreign Secretary himself, so away ye go now, 'til we meet again to make the necessary arrangements, and perhaps Lieutenant Macleod might join us next time? Good evening to you, O'Connor. Well done, and thankee.'

As they approached to shake hands Melville rang a little bell whilst edging Pat towards his inner door. Pat, his heart racing still, gulped down the remnant of his lukewarm tea, shook hands firmly with the First Lord, nodding as he replied, 'Your servant, my Lord.'

He was shown out by the longstanding porter, who handed Pat his hat and coat in the reception room downstairs. He looked hopefully at a not unhappy Pat, who paused in the hall, standing stock still, in reflection, the gravity of his commitment coming home to him. 'Something Bristol fashion, sir?' enquired Old Tom, gently. He knew almost every officer in the Navy; and by longstanding tradition was perfectly entitled to a tip if something had come up to the satisfaction of the visiting officer.

'Indeed, Tom, thankee,' whispered Pat absently, his mind whirling. He pressed the only coin he could find in his pocket, a long-forgotten two pound gold sovereign, into the porter's hovering hand. An astonished Old Tom rushed ahead to open the door for Pat, gabbling with gratitude.

'Thank you, thank you most kindly sir; obliged, thankee.'

But Pat was already marching across the cobbles, and deep in deliberation now that he was committed, as came the alarming thought, 'On my life, how am I to explain this to Sinéad?'

Pat and Duncan arrived by carriage in the late evening at Sinéad's aunt's Truro home, their temporary abode, and settled before the fire, a brace of fine port bestowing relaxing contentment upon them after their supper. They intended a speedy return to the Feathers and the Admiralty, planning only the briefest of interlude at Truro, and allowing for just enough time to alert Murphy to proceed with all haste to raise a crew for *Surprise* from former *Tenedos* crewmen, many of whom lived in Falmouth, and, with luck, for Pat to persuade Sinéad of the merits of the scheme. She had accompanied Pat from Connemara, her mind filled with trepidation at what she might find the purpose of Pat's invitation to be, her acerbic tongue exhibiting the greatest truculence, shrill and unceasing for the whole of a most uncomfortable journey; at least that was how it seemed to a subdued Pat, the Truro arrival coming not a minute too soon, his nerves at breaking point.

Pat, after some minutes of contemplation, lifted his gaze from the fire's flames and looked across to his longstanding friend. 'Duncan, I dare say Murphy will raise a good many men for *Surprise* in Falmouth these next few days, and doubtless enjoy his time spending my shillings, indeed my guineas, in the taverns: most likely in doubtful company; but we must go ourselves and recruit the best of our old shipmates. We cannot offer them any prizes since Boney has long gone and our American cousins no longer truckle with our commerce, but Falmouth has been hard hit since so many of our fleet was struck off and so many more laid up in ordinary. With commerce being so down these past few years 'tis sure we will have our pick of the best seamen.'

'There is nae doot, nae doot at all, brother,' murmured Duncan, most pleasantly surprised to find a glow of enthusiasm, lost since these four years past, rekindling deep within his heart.

'I must speak of this with Sinéad afore she hears of it from Murphy or anyone else,' this spoken with some slight anxiety.

'Gently, Pat. Given time to consider o' it dootless she will come roond, though ah beseech ye, please dinnae press her.'

Sinéad was no different from any other naval wife, accustomed to the lengthy absences of her husband at sea, but dearly enjoying his company during the interludes at home. After the unprecedented near four years of Pat being in Connemara it was all the more an unwelcome shock when Pat broke the news of his aspiration to go to sea again. Her reaction was one of the utmost vexation, followed by many hours of sobs: her contentment and accumulation of peaceful quietude in having Pat at home now proving so very fragile and temporary that it was more than she could cope with. She had made the journey from Connemara to Truro most uncomfortable for Pat, and now that a new commission seemed imminent her vexation knew no bounds. In vain did Duncan too consider how best he might help comfort Sinéad; pleas in support of Pat's career seeming wholly inappropriate given the proposed changes in Pat's circumstances.

'He has been offered a command, he is going to sea. Is such so very disagreeable to ye, ma dear?'

Sinéad's withering scowl gave him his answer, her reply scarcely necessary. 'I have endured many long years of his absence, Duncan. Until the year nineteen the twins did not know him. Our farm is now strewn with dross, mounds aplenty across all our fields, no precious metals have we ever found; our potato crop has failed these past three years: home, in Claddaghduff, is where we need him.'

'Ye spoke of dross, dear?' Duncan was puzzled; Pat had never mentioned such to him.

'Indeed, Duncan; vile promoters from Dublin it was. Gold aplenty assured. there was no doubt, so they said,' Sinéad's despairing reply.

At that an astonished Duncan, blinking, could find no words at all for some minutes. 'How little ah ken o' commerce,' his eventual and rather inadequate reply.

Later that day, Pat himself tried desperately to convince her to accept his looming return to sea. 'My dear Sinéad, for near two years I have fretted ashore, ne'er commanding more than a Galway hooker, my uniform collecting dust, all the officers and crew of *Tenedos* thrown on the beach. The fleet continues to be paid off; my dear friend Duncan will again be afar in Stornoway; my other, Simon Ferguson, I have ne'er seen these four years; the twins become ever more feckless; Murphy is more than ever a mumping nuisance; and even my horse tires of me. 'Tis a chance to be at sea again, with a ship, with Duncan, Simon perhaps, Murphy and the crew afloat once again. Full pay restored, and I don't ask better than that. It will surely make our life easier. My dear, the Ionian isles are a pleasant enough place for you and the twins to spend a summer.'

It was Pat's last plea, a quite desperate throw to recover a losing position, which was obviously the case as he readily saw; all this to a distinctly frosty Sinéad.

'No, Pat; I will not have this. The twins are in need of your presence, your guidance. The farm is failing, we have ne'er seen a potato crop worth tuppence these three summers gone, and I will not stay there without you for more years: I will not!' With that she dissolved into tears and refused Pat's embrace.

Despite Pat's most persuasive and heartfelt efforts, with Duncan maintaining a most diplomatic silence, it was an unexpected and wholly coincidental letter from Sinéad's sister, Kathleen, written and posted weeks before from Stornoway, that ultimately swayed her. The letter expounded on the prospects for the twins to travel, perhaps to visit her in Stornoway or further. She wrote of an imminent visit to Port Mahon, and suggested the twins might gain a little worldly experience; perhaps more rapidly mature in mutually reinforcing new and unfamiliar family surroundings; and yet stay close to and see more of their father, were he to accompany them. She urged Sinéad to embrace wider prospects for the twins in comparison with the recent years wholly spent in Connemara. In short, Kathleen had suggested that the twins would, in travel, grow up and out of their adolescence and their petty jealousies of Brodie, and would develop into the young adults that they so nearly had become. Sinéad could not deny these points, and at the end, after several days, had quite accepted them as the benevolent advice that she had become accustomed to hearing from her older sister.

After this changed conviction had finally been embraced by Sinéad, preparations for departure were adopted with a bustle and enthusiasm Pat could scarcely have imagined: copious orders being issued by the lady of the household, Sinéad's aunt Nora – a wealthy and greatly excited old woman – with letters to a myriad of local tradesmen: for clothing which Pat could hardly credit as suitable, but to which he made not a whisper of protest; and for foodstuffs by the wagon, ordered for delivery to Plymouth Dock, where *Surprise* was being slowly refitted. All despite Pat's attempted but wholly disregarded protests that a crew was yet to be found and there must be some doubt about how far the caulking had progressed, never mind the restoration of the hull's copper-plating.

'Ah congratulate ye, brother. Ne'er did ah think fer a moment that it wid be Kathleen that wid bring her roond,' said Duncan, delighted, satisfaction flowing throughout his very being.

'She had pressed me to consider of command of the old seventy-four, the Plymouth receiving-ship. Full pay assured - to be sure there's a great deal to be said for that - and all my nights ashore ... but 'tis no ship for a proper captain, Duncan, and I would surely be yellowed, in time. To be sure, we have the blessing this day,' murmured Pat quietly, great relief in his voice and coursing through his every fibre.

Wednesday 7ᵗʰ May 1823   *Truro, Cornwall*

It was with some relief mixed with great joy that Pat and Duncan mounted their horses early in the morning to ride down to Falmouth on a very fine spring day to assess the likely crew numbers to be engaged there. Not more than two hours of gentle riding brought them into the town where they had taken rooms for the night at James Wynn's Royal Hotel. Time enough during the day and on the morrow to interview applicants, of which Murphy had gleefully reported to Pat: 'Well, there is plenty enough, even were we a seventy-four.'

The port's population of ship owners and mariners generally had been much concerned in recent years by the speculation that the packet ships would transition from being private vessels to Royal Navy ones, and the recent April takeover of the service had only served to heighten such fears within all the Falmouth seafarers and merchants. The near neighbouring and long established port of Plymouth Dock hosted much of the Royal Navy, and hence the town's greatest fear would be losing the packet trade entirely to that place. The French war had meant the loss of any sure and significant opportunities for the few remaining local fishermen, leaving many to engage in smuggling. The Revenue watchpost on Pendennis Point was a successful deterrent, save when the weather in the Channel was inclement and no shore watcher could see the slightest movement through the fog or discover landings on nearby Maenporth Beach. Even so, the economy of the town was not prospering, the pilchard catches being so much down, and many seamen were idle for want of a job.

Pat had sent letters to several of his former officers, and whilst any replies had yet to arrive, let alone any of them actually reach Falmouth, he was determined to press on and personally engage the crew. The fame of Pat O'Connor as a fighting captain and *Tenedos* as a lucky ship was well known by all the locals: no crew member had ever returned without a sizeable purse from her cruises in the French war, and so there was no lack of volunteers to the call – which Murphy had spread throughout the popular and well patronised public houses of the town for several days, even diligently speaking at length over necessary refreshment, as he saw things, with several of the ladies of less certain repute to be found in them. Pat and Duncan therefore had the greatest difficulty passing through the thick crowd awaiting their arrival. The ostler at the Royal Hotel having taken their mounts, the two old friends walked down to the Fish Strand Quay, cheerfully recognising many familiar faces, and greeting with pleasure old hands, veterans of prior voyages, prime seamen by the score presenting themselves; both shaking so many hands that the flesh became sore and the bones ached. At the end of the quay; Pat, Duncan, and Murphy were astonished to see a most unexpected figure: a man of between forty and fifty, of medium but wiry stature, ill-dressed but radiating an energy, a joie de vivre, all about him; exuding a feeling of well-being which was captured and reciprocated by the excited, voluble throng of seamen in whose midst he stood. A gathering of old Tenedos's stood all about Doctor Simon Ferguson, boisterous and loud in their shouted exchanges.

'Simon!' shouted Pat as the same sense of joy spread through his every fibre, not having seen his close friend for four years. He quickened his step and gently pushed through the seamen; all of whom recognised their former captain and beamed and gabbled, with great joy in their hearts at this unexpected reunion.

'Greetings, brother,' smiled Simon, as the two embraced, arms about each other, no words of adequacy found in the immediacy and warmth of their reunion.

'Joy be with you, old friend,' said Pat after some moments, in great exuberance. 'It makes me so happy to see you.'

'*Ceud mìle fàilte*[(i)]' beamed Duncan, pumping Simon's hand even before he could extract himself from Pat's embrace.

'*Tapadh leat, ciamar a tha thu?*[(ii)]' was all that Simon could reply before Pat released him from his grip, and seized his hand immediately upon Duncan's release of it in his enthusiasm to perpetuate his greeting of his old friend.

'We will speak the Gaelic then. *Gabh mo leiscéal, Duncan! Ní fhaca mé le fada thu,*[(iii)]' Pat interjected.

'Ye have the Gaelic, Pat. Ah wid ne'er have thought it,' said Duncan, in mild surprise.

'Oh I speak it so little, perhaps with the villagers at Claddaghduff. A very few of them speak no English, and so it lingers there still, in the hamlets of the bog and on the islands. It is so very close to the tongue of the Western Isles, and I imagine that your Hebrideans would understand my neighbours. On *Tenedos* I would hear it occasionally spoken by some of the hands, the men of

[(i)] '*A hundred thousand welcomes*'   [(ii)] '*Thank you. How are you?*'
[(iii)] '*Excuse me, Duncan! Long time no see.*'

57

Clare and of Galway, sometimes speaking with our marines who hailed from the Uists - the dialects are tolerably close, and it would always bring a little cheer and remind me of home. We have a ship, a ship again, Simon; ain't that the wonderful news of the world?'

'Why certainly it is a capital development; there is no doubt, no doubt at all. I received your letter only yesterday, Pat, and came immediately. I had long ceased to contemplate going to sea again, and so your letter was welcome indeed.' Simon, smiling, pointed to his companion. 'Mr Tizard, ship's carpenter and a native of Falmouth, is here with me. He is a veteran of the old *Surprise,* and so shifted to this successor ship.'

'My duty and best respects sir; if you please. Stuart Tizard, carpenter; in the old *Surprise.*'

'A pleasure to meet you, Mr Tizard,' said Jack, proferring his hand, and shaking the carpenter's vigorously.

'Murphy!' exclaimed Simon, 'How are you keeping? Tolerably well, I hope?' He enthusiastically seized and pumped the steward's hand.

Murphy was revelling in his role bringing about the reunion of so many old shipmates, his gap-toothed smile never absent this day but usually seen only on the rarest of occasions. 'All fine and dandy, sorr, and you look spry if I may say so. Well, ain't it grand to be goin' back to a barky?' he beamed, the great pleasure so much evident in his face and in complete contrast to his customary bearing as a sour curmudgeon.

'Indeed it is, for sure,' replied Simon, the pleasant prospect becoming more real to him by the day.

'Well, the whole town is a'fired up, sorr, with the news; none better has been heard these five years past. I ne'er knew so many in Falmouth afore these few days: prime seamen aplenty all pressing me for news; old *Tenedos* lads and many others; wives too. Well, I was ne'er so popular with the ladies, yer honour.'

'Take no liberties, Murphy,' laughed Simon. 'The ship is a small place to share with any husband with a grudge. I collect you had a wife; in Pompey was it?'

'Well, only in the rovin' kind, sorr, if you know what I mean.'

'And was there one in Mahon too?' this asked quietly with a whiff of suspicion but none of reprobation in Simon's voice.

Murphy laughed. 'Well, I 'ad wives in Wapping Dock and Plymouth Dock as well, though only when we was in port, like.'

'Browster wives, all, Murphy; a crabbit auld laidron ye are,' said Duncan, alongside Simon, the exchange catching his ear.

'To be sure, there's a deal of sense outside your head, Murphy,' added Pat, smiling.

'Well, sorr, empty and cold is the house without a woman.'

Amongst the Falmouth seamen, Pat's reputation for his ship handling, his plentiful and profitable victories – tactically so well managed as to be won generally at very little cost to his own men – and his kindly and considerate crew management meant that *Tenedos* had always been filled with willing Falmouth hands, embarking not solely for financial gain but also in a spirit of adventure. The seamen were long accustomed to the often poor standards of food and accommodation aboard a fifth rate, but Pat O'Connor offered a harmonious regime without the starting or hazing customarily found on many Royal Navy vessels, and so, for the old *Tenedos* hands, the self-imposed mutual discipline of professional seamen was a great part of their keen interest in joining up again. As most of the old *Tenedos* crew were well known to Pat, Murphy had already, with the aid of a clerk, constituted the prospective crew list for approval. Pat spent the day meeting many of his former shipmates and others brought along by them; every prospective crew member vouched for by veteran shipmates until, by 8 p.m. when they stopped for supper, over one hundred and fifty had been interviewed – albeit very briefly in the case of those well known to Pat – and over one hundred and thirty men had been engaged; only the old and infirm being turned away in kindly fashion and with the most gentle words of reluctance. Simon Ferguson, meanwhile, was consulted by several old shipmates with minor ailments, and one or two with social diseases, which he was able to treat, having brought with him the basics of his medical chest in anticipation of just such a necessity.

By eight o'clock in the morning there was gathered a further queue of hopeful applicants to complete the crew of *Surprise;* all keen and filling the public room of the Royal Hotel to capacity, scores more outside; for the most part former shipmates from *Tenedos's* years in His Majesty's service, particularly from the more recent voyage to South American waters: more men even than had been present to welcome Pat on the quay the previous day. Pat, Simon, and Duncan, with Murphy, struggled through the loud gathering at the public bar to the street outside; the bar proving wholly inadequate in size for all the seamen gathered within and without, anxious in every case to know whether they could make the crew roster.

'I will tell you what, we will have no want of shipmates, Duncan, the line since this past hour is a hundred yards if an inch,' remarked Pat.

'There is a deal o' prime seamen like masel' wi' nae work since so many ships were paid off.'

'We will have no need of the Press then?' asked Simon.

'There ain't any Press anymore, Simon, all long gone these eight years. With so many men seeking a berth we shall have no need of any scrovies in our crew: we will have no froward troublemakers; we will take none but prime seamen, the pick of Falmouth's tars.'

Murphy, glorying in his role as recruiting sergeant, stepped up on a bench brought out to the quay, and, at Pat's nod, commenced calling out the roll of men in the line which had been prepared by the attendant clerk. 'Adams, Bailey, Bartlett, Benson, Bluett, Bolitho, Boscowen … Bower, Brompton …'

'Capital gunners,' said Pat, with a wide smile, recognising many old *Tenedos* hands. 'Welcome Boswell, welcome Brompton.'

'Thankee, sir,' the excited replies came back with huge grins.

Murphy resumed. 'Beer, Belker, Boulderson, Bown, Braithwaite, Browne, Bull, Carne, Clies, Collins, Corker, Courtney, Currie T, Currie W - Tom's younger brother, sorr.'

'Do you vouch for him, Tom?' demanded Pat of one of his oldest *Tenedos* veterans.

'Aye, your honour. He is right masterly on the yards, sir; a grand man to have aloft. He came d'reckly all the way from Pompey as soon as he heard you was recruiting.'

'I will take him, Tom. Murphy, enter young Currie as able, topman.'

'Aye, aye, sorr. Daniels...'

'Daniels! Welcome back,' shouted Pat to his captain of the maintop of long ago, 'Grand it is to see ye.'

'Thankee, sir,' came the cheerful reply.

'Dalby,' continued Murphy, shouting loud, trying to make himself heard above the general babble.

'There you are, Dalby. Welcome back!' shouted Pat, with just a shred more enthusiasm than he felt.

'An honour, sir,' bawled 'Clumsy' Dalby: probably Pat's most devoted crew member of many voyages, but a man with a fully deserved nickname. He looked very pleased to be acknowledged by his captain, and touched his knuckle to his forehead.

Murphy, the interruptions restoring his face to its customary scowl, tried again. 'Dillon, Dodd, Enys, Ferris, Foster, Fowler, Fox, Gilbert, Goodridge, Gott, Green, Fisher ...'

'Good to see you again, Fisher!' shouted Pat across the crowded street.

'Gear, Gray, Hancock, Harkett, Hemming, Hodgkin, Hartley, Hinks, Hinton, Horsey, Hyde, James...' Murphy struggled on.

Pat shouted across the throng to several of the old Tenedos's who customarily served two of his great guns. 'Abel James, William Horsey, home again to our new barky. We will be well with our guns now lads!' His greeting raised a great cheer.

'Jenner, Johns, Johnston, Kelly, Kelvin, Kitto, Knightley, Lake, Lemon, Lovell, Maclean...' Murphy pressed on at best speed.

Maclean pushed forward, 'Douglas Maclean, gunner and topman on our auld _Tenedos_, your honour. I hope I see ye well, sir?'

'For sure 'tis a pleasure to see ye, Maclean; that it is.'

'Marder, Millett, Mould, Mumford, Nankivel, Oakley, Pease, Pender, Pendlebury, Pennington N, Pennington P, Penrose,'

Murphy battled on, valiantly persevering for a full two hours, his voice cracking, his throat sore despite his plentiful swigs from a quart flagon of ale kept nearby, until the end of his list of more than one hundred and fifty names approached, with Pat greeting many more old shipmates with a kindly word or two. 'Robertson, Rowe, Richardson, Robilliard, Scott, Slate T, Slate J, Sly, Smith J, Smith P, Sturmey, Symes, Timmins, Trevenen, Tweedy, Vining, Vivian, Warehope, Wagstaff, Ward ...'

Pat shouted over the hubbub, 'Welcome, Mr Wagstaff; shipshape, I trust!'

'Prime, sir, thankee, sir,' came back the enthusiastic reply.

'Warden, Watson, Walford, Weston, Whitaker, White, Wilkes, Wilkins...'

'Wilkins! Grand to have you back,' shouted Pat, beaming, to his personal cook of *Tenedos* days. 'Praise the Lord, we will not have to count on Murphy for my dinner!' Wilkins smiled and touched his forehead as Pat laughed loud and long and Murphy scowled.

'Wood, Wright N, Wright R, Wyatt, Wynn, Yescombe, Young, Zabinski..., sorr, 'tis the last,' croaked Murphy with considerable relief, his voice beginning to fail him.

'Make your mark, here, Zabinski,' said Pat, amiably, to an old Tenedos, 'and welcome back.'

'Thankee, sir; a happy day this is, so it is; thankee, thankee.'

'There is no man here happier than me, Zabinski. Deeply pleased I am to see so many old shipmates. Will you wait on 'til we are finished here when I have a few words to say to all our lads?'

'Aye sir, for sure I will. We all will. Thankee, sir: thankee.'

The second long day had now passed with barely any pause. Early evening was near upon them by the time Pat had interviewed all one hundred and fifty candidates to select the hundred and ten or so needed to make up his crew of some two hundred and forty men in all, plus officers and warrant officers. At the end he was very satisfied. 'Well done Murphy. Well done indeed; a capital job!' Pat then shouted across the street, 'Lads!' The hubbub faded and ceased. 'Lads, we cannot be sure of any prizes on this voyage,

Boney long being dead.' A great cheer arose, fading after a half minute. 'We will not start in the thick of any war... and our particular circumstances will be for us to discover... but I can assure you of timely wages...' Another huge cheer rose. '...good commons, safe lying...' Pat, his own throat dry, seized Murphy's flagon and took a deep draught. '...the companionship of a sound crew, kindly officers, and an adventure for sure. What say ye lads?'

The cheering resumed, tumultuous for several minutes, reverberating along the quay, the atmosphere of the gathering jubilant, all standing in the warm evening air, women staring out of all the opened quayside windows, waving, laughing. Very slowly the roar abated as Pat raised his hand, in happy acknowledgement, in joy, his face radiating happiness.

From the back of the crowd, from Wright, a very stout former Tenedos and a prime gunner who Pat had been particularly pleased to re-enlist there came a loud shout of 'Off hats.'

The street filled again with resounding cheering, continuing for some moments, blissful to all present, until Pat slowly raised his hand again, and waited for the din to subsume. 'The bar is open this evening lads, on my purse for all the crew.'

This brought further cheers from the contented assembly, loud shouts of, 'Hurrah, hurrah, hear the Captain, hear him,' interspersed with scores of whistles; all shipmates, for that is what the gathering all now felt themselves to be, vigorously clapping; the cacophony only diminishing after several minutes when an obviously tired and emotionally moved Pat raised and waved his hat in salute to them all.

'Does it not lift your spirits mighty high, Simon, our old Tenedos's here again, a prime crew, not a landman amongst them, not a one. Almost all rated able, and the barky being readied for sea?'

'And we will have no hallions; we will have none of the sad gomerels inflicted upon us in *Tenedos* by the Press.'

'Is this not our happiest day for many a year, Duncan?'

'Ah wholly share yer sentiment, brother: nae brighter day e'er arose in all ma time in the Isles.'

By 6 p.m. a very happy Pat prepared to leave for Truro with Duncan. An extra horse had been procured for Simon. Murphy, being no rider, was to settle the bar account next day and follow on by coach.

'A prime set of lads, Duncan, prime. So many Falmouth men are competent sailors, and many of them navigators too; we will not want for a good crew,' Pat said as they mounted their horses. The sun was sinking beyond the higher town behind them, quietude beginning to descend over the quay as the gulls settled for the night, the masts and rigging of the smaller ships tied alongside the quay still just illuminated by the sun's fading rays, dark shadows reached out from the walls of the buildings, the vapours now beginning to rise from the water into the cooling evening air, the more distant and larger ships in the Carrick Roads disappearing within the rising mists.

'Ne'er in doot, ma dear,' said Duncan, pleased to see the deep satisfaction so evident on his old friend's face.

Near two hours of wearying, slow riding brought the now deeply fatigued Pat, Duncan and Simon back to Truro where they sat in front of the blazing log fire, the later hours of the early spring evenings still cooling quickly. Within a short time they were delighted to enjoy their favourite supper of toad in a hole, prepared by Freeman, washed down with a bottle of excellent Madeira from the wonderful vintage of seventy-five, which Pat eked out from his travelling dunnage and brought out from his private cellar only on the most particular of occasions.

Pat explained recent events to Simon: the call from his cousin, Canning; his interview with the First Lord, and the offer of *Surprise* for the Greek venture. 'Tomorrow, I must away to Plymouth Dock and see what can be done to speed the refitting. Would you both care to join me?'

'I should like it of all things. Pray, is there much yet to be done, tell?' inquired Simon, who had not heard about the venture in any detail.

Pat set down his glass, and recounted the refit progress, the minutiae of it all so clear in his mind. 'The hull copper sheath fixing must be nearly finished by now. The rotten keel bolts may not all be out and replaced yet. New sailcloth has come but recently from Pompey, and the yard are making new mainsails and jibs. Some cordage is to be replaced, the rats having inflicted grave damage on it whilst she has been lying up, and there remains the decking to be recaulked in some few places. Some netting is very old and will need replacing ...'

Duncan interjected, 'Och, 'tis all in good hands at Plymouth Dock, nor any other place wid scarcely do better?'

'Oh yes, *Surprise* is in the best possible place, and in very good hands for her refit, dear friend, be assured of it. On the whole she is not far from being shipshape and all Bristol fashion. She is a prime ship, I dare say she may be the very finest fifth rate afloat. Perhaps another week or two,' Pat replied, with an undisguised tremor of growing enthusiasm in his voice.

'Ah am most heartily glad. What better prospects could we have, ma dear?' said Duncan, sharing his enthusiasm.

Pat resumed, 'The report I have received from the Master Attendant explains her state as she was and as she lies now. The yard in her refitting has installed strong cross bracing within the hull and even new knees where there has been any doubt of the originals.'

'She has knees then?' asked Simon.

Pat paused, as if deliberating on how best to reply to his old friend's plainly absurd question. He stared at him with sincere kindness, affection. 'Of course she has knees, have I never explained ships' structure to you afore?'

'Oh, I dare say you may have mentioned it.'

'Not above a score of times.'

Duncan replenished the glasses, and all sat back in utter contentment, the pleasure so much more in all being together for the first time in years.

'I have never doubted the Plymouth men. Though there be many rascallions in that yard, as I have found these four years, there can be no doubt at all of their abilities, none at all,' said

65

Simon, sipping his Madeira, the glow of satisfaction spreading within him.

Saturday 10ᵗʰ May 1823   *Plymouth Dock, Devon*

With the warm and fine spring weather persisting, Pat, Simon and Duncan had set off from Truro after a very early breakfast, all in good cheer, and ridden the Friday to Liskeard, resting there overnight; and riding through the bright morning at a gentle pace to reach the Hamoaze at noon the next day. With a rising sense of anticipation they stared across the grand, sheltered river where three seventy-fours and two frigates were anchored, gazing for long minutes in the bright sunshine to take in the satisfying sight of the familiar naval ships, something about them so reassuringly strong and substantial even as they remained stationary on the sparkling waters. They crossed over via the New Horse Ferry from Torpoint and walked the horses through the fort gates, passed by the barracks, and on to the Dock gate. They were directed along the length of the rope-houses, past the mast pond, and so to the waterside, the yard busy with many men moving all about it. Carefully they picked their way through timbers, ropes, and materials of all forms, strolling amidst the aroma of boiling hot tar, staring about them as if to drink in the pleasure of being amongst ships once again; stepping slowly a hundred paces further in their excitement, all the while staring everywhere about them; and so to *Surprise,* propped majestically on the slip; quite resplendent even though her masts were absent. They stared in silence for some minutes, each in private contemplation, the pleasure so very deep.

'Look, Duncan, Simon. Ain't she the prettiest sight of the world,' exclaimed Pat, eventually, the ship so significant, right in front of him, his thoughts formulating only slowly into his words.

'Och, there is a sure resemblance to oor auld *Tenedos*. She is practically indistinguishable ah find,' said Duncan, quietly, finding the moment so moving, a return to sea after long years now so imminent, so real.

'Magnificent: nothing finer could we behold,' Simon added, finding his own spirits soaring.

'Step carefully now, let us find the Master Shipwright, Edward Churchill. Simon, *mind that yard!*' shouted Pat when they moved off after some minutes towards the ship.

They went onboard to find Mr Churchill, a grizzled old man approaching seventy; still with a plethora of white hair, wrinkled hands, and the florid, wind-burnt face so customary to those engaged in outdoor working. He was inspecting the new deck caulking, and when they asked of the works he pronounced himself delighted with progress, declaring with immense enthusiasm, 'the ship's hull is as sound as the strongest bell', and having expertly assessed the bracing he deemed it 'as firm as the day it was installed'. In the preceding week he had scrutinised the keel on the slip with the utmost care, and so assured Pat that every single keel bolt had been changed so as to hold not the slightest doubt about the hull strength, even all seemingly sound bolts having been pulled out and replaced. 'To be sure, 'tis the iron of the bolts and the copper of the sheathing, and they don't get along. Best change 'em all whilst she is out of the water. She be good for at least another five years now,' he pronounced with unfaltering confidence. 'Her masts are in good order, and my lads will begin to refit them on the morrow. The sails will be ready next week; the new Riga cordage will be here come Monday, and fitted too by Friday - we will have no twice-laid, rotten rubbish. Just you be leaving us to it, Captain O'Connor, sir, and we will see all is finished, timely like, afore Whit.'

'That is very welcome news, Mr Churchill, and I thank you kindly for your progress thus far,' said Pat, gratefully, trying hard to keep his face turned towards Churchill, everything about the ship, *his* ship, demanding his eyes. 'Sir, 'tis our intention to be away to sea on the Tuesday after Whit, as doubtless we will find few crew happy to sail on the holiday.'

'No sir, neither will any of my lads be here in this yard 'til the Tuesday,' the Master Shipwright replied.

'Duncan, we will have to fetch a crew here afore Whit Monday to ready her for the passage to Falmouth, and that means at least forty men. We will use *Eleanor*; we can accommodate them aboard

Surprise as she will be off the slip and berthed in the water by then. It will be no bad thing to have them here by the Friday so as to check and tighten rigging, and to load some small stores and water. She will receive her full complement of stores from the Plymouth victuallers: we have none of significance in Falmouth,' said Pat.

Two hours later and satisfied that *Surprise* was in good hands and the refit proceeding admirably, Pat, Simon and Duncan left the yard for dinner, the horses resting and being fed at the yard's own stable. A pleasant stroll past the New Basin and the drydocks brought them to the Steam Packet public house.

'Have I acted in haste, Duncan? This new venture decided upon out of my own frustration, not being at sea these four years past?' asked Pat, pausing from a very welcome steak pie.

'Nae, ma dear, ah dinnae suppose ye have,' replied Duncan. 'It seems very much akin to Lord Cochrane's voyages fer Chile and ye are to consider we will be accompanied fer the most part of oor time by oor close friends an' family. What more could ye ask? Give ye joy with all ma heart.'

'I will be very happy. Thank you, Duncan,' said Pat, quietly.

Friday 16ᵗʰ May 1823   *Falmouth, Cornwall*

Early on the Friday morning before Whit, the sun emerging, weak and low in the sky, Pat, Duncan and Simon were at Falmouth with their dunnage already loaded aboard *Eleanor,* a Garmouth, Geddie-built, two-masted, topsail schooner belonging to Pat. Bought on Duncan's personal recommendation, and fast, even when sailing close-hauled; she had served as tender to *Tenedos* in her latter years under Pat's command. With *Eleanor's* small crew were a forty-strong nucleus of old *Tenedos* veterans, many of whom were members of the Wesleyans of Falmouth, an ecclesiastical movement, recent in origin but not the only one in the town, which was also home to many other nonconformist chapels. Men from most of these chapels had been represented in the crew of *Tenedos* on prior voyages.

Whilst the last of *Eleanor's* stores were loading, Simon engaged the master in conversation, a scrupulous man and a Wesleyan elder.

They sat on small kegs along the Custom House Quay, water butts for the boats. 'Mr Prosser, good morning to you; the crew seem to be in prodigious fine spirits this morning, very pleased to be serving again and with Captain O'Connor too, I venture?'

Jeremiah Prosser was old in comparison to the average seaman: a veteran of many voyages aboard *Tenedos*, his face and arms were burned brown by long years of exposure to the sun, deep wrinkles covered every visible area of his skin, his hands were large and muscular, yet from his eyes, still bright blue, shone an energy, a spirit, which radiated confidence to all aboard the ships in which he had served. 'Why to be sure, Doctor, there is no doubt. We have all of us given thanks to Our Lord every day in our chapel since Murphy brought news of the Captain returning and *Surprise* coming out of ordinary at Plymouth to go to sea again. These past four years have brought hard times to this town. After the French were beaten most of us were turned ashore: even our kin working away in far Pompey dockyards have been laid off, precious little work to be had, and our families all long since on short commons. Little or no fishing left anymore... no privateering anymore, no money hardly at all, and no brandy smuggling worth a candle this past year since them new Revenue cutters were built in Poole: very swift indeed they be, Doctor, and the rumour in the town which all have long feared was that the packets will all be handed over to the navy. No, we all gave praise to Our Lord when we heard that the barky was coming out again, to Falmouth, and the Captain seeking a crew for a year or two; 'tis a chance again for pay and to put some bread on the table.'

'Mr Prosser, did Murphy explain to you and the lads that this was not to be another surveying voyage? *Surprise* is no longer a Royal Navy ship, and we are to be privateers, mercenaries, in the service of the new Greece,' Simon enquired, cautiously.

The master's smile stretched all the way from one luxuriant sideburn to the other, unkempt sideburns being common to the Wesleyan seafarers of Falmouth. 'Oh, yes, sir, 'tis clear, and nobody cared, nobody cared at all. Even were we to be sailing agin the French, agin the Yankees, or even the Spanish, sir, just as long as we could get back to sea. The same pay as our brothers still serving on His Majesty's ships and the prospect of some prize monies as well: it seemed too good to be true. We thanked Our Lord.' There were nods all round from the hands coiling away *Eleanor's* cords, and Prosser continued. 'We all hurried to make our preparations, to tell our wives, mothers and fathers. Off to sea again, praise Our Lord and be thankful.'

'We are all thankful of that, Mr Prosser,' Simon said, warmly.

'When the Captain himself arrived, sir, it was all that many of us had hoped for, and for a very long time; and then *Eleanor* came into the harbour. When she came alongside the quay there were already more than a score of us to help tie her up, and a goodly cheer was raised when the job was done. Mr Reeve, her skipper, is a Falmouth lad, sir, born and bred. A grand day it was, indeed. Plentiful ale was drunk in the King's Arms later, and the chapel was full that evening, Doctor, I can tell you.'

'I am sure of it,' Simon replied, heartily pleased to hear of the good spirits pervading Pat's new crew.

At last *Eleanor* was ready; the tide was high, just past slack water, and she was set fair for the ebb current. Pat was perfectly at ease leaving master's mate William Reeve, a native of Falmouth, to take her out. The lines were cast off, and with just her topsail and jibs to drive her, the schooner's men standing ready to hoist her fore and main sails, with only the faintest of north-westerly zephyr acting upon her, *Eleanor* slipped gracefully away from the quay, moving slowly out from the inner harbour towards the Carrick Roads. The Falmouth men were all waving to their families, a happy multitude still thronging the quay, all of them still waving back to *Eleanor* as she passed the Bar and receded a mile distant into the Roads, many anxious hearts left far astern in her wake.

The master hovered at Reeve's elbow in a schoolmasterly fashion, not wanting to utter a single word of guidance unless it became absolutely necessary; not that he thought it would be. The Falmouth men, the Surprises, some forty or so now aboard, lined *Eleanor's* sides, as if in a kind of wonder, all striving to savour the realisation, that fleeting moment of joy, that they were at sea again, on a respectable venture and departing in the full glare of daylight. Several still gazed back for long, thoughtful minutes to their now distant family and friends; most simply savoured the moment, basking in the pleasurable realisation that they were going to sea once more. Once *Eleanor* was in mid-channel, and Pendennis Castle off her starboard beam, Reeve ordered the fore and main to be hoisted, the Eleanors aided by the Surprises and making light work of the sail handling: *Eleanor* was now sailing for Falmouth Bay.

Pat was watching events with the utmost delight, and not a word passed his lips until he spoke to Duncan as they passed the Black Rock to starboard, 'William is a splendid man to have with us, Duncan. Ne'er a better master could we ever have for *Eleanor.*'

'Nae doot at all, Pat,' said Duncan, pleasantly engrossed with the spectacle of their departure.

'I should take it very kindly if you will join me for dinner, Mr Reeve,' said Pat, 'when she is set fair on her course.'

'Oh, with great pleasure, sir, thank you.'

Both fore and main sails were now full, and *Eleanor* swiftly picked up speed. 'Nicely done, William, most uncommon neat indeed,' said Pat as she passed St Anthony Head. With a strengthening north-westerly wind behind her, and a very pleasant sea state *Eleanor* made short shrift of the bay crossing to Plymouth. By early afternoon Eleanor approached the emerging new breakwater, and sailed on past Saint Nicholas's Island, Devil's Point, and so to the shelter of Mutton Cove; *Eleanor* tying alongside there, neither Reeve and the master being greatly familiar with the Hamoaze, and both anxious not to foul any ship's cables by approaching that busy, oft crowded anchorage.

It was but a brief walk for the Surprises, a short half mile from *Eleanor's* berth to where *Surprise* had previously been on the slip. She was now moored within the Hamoaze, still very near the New Basin. The men shuffled along the quay, and through the yard, chatting away in prime good humour, all eager to go aboard the frigate, so near identical to *Tenedos* which, for most of them, had been their home afloat for many a year. Their rising excitement was palpable as they were rowed out to *Surprise* in the yard's boats, their jocular comments and good-natured banter so endemic. Pat could not bring himself to call them to order, feeling precisely the same himself. He was the first to climb aboard. There was no formal, welcoming guard of marines, nor could there be on this *unofficial* voyage, but he cared not a jot. He gazed slowly all about him, subsumed in his happiness, his mind swiftly registering the yard's restorations. Her guns, masts, and spars were all restored; and half a dozen yard workers were still aboard, making small, final touches to cabin painting. The Master Shipwright himself, Edward Churchill, was aboard, keeping a wholly unnecessary eye on his team, of whose workmanship Pat had never seen the equal.

'Upon my word, Mr Churchill, she does look prime!' Pat gazed about him, noting the masts and spars all a-tanto, rigging restored, and the deck all freshly caulked, only in a very few places yet to be holystoned to remove the little surfeit of pitch – a task for the Surprises on the morrow. The new sails were for the most part all loosely hung and strapped from the yards – not in any ways that any other than a yard crew would be happy with, but hung nevertheless. The cordage was everywhere new, nicely coiled where it lay on the deck. Pat and the old Tenedos's were immensely gratified to see that the yard – somehow knowing that *Surprise* was bound for Greece as her primary warship, the Royal Navy grapevine being what it was – had hung a fluttering long, blue pennant at the mizzen. Not a pennant that could be considered official of course, and one that Pat would swiftly strike down as soon as *Surprise* left the yard, but a visible and generous token of the esteem in which Pat was held in all the West Country ports.

'I am infinitely obliged to you, Mr Churchill. A finer and faster refit no other yard could have accomplished in the time. Thank you kindly, sir, she is a beautiful sight to behold,' said a delighted Pat.

'The task has been a great pleasure for us all here in the yard, Captain O'Connor. Indeed my lads all think of her as *their* ship, since she has oft been in and out of this yard in the past. 'Twas my lads, bless 'em, that fitted her new knees, and no other ship has ever given them so much pride in their work,' offered a deeply moved Churchill, so obviously and genuinely pleased to see a ship

72

returned to active service rather than the now far more customary work of his yard of hulking ships – ships that in many cases had many more years of useful life left in them, and *Surprise* now saved by his yard, by his own lads, from that ignominious fate.

'Allow me to say that she is a credit to you and your lads, sir, no doubt, no doubt at all.'

The Surprises, for that is how they all immediately felt themselves to be, were now swarming over the quarterdeck, the gun deck, and the rigging. Some were already preparing to shave and holystone the new deck caulking, prominent in its seams. The cook had gone below to light the galley fire, others were checking the water butts, inspecting the bilges, testing the pumps, and generally busying themselves in every conceivable task: all to a man delighted to be aboard a ship once more.

It was gratifying to Pat to see all the activity happening, quite unbidden. 'Simon, dear friend, ain't it very like a homecoming?' whispered an emotional Pat O'Connor.

'You are of my way of thinking entirely, soul. I do not believe I had expected this ... this deep satisfaction. Though Dr Tripe at the Dock is a fascinating man, and a member of the Royal College - I have oft enjoyed the most cordial of hours with him in examination of his collections, his stuffed birds most particularly - and his wife, Mary, is the most kindly treasure, I admit I have long tired of that place.' He gazed all about him at the ship. 'She is remarkably beautiful, for sure. Never afore did I have the same pleasure in simply stepping aboard ship. But is she not now an auld lady?'

'Old?' Pat stared at his friend, mildly affronted, 'Old? She ain't old Simon; only a scrub would say such a thing. You must never say that. Sure there are some who would say she may be old-fashioned, long past mark of mouth, and too puny to engage with her modern sisters, forty-fours and the like; that she is too small for the current age. These opinions have credence for the most part in those lubbers who have ne'er found themselves spitting out the salt air, wipin' their eyes of the powder smoke when the shot is flying, or firing three broadsides in five minutes. She is but thirteen years old, and has been looked after tenderly, like a maiden aunt; handled gently like a risen pudding afore it reaches the table, since ever afore she was laid up for so long. No, she has a long life in her yet, our dear *Surprise*. I am cast down and mortified to hear you say such things, shame on you.'

Simon looked anxiously into Pat's face. 'I am so sorry, Pat, I use the term only as an endearment, akin to making the acquaintance of a long lost, auld friend, a dearly beloved, auld friend: one who perhaps had been thought lost and was found again, the pleasure being so much more in the finding, the return. Doubtless you are correct as to her longevity. Forgive me brother, I meant no other inference. I find I love the ship as much as you, and there you have my confession; coming from a mind of a generally scientific persuasion, though assuredly our dear *Surprise* now brings the nature of a philosopher to the fore. Give you joy of our homecoming, brother.'

At that moment Pat was distracted by Murphy, struggling by himself to hoist Pat's two bags up from the boat, loud cursing evidencing Murphy's return to his customary form. 'Murphy! Belay that whingeing. Stow 'em away in the cabin, handsomely does it! Hartley! Currie! Bear a hand: bring the Doctor's dunnage aboard. No need to pay any attention to the great guns just yet, lads,' Pat shouted to two of the crew of one of the aftmost starboard eighteen-pounders, who were engaged already in chipping away peeling black paint from a gun, the equivalent gun to the one on their former *Tenedos*; their gun, as they now considered it to be, and scraping away just a little crusted salt from the carriage woodwork. 'Murphy! Pass the word for the cook; plenty o' bacon and soft tack for the crew in half an hour, and grog to wash it down. Freeman! Light along there and see about some coffee and kedgeree, if you will,' Pat said, rather more politely than his customarily more abrupt orders to his servants, for nothing would be allowed to spoil his enjoyment of this particular day.

'Well, just aboard and no bleedin' peace already,' grumbled Murphy, standing with Freeman to recover from his exertions hauling up the baggage before going to the cabin, and awaiting Pat's further rebuke.

"'Tis comin', massa!' shouted Freeman.

'Waites! Fisher! See how much water is in the well.' Pat was once again in his natural element.

'She's nicely tight and dry, sir, barely an inch or two,' came back the report within minutes.

'Very good; get yourselves some grog, lads.'

After a further two hours had passed with a myriad checks completed, and as the crew were sitting on the deck with their grog and finishing up their bowls of burgoo, Pat, standing amidships on the gun deck, and, as was plain to all, marvelling at his good fortune, called them all together. 'Lads, we will be taking on stores tomorrow, we will hold church on Sunday; on Monday we will bring aboard our water and livestock, and load powder and shot from the hoy. We will leave on Tuesday's ebb, over to Falmouth. Let us have no riotous drinking here in Plymouth Dock. Any hand who is drunk will be left ashore. There's ten shillings each for all hands for your needs until we depart on Tuesday. Anderton! Belker! You will keep those lines just fine and dandy.'

'Aye aye, sir,' they acknowledged, grinning happily.

Saturday 17ᵗʰ May 1823   *Plymouth Dock, Devon*

All day preparations continued to take *Surprise* to sea once again. The forty or so Falmouth seamen, the majority of them Wesleyans, worked from sun up, several of them nursing thick heads from over-indulging in the taverns of Morice Town the prior evening, but not a man missed the early start. Mr Tizard, the veteran ship's carpenter, checked the yard's workmanship with an experienced eye. Deck holystoning continued incessantly; the great guns were cleaned and oiled, several men continued to chip away at their lingering remnants of peeling black paint. Below deck was aired, as the deck gratings were all lifted away. The galley was cleaned and the fire relit, bilges were freshened with a little clean salt water and pumped dry, and so it went on: the crew industriously pausing only occasionally for water, grog, and the cook's burgoo; a great pot of which was maintained steaming on the galley, repeatedly fed with fresh milk and more oats.

From nine o'clock onwards a constant stream of coaches and wagons arrived on the quay with stores from the Plymouth victuallers, brought onboard by *Surprise's* boats: casks of salt pork; salt beef – every man entitled to six pounds a week, gristled, bony and fat as it was; bread, beer, suet, oatmeal, oil, ship's biscuit, dried peas, flour, salt, onions, carrots, turnips, sugar, cheese; great barrels of lime and lemon juices, and kegs of vinegar and rum. Much baggage had also been sent down by Sinéad from Truro, anticipating *Surprise* being in Falmouth for the very shortest of stays, and likely leaving little time to take the family's necessaries, as she deemed them, aboard. There were many and varied outfits of clothing, boots, wet-weather gear, hats of all sorts, woollen gloves, leather gloves, calfskin gloves, belts, crockery, even a silver dinner service. From the local vintners there were cases of good burgundy, fine French brandy, malt whisky so as to please Simon and Duncan; Pat's cello, Simon's viola, music stands, rugs, blankets; many and varied chests with Sinéad's accoutrements; clothing for Fergal and Caitlin, further clothing for Kathleen and Brodie; and so it went on for many an hour, all Pat's family's personal chests being manhandled aboard by Murphy and Clumsy Dalby.

'Well, I ain't ne'er seen so much bleedin' dunnage afore, and where is it all to be stowed? A dozen o' shirts for the Captain! Well, all will need pressin', an' we ain't ne'er 'ad more'n six aboard afore. We ain't some dandy Indiaman. Dalby, stop yer blathering, get yer nose and paws out o' that chest you graspin' sod,' grumbled Murphy, in his high-pitched, nasal whine.

'Well sorr, if you please, now here is yer second-best breeches,' said Murphy to Pat, later in the morning when unpacking in the cabin. Murphy had served with Pat for many years. Never a master mariner but originally a passable foremast hand, his very few abilities and perpetually complaining attitude as the captain's servant left absolutely everything to be desired. Yet with his old-maidish skills for sewing, silver-polishing, and pressing Pat's clothes, he had inexplicably overcome all rational selection processes to become Pat's valet and servant, performing the same service for Simon. Since Pat had apprised him of the imminent

76

return to sea on *Surprise* Murphy was a new man – almost. He had taken on the task of rousing out the old *Tenedos* men in Falmouth with an enthusiasm never before seen by Pat or Simon. Such stores of wine and brandy that had so far come aboard had, inexplicably, not suffered from any accidental breakages. Even his disagreeable, righteous whining had gone by the board, for the most part, to the astonishment of Pat and Simon. Still, Murphy could not quite rein in his matronly concern for his captain, as he stepped up to the busy quarterdeck, distress mixed with anger as he cried 'Mind yer breeches on that 'ot tar! Oh bejabers, your honour has sat on it and you'se ruined 'em: your best bloody breeches, for shame. 'Twill ne'er come out, nor I spend a week a'washin'. Ain't I fer ever tellin' you yer sleeve is in the soup, and that takes a deal o'scrubbin', and now 'ot tar on yer breeches. Ruined, quite ruined they be. Well, I laid out them very old breeches this morning, and they be still there. Well, what yer wife would say - were she here, the Lord only knows …' adding a proper, 'ax pardon, sorr,' after but a moment and 'coffee's up, sorr.'

'Thankee, Murphy. Now cease your blathering and make a pot of coffee,' replied Pat patiently, long accustomed to Murphy's irritating idiosyncrasies. He turned to the master who approached from the wheel. Prosser had listened with barely contained pleasure to Pat's exchange with his steward, and was striving diligently to avoid laughing aloud. They went down to the cabin. 'Mr Prosser, our old Tenedos's are working uncommon well these two days past. You are familiar with all of 'em and the new lads. You would favour me most deeply by proposing one of them as my cox'n.'

The master paused momentarily, staring at Pat for several seconds as if weighing his reply carefully, and touched his hat before replying. It seemed to all the onlookers as if wisdom was radiating from his wizened, old face as the master spoke, 'Aye, sir; there is but one man I would favour as cox'n.'

'Who is this man, Mr Prosser?' asked Pat.

'He be coming from Pompey on the mail coach today, and will be here presently. I took the liberty, sir, of sending for him when we was in Falmouth.'

'Pray send him in directly, as soon as he arrives, Mr Prosser, and we will ask his mettle,' said Pat, concealing well his curiosity, his deep respect for Prosser, a veteran of many voyages together, bestowing unquestioning confidence in his selection. 'Murphy, where is Doctor Ferguson,' shouted Pat, wholly unnecessarily, as Murphy was still in his customary position whenever Pat conducted an interview in the great cabin: that is to say with his ear pressed to the door.

'Below sorr; in his store.'

'Perhaps it is a timely moment for an inspection of the lower and orlop decks?' said Pat to himself, and he paced out of the cabin and stepped down the companionway into the gloom of the lower deck. He looked about him; there were no men below, all were working above; and he was about to descend the steps to the orlop when Simon stepped up from below. Both were crouching in the low space afforded them, scarcely more than five and a half feet on the lower deck.

'Ah, Simon, there you are. Will you come up to the cabin and take second breakfast with me?'

'It is a benevolent offer, but not now, Pat. I am engrossed at present. I am mixing my stock of Paré's digestive.' Seeing Pat's blank look he continued, 'It is an ointment, a most excellent remedy in the case of gunshot wounds, and I am in need of fresh egg yolks - would you think the cook will spare some?'

'I hope you will leave Wilkins at least a brace to accompany my bacon, it ain't the same without eggs,' Pat laughed. 'The crew have done tolerably well, and the ship nears readiness for sea. We will load our powder from the hoy on Monday, and be away with the tide for Falmouth on Tuesday for the rest of our men - should we have any room left that is for the crew and family; ne'er did we ever see so much in the way of stores loaded aboard. The master has proposed a cox'n, and I expect him directly; after that we will repair ashore for supper at the Steam Packet. Tell, eggs and ointment aside, are you now prepared with your customary medical supplies for our voyage? Is there anything you lack?'

Before Simon could answer there came a voice from the top of the companionway, and Murphy's shrewish visage appeared; but instead of his customary high shrilling nasal whine it was almost a whisper, 'Beg pardon, sorr, yer visitor is here; Mr Prosser's cox'n it is.'

'Send him down, Murphy. At once, if you please,' commanded Pat, intent on continuing with at least some small survey of the hold. The sight of the man who stepped down from the companionway, in the moment that he turned towards them, stopped Pat and Simon in their thoughts in an instant. The shock was overwhelming; heartbeats were missed, eyes widened, words left unformed. For the first time ever in his ship, in the moment of the profound shock, Pat instinctively straightened bolt upright. He cracked his head on the low deckhead beam, shouted in some pain, and fell back into a crouch against the gun-room door, nursing a sore and bleeding head. He gasped in astonished disbelief. He stared for long moments before he could find any words at all, finally uttering, his voice barely more than a whisper, 'By God, Simon, 'tis Barton himself here before us.'

Murphy, further words failing even him, scrambled in haste down the steps even as Pat recovered himself and stood staring, open-mouthed, at this so shocking sight. Pat's coxswain of ten long years, Brannan Barton, had been killed alongside him in the year thirteen in the boarding of *Chesapeake*, and Pat simply could not believe his eyes; was in shock even. Murphy stood there in dumb show, unable to shift or speak: never before had anything like it happened aboard.

Simon hastened round to Pat's side, wiping the blood trail away from above Pat's eye on his shirt sleeve, all the while staring at this apparition, and whispering to himself, 'Oh, my Lord.'

Before them the unassuming seaman spoke up. 'Barton, sir, it is. George Barton, cousin of Brannan Barton. Mr Prosser sent for me.'

'Barton! 'Pon my word, ne'er did two peas more resemble the same pod,' exclaimed Pat, struggling to find suitable words and trying unsuccessfully to come to terms with the sight of a man so utterly indistinguishable from his former coxswain.

Barton bravely resumed: 'Well, sir, Brannan Barton was my

twin but I was placed with my aunt when aged one on account of my mum having no breadwinner, our father having died afore I was born like. She could not afford the upbringing of both of us, and so I have always been called cousin, even as we grew up not half a league apart in Falmouth,' explained George Barton. Seeing that Pat was still agape, he pressed on with the details of his naval career. 'I started at sea in the time of his Lordship, Admiral Jervis, in the year ninety-seven, sir. I was a powder monkey for him at Cape St. Vincent on *Victory*. I was promoted able when serving on *Royal Sovereign* at Trafalgar. I was standing alongside Admiral Collingwood when *Santa Ana* struck to her, sir. The next year I was promoted to captain's barge crew. I served with the Admiral until the year ten when his Lordship passed. I was tie mate with Bill Mindham, gun captain on *Shannon*, in the year thirteen when we captured *Chesapeake*. Bill opened the firing on *Chesapeake* that day, sir, and we boarded her together, Brannan alongside o' me. He was serving on *Tenedos* when Captain Broke sent her away, and she left 'im and a score of others aboard *Shannon:* her second and third were there too. We was rushing to help the cap'n who was downed when the prisoners broke out. Bill and one of the officers from *Tenedos* saved the cap'n, sir. I ne'er knew who he was. Bill and he reached the cap'n when he went down, one or t'other struck down the Yankee about to kill the cap'n. Bill I think it was, and we stood over him together 'til our marines came. It was a bloody business, sir. When the cap'n led the boarding he was followed by Mr Dunn his clerk and Mr Aldham the purser. Can you believe it, sir? Both were shot down dead behind the cap'n even afore they reached *Chesapeake's* deck. Tom Stevens, the bosun, had his hand hacked right off while 'e was lashing us alongside, though 'e carried on with his other hand 'til he was struck down by a musket ball, bless 'im; I have ne'er seen his like since. Poor Tom lingered for near three weeks, sir, and died in Halifax. I was wounded dragging the cap'n back to *Shannon*, a ball from the tops; two mates and my brother Brannan killed alongside o' me. I spent three weeks laid up afterwards, below in the sick bay and in the Halifax hospital. I am glad I was able to give old Tom some little comfort there, sir, afore he passed. I was promoted bosun by Lieutenant Wallis on *Shannon* after I recovered, to replace old Tom. After *Shannon* went into ordinary, sir, I joined *Spartan,* and served on her as cox'n until the year twenty when she also went into ordinary. I haven't found a berth these past three years, sir. Been working at the Pompey dockyards on ship refitting since,' Barton concluded his truly exceptional record of service.

'Barton, Barton: admirable, admirable; indeed, it seems we have already served together,' said Pat, still in a state of some wondrous disbelief, nodding to Duncan. 'Mr Macleod here and I came aboard *Shannon* from *Tenedos* just a day or so afore *Chesapeake* struck to her, your brother Brannan with us. I was second and Mr Macleod was third on *Tenedos*. Captain Hyde Parker sent us aboard with twenty men to assist *Shannon* before Broke sent *Tenedos* away. 'Twas I with your gun captain that saved Captain Broke, and you were directly behind us, you say. I have five guineas in my dunnage for you, Barton. Mighty pleased I was to have half a dozen good fellows behind me when I reached Captain Broke: 'twas a desperate moment ... a very bloody business indeed. And you were wounded in the boarding you say? Alas, I never saw you, nor anyone else I would collect after Broke was cut down; 'twas every man for himself for a few minutes there. As you say, we lost your brother Brannan that day; a painful loss to all of us on *Tenedos,* good man that he was. Lieutenant Macleod and I shifted to Halifax after the battle. And you served with Old Jarvie himself. 'Pon my word: that is a prodigious fine record, Barton, a handsome record indeed. The master speaks well of you: I need ask no more. You would favour me most deeply by shifting aboard directly as our new cox'n,' beamed Pat, seizing and shaking Barton's hand in a vice-like grip. 'Murphy, lend a hand there, trundle Barton's dunnage aboard, smartly now. Take him to the galley for a pint of grog and show him the barky.'

'Thankee kindly; I will not let you down, sir.' Barton touched his forehead and left in the company of a still dumbstruck Murphy.

'You seem taken aback, brother,' said Simon, who had heard the story with great interest.

'I should scarcely have thought it possible... Barton, standing

81

there in the flesh, and hard to believe 'twas not really him,' Pat heard himself whispering, still in some small state of shock.

'To be sure, the twin's resemblance was assuredly so completely indistinguishable from that of our old shipmate, Pat, but it is not as rare as you might think. Perhaps one in three hundred births are identical twins,' replied Simon. 'If I may venture a suggestion, my dear, would it be improper to suggest we get off this vessel and step out for our supper now?'

Sunday 18th May 1823   *Plymouth Dock, Devon*

At first light, Pat roused himself, dunked his head in the washbowl, applied just a very little of Number Six cologne, it being Whit Sunday and no work being intended; the perfume being a present which had been given to him many years before by a particularly friendly local young lady in Halifax, Nova Scotia, and which had remained unremarked by Sinéad in the intervening years, being in his old shipboard dunnage. 'That will have to go to the deep six 'afore Sinéad comes aboard,' he thought, absently. He dressed swiftly, his best coat and breeches having been pressed and left out the night before by Freeman. 'Freeman!' Pat shouted. 'Light along a pot of coffee, and do we have bacon left?'

Freeman appeared immediately, muttering, 'Pot 'im ready this five minutes, massa.'

Some little time later Duncan entered the cabin, sniffing the twin scents of coffee and bacon with undisguised delight.

'There is a whole pile of bacon; eggs too, in that pan, Duncan; Simon has left us a few.'

'A most handsome prospect, fer sure: ah will gladly share yer breakfast wi' the utmost pleasure.' Duncan settled at Pat's table, and swiftly piled his plate with generous helpings.

'Freeman! Bring some more soft tack for Mr Macleod, and pass the word for ... for Murphy.' Pat remained still in some disbelief at yesterday's shock, his thinking since oft slipping into small muddle. 'Will you not regret staying in the Hebrides, Duncan?'

Duncan paused from his obvious satisfaction with the fried

breakfast and looked up. 'Och, ah am sure they have their charms, but how greatly pleased ah am that we are back here, aboard oor new hame, at sea agin, aboard the barky, oor dear *Surprise*. Pat, how agreeably homely it is, there is nae doot,' the deep conviction so plain in his voice.

'*There is no doubt*... Duncan... so long ashore now I had near-forgotten.' Pat looked wistfully into Duncan's face. 'A ship, Duncan.... once again. Oh how I have longed these past three years for this moment to come; my hopes near dashed, and here we are.'

Duncan merely smiled and nodded, chewing with great satisfaction, his mouth full. Pat sat down again in his chair and poured himself more coffee. 'Allow me to help you to a few more rashers; would you care for another egg or two?'

'Most certainly: ah will finish the last three in the pan, if ye will. Wid there be another wee drop o' coffee left, at all?'

'Murphy! There you are. We will rig church, and I believe we will hoist the church pennant, if it is in the locker? Rouse out all the men, if you will. We are too few to muster to divisions, though it being Sunday I am minded to speak to the lads when we hold church. I fancy I will preach the sermon.'

'What? Ye will preach the sermon?' Duncan could not conceal his astonishment, laughed aloud, slapped his coffee down on the table, and clapped his hands together three times in merriment, as if in applause.

Pat glared at him. 'We ain't at war, Duncan, and the Articles don't seem right. I have long had a copy of The Good Book, in my dunnage all these years, and there are plentiful things in it which will suit when you trouble to look. It was plainly written by some honest fellows, fishermen and the like; doubtless many others were mariners too.'

'Aye an' was Jonah nae one of 'em, Pat? Ah collect he spent much time asleep. Ah doot ye should mention him to the men,' Duncan retorted, followed by his hearty laugh.

Rather than below in the customary lower deck location, church was rigged on the gun deck. With so few crew aboard and no chaplain either, *Surprise* not ostensibly being a Royal Navy ship, and the weather promising to be clemently warm, Pat felt a more informal occasion was called for. The ship's bell struck four bells.

'Murphy! My best scraper if you will.'

Murphy, looking unusually spry himself, was there in an instant. 'Well, 'tis on your table already, sorr.'

On stepping up to his quarterdeck Pat and Duncan were greeted by the Wesleyans, two dozen or more of them all lined up near the wheel, all scrubbed up, pigtails all newly plaited, and mystifyingly all garbed in a myriad of shades of red; evidently prepared and awaiting the service. The other crew members, tailing back to the ship's waist, were all also looking particularly prime.

'What's afoot, Duncan? Has the fleet adopted a new uniform since we were last at sea, forgetting to tell us?' joked Pat.

'It is the biblical colour fer Pentecost, brother, an' the Wesleyans are particular aboot the auld traditions, as ye may collect.'

'I do not believe I have ever heard it remarked upon before. Very creditable in them, indeed,' said Pat, pleasantly, being something of a traditionalist himself.

The skeleton crew, barely four dozen men including the Eleanors, assembled in front of a sea-chest over which was draped an ensign to serve as a makeshift lectern. Pat was not a conventionally religious man, but he was a pious traditionalist by nature. Lacking deep familiarity with the scriptures, he generally contented himself when required to give the sermon at sea with reading the Articles of War, which had become almost a venerable substitute for an appropriate ecclesiastical script. On this occasion however, *Surprise* not really being, officially at least, in His Majesty's Service, Pat considered that he should not read the Articles, but expound on their particular circumstances before they sang the hymns.

Stepping to the sea-chest, Pat paused long to look around, taking a deep draught of the salt air borne on the early morning chill breeze, and he gazed up as if towards the heavens. Finally, he tucked his hat under his arm and began to speak, quite softly as there were so few present. 'Good morning, lads. As we are so very few today, and not quite yet in commission, I am minded to speak just a short piece to you. I ain't one for speeches, as you know, but allow me to share a trifle of my private thoughts from these past few days with you. Here we be, aboard our new home, our friend, our dear *Surprise*. It does my heart good to be aboard ship once again ...'

There was a general but softly spoken murmur of agreement from the assembled crew.

'Lads ... most of you have been with me through the dam ... the gravest of hard times: fighting Boney's ships and others too. We have been round the world together, through storms and the vilest of seas. We have shared hard tack and short commons ...,' Pat was speaking quite slowly now and with some deliberation, as if searching for the right words. 'We have lost some fine shipmates along the way...' He paused for a minute or two, looking round at all his crew, studying each of their faces, remembering most of them from long voyages in years gone by, until his gaze alighted on his new cox'n, standing to the fore, and in that instant his heart moved within him, a huge physical tremor rising from deep down, his throat drying, and his mind painfully flashed back, recalling lost comrades, one of them in particular very much at the forefront of his thoughts at that moment. A long further minute passed before he could speak again. He swallowed hard and forced his mind to focus. Quietly he resumed, 'I am minded of one lost shipmate ..., Brannan Barton was with me – *with us* – since my very first command, the gun-brig *Starling* in Portsmouth in the year three. In the year four I will ne'er forget boarding *El Valiente* with him alongside of me, and when I was felled by a pike he saved my life, pistolling the Spaniard ere he could stick me again. Brannan Barton in those years became my friend ..., *our* friend, and served with us until he was killed in the year thirteen. I have oft thought of him these ten years gone.' It was obvious to all the assembly that their captain was struggling, in some considerable difficulty, as he resumed: his words, still very quiet, now not more than a whisper, wafted across, as if borne by the breeze to reach them. His head lifted and he spoke again, the very few words revealing his thoughts with brutal clarity: 'I miss him greatly.' Pat paused again amidst a soft echoing of accord from the crew. 'Today, as you know, 'tis the day of Pentecost, the day our Lord Jesus returned to us …,' Pat faltered again: his knowledge of the scriptures was a little hazy. With only the familiar, shrilling noise of gulls in the background, the crew, bluff seamen all, their whispered exchanges now brought to silence by his words, he continued, 'And perhaps we too have seen someone come back to us yesterday: 'tis Barton here who reminds us that from our tragedy, out of that ache of our despair, will always come hope afresh.'

Not even the quietest murmur now disturbed the moment, all present were listening intently, unaccustomed as they were to words of such poignancy: a long pause of several minutes followed, as Pat once more gathered his thoughts, and, as if realising that he had been speaking very quietly, he swallowed and continued, raising his voice, 'Afore we venture out again, lads, aboard our new home at sea, our dear *Surprise,* let us welcome aboard *George* Barton: our new shipmate, cox'n, and *brother.*'

Pat concluded his address to hearty cheering from his men, 'Hurrah, hurrah, hear the Captain, hurrah'. As he looked up again and across to his crew, the wind having shifted round to the exposed south-west since the start of church and the sky having become progressively darker, a fine rain began to set in, quickly wetting the faces of the assembly: a minor inconvenience, for which Pat found himself profoundly grateful, and obscuring, or so he thought, the flood of tears now streaming down his cheeks.

All hands had noticed that in the lattermost of Pat's address his voice had taken on a halting, softer tone than was usual on these occasions, and much more so than the very firm tone he customarily adopted for reading the Articles of War, and despite the rain none could miss their captain's tears. Mr Prosser, the master and elder of the Wesleyans, stepped up to the makeshift lectern – quite unbidden but understanding perfectly the moment – and waved the now chattering crew to silence once more. 'We thank you most kindly, sir, for your very 'andsome words.'

'Carry on, Mr Prosser,' said Pat, very quietly.

After two hymns had been sung and church concluded the

bosun piped the hands to dinner, and the crew returned to the lower deck for the customary Sunday pork followed by plum duff: the culinary highlight of the week aboard His Majesty's ships. It was a tradition that Pat would never change. Shortly thereafter Dalby beat *Roast Beef of Old England* to signal readiness of the officers' dinner. Back in the great cabin, Pat awaited his dinner with Duncan and Simon, attended intermittently by Freeman. 'Allow me to fill your glasses, gentlemen. This is rather better than our ordinary I believe?' Pat offered, from his dwindling private stock of the Madeira seventy-five.

'I am entirely of your way of thinking, Pat,' Simon replied, 'an exceptional wine. What are your present thoughts, tell?'

'What butter or whiskey does not cure cannot be cured,' declared Pat, rather obliquely, not quite ignoring his friend's question. He paused before adding (twenty minutes having elapsed with nothing to eat in sight) 'I wonder if there *is* any pork left or whether Murphy has eaten it all up?'

Just at that moment Freeman appeared at the cabin door with a large and overburdened silver tray. 'Vittles is up, massa, if you please. Cook sending best underside for dinner, massa: here 'tis.'

'Thankee, Freeman, my compliments to my cook.'

After Freeman had busied himself piling the most generous of portions on silver plates he left the cabin.

'I heartily commend you, Pat; those were very fine words today, most commendable words. None finer have I ever heard uttered afore aboard this or any other vessel, and 'twas most particularly well received indeed,' said Simon. 'Nothing like it have we heard before, and forgive me, brother, I should scarcely have thought it of you. I have a certain, perhaps unfounded, impression. Pray tell, dear soul, is there some uneasiness on your mind?'

'Never in life, Simon; will I help you to some stuffing?' Pat retorted, a little too quickly to pass Simon's notice.

'Forgive me, brother, if I might be permitted an observation. You were tolerably eloquent today, using very fair expressions which I do not generally expect to hear from you.'

'Sure, I never was one for speeches,' replied Pat, smiling a little more broadly now, 'though I can bring something out now and then, given time.' And nothing more could Simon extract from him on the subject.

Tuesday 20ᵗʰ May 1823   *Plymouth Dock, Devon*

The fair weather of the weekend had deteriorated into a mid-grey sky with dawn bringing a prevalent westerly, light wind accompanied by soft steady rain: all so typical of the south-west of England at virtually any time of the year, but moderated, as is so often the case in those climes, by a warm temperature. The crew were assured that all was well for the bay crossing to Falmouth, though it would be a difficult task were the wind to strengthen exceptionally with a crew of just four dozen, capable hands though they were. The Admiralty had denied Pat any serving Royal Navy seamen from Plymouth, maintaining their separation from this covert venture, and so, for the very short voyage, he had decided to rely on those few Falmouth volunteers who were immediately available. As four bells struck, signifying the master's choice of time for departure just after high water, a few of the yard shipwrights were still onboard, though finishing up and removing their tools from about the deck as the Master Shipwright, Edward Churchill, accompanied by the Master Attendant, George Sidley, stepped aboard from the Yard's cutter, and paced up to Pat's quarterdeck to bid their farewells. They shook hands solemnly with both Pat and Duncan before looking about the decks and gazing at the masts and rigging as if in final inspection, and then Churchill spoke to Pat, pride so very evident in his face and voice. 'Just you be very careful with her, sir, and bring her back to us in good time.'

'Never in doubt, Mr Churchill: never in doubt. My thanks to you again, sir,' Pat replied, smiling broadly.

'I bid you all safe passage, Captain O'Connor. Goodbye sir,' said the Master Attendant.

'Thank you, Mr Sidley. Goodbye.'

Pat watched his visitors disembark, and then with the deepest sense of satisfaction he gazed all about *his* ship, as she now seemed.

He allowed himself a few minutes to study those faces of his crew nearby, competency and experience so very evident in all of them; he watched the remainder as they busied themselves with final preparations, some glancing occasionally to the quarterdeck in anticipation of the imminent commands for departure.

The shipwrights were now all departed, rowing towards where the yard crew, dozens of men, all lined the quay. From the launch, Churchill and Sidley gazed back, not wishing to miss any of the spectacle of *Surprise's* departure. Barton, with two of the Wesleyans, was at the wheel, Mr Prosser, the master, alongside them. Simon stood at Pat's side on the quarterdeck, gazing at the final preparations. Despite witnessing many such departures the nautical nomenclature had never rooted in his mind and the ship handling procedures still left him largely mystified. 'To be sure, we are particularly few, Pat, in comparison of our customary numbers; short-handed, I dare say? Will this present any difficulties for our leave-taking, would you think? I only throw out the remark,' queried Simon.

'Why certainly it will, Simon. Be a good fellow for once, and lend a hand there on the capstan, and push hard when I give the word, will you?' replied Pat with a suppressed smile.

The old hands at the wheel looked at each other, barely concealing their astonishment.

'Certainly, brother, I have oft heard you mention that particular device, but be so good as to remind me: where *is* the capstan? My familiarity is lacking a trifle in these nautical, these *mechanical*, devices, Pat, as you may have noticed.'

'No, not at all.'

'Pray point it out if you will,' said Simon, falling wholly into Pat's little trap. The helmsmen tittered, stopping only when Barton kicked them. 'I see you practice upon me,' said Simon.

'You are a hoot,' laughed Pat, his good humour plain.

'I am no mariner.'

Pat gazed with deep affection at his friend. 'Oh, I should never say that. For sure you're an odd one; none finer in the philosophical line, a capital man with the Latin, and to be sure the only sight all

89

aboard the barky would pray to see were they ever carried down to the cockpit; yet for all these years at sea you scarcely have any notion of the bow from the stern, or your larboard from your starboard. If you will, pray see if that rascal Freeman might find us a pot of tea in about ten minutes.'

'I find you in tolerably better humour this morning, brother,' replied Simon, in good spirits himself.

'I am uncommon happy, Simon. Afloat again, a fine ship with a goodly set of hands, Falmouth bound we are, and a prospect of some proper seafaring ahead; 'tis a fine day, none better.'

Simon left the quarterdeck and Pat turned to Duncan and the master, both waiting patiently alongside him. 'Our time is come to depart, Mr Macleod.'

'All hands prepare to make sail!' shouted Duncan.

'Lay aloft!' shouted Prosser, and the men scrambled up to the yards. 'Rig capstan bars and bring to the messenger,' he bawled, and within a few minutes, 'Man the bars!'

Surprise was anchored larboard side on her best bower, the cable hove short, her starboard side towards the quay as she was beginning to be drawn by the current, the tide beginning its ebb; the wind veering to a north-westerly, fine on her larboard bow.

'Breast the capstan,' shouted Prosser.

'Up anchor!' ordered Pat.

'Up anchor for home!' echoed the master.

'Heave and a-weigh,' cried Duncan.

The cable began to be wound in on the capstan, the sounds of a shanty coming from the men '*walk her round and round she goes, way oh, way oh.*' It was a vociferous departure from Royal Navy practices, and one to which Pat paid no heed, for nothing short of King George himself stepping aboard could possibly impinge on his genial and deep satisfaction this day. Even the old *Tenedos* veterans had departed from their customary, restrained '*two-six, two six*', all swept up in the enthusiastic fervour. The capstan men, their singing now general, ran the cable in just fast enough for the few tierers present to keep up.

'Up and down!' came the shout from the bow.

'Thick and dry for weighing!' shouted Duncan.

The topmen meanwhile had shifted out on to the yards; cast off the gaskets, the lines that held the sails tight furled to the yards. They gathered the canvas under their arms, and waited. The tierers were coaxing in the remaining cable until all was swiftly stowed, and the best bower appeared, just hauled out of the water.

'Stand by aloft, let fall,' ordered Duncan, and with his shout came the howling peep-peep, peep-peep from the bosun alone, no mates available whilst so short-handed.

'Let fall! Sheet home, sheet home, hoist away!' the master shouted.

The topmen standing ready at her topsails let fall the sails: down they tumbled, unfurling, loosely flapping; the men hauling on the halliards. *Surprise's* afteryards were already braced ready for the tack to turn her gently to face downstream in the ebb tide, the headyards abox, headsheets hauled to larboard: she would come round slowly but afforded little steerage for the first few minutes.

'Hard a-lee!' Duncan commanded the men at the wheel.

Surprise now backed slowly, stern coming round to larboard, as she gained sternway, her bow coming round to starboard, turning faster now without the anchor constraint, her fore topsail pushing her, back, back, the main and mizzen flapping until she came further round and they filled.

'Helm up!' shouted Duncan when her bow faced the yard and she was beginning to be driven forward.

The combined wind and ebb tide were pushing her now with greater momentum, and the rudder was kept hard over until she was fully turned about and facing down the Hamoaze.

'Helm amidships!' The wind and current now combining to give her speed, she swiftly moved away downstream. The deck crew heaved the remainder of the cable in, and the anchor was quickly catted. Within a very few minutes *Surprise* was well underway in the fairway, the Hamoaze, and all along her sides there creamed a ribbon of white water.

'That was handsomely executed, and with just two score hands. 'Pon my word we have some prime seamen aboard, Barton,' Pat shouted across to the wheel, slipping without thinking into the easy manner of past times with his old cox'n.

'Aye, sir,' Barton shouted back, mightily pleased to hear his captain's compliment.

The master kept *Surprise* firmly in the deepwater channel, and well within the half hour she came out through the Narrows, the small crew making good work of the sail handling tasks. *Surprise* came swiftly out into the Sound, making a south-south-west course, and sailing close-hauled with the westerly wind, passing the new breakwater, and so to Penlee Point.

As Rame Head came up on the starboard beam the ship's bell rang eight bells, and half the crew disappeared below for dinner. The rain had ceased and the sun broke through the clouds, bringing welcome warmth and good cheer to the hard-working crew.

Pat turned to his long-serving companion and first, 'At sea again, a frigate of the very first order, our old lads aboard; don't it give you a shiver down your back, Duncan?'

'Aye, fer sure it does, there is nae doot, Pat, nae doot at all,' whispered Duncan with some emotion. 'Ah dinnae e'er collect a bonnier day fer many a year. Ah widnae exchange it fer a barrel o' gold pieces.'

Later, in the great cabin, Pat, Duncan, and Simon shared a pot of tea with sizzling-hot white pudding, brought aboard fresh that morning. '*Eleanor* is to follow us tomorrow, and William will bring her over to join us in Falmouth with his small crew. We are still short of officers. With the fleet now so reduced I have no hope of serving officers leaving their commands to join us. No, our best prospects lie with those of our old friends who have been these past years a'fretting on the beach; lieutenants on their paltry half-pay, with no prospects of a ship, and no hope of being made post. I have hopes that James Mower may join us yet. I have written to him, his family has long lived in Falmouth; and to Tom Pickering; what a wit that man has. Doubtless the merchant service may have taken one or t'other of 'em. Do you collect them both on our first cruise together, Duncan? Master's mates they were, on our old *Starling*: my first command, back in the year three. Happy times, Duncan, happy times they were.'

'Aye, ah collect the twae, brother, but we were poor, widnae a dollar between us.'

'To be sure, yet I collect that sense of adventure, so long now lacking. Dear God, how good it was to be alive in those years. All of Boney's ships agin us, and fleets afloat that we shall ne'er see the likes of again.' A nostalgic Pat turned to the other side of his table, 'Do you miss those days, Simon?'

'The sentiments of adventure, and much later, of anticipation of profound political change that came about, but which was so sadly snuffed out in Scot ..., that is to say in Spain.' Simon suppressed distressing recollections of Hardie, Baird and Wilson, all hung and beheaded after the failed rising a mere three years previously. 'Those feelings I miss most dearly, Pat. Since Agnes's death I have felt only the cold chill of disappointment in my bones and melancholia in my bosom. This new expedition comes with great hopes for me, even a rekindling of purpose. These are aspirations and feelings which I had long thought dead these ten years past. For sure it will also be a pleasure to see our auld shipmates again.'

'All have been laid up ashore for some years since, and with none having any connections they are unlikely to find any berth. It has reached my ears that William Codrington is hiding from his creditors and near bankrupt this past year. I gather that allegations of his severe gambling losses are well founded. He has been losing badly, as so many sailors do when ashore with a pocket full of guineas, and might well relish an absence from home: doubtless some foreign service would be particularly welcome. We are to meet with the First Lord on Friday, and sail on Sunday week, come what may,' said Pat.

'I do not like to sound forward, brother, but might I trouble you and suggest it may be useful to our expedition were we to engage a proficient surgeon's assistant: one would hardly be a supernumary? Have you, perchance, also considered engaging a member of the cloth?' Simon ventured.

Pat looked doubtful, 'I believe there is something in what you say, Simon. Our time away is uncertain, and our particular efforts may not signify for a long time. Yet there ain't room enough in the gun-room for all these extra fellows, should we find all our officers awaiting us in Falmouth.'

'Allow me to raise the possibility, the very slight possibility, dear, of finding one single person to fit the bill for both these capacities. I have received a letter from Michael Marston: you collect him, an auld shipmate of ours? He has been fretting to find some means of employment these four or more years. Would you consider of him, Pat?' asked Simon, a little apprehensively. Marston's presence on board *Tenedos* previously had not been an unqualified success - Pat not greatly taking to Marston in his role as a chaplain aboard ship, and the crew considering it unlucky to have one aboard - Pat had admitted him only in his capacity as Simon's surgeon's assistant.

'Let me consider of it, Simon. We will speak further about it at supper,' Pat replied, noncommitantly, hedging; Simon content at that moment to ignore the evasion, plain as it was.

The afternoon passed pleasantly, the sun staying to warm and cheer them as *Surprise* tacked through Whitsand Bay, passed Dodman Point, and left Gull Rock in her wake, coming up to the approach to Falmouth. Seven bells struck as Pendennis Point came into sight directly off the bow. The master was back in his home port, and carefully brought *Surprise* past the Black Rock to larboard and into the Carrick Roads, the wind now south-westerly, abeam, her double-reefed topsails alone driving her on a north-westerly tack, her courses long since furled before her approach to the inner harbour. Pat had decided to bring her as close as the master thought fit to the town, and the topmen, skilled as they were and needing no bidding, gradually checked her braces to deaden her topsails, so slowing her momentum to a snail's pace, her course shifting closer to westerly; she could not get closer to the wind. Simon stood alongside a silent, but plainly pleased Pat on his quarterdeck, Barton at the wheel, as *Surprise* crept closer towards her intended anchorage, passing Killigrew's original Town Quay, the Custom

House Quay, to larboard, the master ordering her course changed again, to north-westerly once more, the town now abeam and her bow pointing in the direction of Flushing village.

'It is a great while since I saw you so happy, brother,' Simon remarked, conversationally. 'In such moments I could wish our voyage would go on for ever, all together in our contentment.'

'Fiddler's Green ain't in it,' whispered Pat, a little overwhelmed by the emotions engendered within him during the day.

There was barely a breath of wind, and the sound of her hull through the water, albeit now with the smallest ripple at her bow, was plainly audible, even on the quarterdeck. Inch by inch, *Surprise* approached the master's intended anchorage, the King's Road, the ship near silent now, sliding along, the tops'ls all backed, until the Fish Strand Quay lay two cables off her beam, the master declaring further beyond which he would not wish her to lie at low water. *Surprise* slowed as her way began to fall off, the current acting upon her, making a little leeway, slowing... slowing... stopped, no longer any forward movement at all upon her.

'Let go!' shouted the master, and the best bower was dropped with the distinctive sound of its splash heard all about the ship and the harbour. Pat looked about him, and then over towards the town, and saw, to his astonishment, lining the Market and Fish Strands, hundreds of Falmouth people, recognisable and familiar faces prominent amongst them through his glass even at that distance: many former *Tenedos* crew, old hands from prior voyages, and new *Surprise* crew members too; for the most part standing together with their wives, sweethearts, and numerous excited children. Suddenly the throng were roused as one, and broke into wild shouts of greeting, then cheering, all waving exuberantly, clapping and shouting, to greet *Surprise*, *their* ship, as they now considered her to be, their menfolk now her crew, come home.

Pat was standing near the wheel, very moved by the spectacle, a deep sense of gratitude for such a welcome swiftly arising within him and a heartwarming feeling of well-being quite overcoming him. 'Welcome home, Barton,' Pat turned to his cox'n, grasped and shook his hand with enthusiastic vigour, 'welcome home.'

Frigate, casting (falling away from the wind so as to shift away from anchor)

Source: Serres, Liber Nauticus

Chapter Three

And where are they? and where art thou,
My country? On thy voiceless shore
The heroic lay is tuneless now —
The heroic bosom beats no more!
And must thy lyre, so long divine,
Degenerate into hands like mine?

Wednesday 21ˢᵗ May 1823   *Falmouth, Cornwall*

After breakfast Pat and Simon remained in the great cabin with a fresh pot of coffee, reviewing the expedition preparations and awaiting the arrival of the mail coach from Truro; both keenly anxious to discover whether at least any letter of reply might be received from any of Pat's former officers. Duncan was away to the harbourmaster's office, attending to the port formalities. It being high water *Surprise* had been towed by her boats a little nearer to the Custom House Quay to facilitate the loading of her remaining stores and to allow boarding and disembarking for shore-leave of her all-volunteer complement, all Falmouth men with few exceptions.

'Art happy, brother?' asked Simon, looking up from his papers. 'Tell me of your contemplations. I have the impression - will I say - of a trifling lack of contentment about your person, a certain anxiety, if I may venture so?'

'I am a little put out, I confess.' Pat seemed to welcome Simon's interruption of his thoughts. 'I have been considering of our prospects, but there is one damn matter I cannot shake.'

'How do we stand without our customary complement of officers, if their arrival does not eventuate? Is it that which is oppressing you? Surely they are still to be expected, if a trifle late?'

'I do not like to count all my eggs before they hatch.'

'I suppose not. It would seem we have only Macleod in the basket. If the others do not arrive, would you suppose this will present us with insuperable difficulties, being so short-handed, tell?'

Pat exhaled deeply and nodded. 'Oh, without 'em we can sail the ship, of that there is no doubt; but to fight her, now that is a different matter; no officers on the gun-deck and Lord knows how we will fare. A hundred and eighty men, let us say, to fight the guns, both sides together; forty more to sail her, and a dozen aloft with small arms and in the magazines; two hundred men and more but ne'er a one of officers, save for Duncan - and me - on the quarterdeck. And if one or t'other of us should be wounded... I will not say knocked on the head; I fancy I will never say anything as unlucky as that, I will not tempt fate; no, we could not fight her, that is plain.'

'I dare say. So if not a one arrives this day, on the mail coach, we are to pass a summer here in Falmouth. Surely not?'

'You cannot have a ship sailing about without officers, it won't do.'

'I am no great navigator, but that is undeniable; a most commendable observation.'

Pat raised his eyebrows at Simon's jest, but continued, 'We will lack midshipmen too, and without officers I fear we will sit idling, knocked back on our heels, festering in some Ionian port; and that won't do; no, that certainly won't do. Why, I don't need no mumbo-jumbo seer, no astrological quack, nor any damn necrom... nec... necrophile to tell me what the Greeks will think.'

'Let us hope not.'

'Damned poltroons and cowards we will look, and what could we say to that? Precious little! Is there a tint of coffee in that pot?'

'There is none, will I send Murphy for fresh? Or perhaps we may enjoy a last glass of stingo while we remain in port, if it is not too early? The Globe is a commendable tavern over there on the quay. Let us await the mail there, Pat; perhaps your concerns will prove unfounded, and this principled scheme of yours can still be delivered, the departure of this vessel as intended?'

'The mail is disgracefully late, we will wait here a trifle longer, and if our officers ain't on it we will go ashore the moment it arrives.'

The crew, now that they were at full strength, and numbering more than two hundred and forty men, busied themselves with the many and varied preparations for the imminent voyage, all to a man supremely pleased to be onboard ship once again, and with a particular favour for *Surprise*. From all quarters there came the familiar noises of shipboard activity and bustle, so satisfying to Pat not having been to sea since four years or more: the resounding thump of the 'Bible' holystones on deck, as they were shifted from place to place, the hails aloft from the seniors of the crew on deck, and the general to-ing and fro-ing of men busying themselves in a myriad of routine tasks. From below there came the rhythmic noise of the pump. Even the shrill calls of the gulls were pleasurable and welcome to Pat's ears, the ambience of the whole, aside from his concern for the lack of officers, bringing about a quietude and relaxation within him which had been lacking for a considerable time.

Simon, never the most organised of souls, was similarly pleased to return to contemplation of the emerging and particularly tidy inventory of his medical supplies; at that moment calculating his stocks of portable soup, a glutinous jelly requiring melting before it could be imbibed, and which was a standfast of very doubtful welcome to all occupants of the sick berth. Also within the great cabin was Murphy, cleaning the windows, the lights as they were termed.

There came a pause, a suspension, in the customary shipboard noises, and a rising babble of voices, becoming louder and louder, could be heard coming from the quarterdeck. Pat, noticing after but a moment, his contentment broken, shouted with some irritation, 'What is that infernal row? What is that din, Murphy? Tell 'em to clap a stopper over it. What's afoot?'

'Well, it's the mail coach arrived, sorr, and some visitors be here,' replied Murphy, looking through Pat's glass, staring intently through the lights and across to the Custom House Quay, his naturally excessive curiosity piqued.

Pat and Simon broke off to go up on deck. The mail coach had disgorged its passengers. Even at the distance of almost two cables, the figures were recognisable and confirmed with the glass. To Pat's great pleasure two of them were Tom Pickering and James Mower, both former midshipmen with Pat on *Starling*, Pat's first command, and Pickering a lieutenant on *Tenedos* with Pat after that. The crew had ceased work and were standing about, animatedly gabbling amongst themselves, as pleased as Pat to see two old shipmates, both held in the very highest esteem. Of William Codrington, Pat's third invitee, there was no sign. In high delight to see such welcome arrivals Pat beamed with pleasure and waved across to the quay. 'Barton, you are to bring them aboard directly.' He turned to Simon, 'Why, Simon, ain't it a grand sight?'

'To be sure, Pat, a most pleasing event, indeed it is. A more joyous development cannot be imagined,' Simon replied, smiling broadly.

The barge swiftly brought Pickering and Mower aboard, the two saluting the quarterdeck, as was the old custom, their faces shining with self-evident happiness.

Pat greeted his former lieutenants with vigorous handshakes, his enthusiasm unrestrained, 'Very happy, most exceedingly happy to see you both. Tom, James, come into the cabin. Murphy, bear a hand there, bring Mr Pickering's and Mr Mower's dunnage aboard. And ask Freeman to bring a brace of burgundy too, if you will. Shift along there. Come in gentlemen.'

'Well, I ain't got three hands', muttered Murphy, irritably, under his breath, and left in search of his mate, Old Jim Lamb.

'Tom Pickering, by George, it is grand to see you,' from Pat, shaking his hand again with a vice-like grip as they came into the cabin. 'And James Mower himself: upon my honour, how do you do? Please be seated. Allow me to press you both to join me for dinner. Freeman! Freeman! Where is that mumping villain? Ah, Freeman, there you are. Tell cook we will be dining a little earlier, and there be five of us eating now. Please to put dinner in hand directly. Pray tell; where's the wine, Murphy?' The steward had swiftly returned, anxious to overhear the reunion.

100

'Well, it's just coming up, ain't it, sorr,' grumbled Murphy, without the slightest of genuine discontent, as pleased as Pat to see Pickering and Mower come aboard once again. All sat at Pat's table, each gazing amiably at the others, their mutual joy in reunion so very evident, and none wishing to disturb the deeply satisfying moment of contemplation with questions. Murphy returned with and poured the wine.

'If I may be so forward, Tom, pray tell us of your experiences since *Tenedos* was laid up,' coaxed Simon, eventually.

Tom Pickering was neither wealthy, nor well-connected, and so his recent four years ashore as a half-pay lieutenant did not facilitate his financial obligations to his family life, being with wife and four children: his lack of connections, as Pat had presumed, precluding him from finding another ship. 'Why, Doctor, so very dull years they have been, no prospects for a ship at all, my letters to their Lordships bringing the very briefest of acknowledgements, but sadly no promises. Half-pay at six pounds five shillings a month; just a little work in the Portsmouth dockyards to be had, and in the most tedious of tasks: negotiating on behalf of the port admiral with the repairers, the sole consolation being time with the family, and seeing the children grow up. I oft wonder if prosperity is the surest protector of happiness,' replied Pickering, in a downcast tone, the sparkling wit of many years ago seemingly absent. All felt their prior contentment just a very little diminished.

'Tom, let me offer you a glass of this delightful burgundy, if you will,' said Pat, jovially, to restore the mood. 'James, what of you since *Illustrious*, when you last departed of us in the year ten? By God, so long ago: fully thirteen years since we were shipmates!'

'Aye sir, so it is, and in ne'er a one have I not thought of those days aboard *Starling,* and all her crew. Many a poem have I toyed with in my thoughts since, fondly remembering of her,' Mower replied, nostalgically, with the barest nod. He had left *Starling,* having been promoted to first lieutenant with *Illustrious* in the year ten, voyaging with her to the East Indies where she gained battle honours at Java. 'Well, sir, *Illustrious* returned from Java and the Indies in the year thirteen to Portsmouth, and since then she has been in ordinary; the crew for the most part laid off; all the officers on the beach. I came back very sick, and stayed ashore for two years with the flux until I joined Captain Mould aboard the brig *Mutine* in the autumn of the year fifteen. I served aboard as first on the expedition to Algiers in sixteen, alongside *Impregnable* during the bombardment, and was discharged again sick when we came home.' The collective mood was diminished just a little further as all wondered what the implications of long term ill health might be.

Simon, ever the physician first, and concerned for all his shipmates in case of anything contagious being introduced so soon before departure, prompted quickly, 'My dear James, I am sure you will forgive me for asking, art thou still sick? Please to describe your sickness. Excuse us but for a moment, gentlemen. Mr Mower and I will shift to the gun-room for a more private consultation.' Simon, without hesitation, swept up Mower with a broad grasp of his shoulder, and moved swiftly through the cabin door, no murmur of objection being heard from him. Their departure and the subject left the prior cabin ambience of deep contentment entirely absent.

'Tom, allow me to fill your glass,' said Pat, striving to recover the mood and smiling broadly to Pickering. 'We are sailing on Monday and I have but a single officer, Duncan Macleod as first. Though we will be accompanied on this voyage by *Eleanor* – you may collect her, my schooner – she will serve only as tender and messenger, and so I should look upon it as a most particular favour were you to join us on *Surprise* as second. I explained in my letter only the bones of our purpose, which is to return to the Ionian Islands; to render assistance to the forming Greek government, resisting the Turk. Mind, 'tis not a mission for their Lordships, 'tis quite unofficial. Our status will be as a letter-of-marque for the Greeks. 'Tis akin to how Cochrane operated for Chile and now the Brazil. We will be away for a year or two. We can offer full pay and but the slenderest prospect of prizes. What say ye?'

'I am most heartily glad of your offer, sir. Most grateful to you for remembering of me, and would dearly wish to join you again: and on *Surprise* too, *Tenedos's* sister ship; doubly pleased, sir. If this crew is not the finest of company, where will I ever find it?'

'Capital, Tom! I am most heartily thankful to hear it, and welcome back, old friend, welcome back. Murphy will stow your dunnage in the gun-room, and after dinner we will take a tour of the barky. Murphy! Murphy! Trundle along to see cook, and ask after our dinner, if you will.' Murphy was pleased to see Pat still in exceptional good humour, albeit for much of the interview his ear had scarcely shifted from the door.

In the gun-room Simon and Mower were conversing in near whispers, there being no place on a ship the size of *Surprise* for assured privacy of communication. 'You will forgive me, Mr Mower ... *James*, for pressing you to explain your sickness. Whilst I naturally rejoice to see you again, I must be sure there can be nothing of any contagious nature introduced to this vessel. Particularly not just before we sail, and what I am minded to know is whether your long-lasting illness might persevere still, and what may yet be done, or be necessary, and – if anything – what help I may provide. Tell me of the very nature of your sickness.'

'You are very good, Doctor, and thankee for your kind interest for me. In the Indies I was struck down with the most severe flux, persisting for week after week until I was so ill I could hardly rise from my cot in the sick bay. I was in fear of my life, but the surgeon, good man that he was, could do nought to help me. I was bled four ounces every other day. For six weeks I was given no food save for onions, lemon juice, fresh fish and ship's biscuit aplenty. I recovered slightly afore we left Java, and became a little stronger during the voyage home, but the dysentery was so bad that the captain took pity on me and allowed me to shift into the great cabin, where I spent more time in his quarter-gallery, on the seat of ease, than ever on deck. The second was obliged to assume my duties, the third his, and so forth. When we arrived back in Portsmouth I was discharged sick. My wife, good lady that she is, bless her, nursed me back to health, but it was a full two years afore my strength returned such that I could beg a place on *Mutine*; but three months later, at sea again, and my flux was back,' Mower recounted the sorry tale, his voice full of worry, and clearly ill at ease even speaking of his illness.

'Pray, how are you at present?' asked Simon, tentatively.

'All a-tanto, Doctor, my wife has again nursed me back to good health.' Mower tried hard to smile, but his determination could not quite overcome his anxiety, so very plain, his low voice betraying a concern, a fear that he might not be believed, and so might be left ashore, in desolation.

'Console yourself, dear James,' Simon's voice carrying the conviction of kindness and friendship. 'The flux and dysentery are present on all His Majesty's vessels, more prevalent on some. Disease on His Majesty's ships has struck down many more men than Boney's sailors ever managed. You appear to have been singularly unfortunate, being stricken and incapacitated for so long, and so very severely. You will subsist only on a light diet, the basis being that which my colleague specified for you in the Indies, onions being an excellent antiscorbutic, lemon juice, oranges when we can find them, and fresh fish, which is excellent for the fibres. We will allow you neither salt pork, nor any salt beef. Vegetables you may eat aplenty, but no butter or fats. No water unless it be of the very freshest, only small beer for you should there be any doubt of its provenance, and I venture we will keep you in fine fettle. A glass of wine or brandy will do you no harm, it will doubtless rectify the humours,' Simon concluded his reassuring prescription.

'You do me the greatest kindness, Doctor, thankee,' Mower replied, brightening; realising he was not to be tossed ashore, his acute anxiety dispelled with the greatest of relief, and greatly heartened to find himself under the care of Doctor Ferguson, an infallible legend amongst his shipmates, and well regarded in much wider circles, having been consulted by the First Lord.

When they returned to the great cabin Pat was pleased to find that Simon had not discharged Mower, and insisted he take another glass of burgundy, to which Simon nodded, near imperceptibly, to Pat. 'You would do me the most essential service, James, were you minded to accept the duties of my third, Tom here having joined us as second,' said Pat, beaming now, considerably relieved by Simon's verdict, and finding his satisfaction in securing another of his old officers now preserved.

'Gladly sir: it would give me the utmost pleasure to serve again with you,' came the unhesitating reply from Mower, his joy and relief evident for all to see. At that moment Freeman and Old Jim Lamb arrived, carrying the dinner, steaming on Pat's silver plate. They set it down to delighted looks all round, and hastened away for more burgundy, the first two bottles being quite empty.

A little later, the main course having been eaten, a brace of bottles of fine port consumed, and with all about the table settled in the most amiable of moods, all present settled in comfortable languor. Pat looked around his cabin, his mind absorbing the entirely restored comfortable ambience and the genial satisfaction of all present, himself included, before his gaze settled on Simon. His mind continued its cogitations even as Freeman cleared the table. 'Simon, I have given thought to your proposal to take aboard Mr Marston, as your mate and as chaplain, and I would be pleased were you to send our invitation to the gentleman, if you will,' proffered Pat, as the pudding emerged. Simon allowed himself a private smile, merely nodding to Pat by way of confirmation. 'Will you take a little of pot still with me, gentlemen?' asked Pat.

'Pot still?' queried Duncan, who had returned aboard.

'Whiskey: from the son of MacManus, of Kilbeggan, in the fine County Westmeath; I have a bottle or two which Murphy ain't found; the glory of the world, so it is.'

'Och, certainly ah will take a wee dram wi' ye,' Duncan replied, grinning broadly; heads nodded emphatically all around the table.

'Mr Mower… *James*, perhaps you will grace us with a verse of your poetry?' suggested Pat, in high good spirits.

'Why, yes sir. I have a new poem underway, the first stanza completed only yesterday, a return to sea and the parting with my wife prompting it.' Mower extracted a much creased paper from within his jacket,

'Amidst the rolling waves of oceans comes the lovely thought of you,
Through the soughing of the breezes and the sparkle of the dew,
In the shining light of morning and the blackness of the night,
Come wondrous recollections and dreams of past delight.'

'Magnificent, to be sure,' complimented Pat as all clapped, 'though a trifle short. Would you care to scrape a little, Simon?'

'With all my heart, brother.'

'What do you care to play?'

'That is for you to choose.'

'Allow me to suggest our old favourite, *St Patrick's Day* or *Bacon and Greens* as we mariners refer to it, and then we shall play *the Rakes of Kerry:* I have a hankering for a reminder of the Emerald Isle; 'tis plainly far too long since I have gazed over the green hills of Galway and the fields of Connemara, so it is.'

'An inspiring choice, without a doubt.'

'Capital, Simon; have you seen my rosin?'

Friday 23rd May 1823   *Westminster, London*

On the day after the happy reunion with his officers, Pat and Duncan posted back to London, having arranged with the local carter in Truro to deliver all the remaining baggage packed by Sinéad to Falmouth on the morrow. The following morning the two friends presented themselves at the First Lord's private residence in Arlington Street. Mr Lowrey of the Foreign Office, George Canning's aide, was present to discuss all the political limitations associated with the arrangements for the expedition and to finalise the exact terms under which *Surprise* would be engaged and funded. The introductions were made without delay, the servant bidding them all to be seated around the large dining table when the discussion proper began. It continued for an hour, ranging over the most diverse aspects of the venture, including the readiness of *Surprise*, her victualling, the escort of Lord Byron, their intended port of arrival in Greece, contact with the Greek authorities, communications with London, and eventually the necessary secrecy of their arrangements.

Melville, anxious to wind up, rapped his spoon on his cup to gain their attention. 'O'Connor,' said the First Lord, 'until such time as you are engaged in Greek service and with a proper letter-of-marque from the provisional Greek government – not that such will count for much should ye be taken by a Turk I venture – I am minded to suggest that *Surprise* ostensibly be engaged in hydrographical surveying. We have a first rate man there in Smyth, *Mediterranean Smyth* as he is known at the Hydrographical Office, in command of *Adventure,* a sloop engaged in charting those waters.'

Pat merely nodded: the sophistry of the scheme not appealing to him in the slightest. After a further hour of negotiation and discussion had passed, the First Lord summarised, 'Weel, gentlemen, we are in consensus now. It is incumbent upon me to remark again upon the strict political limitations of our association with the provisional Greek government in that no connection with His Majesty's Government will be admitted in any circumstance. The first task for *Surprise* is to escort Lord Byron, who has joined the Greek Committee, and wishes to go to Greece himself, to Zante, and thence to establish contact with the Greek military authorities – such as they may be – with the intention of offering the assistance of *Surprise,* which must, note well O'Connor, be formally arranged. His Majesty's Government cannot become the recipient of any allegations of piracy from the Porte, and hence *Surprise* must become a Greek ship of war only after formal notarised request, and at the behest of the Greek authorities. Mr Lowrey will provide to you further instructions, as may be necessary from His Majesty's Government, in the strictest of secrecy and under cipher. He may deliver instructions of the first importance personally, or via a representative known to yourself and Lieutenant Macleod, commencing with your arrival in the Ionians. In the first instance, Mr Lowrey will provide to Lieutenant Macleod the appropriate code books in order that he may decipher any instructions that you may receive. Mr Macleod is also to write and return encoded reports of all political and military developments to the Admiralty. In that respect it is anticipated that he may seek to closely associate himself with the highest of Greek political and naval authorities. A suitable translator will also be sent to assist him in that task. Their Lordships will further commit from the secret fund a sum sufficient, as we have discussed, for the maintenance of *Surprise* and her crew during the expedition. These funds will be paid to your account, O'Connor. It will be for Mr Lowrey to remit funds to you in specie or any other form of your choosing via His Majesty's Consul in Zante, as you will call for it. The value of any prizes taken will be deducted, less forty per cent, from the agreed subvention, which will leave an adequate sum for the payment of prize shares to the officers and crew. Should there be any capture by the Ottoman authorities of *Surprise*, gentlemen, know you well that their Lords and His Majesty's Government will disavow any knowledge of these arrangements; will plainly state that *Surprise* is your private vessel; and I suggest, O'Connor, you will be festering in a Turk prison with no prospect of release, and will probably be hanged, or worse,' Melville concluded, on a dark and sobering note.

'My Lord, if you will, please to authorise a draft on my account. There are many pressing calls for considerable funds, very large calls indeed, and I must have this immediately if I am to complete all our preparations and make my tide. There is not a moment to be lost.' Melville merely nodded at Pat in acknowledgment, and turned towards Lowrey, his hand raised and pointing.

'If I might be permitted a question?' ventured Lowrey. 'Captain O'Connor, may I enquire: who are your bankers, sir? It is in order that deposits to your account may be arranged.'

'My principal bankers here in London, sir, are Hoare's, and since Smith failed some years ago I also have an account with Pole, Thornton, Free, Down and Scott of Lombard Street,' replied Pat, adding, 'I also hold some small funds with the Plymouth Dock Bank, for the purchase of local provisions should any ship I serve with ever require to dock in Devon or Cornwall, as has occurred from time to time.'

'Very good, sir; I think it would be convenient for the funds to be deposited in one of your principal accounts here in London, and Mr Thornton being well known to the Foreign Office, and he being accustomed to such careful transactions, Pole's would seem to be most appropriate,' concluded Lowrey.

'It leaves me, O'Connor, only to wish you well and good fortune. I must away now to dinner with the Foreign Secretary, and so I bid you all farewell,' concluded Melville, soberly.

Pat and Duncan left together, intending to overnight at the Feathers. Canning left accompanied by Lowrey, wishing them God speed. 'A rum venture, Duncan,' opined Pat, walking back along Pall Mall. 'I should scarcely have imagined it but a month ago. Am I not too old to be engaging in such capers?'

'Why to be sure 'tis certainly unorthodox, brother, but ye are to consider that it has brought us, Simon, Pickering, Mower an' all, back to sea, to oor new home, oor dear *Surprise*: a concentration o' endeavours o' which we have nae seen the like fer many a year an' there is certainly somethin' to be said fer that.'

'I am very sensible of it,' Pat replied, quietly.

Sunday 1ˢᵗ June 1823   *Falmouth, Cornwall*

The rising dawn sun cast its weak light over sleepy Falmouth town, the air dry but chilly as Pat stepped up from the great cabin, shivering a little as he paced about on his quarterdeck. A thin mist arose about the ship from the warmer harbour waters. Pat drew a deep draught of the cold salt air into his lungs and gazed up at the rigging, masts, yards and sails, his keen eye finding no fault with any of the arrangements. He looked through his glass towards the town. There were fishermen and merchants on the Fish Strand Quay but barely a soul to be seen on the Custom House Quay. He stepped along the deck to the bow, nodding pleasantly to the three men on duty. Contentedly he paced back to his quarterdeck. Barton was one of the very few persons on deck as Pat gazed about, standing near the wheel and chewing his quid, only the three other crewmen forward being about so early. He was a constant reminder to all aboard of his late brother, a reminder that oft prompted Pat's recollections of his lost cox'n; even now, memories of those days ten long years ago still returning so clear, and in his dreams too.

'Good morning, Barton. Tell me, did you know your brother well in his last years?' asked Pat, conversationally, still reflecting on his sleeping thoughts.

Barton, pleased to be asked, smiled weakly and nodded. 'Like my right hand knows my left, sir; I cannot say it any closer. Every possible leave we stayed together at our mother's house, our other brother, Robert, having been killed on *Irresistable* in the year twelve. Mother passed but a few months after he was gone: a broken heart, 'twas said.'

'He is, even now, mightily missed by his friends aboard too, Barton. A capital man, he was, 'pon my word,' Pat left the subject there. 'Be so kind as to rouse the bosun to pipe the hands to breakfast.'

'Aye aye, sir.'

Back in his cabin, Pat passed a few minutes in pleasant solitude gazing through the lights, abstractedly watching a lugger coming in towards the Fish Strand. She was rolling in the smallest of swell, two score or more of frantic, swirling gulls behind her, their shrill squeals bringing his mind back to the day ahead. He sipped his strong, black coffee whilst gathering his thoughts in preparation for *Surprise's* looming departure before shouting for his steward, 'Freeman! More coffee, if you please, and perhaps some soft tack and kidneys too; butter as well, if you will.'

'Coffee's a'comin' d'reckly, massa, an' cook 'im relightin' galley now,' came Freeman's cheery reply from the door.

Murphy too peered quickly round the door of the great cabin, looking crisper than his customary self so early in the morning, or at any time for that matter, thought Pat absently. His thoughts were interrupted by a still sleepy Simon coming into the cabin.

'Ah, Simon! Good morning, brother; give you joy of our departure today. Will you take some coffee with me? So much to do. Sinéad and the family are expected at four bells, the mail coach at five bells, and we will then be away directly on the tide.'

'And what o'clock would that be, brother?' croaked Simon, his grasp of nautical horology quite failing him so early.

'Why, Simon, ain't I explained that to you no more than perhaps two hundred times?' quipped Pat, mercilessly joshing his old companion.

'I believe you may have had occasion to mention it, soul. You navigators are sadly given to jargon, and a devotion to clocks and bells, so very incomprehensible to those of us whose genius is plainly more akin to the land-oriented kind. Pray, where is the coffee?' asked Simon, yawning. At that moment Freeman returned with the pot, clutching too, with a little difficulty, the soft tack and butter.

'Freeman, another plate for the Doctor, and ask the cook to double up the kidneys. Look alive there, and send for Murphy,' Pat said, in a very mild way, determined that nothing at all was to dampen his pleasure on this bright day of departure.

'Well, there ain't no bleedin' peace on this barky,' muttered Murphy, almost inaudibly, and only to himself, or so he thought, as he shuffled in to the cabin.

'Murphy! Top your boom there, you scoundrel, and you are to lay out my best coat and breeches athwart my cot when Freeman has served breakfast; and nicely pressed, mind,' shouted Pat to a sour-looking Murphy, departing in haste.

The early morning passed swiftly, the mist clearing, a brightening sun rising to warm the quays, the myriad of gulls still calling, orbiting the later returned fishing boats awaiting their turn to tie up at the Fish Strand Quay with their pilchard catches. With the high tide bringing plentiful depth of water, *Surprise* had been towed so as to be nearer the more spacious Custom House Quay where the families of the crew had gathered to witness her departure; her best bower and a kedge anchor now holding her position near two cables off the quay. The crew in their entirety were passing to and fro' the ship and the quay, all the ship's boats employed for this purpose, the men making their farewells to family, friends, and numerous other interested onlookers, a growing multitude of them gathering as the clock marched on. At the foretop the Blue Peter flapped vigorously, and at ten o'clock – four bells in the Forenoon watch – the coach arrived with Sinéad and the twins. Pat, in his best captain's attire, had previously stepped ashore to await and greet his family, now aboard *Surprise*. The ship's final preparations were left to Macleod, Pickering and Mower, the latter two sharing their time between their own families on the quay and their duties aboard; gently hustling along crew members dallying with their own kin whilst awaiting the mail, and minding the tide. The crew had also made an extra effort for such an important event. Their own best clothing, having no uniforms as such, had been washed, starched and pressed. Their pigtails were all replaited, as they sought, as much as their captain did, to look their very best on departure. The Wesleyans stood prominent amongst all, still garbed in their red attire.

Pat had returned aboard and, now standing on his quarterdeck, contemplated the late arrival of the awaited mail coach. He was mindful, with the very mildest of anxiety, of the imminent ebbing of the tide. 'This is cutting it pretty fine, Mr Macleod; we will strike the Blue Peter.'

Sinéad and the twins were all standing on Pat's quarterdeck, and in a high state of excitement as the final preparations for departure proceeded all around them. Pat had no time to pass with them, his attention was all for the ship: 'Mr Macleod, the bosun is to send the topmen aloft,' he ordered, adding to himself, 'The mail coach is hellfire late.' He was hardly conscious now of his family's presence, as his professional routine pressed in upon him, but he beamed in every direction, his own spirits never higher. Five bells came closer; the officers having called all the men aboard - only the arrival of the mail coach was still awaited. The quayside families continued to wave and shout excitedly to their husbands and sons; more than a few tears being shed by many of the wives and sweethearts. The crew strived to look busy, making ready to depart, but all was ready. Many were still shouting last farewells, and waving to the excited, assembled throng when they could. Only the barge with six rowers now still waited at the quay for the mail.

As the minutes ticked away, from the Custom House Quay came the distant clippety-clop sound of hooves and the distinct clatter of metal wheels on the cobbles. The mail coach approached the quay, brought to a halt amidst the excited throng. Two figures stepped out: the first a rather short man in His Majesty's most elegant uniform, the second plainly a civilian. 'By God, Simon, 'tis William Codrington!' shouted Pat.

'And my colleague, Michael Marston! To be sure, we have the blessing this day,' exclaimed Simon.

Pat shouted through his speaking tube to the quayside barge crew. 'Barton, bring those gentlemen aboard with their dunnage; swiftly now! There is not a moment to be lost.' He turned to the master and murmured 'Mr Prosser, stand by.'

Within five minutes, Codrington and Marston had scrambled aboard, two of the barge crew passing up the arrivals' baggage and following swiftly behind them, the barge swiftly hoisted up. Pat waved his hat briefly to the two men before turning to his steward. 'Murphy, my compliments to Mr Codrington and Mr Marston, and will you kindly take their dunnage below.'

The high tide had passed near two hours ago, and the ebb was about to succeed slack water. Before *Surprise* could begin to swing on her best bower - her bow still faced east towards the Carrick Roads, a kedge anchor keeping her station - Pat had decided that she would sail as soon as the ebb commenced; the gentle westerly breeze and lee tide would greatly facilitate her leaving. All along the Custom House Quay the crowd, sensing the imminence of *Surprise's* departure, cheered loud and shouted vigorously, tears and joy all a-jumble. The crew, those that could spare a moment, their hats tightly gripped and furiously waving, shouted vigorously back, and exuberant, loud whistling was heard from atop all the yards. Pat was immensely pleased himself, and minded not a jot this joyous breach of the customary, orderly routine of departure. The crew, many more hands in comparison with her departure from Plymouth Dock, made light work of all their tasks: the kedge was brought in, tops'ls unfurled, yards braced, the best bower swiftly catted, and slowly *Surprise* shifted away from her anchorage, a very happy Pat content to leave her control to Duncan and the master. She moved off, the two cables distance between the quay and the ship swiftly increasing. *Surprise* was gathering momentum, the wind acting upon her tops'ls, the ship now being driven across the inner harbour in the strengthening ebb current. Gradually, *Surprise* picked up a little more speed, but still the families ashore could be heard shouting fading farewells from the quay.

After a further ten minutes *Surprise* cleared the inner harbour and entered the Carrick Roads. Pat turned to his second lieutenant and the master. 'Mr Pickering, please take command if you will. Mr Macleod, Doctor Ferguson, and I are going into the cabin to greet our late arrivals.' This to Pickering as a convention and courtesy, but mostly for the ears of Mr Prosser, in the knowledge that no sailor knew the harbour and Roads better than the master, a native of Falmouth. 'Please excuse me, my dear,' Pat smiled as he spoke to his wife. Sinéad remained on the quarterdeck with the twins, quite fascinated by the spectacle of *Surprise's* departure. Pat was quite out of his depth as to how to manage his son and daughter, hurtling with great excitement around his province, the quarterdeck. To Simon, Pat muttered, with some little exasperation, 'Anyone might think we were aboard the Margate hoy.'

Simon said nothing, and simply smiled. Pat was more than a little relieved to go below, prompted by Simon's earlier and gentle suggestion that it was not a day to stand on the strictest of shipboard custom and etiquette. Pat and Simon came down into the great cabin, the new arrivals already seated and sipping tea, Freeman hovering near the door.

'William Codrington, joy be with you, 'pon my word it is good to see you again. Mr Marston, how well you look, sir. Welcome aboard. Freeman! Rouse out two bottles of the best Madeira, if you please; the seventy-five.'

When Freeman had returned, and was pouring the wine, all in the cabin had settled round Pat's table. Codrington explained that he had been away visiting relatives in the North Country; avoiding certain gentlemen of whom he declined to speak further, and had only very recently received Pat's letter. He had rushed immediately to Falmouth upon receipt of it, pausing only to don his uniform and pack the most meagre of baggage. Further necessities could be bought at their first port of call, and yes, he would be honoured to shift to *Eleanor*, as Pat suggested, most honoured and pleased to do so. Codrington hurried on, explaining that his finances were in an assuredly temporary state of dysfunction, but he was in no doubt that a successful voyage would restore his treasury and his standing. Pat had not anticipated all his officer invitees would become available in response to his invitations, and so, the appointment of a fourth lieutenant for *Surprise* being somewhat superfluous, the surplus of officers had been satisfactorily resolved by Codrington shifting to *Eleanor* where Pat was very pleased to have him as commander.

Michael Marston had heard from his parishioners in his Cornish benefice of Pat O'Connor's planned return to sea two weeks previously. An educated and intelligent man, the past four years he had found increasingly tedious as parish parson to his tiny and generally unlearned congregation. His subsequent letter to Simon in Plymouth had enquired of the prospects for employment of any kind. His letter had reached Simon at precisely the moment that he had realised the necessity for a surgeon's mate, Pat more conventionally considering first of his need for sailors. In anticipation of the possibility that he could be called away from the ship, Simon had deemed it wholly prudent to engage a surgeon's mate. Hence Marston's letter was opportune. Upon Simon's affirmative reply, Marston had leapt at the opportunity to volunteer his services. Marston was a proficient surgeon's mate who had assisted Simon through a particularly bloody battle aftermath with serious casualties requiring immediate surgery during one of his voyages aboard *Tenedos*. Simon was thus assured of his competency. The fact that Marston was also a knowledgeable naturalist further weighed significantly in Simon's considerations: finding on occasions that the company of nautical men could verge some way towards the tedious, Pat and Duncan being the exceptions. Marston could also play the violin, albeit he had not been the most accomplished of musicians when last aboard *Tenedos*.

Pat gazed out though his cabin lights, the large windows at the stern of the ship. *Surprise* was well out into Falmouth Bay, experiencing the customary chops of the Channel, sailing in a strong wind under all sail, white horses everywhere over a vigorous grey swell, spray spicules sweeping through the air and splashing on the glass. *Eleanor*, under the command of Reeve, trailed a mile behind in her wake. He turned to his table. Duncan, Pickering and Mower had left the master in charge on the quarterdeck, and had come into the great cabin at Pat's invitation to greet their former shipmate, Codrington.

It was a strict convention within the Royal Navy that no one spoke at the captain's table unless in reply to the captain. In this instance the tradition had seemingly gone by the board, as Pat's four lieutenants and two surgeons happily engaged in an animated babble of mutual reminiscences and told of their experiences since last meeting. Pat did not mind in the slightest since he was as interested as they all were in hearing their stories, and particularly delighted that all three recently arrived former lieutenants had accepted his invitation. Of Marston he was not so sure, but it was inconceivable that anything could shake his pleasure in this particular day. After half an hour, and Freeman having coughed at least three times at the door, and having brought in, after the captain's nod, two large pots of coffee, Pat rapped the table with his knuckles to call them to attention. 'Gentlemen, I am very much obliged to you all for accepting my invitation to join me, to serve aboard *Surprise*. Freeman, please pour the coffee. Only a very few days ago I had a fine crew and but one officer, and here we are, today, three more former comrades with me once more, together with our old friend and surgeon Doctor Ferguson ... Simon, and Mr Marston too.' Pat could not quite bring himself to speak of Marston as Michael, cordiality between the two in the past never having progressed that far.

Simon, in quite flagrant breach of convention, but in the knowledge that the new officers knew precious little detail of the voyage, its purpose, or the obscured drivers of it, interrupted Pat in his momentary pause, 'Be so kind as to outline your clearer view of our voyage, Captain.'

'Thank you, Doctor,' Pat reverted to a customary minimum of formality. 'I must tell you, gentlemen, that I am no longer a serving Royal Navy captain: I have resigned the service.'

There was an audible sharp intake of breath around the table.

'I have accepted the invitation of the provisional Greek government to advise and assist their formative navy on its methods to counter the Turk in the current struggle for Greek

116

independence. Gentlemen, upon our arrival in the Ionians, *Surprise* will commence operating under a Greek letter-of-marque. We have plentiful time afore we reach the Ionians in which to prepare: there is the Bay to traverse, we will touch at the Rock, the Straits, thence briefly to Port Mahon. From Mahon we are to visit Genoa for stores afore our voyage continues to Zante. The Governor there will provide us with victuals before we temporarily assume our ostensible mission: a survey vessel in Ionian waters. *Eleanor*, however, will at all times retain her status as an English ship, sailing as a private vessel, and thereby enjoying protection from Turk interference. She may be very useful to us with that safeguard and capacity should we need to separate our activities. As you know, gentlemen, I am accompanied by my family, who will become resident in Zante; and so on this first day aboard I must attend to them.

'Gentlemen, you will forgive me if I leave further explanations until the morrow when I hope you will all give me the pleasure of dining in the cabin, and we can speak further of these matters,' Pat concluded.

There was a murmur of further pleasantries before the officers shuffled out to settle in to their accommodation in the gun-room, and to reacquaint themselves with the crew.

'Murphy, my wife will take my cot, please rig another in the cabin for myself; the twins will berth in the spare officers' cabins. Be so good as to shift their dunnage down there, afore supper if you will, thankee.'

Murphy, only too pleased to be asked on matters of this nature, indeed in the most polite manner, even thanked by his captain, being mindful of Pat's imminent dinner busied away in some haste.

Pat returned to his quarterdeck where Sinéad and the twins were still evidently enjoying the novelty and vivid sense of adventure. The weather was particularly clement now that the sun was full up, and the wind, a gentle westerly, propelled *Surprise*, close-hauled but with her clean hull, at a steady six to seven knots. *Surprise* had passed the Manacles at noon, she was making good progress. By supper time and Lizard Point far off to starboard, Pat sat down at his table to eat with Sinéad and the twins. The youngsters were plainly excited at the adventure they had embarked upon, and had busied themselves all day speaking with many members of the crew, engineering encounters with them, asking many and varied questions about *Surprise*, their past voyages, and the crew's past experiences with their father. To all enquiries they received only the most glowing of positive answers, all mention of blood-curdling events or setbacks being most diligently expunged in the telling. Sinéad, more soberly, investigated the domestic arrangements for the voyage, and queried all on the prospects for the weather: not that anyone could vouch anything more than generalities and platitudes. After supper, before leaving the table, Sinéad pressed Pat for his views on the potential dangers of the expedition, but could glean near nothing about that, and so she ultimately contented herself with the short term prospect of the voyage to Greece – via Mahon, via Genoa, and via anywhere else that wind and weather might take *Surprise* – as Pat laboured to explain the vagaries and vicarious nature of weather at sea.

As the twins, finally exhausted, went off to their berths below, Pat settled Sinéad in his cot, and decided on a little time for quiet reflection on his quarterdeck, the late spring evenings being pleasantly warm. It was these tranquil last hours of the day, the sun having set and dusk fading into the near total blackness of the approaching night that Pat, being a passionate astronomer, particularly enjoyed. At home, he had a telescope established in his own observatory. Aboard, he had a powerful glass which doubled for his military and astronomical purposes. The ship was now quiet, supper having concluded, and on deck there remained very few of the crew. It had been a relaxing watch for them, the wind having being steady and westerly since sunrise, though veering north-westerly as the day progressed, and no tacking had been necessary for much of the day. Pat, Mower, the master, Barton and two helmsmen were the only ones present on the quarterdeck. Pat gazed back over her stern, her wake still visible for miles behind her with its trail of sparkling silver phosphoresence, her course so straight, unbending: two points west of south. He looked up at her yards, all braced to catch the prevailing north-westerly, since late afternoon so constant in its strength and direction; the helmsman with little challenge to maintain her course with hardly any leeway. Pat slowly paced the length of his ship, enjoying the quietude of the moment, *Surprise* pitching very gently in the exceptional tranquility of the Channel sea state, and with only the slowest and smallest of roll, near unnoticeable to any seasoned mariner. A few minutes passed before he stood on the forepeak; he swept the southern sky through his glass: the brightest of the stars already visible; the constants of *Vega*, *Cygnus* and *Altair* were shining brightly; the planet *Saturn* faintly emerging. Ten minutes passed, Pat gazing at the night sky in all its emerging splendour until, with a deep sigh of satisfaction, he retraced his steps and regained his quarterdeck.

'A prime day, Mr Mower, Mr Prosser, Barton; I bid you good night, gentlemen, lads,' remarked a very contented Pat, pacing slowly past the wheel.

'Proper, sir, none better,' replied Prosser in his slow Cornish intonation.

'Good night, sir,' from Barton and the helmsmen.

Below in the gun-room, the officers were engaged in vigorous debate about aspects of the voyage that loomed large in their minds, principal amongst which was their captain's resignation. Simon, with possession of many if not all of the answers, could not freely comment, and politely demurred from doing so when pressed, claiming scant knowledge. A strange look from Marston, peering out of his cot where he remained prone and in some little discomfort, the sea sickness claiming him after such a long absence from sea rather suggested that he believed Simon to know more than he was prepared to let on.

Monday 2nd June 1823   *Bay of Biscay*

The Bay of Biscay weather was pleasantly clement, exhibiting none of the violent horrors that the crew had experienced on many a prior occasion. *Surprise* sailed on steadily at a comfortable five knots, the air temperature rising slowly as she made southing. From the gun deck came the sound of clicking hammers, as the crew sat about, chipping away at the round shot that had been resurrected from the damp stowage of the hold, having gathered a patina of rust, smoothing before oiling them with slush begged from the galley, it being a valuable perquisite of the cook. On the forepeak three men were polishing one of Pat's two personal chasers, *Lucifer*, all its old brown paint now gone, and its bronze restored to a lustrous shine.

At his customary dinnertime Pat sat at his table in the great cabin with his officers: Duncan Macleod, Tom Pickering, James Mower and William Codrington all present. William Reeve, being master's mate in rank but for so long in Pat's service, and entrusted latterly with *Eleanor,* was also in attendance; Mr Prosser skippering *Eleanor* in *Surprise's* wake. All were in a high state of anticipation and curiosity. Finally there was Simon, seated alongside Pat, and savouring the remnants of his coffee. Michael Marston, still indisposed by sea sickness, remained in his cot in the gun-room.

'How does Marston fare, Simon? I gather he is laid up, indisposed, the sea-sickness. Will we put him ashore at The Groyne?' This said with a smile and a wink, Simon well aware of Pat having no prediliction for the clergy aboard his ships.

'Certainly not: he is merely incommoded at present, a temporary state; the rhythmical motion of this vessel it is, after years ashore on firmer standing. He sends his compliments. A low diet will answer, and he may return to his duty on the morrow.'

'I am gratified to hear it.'

After a most cordial dinner of the first quality, fresh provisions being in plentiful supply so soon into the voyage, and a pleasant hour spent in the most delightful of reminiscences, Pat caught the air of restrained anticipation and so began the briefing. 'Gentlemen, we are bound for Genoa for provisioning, beforehand touching at the Rock for fresh water, and calling also briefly at Port Mahon. Thereafter we sail for the Ionians where we will make contact with representatives of the provisional Greek government, and so formally enter their service. Whilst we are awaiting our letter-of-marque we shall engage in surveying the Ionian waters. Mrs

O'Connor, my son and daughter, Mrs Macleod and Mr Macleod's daughter will remain in residence at Zante whilst we are engaged in that task. Only when we have our letter will we become a combatant ship, and then we will be officially entitled to any Turk prizes we may capture. Note gentlemen, we do not serve in any official capacity on behalf of His Majesty's Government, and therefore none of us may legally continue with our service rank, and so all must resign. The First Lord has, so you all will know, pledged to restore all of us to our former rank and seniority when we have completed our service for Greece, but note also, this particular aspect is to remain confidential, known only to those at this table, and may not be communicated to anyone else. I trust you will remember of this, gentlemen.'

There was a general and concurrent affirmative response from everyone present, all mulling over questions that had come to mind, but in the more formal ambience prevailing now that they were at sea all observed the long familiar protocol of the captain's table, withholding questions and comment until asked directly.

Pat continued his briefing, 'The Greeks have precious few ships with which to fight the Turks bringing reinforcements and stores to their troops in Greece. Two years ago the island of Chios was sacked, and thousands of Greeks taken from that place as slaves. The Greek islands of Psara, Hydra and Spetses provide the only Greek warships, and these are generally armed merchantmen only, no regular warships being available to them. Their crews insist on payment in advance, and will not sail without it. Most of the shipowners will not hazard their vessels against Turk warships; they will only fight merchantmen. There are, however, senior and brave Greeks, Admirals Miaoulis and Canaris being principal amongst them, who will fight the Turk warships with what little they have to command. The Greeks have become adept at using fireship tactics to make up for their lack of numbers and ordnance. New Greek warships *have* been ordered, notably two heavy frigates and six steamships, yet none are expected to arrive for some time, years even. Until then, gentlemen, *Surprise* will be the sole purpose-built warship fighting in the Greek cause. Our adversaries are many, and the Turk frigates may substantially exceed our size and ordnance; we will therefore choose our engagements with the utmost care, and flee before great odds so as to remain intact and effective for another day. Mr Macleod has, in these past few weeks, studied the political and military situation, and has some knowledge of the current circumstances. Will you comment please?'

Duncan followed on: 'There is near civil war amongst the Greeks. Koloktronis is chief in the Morea, Odysseus in the East, an' Mavrocordato 'tween the twae. Messalonghi is under siege, Athens is in the hands o' the Turk, an' the provisional Greek government resides in Nauplia in the north-east of the Morea. Och, the situation, gentlemen, is bleak indeed fer the Greeks. It is to be hoped that the Turk resupply by sea can be hindered, so weakenin' their forces in Greece until the Greeks can act resolutely as one, their infightin' ceases, an' ultimately their wee state becomes more firmly established, wi' greater political support. If an' when this occurs, gentlemen, it might be hoped that significant pressure might then be brought to bear on the Porte.'

'Thank you, Duncan. Let us for Heaven's sake return to our humble level of honest mariners and our shipboard intentions else we may run foul of politics, the politics of foreigners even, and that is the end of all comfortable talk. As can be seen, the Greeks are in a proper lather; a greater dog's breakfast can hardly be imagined, and it is we who are to pull their chestnuts out of the frying pan,' Pat concluded.

Tuesday 3rd June 1823   *Bay of Biscay*

It was the morning of the third day out of Falmouth, and Marston was feeling sufficiently recovered to take some solid food for the first time. 'I am most thankful for your ministrations, dear colleague,' he said to Simon. 'Ne'er did I think I would suffer so, and after so many prior voyages at sea.'

'A few days aboard will answer tolerably well. Allow me to offer you a trifle of this burgoo, Michael. Eat it whilst 'tis hot; here is a glass of the most excellent and medicinal Madeira to follow, then we will take a turn on deck,' replied Simon.

The fresh sea breeze and warm, morning sunlight both being so reviving, Marston recovered some colour after a few hours, and so was able to walk unaccompanied, and to stand on the lee side, leaning on the bulwark and gazing at the Spanish coast.

'Mr Marston! I hope I see you well, sir,' shouted Pat, seeking an opportunity to extend some hospitality and cordiality to him, and looking forward from his quarterdeck. 'What do you say to a pot of tea with the Doctor and I?'

After a few minutes they descended to the great cabin, Pat shouting for his steward, 'Freeman! D'ye hear me? Bear a hand there; bring another chair for my guest and a fresh pot of tea, some eggs and bacon too. Send the word to the cook. Mr Marston, pray sit down, sir, you do not look well.'

It was a statement which struck fear, great fear, into Marston: for a brief moment the fleeting thought that he might be set ashore flashed through his mind. 'Oh no, sir! It was only a passing malady, quite transient, and gone now. Dr Ferguson assures me that the remedy is sea air, plentiful sea air, as much as possible; being aboard ship and far from land being the surest of cures.'

'I hope you will give me the pleasure of joining the Doctor and myself for supper today, after which we will practice a little scraping; you *did* bring your instrument?'

'Why, sir, thank you, thank you; indeed it would give me great pleasure to accept your kind invitation, and yes, I have my violin, I am very pleased to say,' Marston beamed, the invitation so significant, so welcome, and his face for the first time shifting from the mask of strain.

After Marston had left the cabin, considerably reinvigorated, bacon and eggs heartily consumed, Pat remained with Simon. 'What do you say to a fresh beefsteak, with beans, and a second pot of tea, Simon?'

'With all my heart; and conceivably might there be onions too? I venture the suggestion in the medical context: they are an excellent antiscorbutic, as you will doubtless collect.' Simon laughed as the recollection of such banter came back to him from their former voyages together.

'Freeman! Show a leg, and rouse out a bottle of the good Madeira,' shouted Pat, perfectly aware that Freeman's ear would be hovering close behind the door: he had learned well from Murphy.

'That was an exceedingly cordial gesture, Pat, if my memory does not fail me. The more so as I collect you did not favour my colleague's playing when he was last aboard?' remarked Simon.

'I am so happy, old friend, being at sea once again, a prime crew, fine officers to a man, Sinéad here, the swabs happy, the Bay behaving herself; Marston's playing, bad or worse, is of no consequence. Simon, a toast, if you will,' said Pat, raising his glass, 'To our venture, and may no new thing arise!'

'Our venture, and may no new thing arise,' echoed Simon, smiling.

After supper Pat, Duncan and Simon were astonished by Marston's playing. They started with the old Royal Navy favourite, *Bacon and Greens,* and shifted to *Corelli,* Marston's violin bringing a pleasing high end sharpness to the pair of Pat's cello and Simon's viola, greatly contributing to their enjoyment of the melodic sound of the *Concerto Grosso Adagio Opus 6 No. 8*, Simon's particular favourite. The evening's ensemble, even allowing for Duncan's sometimes indifferent improvisations with the whistle, excelled everything previously heard in the great cabin, so much so that they were all greatly delighted, and expressed volubly the most flowing of compliments at the end. 'Mr Marston, may I praise you most heartily on your violin,' said Pat, much to his own surprise.

'I am much obliged, Captain O'Connor, deeply obliged, thank you sir,' Marston replied, a little overwhelmed by the warmth of his inauguration to the cabin social scene.

'I give you joy of your nautical parish. Pray tell, sir, how did you impr … *achieve* such an excellent talent since last aboard our barky?' asked Pat, still incredulous at the very substantial improvement.

'The melancholia, sir, long winters, dark evenings; the dwindling congregations in my benefice; my parishioners struggling to make ends meet, their long hard days working to earn a living, the cost of bread now so very high, and Sundays tending

124

their vegetable plot, those that had one after the enclosures that is. Great poverty abounded in my parish. For a while I took to drinking the local cider: it started at harvest festivals, from flagons left as my gift until I decided one day to stop before things got out of hand. To cheer myself, I took to my violin, practising every day, and sometimes I would have a visitor, accomplished in the strings, who would encourage me until I mastered all the sheets I had. Then I gave solo concerts in the church, and my parishioners trickled back, but their numbers were still so few, many so poor and gone to the workhouse, husbands even selling their wives for lack of even a shilling. That, sir, is why the news of your voyage was so welcome to me, and I am here with the blessing of my good wife, Mary, to seek a new purpose, a re-invigoration, Captain O'Connor.'

The latter comment struck a most sympathetic chord with Pat, and being a landowner himself, albeit in a small way, and an Irish Member of the House, he understood full well the implications of the accelerating agricultural changes, post-war: particularly the enclosures, and worst of all, the very high taxation regime imposed on corn imports and the peasants' staple, bread - consequently so costly. He commiserated wholeheartedly with Marston: 'Ah, the enclosures; the Corn Laws; the interest on bonds now reduced to a trifling three and a half percent whilst tax has risen to thirty-four shillings a quarter on corn. Boney is long gone yet income tax is still at two shillings in the pound. How is an honest man to feed his family? 'Tis a pretty kettle of fish when bread is so dear. Mr Marston, I have so much enjoyed myself this evening; I thank you again for your company. Might I enquire if you would favour us with your playing after supper each evening, for an hour or so perhaps, as we cross the Bay?'

The captain's transformation was quite incredible to Simon who in past times had come to accept that Pat could not bring himself to favour the chaplain, even in his capacity as assistant surgeon.

'Why, sir, I thank you most kindly. I will look forward to tomorrow with particular enthusiasm,' Marston replied, as much taken aback as was Simon by his captain's gracious compliments and invitation, his face shining with pleasure.

Murphy was less overwhelmed, as he complained to his sometime assistant, Old Jim Lamb, whilst helping Freeman and clearing the dishes back to the galley. 'Well, there be another of 'em now, all caterwaulin'; four of 'em, dinning away. 'Tis enough to drive a man to the captain's liquor store.'

'Would you be meaning *more often*, Murphy?' asked Barton, who was also Old Jim Lamb's cousin, and consequently privy to certain shipboard practices, overhearing Murphy as he was helping himself to cocoa off the galley stove.

By Corunna the quartet had become well established: before Cape St. Vincent Sinéad had returned from keeping the twins company in the sick bay after supper to attend the playing; by Cadiz the ship's officers were invited to join them for toad in a hole and to enjoy the increasing ambience of informal bonhomie in the cabin after supper as the quartet played.

'God help us,' said Murphy, taking advantage of the absence of all officers from the quarter-deck, all being in the cabin, and chatting to Anderton, his cousin and one of the helmsmen, 'what a caterwaulin' they do make, to be sure, 'tis a din worse than the bar o' the King's Head in Galway Town of a Saturday night.'

Tuesday 17th June 1823   *Gibraltar*

Surprise had come into Rosia Bay at Gibraltar in the late afternoon of the previous day. In the brightness of the following morning, Pat, his officers and most of the crew had gone ashore: Pat to show Sinéad and the twins his old haunts; Simon and Marston had left to climb the Rock and observe the wildlife; Reeve and Barton remained aboard with a few hands, supervising the loading of fresh water.

Marston, by now fully recovered from his seasickness, and his morale restored substantially by his welcome and playing popularity in the cabin, exuded enthusiasm for all things, including O'Connor, the officers and the crew. Duncan, Pickering and Mower he had become accustomed to many years previously, and both had extended a friendly welcome to him upon his return. Codrington and Reeve were also very amiable with him, and unsurprisingly he

126

contrasted the lonely times in his small rural parish with the companionship aboard ship, in which he delighted. Ships fare whilst plain for the most part was plentiful and invariably accompanied by wine which, although varying from indifferent to excellent, was not the norm at his Cornish home, and contrasted so much with his recent hard times.

Upon gasping their way up the final yards to the summit of the Rock, Simon and Marston collapsed for respite, sweating profusely and gulping the last of the water from their flasks. As their breathing recovered they sat enjoying the magnificent views, and recounted fond recollections of their last time at Gibraltar, when they had also climbed the Rock to observe the vultures, storks and even eagles: all of which were still present and plainly visible. They sat basking in the hot sun, not a single cloud in sight, and when fully relaxed from their exertions supped from a brace of red wine bottles which Simon had brought along, reclining and eating plentiful cheese sandwiches, munching on large and crunchy red onions purchased that morning, and cracking Gibraltar walnuts, a particular favourite of Simon's. 'Marston, art happy? I am considering of a particular matter.'

'Pray tell, Ferguson; we have known one another long enough to speak our thoughts without giving offence.'

'Listen, Michael, will I tell you something? You will know that O'Connor has resigned the service?' Simon volunteered, 'This venture not being one in which His Majesty's officers can lawfully serve.'

'I am not unaware of this, this … development. The officers speak of it in the gun-room, and there is a singular want of privacy for such discussions, as you know full well. The Captain must surely be cast down fearfully by such a change, the service being his life, even his very being?'

'To be sure, O'Connor did not choose this course lightly. It came about only after several years ashore, and his dissatisfaction with their Lordships keeping him cooling his heels on the beach whilst all around him the fleet was shrinking. It has been a tolerably good decision on his part, I find. I do not collect seeing him happier than these past weeks. May I say, as you have now so fortuitously engaged with him in a social capacity, joining our scraping at supper, O'Connor could not be described as a philosopher, being something of a plain speaker in his honest tarpaulin way. You should mind where any dialogue might lead us: in particular you would be well advised never to let the term *privateer*, or even worse, *pirate* – God forbid – cross your lips, and though one must never become the prisoner of words we must content ourselves with the term *letter-of-marque* should the subject of our capacity in Greek service ever arise. I collect we may have spoken of such afore, though these matters of mere procedure, of protocol, I find, oft slip the more – will I say – philosophical mind.'

'Is the nature of the privateer somewhat discreditable? I would be sure of my understanding in such a delicate matter.'

'Of course the privateer fights for what O'Connor and his colleague officers would consider as the basest of motives: he fights solely for gain, for profit; purely mercenary are his interests.'

'And prizes hold no interest for O'Connor? I collect great joy abounding when prizes were taken in the past, the Captain being particularly pleased: surely so?'

'That is plainly undeniable, Michael. Yet the Captain would consider the two to be wholly different: the taking of prizes in His Majesty's service bestowing a legitimacy which is morally absent from the perspective ... from the thinking, of the privateer.'

'Why, there is a distinction of course; no one would deny it.'

'Conceivably, your role will become of the utmost significance for our venture, and it would be a particularly unwelcome development were anything to arise so as to bring even the slightest of rift between you and O'Connor.'

'Never be so concerned, dear colleague: after years of shivering in Cornish winters, no fuel to be had save the odd windfall along the lanes, nothing of note ever occurring in my daily routine, no person of any education with whom to enjoy any meaningful discourse, this is most certainly the life I aspire to: interesting companionship and good commons. Be assured I will never cross O'Connor; such is inconceivable, you may be certain of that,'

Marston nodded as he spoke, in emphasis of his understanding, whilst both stared intently at the whirling vultures overhead, entirely distracting Simon. His point made, Marston looked about him, his interest returning to the fauna, before loudly exclaiming, 'Over there; apes! Why, the rascals have seized our sandwiches!'

Wednesday 25th June 1823   *Western Mediterranean*

The wind was blowing a very favourable, gentle southerly as *Surprise* neared Port Mahon in the early afternoon, greatly facilitating her entrance to the harbour, a long and winding passage, no great width available, and hence safe access so dependent upon the wind direction. Slowly she slipped past Fort Marlborough to larboard, and Cape Mola to starboard, shearwaters flying in a multitude about them, as they passed by with her courses furled, coming up next past the Lazaretto Fortress to starboard; now sailing on reefed topsails alone, keeping to the north side of the channel, passing Cuckold's Reach, gliding through the narrow passage to the north side of the hospital island of Sant Felip Fort, and approaching the Town Quay. The northern side of the great length of water was devoid of buildings for the most part, and presented a dry and brown landscape covered with the scrub oak native to the island, contrasting so starkly with the cultivation amidst the scattered buildings set back from the harbour. Orange groves covered with white blossom stepped back up the hillsides overlooking the town, the wind gusts bringing occasional scintillas of their scent, alternating with wild jasmine, wafting towards all on deck. *Surprise*, her topsails now double-reefed, slowed to a near stop as she turned hard to larboard with the last of her momentum just as she came abeam the Town Quay and Pigalle Steps, no other ships being tied up. The southerly wind now pressed upon her at the bow, her topsails backed, and she came quickly to a stop, and let go her small bower. The cable veered, *Surprise* drifted back slightly to leeward to set her anchor. Long known in the Service as the Pigtail Steps, they led directly up to the top of the town. The whole crew were now on deck: many of them gazing at a port which they had, for the most part, lived in for four years until the year two when the island had been handed over to Spain, a port they had visited many times thereafter. Pat and Simon on the quarterdeck similarly looked hard for familiarities and changes, not many of the latter being evident.

'Why, Simon, 'tis been a long time since we first tied up here: it seems a lifetime ago,' sighed Pat, with just the barest hint of melancholy in his voice. 'It ain't changed at all, save that I see no brigs or frigates, not a one here.'

'It is as if we were never away, Pat. A glorious place it is, there is no doubt.'

'Happy times here, they were.'

'To be sure, that thought is never far from my mind these days, brother. I oft so dearly wish that Agnes could be here to share these peaceful days with us.' Simon said this very quietly, and Pat did not hear him.

'Mr Pickering, be so good as to roster leave ashore for the crew; we will be here two nights. The Doctor, Mr Macleod, and I will be ashore for both of them. Pray take command of the barky, if you will. Duncan, Simon, a walk up the steps, and a pint of sherry in Jeraldo's Coffee House, for old time's sake, on our way to the Royal, I fancy. Are you with me?'

'Aye, fer sure,' said Duncan.

'I will be very happy, dear soul,' Simon replied, wistfully, thinking of his prior, penurious days during numerous visits to Mahon, for many a year after he had first met Pat.

Port Mahon was well known to them all: even after Minorca had been handed back to Spain after the Treaty of Amiens the town and harbour of Mahon had continued to be used as the Royal Navy base in the western Mediterranean. From inauspicious beginnings when they had all first met in Portsmouth in the year three, a deep and enduring friendship had grown and blossomed over the sixteen years afterwards whilst they served together on His Majesty's warships, cemented by many a sociable hour in this town.

Walking up the steps was something akin to a homecoming for all of them. Pat's mind wandered fondly to a discrete dalliance with a lady in Mahon, before he had married, with the wife of one of the based squadron's officers: a liaison perhaps suspected, but never coming into the open; the said officer losing his ship and his life in battle at sea a year later. He also fondly remembered a near romantic encounter with the wife of the landlord of the Royal, the lovely Marisol: near only because of the impromptu and perhaps timely arrival of Duncan who took a disapproving view, almost bringing them to an occasion of honour with seconds in attendance; the inevitably bloody conclusion fortunately averted by an engagement at sea in which Pat was wounded; the passage of time during his healing, Simon's care and intervention, and Duncan's solicitude for him smoothing the rift between them.

Though it was some years since Pat had been in Mahon he felt immediately at his ease; indeed, he was acknowledged still by brief, but friendly greetings from several near-forgotten, nodding acquaintances, as he walked along, few officers ever having brought so many prizes into the harbour. Pat might even now be a welcome guest in many respectable houses of the town.

The appeal of the sherry at Jeraldo's was a nostalgic pull, but the Royal beckoned more strongly: certainly for Duncan, as that was where his daughter Brodie and wife Kathleen were accommodated, and so they resolved to pass by Jeraldo's, and bear directly for the Royal, aware that Kathleen and Brodie, not knowing precisely when *Surprise* would arrive in Mahon, might not actually be there. Kathleen had written to Duncan before they left Falmouth, advising of her love of the island, never previously having left the British Isles, and she was usually engaged in roving far over the interior by horseback, always accompanied by Brodie.

They strolled into the Royal by the familiar back way, through the little courtyard of orange trees; greeting a pair of English mastiffs; Duncan throwing four old walnut halves found in the depths of his pocket before the dogs would rise to greet them, slavering and panting in the heat of the early afternoon. Of Brodie and Kathleen there was no sign, but Marisol was still there: a little greyer, a little plumper, but still the same excitable and enthusiastic person that Pat was never likely to forget. 'Capitano Pat!' she shrieked, rushing to throw her arms around Pat's neck, to his evident joy, as he swept her clean off her feet in the friendliest of embraces, beaming with undisguised pleasure.

It was becoming a little late in comparison with their customary dinner time aboard *Surprise*, and so, after profuse greetings, several fondly remembered Royal staples were ordered: beefsteak pudding, a solomongundy, almond cakes to finish; washed down with refreshing bottles of a very palatable local beer – English beer sadly no longer to be had – and followed by generous brandies accompanied by a large pot of strong coffee, Marisol remembering well their affinity for it.

By mid-afternoon the tiring effects of the food, the several beers and brandies, together with the deep heat of the Mediterranean sun, combined to dictate a siesta, as was the local custom. Pat, Simon and Duncan slumbered comfortably in deep chairs within the draught and shade of the inside of the Royal. They were awakened, as the afternoon began to cool, by an excited babble from the kitchen, Marisol in voluble exchanges with undetermined female voices. Within minutes an excited Brodie burst through the drape separating the kitchen from the public room, running across to greet her father as he rose from his chair.

'Och, ma wee bairn, 'tis so wonderful to see ye, indeed it is,' said a delighted Duncan as he seized her up from the floor and they hugged. He bestowed a gentler kiss on both cheeks for Kathleen, as is the Mediterranean custom, husband and wife settling into animated conversation, the reunion so pleasurable.

Another old Tenedos, Patrick Coghlan, now the ladies' escort, stood mute but beaming behind them before replying to Pat's greeting of: 'I see Mr Macleod has dragged you from the Boora bog, Coghlan!' with his gruff Irish, 'Aye sorr, thankee.'

Friday 27th June 1823   *Mahon, Balearics*

Surprise slipped out of Mahon harbour with the aid of a benevolent north-westerly, which greatly aided her passage along the several miles of channel from her mooring near the quay, past the Lazaretto, and out into the open waters; her courses, topsails, and topgallants together giving her a steady seven knots as she set up for Genoa.

The previous day had been spent in shifting the little baggage of Kathleen, Brodie and Coghlan aboard *Surprise*, followed by their long delayed visit to Jeraldo's. It had changed not one jot since their very first drink there together, of cocoa, more than twenty years previously, many pints of sherry having been shared there since. The day had ended with a celebratory farewell supper at the Royal: Marisol in tearful embrace with Pat at the end, a little to his embarrassment; Sinéad being present, but not caring to ask about Pat's old times in that dimension, recollecting a suspected brief dalliance by Pat with a young lady in Halifax, Nova Scotia, during the war.

Despite the emotional farewells of the previous evening the mood aboard *Surprise* was buoyant: it was sustained all day through to a voluble and amiable supper in the great cabin; Marston and all the officers being introduced to Mrs Macleod and Brodie; the crew welcoming back their old shipmate, Coghlan.

Accommodation aboard *Surprise* was now becoming full, and the officers had kindly shifted around their tiny cabin berths in the gun-room, so as to make space for the two ladies; the twins and Brodie adopting the larboard berths; Duncan shifting temporarily to Pat's cabin; Pickering, Mower, Prosser and Marston taking the starboard cubicle berths, with Codrington and Reeve living aboard *Eleanor*. A little more space was afforded to the ladies because the captain had not engaged a clerk, and neither were there any midshipmen.

As the days of the voyage passed, the quartet of Pat, Duncan, Simon, and Michael Marston, playing after supper time, had already become something of a routine and an event that all four greatly looked forward to. Sinéad, now joined by Kathleen, was nearly always in the great cabin during their playing, and the lieutenants too were usually in attendance. Marston, in contrast to his diffident playing during earlier voyages, was now almost approaching virtuoso. His playing had, over recent weeks, inspired both Pat and Simon to strive harder to follow him. At other times the playing was so relaxed that they ventured enthusiastically and unprompted into surprising variations. Even Murphy by now was lingering close outside the cabin door, helping Freeman serve the toad in a hole, and had ceased grumbling at the much increased cleaning afterwards – except when with his mate Old Jim Lamb, for even Murphy had his position and reputation to consider of.

Sunday 29th June 1823   *Western Mediterranean*

The evening being pleasantly warm, and the four musicians having been playing with great exuberance, Pat had left the great cabin door open through to the gun deck, so as to capture a draught of air to cool the cabin. Sinéad and Kathleen being with the twins and Brodie in the gun-room, the quartet had been playing with great enjoyment, uninterrupted, for more than an hour when Marston paused with a broken string. Whilst he changed the string, Pat and Simon decided upon a brief recuperation.

'Pat, might I suggest we take a turn on deck to take a draught of the cooling evening air,' suggested Simon, and led them out and up the companionway to the quarterdeck, Pat readily agreeable.

Surprise was heeled over slightly to starboard and making, Pat felt, a steady six knots or thereabouts. With no tacking having been required for some hours there had been a pleasing lack of interruption of noise and activity to disturb a certain engrossment in their playing. On deck there was only the noise of the bow wave slapping along the hull and the faintest sound of wind soughing through the creaking rigging. The sun having set just half an hour previously, the early evening being fine, and there being no cloud at all, the navigator in Pat gazed up high over the starboard bulwark at the readily recognisable orange glow of the emerging two brightest of the stars, hundreds more twinkling about them.

'Simon, look there over the starboard side – *the starboard side* – ain't that a prime sight? Are we ever blessed with any finer? Have you ever beheld such wonders?'

Simon stared out, quite unable to fathom precisely what Pat referred to, nothing being visible in the darkness. 'Quite splendid, Pat,' he ventured, cautiously.

'Look *up*: so much to see. Do we have any greater splendours? Look there, our friends, *Arcturus* and *Vega,'* Pat now pointed high into the southern sky.

'Yes, brother, so I had understood. And, one may say, so very significant for you mariners, I believe.'

As Pat's eyes, after the brighter illumination in the great cabin, became further accustomed to the gloaming and shifted from the stars he turned and looked for'ard beyond the mainmast. He could now make out and was astonished that it seemed as if the entire crew – rough and ready jack tars for the most part that they were – were sitting silently along the gangways, backs against the bulwarks, evidently having been listening to the music of the quartet, and all were patiently awaiting more. As Pat paused to take this in he turned, as if to speak to Simon, when a ragged ripple of applause broke out, growing steadily until all on deck were clapping and whistling loudly.

Sloop   *J.J.Baugean*

Chapter Four

'Tis something, in the dearth of fame,
Though link'd among a fetter'd race,
To feel at least a patriot's shame,
Even as I sing, suffuse my face;
For what is left the poet here?
For Greeks a blush — for Greece a tear.

Monday 30th June 1823   *Gulf of Genoa*

The westerly *Ponente* wind blew *Surprise* steadily across the remaining leagues from Mahon towards Genoa. In the gun-room and on the lower deck, as proximity to Greece increased, discussion became rife over the mission. The old hands were wholly unconcerned about the nature of the enemy and the odds against *Surprise*, knowing little of the military balance between the parties. The officers were a little more knowledgeable of the Turk naval resources and those of their Egyptian vassal, specifically the French training of that particular fleet, albeit they were less familiar with the politics of the Greek revolution. Despite the uncertainties all on board remained utterly confident in the judgement and capabilities of their captain. Murphy in particular found himself very much more in demand with the crew, most of whom were aware that he had his ear to the captain's door, and might therefore have gleaned a good grasp of the mission and its objectives. Yet, for all his persistent efforts, Murphy had not been able to eavesdrop with any degree of success, as Pat had been circumspect with his briefings whilst slowly coming to terms with the nature of the mission.

Surprise was no longer officially a Royal Navy warship, albeit she was, in secrecy, *His Majesty's Hired Vessel Surprise*. Nor was she yet actually engaged with the anticipated Greek letter-of-marque, but floating on a sea of rather less certain arrangements: at least until she had arrived in Greek waters and Pat was able to formally engage with the provisional government there. Because of this multiplicity of uncertainties, discussion of the mission within the great cabin was limited in the extreme.

Notwithstanding the unofficial or indeterminate status of the voyage from Falmouth to Greece, Pat was in high good spirits: it was more than simply a return to sea; more even than the satisfaction of being once again aboard a frigate, and with his long cherished aspiration for a crack crew achieved – for assuredly that was what he now had, bar the absence of any marines. No, Pat O'Connor, for the first time in his long and successful sea-going career, felt not the immediacy of seeking out an engagement with the enemy, had no longer to keep one eye ready for an approaching vessel bearing Admiralty instructions, and so he had discovered a deeper inner satisfaction, a calming self confidence, almost a renewal of purpose. All of which made him feel quite at ease with himself and the world, to the extent that he even began to feel at ease with Michael Marston who was now an assured evening visitor to the great cabin, accompanying Pat, Duncan, and Simon in their musical relaxations; an addition to the trio that Pat, to his own surprise and satisfaction, now welcomed.

'What do you say to another pot of coffee, Simon?' Pat prompted as they finished eating breakfast.

'With great pleasure, my dear,' Simon replied, adding presciently 'I give you joy of your present contentment, long may it endure.'

'Freeman! Another pot of coffee, if you will; light along and fetch a bottle of the best Madeira and see if there is anything left of the Sunday cake.' Pat paused for a few moments, and looked closely at his friend of many years before replying to Simon's comment. 'I cannot recollect in all our voyages this feeling of self-quietude.'

'I am entirely of your way of mind, brother. It is only since we left Falmouth that the pain of losing Agnes, which has been sitting ill with me these ten years past, has receded just a very little,' Simon replied, with his small revelation, his heartfelt sentiments wholly concurring with those of his friend.

Ten minutes passed by in silence, and Pat, sensing that Simon's mood was sinking - perhaps reflecting on his last words, prompted, 'A penny for your thoughts, brother.'

'Is that all you care to offer?' this said with a wan smile from Simon, striving to raise his own spirits a very little.

'A penny may seem a trifling thing, but thirteen of 'em make a shilling.'

'Twelve, dear.'

'Thirteen *Irish* pennies are asked for one *English* shilling - you didn't smoke it,' Pat smiled in his little triumph; to no avail, Simon looked glum.

Some little time passed by, both in private contemplation, until Pat spoke again, tentatively, his voice low, gentle, 'I say this in friendship, brother... have you ever, perchance, considered of... that is to say... taking another... another wife... a companion perhaps?' It was a question that Pat had thought of asking for several years but the moment had never seemed right.

Simon raised his head only after a long minute, and looked at Pat in thoughtful silence, the look on his face one of unrelenting distress, of pain, until Pat began to wonder whether he had breached some unstated boundary within their friendship and had now imperilled their close bond. 'I ask only in kindness... if I have offended you...' Pat's voice tailed off. He looked closely at Simon's now expressionless face, his eyes showing a want of some spark, a lack of spirit or light so very evident.

'I take it very friendly in you, my dear, to ask, bless you, but on such a subject I find not the slightest placidity of mind, ever; only the contrary. I cannot conceive of ever possessing again of such contentment as I enjoyed with my beloved Agnes... on this side of... of passing,' Simon replied, the deep conviction of his feelings so firm in his low, flat voice, a tinge of distress creeping in.

'No, soul, never say that,' said Pat, alarmed and concerned for his friend.

'My precious Agnes was one of a kind, a rare and so special kind, and I hold no illusions of finding another.' This spoken very quietly.

'Why there must be a dozen or more colleens in Claddaghduff who would put a smile on your face and warm your heart; there is no doubt, and as for Galway Town...' Pat had found himself some considerable way out of his depth, but he strived valiantly to think of something, anything, to cheer his friend.

'I must not decline your generosity and consideration for my well-being, brother, and blessed hope does creep in, from time to time: perhaps I will visit when we return.' This said with a thin smile, an attempt at enthusiasm. 'For now, I think a generous dram will do all that is necessary, will answer the case, and we will contemplate our evening's musical endeavours. An hour or two with the strings and the world will doubtless seem a more pleasant place, and that is a great comfort.'

Murphy returned at that moment with the fresh coffee, the aroma so inviting, Pat particularly grateful, 'Thankee, Murphy. Will you cut along and find a bottle of my whiskey - if the millers ain't got to it that is,' this in small jest, Murphy's periodic explanations for dwindling liquor stocks being many and varied. He hastened away before levity became acerbity.

As they savoured their coffee, later the whiskey - which had been found, Simon pondered on his friend's so personal question. He considered that all inhabited an inner world, oft lonely for many, and certainly it was for him when he was remembering of his late wife; and the ship's social intercourse, however amicable, however direct, as Pat was wont to be - in his honest tarpaulin way - so rarely, if ever, pierced that barrier between the immediacies of the present, the situation, the subject at hand, and those deeper feelings of the mind: language, mere words; so very inadequate to reach that inner sanctum of the soul. He wondered if it could ever be otherwise: only with music perhaps? He drained his whiskey, black turmoil in his mind, his eyes moist, and his heart all a'tremble; more so than he could ever recall.

* * *

The gentle sea state for most of the voyage, the clement weather, and the contentment that this had brought about, growing with the increasing distance from Falmouth, had created an atmosphere almost of tranquillity for all aboard *Surprise*. No longer, as far as the crew were aware, was she a Royal Navy ship, and hence the customary Articles of War were no longer being read on Sundays, plus there were the families of both Pat and Duncan present. All these changes from regular routine had, quite unexpectedly, brought about great efficiency and sharpness in the crew in a way that Pat had never previously experienced: an attention to every detail in the daily routine of *their* ship, for that is how *Surprise* was perceived. The officers never found occasion to pick up on any defects of the crew, for remarkably there were none. The regular evening playing of the string quartet had considerably enhanced this pleasant ambience, and the musicians had since several days past shifted to playing on the gun deck on warm and dry evenings, as appreciation of their music had become near universal amongst the crew. Morale was therefore exceptional, and not a soul had reported sick since the start of the voyage.

'Freeman! Freeman! Break out a case of the Haut Brion, the one with the long cork, the eighty-nine, in readiness for dinner, and see how it is coming along with my cook,' shouted Pat, sitting on the chest against the stern windows, finishing his coffee, discussing the powder and shot stores with Pickering, and considering his position generally, noon fast approaching. 'Why, Simon; ain't you shifting your old clo's, and shaving for dinner?'

'Must I? I shaved only yesterday or perhaps the day before.'

'I could never introduce you in polite company in those slops. Murphy remarked this very morning that in Falmouth we have cast away old sails, veterans of the Horn and battle, in finer fettle.'

'I am aghast, brother. You oft say that it matters not one jot at sea, that we may wear anything at hand which serves our comfort, and neither is it necessary for our vestments to be washed nor pressed particularly often, more than once a month, let us say.'

'It is Sinéad's day. The ladies will be present, and doubtless in all their splendid finery. You would not care to disappoint them, would you? Perhaps clean clothes might suit?'

'Why, there is only a trifle of fat lingering on the breeks from that memorable sauce with the crubeens and trubs of last week; I forget the day. With such excellent tatties too, though the fat is scarcely bothersome. I will be there presently.'

'Not in them old rags you won't, sorr,' hissed Murphy who was beside himself, seething, and could not refrain from comment, his captain blinking as he heard the uninvited, the unexpected, interjection.

'Simon, doubtless you will wish to present yourself before the ladies in fresh garb, and you will favour me most deeply by changing your clothes. Your sleeves resemble those of our young *Tenedos* snotties. This is surely a day on which our every effort will be remarked upon, our vestments particularly, and you would not wish to be laughed at when we are at the table.'

'I am a modest sort, clothes do not greatly signify in my mind.'

'For the love of God, Simon, cast away those scabrous slops if you will! The ladies may believe that you have stepped out of your store without so much as a lamp and fallen into the stove's coal.'

'I see you will not be swayed. Oh, very well, Pat.'

'Clothes cover a multitude of sins, Doctor; particularly so as we get older, as you of all will know; and naked we have but little influence,' volunteered Pickering, bringing a bemused stare from his captain and a scowl from Simon.

It was Sinéad's birthday, and in the knowledge that *Surprise* would arrive in Genoa on the morrow, Pat had invited all his officers to a celebratory dinner, to join his and Duncan's families. Afterwards he intended to give them what small extent of briefing that he was able. It was therefore an expectant gathering that took its place at the table in the great cabin. All officers were in formal uniform, albeit without Royal Navy insignia, and there being no marines on board each was attended behind their chair by stewards in smart blue jackets with brightened brass buttons and white gloves, near all of the men with gold earrings; all as keen as the officers to glean what might fall from their captain's lips for eagerly receptive shipmates. Before that the meal was to be eaten, to be enjoyed, the birthday celebrated; the captain's cook had been tasked with the provision of something a little above the norm. Pat's private stocks had been severely diminished for the occasion, and his cook, Wilkins, had quite excelled himself. After the customary glass or two of Madeira, very popular with the ladies, Freeman and Murphy, Old Jim Lamb helping, brought out the food on the captain's best silver plate. They began by serving dishes of freshly caught tuna, prepared as floured thick steaks, and served with pureed peas and white sauce. In that expectant instant before anyone began to eat, and as all looked over towards Pat, he raised his glass, rapped the table with his knife, and turning slightly to take in his wife to his right, Simon at her other side, he announced, 'Ladies and Gentlemen, a toast, if you will. To my dear wife, to Sinéad: a most happy and joyous birthday!'

'To Sinéad!' shouted by all.

To Pat's left sat Kathleen; to her left Duncan was flanked by his daughter, Brodie. Simon was at Sinéad's other side, and beyond him Michael Marston. On the opposite side of the table the twins were seated amongst Pat's officers: Tom Pickering, James Mower, William Codrington and William Reeve. Only the master, Mr Prosser, was absent, in command of *Eleanor,* sailing independently for the approach to Genoa. Barton alone remained on the quarterdeck with the helmsmen.

'Mr Reeve, the bottle stands by you,' from Pat, perceiving his most junior officer to be a little daunted by the very full gathering. With the family members present and the occasion being one of celebration the customary formality of dinner at the captain's table, of speaking only in response to the captain, was quickly abandoned, and a vigorous hubbub, the most amicable of conversation, ebbed and flowed around the table. Freeman and the stewards replenished the silver plate with more tuna steaks, eagerly consumed by the officers. Then followed fresh roast pork, one of Jemmy Ducks' number having been killed that same morning; served with crisp crackling and sage and onion stuffing with a brown onion sauce, carrots, shallots and mushrooms, all taken up in Port Mahon – the shipboard millers not yet having got to the supplies, the myriad of cats at Plymouth Dock having decimated their numbers; and the solitary, retained ship's cat, a most amiable cream tabby, successfully keeping their numbers in check since.

'Brodie, my dear, allow me to cut you a little more pork,' Pat beamed across to her, rightly perceiving that she remained nervous throughout the gathering. At least until her covertly consumed wine, from a glass frequently refreshed from the bottle standing in Duncan's place, brought about a relaxation, when she began to converse with a little more animation with William Reeve. The twins were delighted to be attended by Pat's lieutenants, and regaled with tales of *Tenedos's* experiences in the deepest and farthest oceans, all events of severe personal setback and bloodthirsty battle being most diligently expunged.

Sinéad, in particular, passed a most enjoyable time, and commented, her pleasure so very evident, on how much she had been enjoying the voyage, 'The crew seem to be in the finest of form, Pat, and such a pleasant band of men too.'

'To be sure,' said Murphy, letting a plate slip crashing to the table to cover his comment, but raising smiles from the two nearby stewards who heard it and Codrington who pretended not to have.

'Mr Mower... *James*; would you care to read us a poem, your most recent perhaps?' asked Pat.

'Why yes, I have it here sir. 'Tis written for my wife, but will serve for all our wives, and today, with your permission, most particularly for Mrs O'Connor,' Mower replied, clutching a wafer of paper from his inside pocket. The table quieted as Mower began, his softly spoken voice bringing complete silence to the great cabin:

'Amidst the rolling waves of oceans comes the lovely thought of you,
Through the soughing of the breezes and the sparkle of the dew,
In the shining light of morning and the blackness of the night,
Come wondrous recollections and dreams of past delight,
In the horror of bitter struggle when my heart is gripped with fear,
When my soul seems lost in darkness, blind and frantic; you are near,
Giving faith and courage to carry me o'er the steepe roaring sea,
In the bleakest of moments you shine bright in my memory,
Bringing rays of sunshine, my tired hopes restored anew,
I cast aside the darkness and cherish the lovely thought of you.'

There remained a contemplative silence at the table for a few moments, all looking to Sinéad, until she spoke, 'Why, Mr Mower, that is the most beautiful poem I think I have ever heard. I thank you kindly.'

Loud applause erupted from all. 'Thankee, James: a most prodigious talent; genius, nothing less. I congratulate you, sir,' said Pat, amiably, as the applause ended.

'Artistic creativity prospers well in the nautical mind! Congratulations, Mr Mower. Capital wine, sir, if I may say,' said Tom Pickering.

'Thankee Tom; 'tis a particular favourite of mine: Romanée-Conti, a burgundy of the year seventeen. Another glass with you,' replied Pat, swiftly sweeping off the table a bargeman which had crawled out of a biscuit before Sinéad might see it, and stamping it flat on the deck.

'If you insist, sir; nothing serves dinner like good wine,' Pickering replied, smiling broadly at his host.

With the ladies and girls being present, Wilkins had suggested, and Pat had readily agreed to conclude the meal with a huge Jam Roly-Poly, now brought out and presented to the table in front of Pat, by Freeman – a generous portion of it having been put by in the galley for the later enjoyment of the stewards. This sweet pudding was immensely enjoyed by the two girls, in fact by all, and none escaped the plate's return to the galley. When the meal had concluded, with little marchpane cakes – Murphy having pressed the cook to make them, ostensibly at Pat's personal request but in reality the desire originating solely in himself, marchpane being his particular favourite – the ladies and youngsters retired from the great cabin, so that Pat could present what scant briefing he felt able to provide to his officers.

'What are millers, Mr Murphy?' asked Pat's daughter, in a whisper, as they were escorted out.

'Well, they are the very smallest of the ship's complement, Miss Caitlin,' replied Murphy, stretching his tiny reserves of tact to the extreme.

'Gentlemen,' the men alone now in the cabin, Pat commenced

his briefing. 'It may be some small puzzle to you that we are sailing to Greece, but will arrive in Genoa tomorrow. Many reports have come back from the events in Greece to governments and unofficial bodies throughout Europe, from diplomatic missions and non-accredited persons. A Greek committee has been established in London, as in so many other capitals, and emissaries despatched to discover the true nature of the situation in Greece. One such emissary has but recently returned, we are reliably informed, to Genoa, and we are to consult with this individual, so as to ascertain as much as possible afore we arrive in some weeks time in the Ionian Isles to commence our service for Greece. At sea the Greek fleet, such as it is, is fewer than three score of armed merchantmen: principally from the islands of Psara, Hydra and Spetses. The Greeks have two senior admirals, Canaris and Miaoulis: the first from Psara, and the second from Hydra. Admiral Miaoulis has enjoyed considerable success with fireships, attacking the fleet of Kara Ali last year, the Turks withdrawing to Alexandria after five hours of battle. Sadly, the Greek fleet arrived too late to prevent the landings and massacres on Chios, twenty-thousand souls being killed, including all infants of less than three years of age, all boys and men twelve years and older, and all women over forty years; all others, reportedly some forty thousand souls, being enslaved. Admiral Canaris then attacked the Turk fleet in the port of Chios with fireships, destroying the Turk flagship and killing Kara Ali. In October Canaris attacked the Turk fleet again, in harbour at Tenedos near the Hellespont, also with fireships, burning their flagship and driving them back to Constantinople. Yet now the Sultan has commanded his Egyptian vassal, Ali Pasha, to send the Egyptian fleet to join the Turk, and so the Greeks are even more severely outnumbered and outgunned.'

Pat paused to refer to his notes. 'Freeman! Freeman!', and as the beaming, black visage of Freeman peered round the door immediately, Pat remarked 'After such a fine dinner - my compliments to my cook - I find I am in need of a brandy; light along with the bottle, and bring coffee too, if you will.'

Pat returned to his briefing. 'Gentlemen, we are but one fifth rate to face the combined Turk and Egyptian fleets, of which there be several first rates which we cannot expect to profitably encounter. Yet for the most part their fleet will be split into smaller flotillas throughout the islands. These will be engaged upon transporting stores to their forces widely distributed in the Morea, as well as in western Greece. Our mission is to disrupt their commerce, their resupply; to encourage the Greek fleet as much as we can, to discourage the Turk; to bring hope to the Greek peoples throughout the mainland and the islands whilst better organisation and greater resources can be assembled, and a new and modern Greek fleet be raised and trained. There are plentiful stories in high places of loans to be raised for Greece, of new frigates and steamships to be built and purchased; but these will not be here this year, nor next. Yet the war must be sustained with but what little is available until they arrive. We have *Surprise*, and she has beaten many a Frenchman and others. We have a crack crew, and the Turks do not: they being served in large part by slaves, including Greeks. We can go where we please, and appear out of the night to strike hard and disappear; to re-appear where we will; to strike fear into the heart of the Turk: that is our mission, gentlemen. I will entertain your questions, if you will.'

At that timely moment, Freeman sidled in with the brandy and coffee, having dashed the ready boiling water on to the freshly ground beans the instant after Pat's request, 'Coffee here, massa.'

'Sir, may I ask whether we will be serving alongside the Greek admirals or sailing independently?' asked Tom Pickering.

'A very good point, Mr Pickering; I incline to the independent approach, not least as I expect *Surprise* will be considerably faster than the Greek ships; but perhaps on some occasions we will be acting in concert with them.'

'Where will *Surprise* be based, sir?' came from James Mower.

'Afore we begin our active service we will leave Sinéad, Kathleen and the children on Zante, it being a British Possession; where they will be quite safe from the Turk. We will be guided by what we find when we arrive there.'

146

'Speaking without the least authority and with unsurpassed ignorance of all matters naval, may I enquire how long we anticipate voyaging against the Turk, and are we ourselves assured of resupply, Captain O'Connor?' piped up Michael Marston, rather unexpectedly, and with a deal more confidence than ever hitherto demonstrated in the captain's presence, perhaps since becoming a more frequent visitor to the great cabin.

'We will be roving far and wide throughout the Aegean, Mr Marston, and roundabout the Morea. Resupplying in part from our captures, at least in powder and shot, consuming our shipboard stores until such time as there arises the need for a more plentiful re-provisioning, and perhaps a refitting, when we will return to England,' Pat explained, in truth with rather more thinking aloud than he cared to admit.

'Who will pay us for our prizes, sir?' came possibly the most prescient question of all from William Reeve.

'Well, Mr Reeve, I expect that they will be condemned by some Greek prize court, and sold, the monies to be held for our account. The specific arrangements we will have to see when we arrive in Greece,' replied Pat, with greater confidence than he felt. More questions of lesser significance were posed, but as it became clear that Pat had no precise answers at this very preliminary stage in the venture it was with some relief to him that the questions did not persist much longer. Pat brought his officers attention to his final point with a rap on the table, and raised his voice slightly: 'Gentlemen, there is one final point of importance which I will explain. Sailing alone we are very likely to encounter more than one Turk vessel: in such circumstances we will be hard pressed to fight them all, and so flight may be our sensible course. However, it will be of the very first importance for our survival, and will serve us well, were we able to fight both sides of the ship at the same time, keeping our distance so that we cannot be boarded. By that I mean fighting with complete crews for both sides, and none of the running to and fro of the men in the customary way. Remember, we have no marines and precious few sharpshooters to fight with in close. Fighting both sides of the ship and firing all guns, were we to find ourselves between two Turks, will give us the best prospect of surviving and of winning; by all accounts the Turk not being more than an averagely competent gunner. That objective, gentlemen, is where we will direct our training. We will exercise the great guns each day as we approach Greek waters, and damn the cost of the powder. I have some concept of appropriate tactics to fight the Turk, as I will explain when we are ready to exercise our guns. Mr Pickering, you are to consider which crew members we may profitably shift from sail to gun, for our purpose of firing both sides. I believe we will need more gunners. One last thing, gentlemen; as we have no jollies aboard, and so no sharpshooters to send aloft in any engagement, we must find our best dozen marksmen from the crew. There will certainly be poachers and the like familiar with a musket. Mr Mower, you are to talk with the older hands, and see whom you may find,' Pat concluded, with some relief and holding up his hand to stay any questions on his gunnery strategy, before adding as by way of confirmation of the end of the meeting, 'That will be all, thank you, gentlemen.'

After the officers and Marston had left, the families being still on deck, only Simon remained as Pat asked, 'What do you say to a glass of Sillery, Simon?'

'Well, if you insist, brother. I do not like to sound inquisitive, but you seem just a whit uncertain, if I might venture just a trifling observation.'

Pat thought for a moment before he answered. 'I suppose it is no use asking your opinion about the standing of the Greek government and any Admiralty Court that they may possess, and the likelihood of an equitable distribution from any prizes we may take? Young Reeve was, as all saw, quick off the mark there on this prime question; he hit the hammer square on the head, and doubtless by now it will be a talking point all about the crew.'

'None whatsoever, my dear: I am no friend of speculation, and my opinion of that would be as valuable as yours on the prospects for a cure for the yellow jack,' Simon replied to his friend's pessimistic question, rhetorically asked in absence of expectation of any helpful answer, but Simon continued as helpfully as he could, perceiving a worry on Pat's brow: 'In so far as the officers and crew will be wondering about the prospects for prizes, for that is sure to be the case, as sure as Hestia's oath, you may care to collect that they consider Captain O'Connor exhibits the wisdom of Solomon in all matters nautical, and any indication from yourself on this matter or any other will surely remain unchallenged on this vessel.'

Pat seemed to find this helpful, 'Well there is something in what you say, and Solomon was, by all accounts, a sensible cove. Thank you, Simon. I believe I will take a turn on deck.' Deep in thought he left the cabin and had stepped only a few paces along the gun deck when an indistinct noise caught his attention. From for'ard, from beyond the scores of Monday's shirts hung to dry on lines strung across the deck, came the sound of singing, and Pat slowly paced down the deck to hear more, his ear and curiosity intrigued. Beyond the foremast the singing became quite clear, accompanied by an unfamiliar form of stringed instrument...

'So fare ye well, sweet Donegal, our lasses and families all
I'm leaving that fair land, for the great oceans us do call,
It breaks my heart for us to part, where I spent many happy days.
Far away from friends and relations dear I'm bound for Amerikay.

And above all the skies of the port was the blue sky,
and I heard the birds singing for the dawning of the day
but there was no work from this town forthcoming,
just sympathy numbing the going away.'

Pat espied his third sitting for'ard near the galley with three of the new crewmen: Beer, Knightley and Maclean; their singing ceasing as he approached. He wondered briefly of what convention might be the norm for an officer playing accompanied by seamen, but dismissed the thought as he reached the quartet. 'A most pleasing song, Mr Mower, but pray tell me: what is that curious instrument? Is that six strings I see? Is that not a trifle ambitious? 'Pon my word we mere mortals struggle to scrape with but four strings.'

'There is no bow, sir: 'tis customary to pick at the strings with fingers.'

'Well, I never: a rum device, though melodic for sure.'

'It is Spanish in origin, sir. I took it up to set my poems to music, growing tired of the plain words. I bought it in London a few years ago, after listening to a Catalan player, Fernando Sor.'

'A Catalan, you say? Our players will be keen to hear the story, no doubt.'

'Near my last half-pay guinea it cost, but when I heard its tone, so warm, I was lost.'

'Mellow it is, indeed. Your guinea was well spent, there is no doubt. We will look forward to hearing your fine playing and singing in the cabin. Mr Mower, Beer, Knightley, Maclean: good night to you all.'

'Good night, sir,' echoed the reply, as Pat paced away, the singing resuming to the gentle sound of the Spanish strings.

> *'And I wish I was in Falmouth town and seated on the grass,*
> *And by my side a bottle of wine, and on my knee a lass,*
> *I'd call for liquor of the best, and I'd pay afore I go,*
> *And I'd hold my Sally in my arms, with a lingering kiss so slow.'*

Pat's evening was spent very pleasantly with Sinéad who joined him on the quarterdeck until the evening air cooled when they removed to the great cabin, sitting near the window and enjoying private reminiscences of their years together. Duncan and Simon had considerately shifted to their berths in the gun-room. The twins, with Brodie, were being entertained by Kathleen, though they had last been seen pursuing Pat's cook for more marchpane and roly-poly; fruitlessly, Murphy long having removed the first, and his mates having consumed the second.

'You lead a very happy crew, Pat, that is sure, even to my inexpert eye in these matters. And, if I am not wide of the mark, you are yourself most splendidly pleased to be here, to return again to voyaging, in *Surprise* now, and in Mr Ferguson's and Duncan's company too. Will *we* be happy again upon our return to Claddaghduff, do you think?' asked Sinéad, her voice wavering.

Pat gazed into his wife's moistening eyes with deep

benevolence. 'Be not concerned for that in the slightest, Sinéad my love: all my life I have been at sea, since I was much younger even than the twins, in the company of sailors, and fortunately with the very best of companions in Duncan and Simon - Simon has saved my life you know, when I was shot in a cutting out party – did I never mention that to you ... perhaps not. We have seen many a successful cruise in the dear *Tenedos*, success that has been the founding of our home and farm, a place which I very much look forward to coming home to, to be with you there; and I dare say I will not be at sea for many more years, my love, afore I am laid up; *in ordinary*, as we sailors say. Until then, in the few more years I have at sea, it is my dearest wish to see them out in command of a proper fighting ship such as *Surprise*, and since we have long since seen off Boney then there will be but few ventures in which we can profitably engage. All of us aboard do hope that this is one such venture. Nor do I say *profitable* wholly in the mercenary sense, far from it: there are few men in this crew who *need* to serve again at sea, many of them having taken very substantial prize monies to their homes in Falmouth in the years of the French wars. No, I find a sense of contentment in this crew, a contentment founded on returning to our home at sea, for that is how we all feel about *Surprise*. Though usually we have no wives here, nor any of our children, we share the companionship of those that have served with us for many years; we are together, officers and men. All are here not for the prizes, though none would ever admit that; no, we are here because this is where we have all spent the greater part of our lives, and we are comfortable in the traditions of the ship and the service, each man secure in the steady routines of the day – unchanging routines – as sure as the sun will rise in the morning, and that is pleasing to us all. So you see, my love, we are fortunate; all of us, we have two homes, but we all begin to see that we will serve in our shipboard home only for a very few more years, and that is why we are here, all of us to a man enjoying the time we have left aboard, in our *dear Surprise*. We are content also in that we know – *we know* – that we will be coming to our other home, our home ashore, to our beloved wives, to our children, in a near time which will be with us almost afore we know it. Is that a satisfactory answer to your question, my love?' Pat concluded, observing Sinéad's tear-filled eyes with great concern, and seizing his wife into his arms in a crushing embrace.

'Oh Pat, I love you so much,' was all that Sinéad could whisper in reply, blinking rapidly as the tears now flowed in great streams from her eyes and down her cheeks.

During the next day, the final day of *Surprise's* voyage to Genoa, the weather and sea state remained as tranquil as all those that had preceded it. As the warmth of the day faded with the sun sinking into the horizon of the western sky, leaving behind a splendid residual sunset, *Surprise* passed the western mole and La Lanterna to larboard, and entered the harbour of Genoa under topsails alone, slowing as they were backed, and coming gently to a stop, letting fall her anchor three cable lengths off the quay.

Wednesday 2nd July 1823   *Port of Genoa*

After breakfast, the crew lowered all *Surprise's* boats, her proximity to the Old Pier greatly facilitating the taking on board of water and other provisions. With an unknown departure date, Lord Byron's specific plans not being known to Pat or Duncan, the near quayside anchorage was also considerably more convenient for going ashore, Pat anticipating much use of his barge.

'Duncan; pray tell, what news of our task to escort Lord Byron?' Pat asked, after *Surprise* had been tied up, and they, with Simon, were enjoying tea with Pat's second breakfast in the great cabin. 'We will need to acquaint ourselves with his Lordship's intentions. Do you know anything of his plans, his travel plans particularly?'

Duncan looked up from his bacon and eggs, 'Lord Byron travelled previously in the eastern Mediterranean in the company o' his longstandin' friend, Hobhouse; noo a luminary o' the Greek Committee. Ah have a letter o' introduction from Hobhouse, given to me by Lowrey afore we left London, and ah will send this to Byron's residence today. In a day or twae ah imagine we will call upon his Lordship.'

'Until then, Pat, might I suggest that we take a day to see this magnificent city?' Simon interjected, wiping the grease from his chin onto his sleeve. 'It is a tolerably significant city for you mariners. By all reports one Christopher Columbus originated here, a mariner you may be familiar with. Those of us of the faith, of a more devout persuasion, will I say, are visiting the basilica of San Lorenzo, Saint Lawrence in the English parlance. Duncan, Brodie and Kathleen are with me, Sinéad and the twins too.'

'Murphy! Pass the word for Barton!' Pat shouted. 'Why, perhaps I will join you, Simon. I would not wish to appear singular,' Pat smiled, bowing to his friend's arrangements in pleasant grace.

Pat's cox'n entered within moments and touched his forehead. 'Barton, be so good as to deliver a letter ashore for Mr Macleod. You may require a local guide; Mr Macleod will give you the letter directly.' Pat had by now established that Barton was of a similar, reliable ilk to his much lamented, deceased brother, and had begun to pass small tasks of some significance to him. At that moment Sinéad and Kathleen entered the great cabin, in some small state of excitement with the prospect of going ashore and the appeal of an escape from the close accommodation of *Surprise*: the near total absence of personal privacy was beginning to grate after the month's voyage. The twins too, the novelty of shipboard life fading, were beginning to evidence some youthful truculence and impatience with the shipboard routine.

'Will you be long, Duncan?' asked Kathleen.

'Not at all, ma dear, just a wee few minutes, and ah will be wi' ye. We will all be wi' ye. Pat is minded to accompany us, wi' Simon.'

'We will await you all on deck,' said Sinéad, in high good spirits, as the ladies left the great cabin.

'Ah will find the introductory letter fer Barton, it is in ma sea-chest, an' briefly scribe an accompanying note; ah will be wi' ye d'reckly,' said Duncan.

'I will also be ready presently,' said Simon.

'I suppose you could shave and change later,' Pat volunteered, a comment wholly disregarded by his friend.

The visit to the cathedral was a resounding success, the twins being overwhelmed by the grandeur and scale of the edifice and its environs. Never before had they seen a city of such historic substance. Their walking tour continued for some hours, taking in the splendour of the palaces of the Strada Nuova before the long walk the length of the harbour to visit La Lanterna, the ancient lighthouse. In the late afternoon the long day of walking had quite tired them out, and so the twins were considerably more subdued walking back to *Surprise*.

After supper Murphy entered the cabin clutching a letter which he presented to Duncan who swiftly opened it. 'Pat, 'tis a reply from Lord Byron: his Lordship has invited us to attend him on Friday.'

Friday 4ᵗʰ July 1823   *Albaro, Genoa*

After dinner, Pat and Duncan, their wives and Simon, set off to stroll the near three miles to Byron's home, guided by Barton: walking up and down and through narrow streets that only gradually widened as they walked further from the port and higher up the hill of Albaro until, pausing for a brief measure of relief from their exertions, they enjoyed a commanding view over the harbour and the city. They gazed at the splendid panorama of the bay before resuming their climb, eventually coming with some relief to the Villa Saluzzo, as they began to tire in the enduring heat of the late afternoon, all perspiring freely.

The maid ushered them in, and served welcome jugs of punch. After a few minutes, which were most gratefully appreciated for recovery from their exertions, Lord Byron entered the drawing room, walking with a limp on account of his club foot. He was a tall man, in his mid thirties, but looked older, youth having faded from his face, some spark having been lost; his curly auburn hair was now streaked with grey, his thin moustache near white. Yet he nevertheless retained an impression of energy, of quick interest, and his large, luminous blue eyes exuded a sense of restlessness. Byron was accompanied by a man with long black hair, bushy sideboards, and an aquiline nose; dressed in, or so the ladies

154

thought, rather untidy clothing that seemed to have seen better days – a thought which never occurred to Simon.

Pat made the introductions. 'I am Captain Patrick O'Connor. Thank you for your invitation, my Lord. May I present my wife Sinéad; my first lieutenant, Duncan Macleod; his wife Kathleen; and my surgeon, Dr Simon Ferguson.'

Lord Byron appeared to be in fine good humour, and pleased to receive his visitors. 'Your servant, sirs, ladies; we are favoured today, and it pleasures me exceedingly to present my visitor, Signor Niccolò Paganini, the celebrated Italian composer and violinist; a son of Genoa, and residing here at his mother's home to recuperate from recent illness. He has called upon me to discuss my poem, *Childe Harold's Pilgrimage*. He has but a token grasp of English and converses only in Italian and French.'

Paganini bowed to the ladies and shook hands with the gentlemen. Simon scrutinised him professionally. He did not look well, but then again he had treated sailors that looked far, far worse. 'Un grand plaisir, monsieur, enchanté,' said Simon with some passion, being acquainted with Paganini's music, if not his playing.

Lord Byron continued, 'Before Signor Paganini leaves very shortly we are to enjoy the playing of his most recent solo piece. Please to follow me if you will.' Byron led the party to the music room where Paganini took up his violin, and without any preamble began to play. In the five minutes that followed, the most animated playing by a standing Paganini, with unsurpassed and wonderfully dextrous fingering and bowing, his violin seemingly coming to life in his hands, was utterly exceptional to the ear of Pat, a talented cellist, and Simon, a considerably accomplished musician with the viola. The flowing skill of Paganini was of an overwhelming virtuosity, unparalleled in anything that they had ever heard before, the most vibrant long notes held in the air for an age, others intensely resonating beyond that which Pat and Simon thought possible: the flowing continuity of the bow, his wrists flexing and shifting at astonishing speed, the music sublime, his playing infinitely gratifying in its perfection. At the end they were in a state almost of disbelief at what they had heard, before clapping from Sinéad and Kathleen jolted them from stunned silence to vigorous applause.

'Caprice vingt-quatre,' Paganini said simply, and bowed to his tiny audience.

'My dear sir,' said Simon (in French); 'that was uncommon magnificent. We have never heard the like. We are both of us keen scrapers, indeed we are, yet we could never aspire to such wonders; never in life. Overwhelmed, overwhelmed, we thank you most kindly, sir.'

'Merci, merci,' was all that a stunned Pat could utter before turning to Simon to suggest that, 'he should invite Signor Paganini to dine aboard *Surprise,* and perhaps he could bring his violin,' adding as an afterthought, 'Signor Paganini's schedule in Genoa permitting.' To Pat's deep satisfaction Simon's reiteration of his invitation was accepted with evident pleasure, Paganini adding something to Simon along the lines of 'seeking Doctor Ferguson's opinion', but it was beyond Pat's pidgin French to follow assuredly.

After Paganini's departure the ladies remained in the music room, enjoying punch whilst the gentlemen shifted to the drawing room. 'My Lord,' Pat began, 'I have but recently become acquainted with the nascent developments in the Ottoman Greek provinces, coincident with my resignation from His Majesty's service. Lieutenant Macleod and I attended the London Greek Committee some few weeks ago, and having heard of your intended participation as an emissary of the Committee, perhaps we may be of some small service?' Pat concluded a rather brief and vague explanation, not wishing to dwell on the background to his particular circumstances.

'My dear O'Connor: that is most kind. However, my banker has located, and I have already engaged, a ship, *Hercules,* Captain Scott, to convey my party from Genoa to Zante, perhaps in some few days time. It is generally held that the Turks are preparing a large expedition for the suppression of the rising. I am fully disposed to assist the Greek cause, and with every means at my disposal, hence my departure to offer my personal assistance. I now await only correspondence from Blaquiere, an emissary of the Committee who is already in the Morea, before we depart.'

Pat hesitated in thought very briefly before concluding the meeting, 'My Lord, our aspirations are therefore similar. Allow me to congratulate you on your admirable intentions, and we wish you success in your noble endeavours.' With that they took their leave.

The next few days were passed in taking onboard those few stores which had been omitted in the hectic provisioning of *Surprise* in Plymouth and Falmouth, the crew shifting everything about to the satisfaction of Simon's assistant, Michael Marston, he being of an exceedingly tidy disposition. In respect of the sick bay he was striving with an evident desire to please Simon, and ensured every medication was readily at hand. The atmosphere onboard *Surprise* was relaxed, the crew having cleaned every conceivable part of the ship, all revelling still in their homecoming, as they saw it; even to the extent that they had stripped the aged and peeling black paint from all the cannon during the voyage, and then rubbed them down to the iron before repainting, layer upon layer afresh, until the guns looked as if they had left the manufactory that day, their new black paint gleaming pristine in the bright sun. They had also repainted the chequerboard sides of the ship with a precision that impressed every inspection, Pat insisting on the crew painting the Nelson yellow bands along the hull. All aboard concurred that it was a magnificent idea; the few Trafalgar veterans in particular being highly gratified. The officers had barely any need to direct the ship's activities, the crew being volunteers to a man, confident in their assured prospects under Pat's command for substantial prizes.

The ladies, Brodie and the twins were, for the most part, ashore in Genoa each day and even most evenings, enjoying the temperate early summer of the northern Mediterranean latitude, there being little for them to do aboard. They had hardly any domestic duties, Murphy being very jealous of and robustly resisting any attempted incursion into his personal province of care for Pat and Simon's accommodation and laundry – albeit it could have been argued that a little further help might have been justifiable in Simon's case.

During the morning that Pat was to dine in the gun-room with his officers, word was received that Paganini was to come aboard to join them. To the astonishment and pleasure of the hands, the man delivering the message was a familiar face, a former comrade who had served with many of them long years ago in the Mediterranean. Giobatta Repetto was a native of Genoa, retired from sea service, and now, still active in his late sixties, he delivered messages around the town for important personages including Byron and Paganini.

Pat was sure he had met the man and invited him into the cabin. 'We have met before, I collect; yet I cannot fathom your name.'

'Repetto sir, if you please.' The greying, old man touched his forehead.

'Ah... Repetto, yes, it comes back to me ... it must be seven years or more since we were shipmates. Now I collect you was with us when we sank *Iskander* and captured *Half Moon*; larboard watch, *Hurricane* gunner - am I right? It was back in the year sixteen... seven years, so it was. It is pleasing to see you again. You look in fine fettle, if I may say so,' said Pat, smiling, 'Are you keeping well?'

'Splendidamente, Comandante,' Repetto bowed to Pat, beaming broadly, deeply pleased that he had been remembered, and he stood in silence, in awe, and with transparent delight, being once again in his esteemed, former captain's presence. He was pressed by Pat, with whom he soon commenced bantering about past voyages, to enjoy a glass or two in the cabin whilst Simon read the letter in case of any reply being necessary. The subject of the letter revealed, Repetto declared that he was also a keen and proficient cook, and willing to help in the preparation of local Ligurian and Genoese specialities. Without further ado he was speedily introduced to Pat's cook, Wilkins, and pressed to advise on the forthcoming VIP's dinner; the preparation of which then became, for such a momentous occasion, a joint effort with Repetto, Wilkins, the gun-room cook, and even the ladies; all vying to produce a meal of unparalleled excellence for such an eagerly anticipated visitor, Repetto quite comfortable at the galley, overjoyed to be back aboard a ship, and particularly pleased to be of service to his former captain, the famed Pat O'Connor. Murphy, with his mate Old Jim Lamb, fussed about with table preparations, polishing Pat's best silver plate, a task at which he excelled. He put a dozen bottles of Pat's best claret over the side to cool in a fishing net. From Murphy the crew were perfectly aware of the impending visitor. Having expended in Genoa what few dollars they had left, and having little to do, they contented themselves with leisurely light maintenance tasks, in anticipation of the visit, for they had heard from Mower, who played guitar to accompany the singing of several of them, that Paganini was a violinist of the most exceptional talent.

The dinner meandered through Repetto's simply stunning three courses; he had served them well: *zemin de ceci,* a chick-pea soup; followed by *pansoti* pasta with spinach and walnut sauce; finally cod stockfish cooked with potatoes, raisins, and pine nuts in a tomato sauce. The food was a great success: the Genoese cuisine, unfamiliar as it was to the Surprises and the ladies - who marvelled at it - was relished by all in the most convivial of ambience. Several hours passed by in the most cordial of dialogue and banter, Simon translating from Paganini's French to English for Pat's officers who were being very welcoming to their most distinguished visitor ever. Paganini ate sparingly and seemingly with a little difficulty, but he complimented effusively the food and wine (of which he drank very little). Late afternoon slipped pleasantly into early evening with a graceful acceptance by Paganini of Pat's invitation 'to play just a very little – his *Caprice vingt-quatre* again, perhaps' – and on deck to the assembled crew.

With surprising alacrity, some considerable bottles having been consumed during the feast, Mower and Codrington fetched the chairs from Pat's cabin out on to the gun deck, the stewards bringing more from the gun-room. Officers and ladies settled to listen to the maestro; the crew too were gathered about the gun deck in anticipation, alerted by the stewards. The men had already enjoyed their supper and their grog, and with little to do as the day slipped away the impromptu prospect of music was very welcome to them indeed. They settled, sitting about the fore part of the deck, the hubbub of conversation dying in anticipation. Paganini did not disappoint, launching into Pat's particular request, playing with consummate passion and skill, his bow flowing with an elasticity which Pat, Simon and Marston could only marvel at; his fingers shifting to positions that they could not comprehend. His music consumed all those listening to it, its unrivalled and exquisite excellence registering even with the least musically inclined old tars sitting on the deck or leaning on the guns; the sounds reaching deep beyond their ears and striking chords within their souls such that all other thoughts were eclipsed from their minds, and they gazed in wonder and utter silence as Paganini played the piece until, with a final flourish of his bow, it reached its unwanted end. The conclusion of this, the most magical playing that all had ever heard, was followed by raucous appreciation from all the ship's company.

'That,' said Paganini, beaming to his hosts after a bow to his audience, 'is how it plays in paradise.'

Pat, recovering from his absolute concentration in the music, complimented Paganini profusely. 'Very finely played, sir; the beauty of the world; so it is.' The sun was beginning to sink towards the horizon, but the evening remained comfortably warm. Pat inclined towards and whispered to Simon, 'Will I ask him? That is to say, would you think he might play with us? We will never have the chance again.'

Simon simply smiled, his lingering contentment precluding any contemplation of Pat's question. A deeply pleased and now somewhat emboldened Pat ventured to ask Paganini, 'Perhaps Signor Paganini would consent to playing just a very little more, and accompanied by the ship's musicians?' He was delighted when his request was accepted. 'Murphy! Barton! Rouse out our instruments from the great cabin, quickly now, there is no time to be lost,' Pat urged.

'Well, they be here already a'waitin' yer say so, sorr,' Murphy pronounced, with a smile of self-satisfaction; Pat's cello under his arm, and carrying the violin; Old Jim Lamb with the viola and bows. With their instruments, the trio of Pat, Simon, and Marston took their places alongside Paganini. They began, slowly at first as all adapted to their fellows, with Corelli's *Christmas Concerto*, followed by a magnificent rendition of one of Pat's particular favourites, Boccherini's cheerful *La Musica Notturna Delle Strade Di Madrid*, to Pat's mind a piece ideally suited to the collective shipboard temperament. It was a near twenty minutes of the most sublime playing by Paganini on first violin and sheer bliss for the accompanying trio. It was with the utmost satisfaction and shared congratulations that the piece came to its end. Vigorous applause followed from the enrapt crew.

'Och, that was the most glorious piece o' all the world,' said Duncan.

As the applause died down, and the quartet took their bow, Barton, with Evans, a popular Welshman living in Falmouth, and a tolerably fine tenor, quickly stepped up in front of the players and turned to the crew. Barton waved the applause to silence.

'What's afoot?' a puzzled Pat muttered to Duncan.

From Evan's deep booming voice came the stirring first verse of *Heart of Oak*.

'Come, cheer up, my lads, 'tis to glory we steer,
To add something more to this wonderful year;
To honour we call you, as freemen not slaves,
For who are so free as the sons of the waves?'

With only the very slightest of pause the happy and delighted crew, more than two hundred of them now on deck, by way of their own thanks and appreciation, scrambled swiftly to their feet, and without hesitation joined the chorus of the song, the Royal Navy's traditional anthem, singing with great gusto and enthusiasm.

'Heart of oak are our ships, jolly tars are our men
We always are ready; steady, boys, steady!
We'll fight and we'll conquer again and again.'

At the end of the song an animated and impressed Paganini

161

clapped his hands and turned to Simon. 'Bravo! Bravo! Nous avons trouvé un petit coin de paradis ce soir.'

Pat, who had expected nothing like this, such a deeply pleasing and spontaneous gesture from the crew, beamed with evident delight, speechless. The crew continued to cheer Paganini with great shouts of 'Hurrah! Hurrah!' Simon and Marston embraced, slapping their mutual backs while the ladies smiled and clapped until their hands were sore. At the conclusion of this revelry, Paganini and Simon, with Marston, retired to the great cabin in close discussion. Pat thanked the crew profusely for their impromptu singing, 'Barton, Evans, thank you kindly; well done, well done indeed. Barton, please thank the lads for a most generous gesture, most kind indeed, thankee. Mr Mower, an extra issue of grog to the crew, if you will.' He returned in high good humour to the gun-room with his officers, the ladies retiring to settle the girls and Fergal in their cots below.

In the cabin, Simon and Marston conversed with Paganini. He had sought a consultation with Simon when they had met at Byron's house. They conversed in French, which fortunately neither Freeman nor Murphy, both listening behind the cabin door, were able to understand. To put Paganini more at his ease Marston assured him that Simon had an Edinburgh medical degree, had studied Paré, and had been consulted by no less a dignitary than the First Lord, Melville; and it was widely understood that Simon had been considered as a candidate for Physician of the Fleet. A clearly less anxious Paganini described his symptoms and treatment, 'I have been ill since January. I consulted Dr Borda of Pavia during June following weight loss and severe coughing up of sputum. Dr Borda has prescribed opium for my severe laryngeal cough, and mercury for hidden syphilitic infection. I take the blue pill.'

Simon responded cautiously, 'Sir, your account does not suggest any fatal issue, and we are unable to differ with your own physician and his diagnosis, he being presumably more acquainted with your medical history than we. Yet, in candour, I must caution you against excessive and prolonged treatment with mercury, for such will most surely lead to undoubted deterioration of the physical state of the larynx and the gums, and to loss of teeth and general ill health; the consequences of the mercury being far, far worse than the mere possibility of the emergence of hidden syphilitic infection. Mercury is generally recognised as effective principally in the early, *the very early*, stage of syphilitic infection, as we see so often aboard ship. As the finest musician it has ever been my pleasure and great good fortune to hear, I must also caution you that the accumulation of mercury over some considerable time will lead to tremors in the hands. Surely you, the master of the most exquisite violin I have ever heard, would wish at all costs to avoid that?' Simon's voice and mind filled with infinite sadness, regretting bitterly that he could offer no more optimistic a prognosis to this unequalled musical genius.

'Dr Ferguson, Mr Marston, I am obliged to you both for your ministrations and professional advice, for which I thank you most sincerely,' Paganini sighed; his disappointment so evident in his face. All shook hands, the two surgeons lingering in the last minutes with their visitor, as if to save the precious moment, to preserve a recollection of their encounter firmly in their minds.

Shortly afterwards Paganini departed, leaving behind an exquisite musical memory, to be treasured by Pat and Simon for the rest of their days.

'Was your consultation of any service to our guest, Simon?' asked Pat.

'Oh, I could not possibly say. Certainly, Marston and I passed some time contemplating on the efficacies of familiar processes. We may consider further of our interest in mercury, which in some instances will prove disappointing.'

'Yes, he is of little use for navigation, though assuredly of astronomical interest.'

'So I have always understood, but what I meant was the metallic element of mercury, brother. It is used in the blue pill.'

'Oh, I beg pardon. As to our guest's playing, we will never hear finer, never in life; of that I am sure.'

Becalmed in Genoa for several days, and no contact having been established with the anticipated emissary from the Ionians or anyone from the Morea, nor having received any further instructions from Lowrey or Melville, Pat was anxious not to lose more time idling in port. Such inactivity was wont to lead the crew into predictably regrettable diversions. *Surprise* and *Eleanor* therefore now left harbour, preceding *Hercules*. The wind, having risen little above a breeze since dawn, had dropped to a near calm again as two bells were rung. Pat had not left his quarterdeck since rising, the south-westerly *Libeccio* making for a very slow departure from the harbour, and something of a laborious task, with frequent tacking a necessity to make any progress at all until they were well past the entrance and La Lanterna left far astern.

'Precious little wind, sir,' said Pickering.

'Aye Tom, though look to those high clouds, shifting along sprightly. I think we may see a blow tonight; 'til then let us put the fire hoses on the sails and we may see another half knot.'

'Aye aye, sir, engines to wet the sails it is. Mr Prosser, if you please.'

By mid-morning the frigate hardly raised a wake with every stitch of canvas set, including royals, and with her studdingsails boomed out. Pat retired to the cabin for a late breakfast. 'Freeman! Look alive there! Rouse out my cook, and see what can be found in the line of bacon, eggs, plenty of soft tack, and a pot of tea.'

This came as no surprise to Murphy, waiting alongside Freeman, and accustomed as he was to his captain's preferences after so many years, 'Well, it's all been a'waitin' these two hours past, to be sure. 'Tis all ruined,' he muttered as Freeman scuttled away to the galley.

By the time Pat had eaten his solitary breakfast and returned to the quarterdeck the wind had freshened considerably. *Surprise* was now making respectable progress on a broad reach, well heeled to larboard, the necessity for tacking now long gone, huge showers of spray flying, and the wind beginning to whistle loudly in the rigging, the stuns'ls and royals long since taken off her, the royal and topgallant yards struck down, the topgallant masts housed on deck. Duncan Macleod, Tom Pickering and James Mower all stood by. 'I think you are proven right, sir. Not long afore we see the storm,' said Pickering.

Pat gazed about him, assessing the weather and contemplating the sails, 'Mr Pickering, signal *Eleanor* to proceed independently to Leghorn. I smell bad weather coming, and she may not keep station with us. Mr Mower, heave the line.'

The line indicated a not unexpected acceleration to a swift eight knots, according with Pat's growing uneasiness as he surveyed the sky to the west, voluminous dark grey clouds having now near blotted out the sun. The temperature had also fallen noticeably, the storm winds were upon them, and the ladies had long since retired from deck to the gun-room. 'Mr Macleod, we will double-reef her courses. Briskly now: we will brace in the upper yards just a very little. We will have the fore-staysail set with double sheets.'

'Aye aye, sir,' Duncan reiterated the order to the men.

Another hour passed and the storm winds strengthened further. 'Mr Macleod, we will take down the jib and flying jib.'

'A considerable change since this morning, Pat, for sure,' said Simon, who had joined the officers on the quarterdeck.

'I do love a blow, but with the ladies and children aboard we will treat her tenderly.'

Pat's appreciation of a blow was not something with which Simon personally accorded, despite his now long years as Pat's seafaring companion. The rising violence of the waves had, for the past hour, sent spray flying across the waist of the ship, and the few crew of the duty watch that still remained on deck had donned oilskins and awaited the next order to further reduce sail. Two hours passed and the frigate was now making a racing nine knots. She was quite heeled over, her masts and yards showing a gentle curve of load. The crew, needing no bidding, were going about securing the ship's boats, checking the security of fastenings of the great guns, and shifting or tying down anything that remained remotely loose on deck. Since noon lifelines had been rigged along the length of the deck, which canted thirty degrees as she rolled; the rails subsumed and invisible in the spray.

'Mr Macleod, we will reef her tops'ls, 'tis time.' The commands were passed down to the crew who sprang aloft with alacrity, for they had been awaiting the order for the past hour. Pat was now certain of his suspicions and turned to Simon, 'It is coming on to blow hard. If the wind strengthens and if it becomes uncomfortable we may have to lay to.'

'What? What did you say?' Simon shouted into the wind, clutching his still unbuttoned coat, heavy rain soaking him, and the deck rearing up beneath him before sinking as fast into the trough of the steep swell. 'Just how uncomfortable would we have to be? It is very disagreeable up here! 'Tis a dreich day! I am fair drookit. I do not wish to sound discontented, but will this infernal tempest last long, would you think?'

'Why, of that there is no telling. One day: perhaps two or three, if we are unlucky.' At that moment, as *Surprise* rose from the trough, she was struck full by the wind and rolled violently until her lee gunwhale was near subsumed within the furious, boiling maelstrom that was the black water. 'You had best go below, Simon. Look to the ladies. Ask cook for a hot meal without delay, we may extinguish the galley presently. Mind now, clap on; one hand for yourself and one for the ship,' Pat shouted back, his words near drowned out by the wind, wild and constantly shrieking through the rigging. Tons of cold, grey water in vast torrents of spray traversed the quarterdeck, and the gun deck was awash more often than not, clearing only as the bow reared up before crashing down into the next trough, the cycle repeating itself interminably, hour after exhausting hour. The sky had darkened considerably and the light was more akin to an evening dusk than late afternoon.

'An uncomfortable night ahead, sir,' said Pickering.

'No doubt, Tom.'

At six bells of the Afternoon watch Pat made his next declaration. 'Mr Macleod, this sea will have our hide if we keep our sails. 'Tis time to take them in. I think we will pipe all hands on deck.'

'Aye aye, sir.' Prosser, listening, and seemingly very relieved to hear the order, bustled away to rouse his men, almost all of whom had been below for some hours, few remaining on the exposed deck as the sea flooded it frequently as *Surprise* rolled and pitched violently. The order passed along, the men came tumbling up from below in haste, assembling on the fo'c'sle and on the quarterdeck aft the waist, all staring about them, assessing the sea state and the commensurate sails, looking back to the quarterdeck for instruction.

'Mr Macleod, send the men aloft; double-reef all tops'ls and take in her courses,' ordered Pat, Duncan standing alongside him, and the crew hastily scrambled to do so as the first lieutenant bellowed out the order. 'Mr Prosser, luff up!' shouted Pat. 'Bring her to the wind, let her lie, nothing off, handsomely now.'

'Aye aye, sir, luff and lie: nothing to leeward, Barton, steady so.'

The rain, so heavy for several hours, became heavier, fiercer, and so thick that for all on the quarterdeck it seemed to merge with the fury of the sea. Huge black rollers swept all about them as far as the eye coud see, and the most violent of wave tops were perpetually breaking all over the deck, the water never clearing from the lee scuppers before the next wave crashed over them. The fury of the wind about them, its shrill shrieking through the rigging and the crashing all around of the tremendous seas made hearing difficult, and orders near impossible to communicate, yet the wind was noticeably increasing, as was the height of the rollers, white water breaking off their crests, torrents of spray whipping away within the wind's wild fury. *Surprise* was both pitching and rolling: lateral stability now solely afforded by her double-reefed tops'ls and fore-staysail. The afternoon had slipped away into evening and the light was nearly gone under the press of black cloud and sheeting heavy rain, the wind screaming aloft in the rigging: *Surprise* could do no more than lie-to. Yet for all this press of extreme seas and weather, four men now being necessary to hold the wheel, Pat remained unperturbed; indeed his officers still alongside of him on the quarterdeck believed that Pat was actually enjoying himself, for indeed he was. Precious few others shared the feeling: all on deck were soaked to the skin, all below thoroughly uncomfortable. No hot food had been served since the crew ate dinner at midday; no hot drinks were available, the galley fire having been extinguished as a safety measure. Little light now permeated the gloom below deck, and the severe rolling and pitching made even those with the strongest of stomachs nauseous. The ladies and children were badly sick, retching so violently that Simon was called to attend, and he administered a particularly strong dose of laudanum. Marston too had succumbed again to sea sickness and was of no use. At four bells the First dog watch hands disappeared gratefully below for respite and to eat hard tack with grog.

'The carpenter reports several seams working, sir. Eighteen inches in the well,' reported Mower to Pat who received the report with unconcern.

'Chain pumps, Mr Mower, if you please.' By five bells of the First watch and the sky being inky black, Pat retired below to check on the ladies, leaving Pickering in command on deck; Duncan had retired to rest, the sea state and wind having been slowly diminishing for some hours. The reefed tops'ls and fore-staysail had sustained her throughout the violence, and the severe rolling of earlier hours had subsumed to something less uncomfortable. The ladies and twins were all lying in their gun-room cots in a semi-sleeping state, their discomfort having been eased by Simon's laudanum. Brodie alone was sitting up, quite unconcerned, talking in Gaelic to a somewhat discomfited Patrick Coghlan. 'How are you?' asked Pat, smiling to Brodie.

'Quite well, sir, thank you kindly,' beamed Brodie, in obvious good cheer and most pleased to be able to assist Simon tending the sick and distressed.

'The worst is past, my dear,' soothed Pat.

The crew were all well, quite used to storm and unaffected by sea sickness, but grumbling volubly about their supper of hard biscuit and grog. Genoa was near twenty-five leagues in their wake and *Surprise* was well past halfway to Leghorn, Pat calculated. Presently he would alter course, east-south-east, direct for Leghorn. At midnight Pat altered course, the wind now near abreast on

Surprise's starboard beam, its constant strength and consequent wave direction greatly easing her pitching, though there was scarcely any further diminution of her roll with only the double-reefed tops'ls, staysail, and the now restored jib and mizzen to press on her. All through the long night the wind continued to decline, and at six bells of the Middle watch Pat was able to take the reefs out of her tops'ls, which greatly further aided her stability and progress. It was close on dawn before the storm finally blew itself out, the sea state declined, the gale dropped to a tolerable blow, the hatches' battened tarpaulins were removed, and the galley fire could be relit, to the deep satisfaction of the crew, as hot food and drink could once again be served. *Surprise* shook out her courses – a respectable spread of canvas again, and she resumed her voyage.

To Pat's immense pleasure Freeman appeared in the cabin without beckoning, with tea and hot breakfast, and the welcome news, 'Ladies feelin' very better, takin' tea, massa.'

A very tired Pat, for he had not retired all night, was much relieved to hear it, 'Pass the word for Mr Pickering, Freeman.'

As Pickering entered the cabin, Pat asked, 'Tom; is there any sight of *Eleanor* or *Hercules*?'

'None, sir.'

'Well, keep us set firmly for Leghorn, we will doubtless meet them there. Mr Macleod is resting and I will sleep now for a few hours. You have command.'

Eleanor, a most weatherly sailor, had preceded their arrival at Leghorn, but of *Hercules* there was no sign. It was a full three days before she arrived. Captain Scott had returned in the storm to Genoa; the horses having become unsettled, kicking out their stalls in the hold.

Wednesday 23ʳᵈ July 1823   *Leghorn*

Little time was spent in Leghorn other than that necessary to take on water, revictual a few fresh comestibles, and repair the relatively slight storm damage. *Eleanor* had suffered no discernible damage at all and *Surprise* required only the most minor attention. Captain Scott, having rectified in Genoa the stalls broken down by the

169

panicked horses, had no need to dwell in Leghorn. Nevertheless, *Hercules* stayed two full days before departure, Lord Byron fruitlessly seeking news from the Morea and Greece generally, *Surprise* and *Eleanor* leaving in her wake. Whilst in Leghorn, Byron had kindly communicated to Pat that it was now his intention to land in Cephalonia rather than in Zante, upon the advice of his passenger, Hamilton Browne, a knowledgeable Hellenic sympathiser and a friend of the Zante governor.

'Cephalonia, Zante: 'tis all one for us, Duncan,' Pat had remarked with some acerbity whilst playing chess with his first after supper.

'Whining will serve no purpose,' muttered Simon, his head not shifting from his book.

Duncan did not look up from contemplation of his long planned knight's move, merely riposting, 'I think ye are in a wee difficulty. Does the game begin to tire ye, at all? There, checkmate!'

* * *

As greater southing was gained Simon and Marston were keenly anticipating passing by Etna and more particularly Stromboli, in great hopes of witnessing an eruption. 'With the blessing, 'tis to be hoped that we will witness fire atop one or t'other of them,' said Simon in the dispensary one morning after breakfast, as they were strapping up several sprains the crew had suffered during the storm whilst struggling to reduce sail.

'Has Captain O'Connor some worry with which he is pre-occupied, colleague? I have received no invitation to the cabin these past two days. Am I in his disfavour, in breach of some nautical protocol or convention of which I know not?' ventured Marston, a little anxiously, when they had finished up the dressings.

'Not at all, dear colleague; be not concerned: the captain's mind is a military one. Such souls have a predisposition towards order, regularity, and convention in affairs which, to those of us of a more, will I say, *laisser faire* nature tends to morosity, when indeed such is not the case. I fear he finds this venture a trifle unorthodox, and with no channel of communication being apparent to him, an expected envoy never appearing in Genoa, the further distance we are from home the greater his discomfort. Doubtless matters will take their course.'

Pat had completed his breakfast in Sinéad's company, and after she had left to join Kathleen, Brodie, and the twins he hailed his servant. 'Murphy! Pass the word for my officers.'

His lieutenants appeared within a few minutes, and they sat around Pat's table; Simon and Marston attending too. 'Gentlemen, we are but one small frigate, and expected to engage the Turk wherever we can. Most likely we may encounter more than one of their warships. They have several seventy-fours and many frigates, some bigger and more modern ships than our *Surprise*. I have been considering of this during our voyage, and here is my plan to fight with best prospects, not only for success but for flight too. *Surprise* boasts thirty-eight guns. She carries twenty-eight eighteen-pounders and ten nine-pounders including two bow chasers. In addition she has eight thirty-two-pound carronades. All are now equipped with modern flintlocks to preclude misfires.' Pat turned to Simon and Marston, 'That is in case spray were to douse our former slow-match. Our customary complement to fight the long guns is seven men per gun, a first and second captain, two loaders, two spongers and a boy serving as powder monkey. On some ships nine men and a powder-boy are not considered too many. For the nine-pounders, five men for each is plenty. Our carronades require fewer men, perhaps four, and so to man all of our thirty-eight guns and our eight carronades to fight the ship on both sides, as fast as ever would be possible, and with full gun crews, would require two hundred and forty-eight gunners. Yet our entire crew number, officers and men, is but two hundred and fifty. There is plainly a want of men to sail the ship were all to attend the guns. My intention, gentlemen, is this: the six carronades on the quarterdeck will be fought with just two men each; we will quit the two fo'c'sle carronades and the bow chasers as we approach the enemy, and all the quarterdeck nine-pound guns as well; leaving our men to serve only the eighteen-pound guns and the quarterdeck carronades. All the gun crews will be reduced to six men each, and one boy serving every two guns or carronades. In action we will fire the fo'c'sle long nines,' Pat turned again towards his surgeons in explanation, 'That is our *bow chasers*, during our approach from astern of our enemy, and in the hope of damaging her masts or rigging so as to degrade her speed and steering if possible, but as we come alongside of her the bow chaser and for'ard carronade crews, eighteen men, will shift to serve the quarterdeck carronades. We will need one hundred and eighty-two men for the eighteen-pound guns and fifteen for the quarterdeck carronades. Each eighteen-pounder crew of six men will fight their gun, with the heavy physical work associated with running the gun out, for the fifteen minutes only we will fight the ship if we find ourselves in peril, outnumbered. We will fire only nine broadsides in just fifteen minutes, and thence be away at the best speed she will make from 'tween the enemy ships. If my arithmetic serves me well, enough men, perhaps twenty, after leaving aside officers and cooks, will be left to sail the ship. That is at least enough men at the helm and to keep her on course when gunners cannot attend the yards. Not enough men to engage in any complicated manoeuvre, for I plan no such tactics, gentlemen; and no changes of sail can be contemplated, save if necessary to come about were we to find ourselves close in to some coast. Indeed, as my plan assumes that we will likely be outnumbered, it will be necessary to maintain all possible speed at all times, and such will best be preserved by strictly avoiding course changes and any manoeuvring, which would usually reduce our speed. Speed will be essential to our ability to escape from those situations where we are outgunned and for which these tactics have been devised. To take advantage of these tactics, and to repeat myself for clarity, we will make a direct approach: we will *ne'er mind manoeuvres and go straight at 'em*; as Nelson advocated.'

The lieutenants all looked doubtful; Pat could plainly see their glum faces. It may have been advocated by Nelson, but it was a high risk tactic that could be very costly: the approaching attacker could be battered by its prey, possibly even be raked, bow to stern, particularly in the final one thousand yards of closing which was the maximum effective range of ship's guns. The attacker could not reply except with bow chasers, and so the tactic had been abandoned long before the end of the French war.

It was Marston that interrupted Pat, 'I am no sailor, sir, but what will your enemy do with his great guns while *Surprise* strives so to reach him? I beg your pardon, sir, doubtless you have considered of this.'

Pat looked about the cabin before he continued, 'Yes gentlemen, I see your concern, but we may expect that the Turk is not yet as expert as the French and the Americans became. Approaching from astern of them, we will fire the bow chasers until we are upon them, when we will insert *Surprise* between the two for only as long as it is necessary to fire nine broadsides. We will be away at all possible speed if it don't look like they will strike their colours; only changing course once to cross the bows of one or t'other of our adversaries, to rake them, and with luck to shield us from the other's guns. Thus it will be necessary to retain the weather gauge throughout our approach, and preserve all possible speed. The carronades will open with shot only, no grape or canister. For three rounds their fire will be directed low, near the waterline of our enemy. From the close range I intend *Surprise* to open her fire from, no more than two hundred yards, the smashers will assuredly penetrate the enemy hull and start their sinking. After three rounds the carronades will switch to shot and grape, the better to cut their rigging. The eighteens will open double-loaded with shot and with canister, seeking to smash their guns and kill their men. For their second round they will switch to grape replacing canister so as to tear their rigging. One final point, gentlemen; we will not extinguish the galley fire in action.'

This comment drew sharp intakes of breath from the lieutenants, but Pat pressed on, 'I intend to fire red hot shot, and with reduced charges so that the ball will lodge within the target, and so will not penetrate through both sides of her hull. The consequent fire will give the Turk something more to struggle with. Of course, we may only be able to heat a very few shots in our galley. Mr Mower, you will discuss this with cook and the gunner. We shall practice heating and firing red hot shot in our great guns exercise.' With this Pat concluded his briefing; his lieutenants' initial doubts being only partially dispelled, but to some extent replaced with a keen interest to find out if the aggressive, innovative tactics and the increased gun crew capabilities could be developed successfully.

Sunday 27ᵗʰ July 1823   *Tyrrhenian Sea*

After divisions Pat announced a great guns exercise would be carried out, explaining to his experienced gun captains his intentions of fighting the ship from both sides, all the crew listening with manifest interest. '...fighting that is with gun crews serving the great guns on both sides concurrently – *at the same time, Dalby!*' Pat glared at Clumsy Dalby who plainly was seeking some clarity as to his role and muttering to his gun captain, Old Pennington. 'Mr Pickering will command the larboard battery and Mr Mower the starboard. Mr Boswell, Master Gunner, you will favour me by commanding the carronades on the quarterdeck.'

'Yes, your honour, sir,' beamed Boswell, delighted by his captain's instruction.

'Lads, we may find ourselves in situations where the odds are very much agin us. We are but one small frigate, though all of us would vouch the very best of frigates, would ye say?'

There was a barrage of affirmation from all present, as if anyone could doubt it, before Pat resumed, 'We must fight fast, and fire from both sides. Fast! That is three broadsides within five minutes. If we can do that there is not a frigate can stand agin us. Can ye do it?'

Huge roars of confirmation erupted, subsiding as Pat raised his hat. 'Lads, we have not been at sea aboard the like of our dear *Surprise* for four years or more. Doubtless 'twill take time to recover our past form. We start today. Look lively lads and God speed!'

The crew became instantly alert, the spectacle and occasion of firing the guns was always exhilarating, but firing both sides together was a rarely experienced tactic, the crews by conventional training switching from one side to the other. As their larboard gun was reloaded they trained and fired their starboard one and vice versa. Would there be enough men to fire both sides together and still achieve three broadsides per side, all within five minutes; Pat's minimum competency standard, as they all knew well? Would depleting the sailing crew to furnish more gunners diminish the ship's speed of manoeuvrability, a critical function in battle, as they all fully understood? The loss of such manoeuvrability could well bring the potential for catastrophe, which some, including Pat, had experienced personally when *Java*, critically unable to steer, had struck to *Constitution* in the year twelve. For this first exercise, no shot would be loaded and wasted, no targets set afloat; it would be simply running out the guns and firing the powder, with extra wads rammed as shot. They would see what timing could be achieved firing three rounds. Pat had no intention of keeping the new and old gunners wholly separate, a division which would slow the firing rate from many of the guns, and so every experienced crew had been diluted with new men, most with at least some experience of firing the guns – as most men in a man o' war had had occasion to do at some time in their career, even the cooks were retired gunners in many cases. But the new men had been drafted from their customary stations, standing by to make sail and course changes as required - to bring the frigate closer to its enemy, or away, as the battle dictated. Thus the experienced crews all found themselves with a new crew member or two whom the captains invariably instructed to 'Keep out of the way! Jump when I says so! And be ready to heave that gun in and out as fast as fast can be! As if your very life depended on it – as it surely will! D'ye hear me?'

'We will ripple the firing, bow to stern, to spare her timbers,' said Pat to his lieutenants. 'Stand by on my command.'

There was not a living soul below decks as the exercise was prepared, save for the powder crews in the magazines. The ladies and girls – although it had been firmly suggested by both Pat and Duncan that they retire below to the gun-room – could not hold their curiosity in check, and they stood on the quarterdeck in keen anticipation, never having seen the guns firing. The bulwarks forward of the great cabin were also taken down. Pat gazed down from his quarterdeck, reflecting that it had been over five years since *Tenedos* had fired her great guns in anger, even longer for *Surprise*. Five years of near total inactivity, and four or even more years in many cases since any of the crew had even run out a gun, let alone fired one. What would happen? The gun captains shouted encouragement to their men, 'Attend! Look alive! Stand ready!'

It was only with severe cajoling that the lieutenants had switched gun captains and experienced gunners from long guns. Not one had volunteered for the short carronades, considered ugly by most gunners. And who would expect them to transfer willingly, for they were attached to their guns which were all fondly named – aptly as far as their crews were concerned – with such striking names as *The Nailer, Axeman, Dutch Sam, Hell's Mouth* and *Hurricane*. Pat had found the nearest thing to a mutiny on *Surprise* when some gunners had been switched to the carronades, and only personal intervention alongside his lieutenants had smoothed things over. It was not like the Royal Navy of Old Jarvie's day, he thought, but perhaps that was for the better, the morale on board *Surprise* was better than ever he had remarked before, in all the years and in all the ships and oceans they had travelled. Perhaps it was just a reflection of the fact that every gun crew dearly wanted to show their best, and they doubted that they could do so if relegated to a carronade, for that is how they saw things, and who was to say that they were wrong. The carronades were close in smashers, short of range, but absolutely deadly when they were close enough to be fired, firing a ball near twice as heavy as the guns. They could also fire canister, two hundred and fifty balls each of two ounces which could sweep an enemy deck clean if used at the opportune moment; and fire grape, nine balls each of several pounds weight which would tear sheets and rip away rigging and thence substantially degrade the enemy's speed and manoeuvrability with a single broadside. They were usually fought by a crew of four, now reduced to two, so that Pat could implement his plan, spreading his experienced gun crews a little more thinly and fighting both sides of his ship concurrently.

If *Surprise* encountered two ships and was able to get between them, and if both sides could be fought and deliver three broadsides in five minutes then *Surprise* would be the most deadly of adversaries. Of course there was *Surprise's* transitioning to the firing position to be carefully managed. A slow approach could expose her to repeated broadsides from two enemy ships, and depending on her relative speed she could be under sustained fire for up to fifteen or so very unpleasant minutes. Pat had considered this before deciding on his tactics, for they gave *Surprise* – once she was in position to fire her broadside from close in – a potentially decisive advantage: the near certainty of holing the enemy hull. Were they to clear the enemy decks with canister and grape then it would be so much better for the boarding parties, particularly with *Surprise* no longer carrying any marines.

Before commencing firing, the decks had been wetted and sanded, and the magazines protected with thick 'fearnought' screens over the hatches to prevent any danger from sparks. The more experienced crew had stripped to bare chests, stuffed cotton waste in their ears, and wound scarves about their heads to afford a little protection from the anticipated thunder. All stood by their guns clutching rammer, sponge, and powder horn; the slow-matches having been replaced some years before in favour of the modern flintlocks. Pat had adopted this change with reluctance, and still kept slow-matches lit alongside the guns by way of precaution against the flintlocks misfiring.

The great guns had all been aligned with one of several marks Pat had ordered to be painted on the deck, so that every gun's fire would converge on the target at differing ranges. It was an aid devised by Captain Broke of *Shannon*, where Pat had first noted it. His tactical preparations for their mission lacked not the slightest detail: the magazines had been filled with the best red, large grain powder; all guns had been fitted with spare breeching ropes in case of damage to the tackles – a gun recoiling with cut breeching rope or damaged tackles represented a substantial danger; the deck had been wetted and sanded to prevent slipping of barefooted men, straining with every sinew to haul the heavyweight guns through their ports; near each port stood a water bucket for the sponge, wetted each time before it was run into the barrel, prior to loading the charge; behind the gun another bucket was filled with water for the crew to quench their thirst and slake the bitter taste of smoke; gun captains all retained the lit slow-match within a third barrel to keep it dry in case of spray. Behind the gun captains stood the second and third lieutenants, pacing the deck, each overseeing one side, no midshipmen being aboard to share the task.

Pat and Duncan looked down from the quarterdeck. 'Mr Prosser, you will oblige me by hauling our wind three points, and keep her steady at five knots, no more, if you will,' said Pat to the master. At last, after a final survey of his deck, Pat spoke to Simon, 'Be so good as to mark the time on your fine repeater, Doctor.' Pat turned to his wife, 'Sinéad, Kathleen, girls; be ready, we are about to commence.' He then shouted 'Cast loose your guns! Out tompions! Run out your guns!' Within moments there came a drumming, roaring noise as twenty-eight guns were pushed forward over the deck, the six quarterdeck carronades shifting more easily on their wheels within their constraining slides.

'Prime your guns!' Pat bellowed, and finally, 'From forward, a rolling fire … FIRE!'

To the passengers on the quarterdeck the loud, great crack of the guns – for they had never heard it before – and the spectacular jets of shooting orange flame were simply beyond anything they had ever experienced, and they shrank away in awe. The effect of the rippling barrage progressing down both sides of the ship overpowered them as they looked down from the quarterdeck. The noise was louder than the loudest thunderclap they had ever heard. The girls shrieked in excitement, but the ladies cowered. After a few moments the carronades fired, a higher cracking sound in comparison with the deep boom of the long guns. Noxious black smoke enveloped all on the quarterdeck, and Simon shouted to the ladies through the din, 'Come! Come below! Swiftly now, there is nothing here for you, as you can plainly see.' He shepherded them down to the gun deck and on down to the gun-room, the rolling thunder of the continuing barrage following them.

On the gun deck the forward crews, now glistening with sweat, were worming and sponging their guns, ramming in fresh cartridges and wads, though no shot, and re-priming the flashpans as fast as they could go. Newcomers were being cursed by their captains, communicating with gestures, nods and a rare shout. Two had fallen back on the deck, squealing like stuck pigs, not shifting quickly enough as their guns had recoiled, leaping from the deck before settling on their wheels. They had forgotten their captain's instructions to stand clear, and their legs had been struck by the gun trucks. Another new gunner was being berated for dropping the wormer as he leapt back in panic. Two captains were screaming at their powder monkeys for the cartridge. None of this escaped the immediate attention of the lieutenants. As the aftmost guns fired, the lieutenants waved their hats, ordering the forward ones to fire again. The noise was deafening, even below in the gun-room, where the passengers trembled as the second broadside rippled aft, the shaking of the deck being only very slightly less violent than it had been on the quarterdeck. Smoke drifted down the companionway, and they coughed in the noxious air.

Amidst the frenetic activity, the thunderclaps, and the bilious smoke from the guns in action, two men could be seen coming from the galley stove, attired in heavy gloves and carrying a glowing red hot shot between them in steel pincers, moving towards larboard number seven gun, *Hurricane*, the nearest gun to the galley. *Hurricane* had already fired its first shot, and now back inboard from its recoil was being swabbed to wash the barrel before a fresh powder charge was loaded. The gun captain, Old Pennington, was coaxing his crew 'Faster, faster, you whoreson buggers. D'ye think the Turks will wait whilst you fumble about at the breech.' Their evident reluctance to load the red hot shot and their severe grumbling was only overcome by the confidence they had long placed in him; the marked reduced-charge bag was rammed down, followed by the wad, and then the ball, gingerly introduced by a nervous crew, a crew in great trepidation and plainly aghast. Loading red hot shot with just a wad separating it from its powder was surely asking for disaster; another wad followed, and all was rammed tight, the man with the rammer fearing for his hands. The gun crew edged away from their captain, away from their gun, surreptitiously, a pace or two back from their customary stations, as far as they could decently shift. To their astonishment and very great relief no spontaneous detonation occurred. Old Pennington shouted to them, the gun was hauled forward by the crew, the lanyard pulled; the flintlock pan powder flashed through the vent to fire the charge and send the glowing ball out across the waves. No gun crew ever felt more relieved; disbelief reluctantly assuaged.

Some little time later, as the aftmost gun fired its third shot, Pat shouted, 'Avast firing!' and the guns fell silent. Simon had long since returned to the quarterdeck, and peered at his Breguet repeater in anticipation of Pat's only question, 'How long?'

Simon replied with an answer that he knew would dissatisfy Pat, 'Seven minutes forty seconds: would that do tolerably well for our first time after all these years?' One glance at Pat's glum face confirmed his expectation that it would not, not by a long chalk.

'Draw and house the guns, if you please,' Pat, standing above the waist, shouted the command, which was echoed down the gun deck by his lieutenants.

In the evening a glum Pat settled to his supper of toad in a hole with Duncan and Simon. The dish appeared to Simon to be more blackened than the norm, though Pat seemed not to notice.

'Pray tell, brother, what ails thee?' prompted Simon.

'Eh?' Pat looked up, frowning. 'We must fire faster. We will likely be outnumbered, and only the very fastest of firing will preserve us: 'tis clear that the crews are rusty, like a half-baked old hinge,' this in a very strident voice, angst plain in Pat's tone.

To Pat's muddled metaphor Simon could only offer a sympathetic, 'Surely, dear, there is time enough to improve on today's tolerably promising start?'

'Sweat, Simon, saves blood. Very poor, it was. We will be sunk afore we fire our second at that rate.'

'I am concerned to hear it. But would you expect the finest horse, though in want of training, to win the King's Plate at the Curragh? Not even Pat O'Connor, the optimist of all the world, could hold such a glorious hope, and 'tis little different.'

'Optimist of all the world? That is coming it a trifle high, Simon,' the irritation plain in Pat's voice.

'Doubtless you have not forgotten your considerable expenditure in canal stock, in bank stock, and latterly in South American bonds? Indeed, I collect there was mention even of gold mining, Pat. You are assuredly not frittering your capital away in such a venture - eh?'

'Gold, Simon, was found in Wicklow in the year ninety-five, or was it ninety-six? The promoters; Mrs Webster, Mr Mills, and Mr King were introduced to me; they explained that the gold was in the granite, in the bedrock, through which flowed the Ballinvalley River, and from which it was a simple task to pan for it in the water; bountiful quantities awaiting harvesting. Their colleague, Mr Sharp, showed me the nuggets found there - '

'And *sharp* would be right,' said Simon, Pat not listening, not detecting Simon's *double-entendre*.

' - said that some early prospectors had cleared thousands, declared that my farm sat on the very same granite, and doubtless it was only the want of financing of explorations that had precluded the discovery of gold in Claddaghduff itself. Sure, I have a little capital now in the Gannoughs, in the very smallest of mine, on the hill there. Investments, Simon; investments they are, and 'tis a bull market at present; though there is never a certainty in them. There is no sure investment, as all men of commerce will know. There is but little return in leaving precious funds in Consols and Navy five per cents when prices are rising again.'

'I dare say there is not. I do not set myself up as an authority on investments, Pat, I rub along. My father's bequest was so very small, and hence my penurious nature would ne'er permit of such follies. Nor could I tell a bull from a bear, save they were standing alongside of me. Doubtless I have been too long immersed in the medical world and that of the naturalist!' Simon laughed out loud.

'You would surely never say I was rich? I have but scarcely more than a dozen acres; three quarters are bog, and the remainder provide but the smallest of potato crop, and that only in a good year – it has failed these past two years – and 'tis only the accumulation of prize monies that has kept us from the workhouse: my half-pay could never feed even the wife and wains.'

'For God's love, it seems to me that if the boggies will believe our beloved Jesus did raise Lazarus from the dead then 'tis not remarkable that unscrupulous sharps will always find plenty o' blunties to gull. Gold, Pat; gold? In Ireland? I am amazed. Do you leave your precious sense in the cabin when you step ashore?'

'John Darcy did assure me there is gold in Galway; in Mayo too, on Inishturk island it has been found; many a day have I fished near that place; and the prospects for this promising enterprise have been scrutinised by the most sagacious of advisers.'

'I fancy salacious might answer better than sagacious.'

'Salacious, of course. I knew there was something not quite Bristol-fashion there. Salacious, a prime word, I dare say that is with an L?'

'An impecunious man should never indulge in speculation, brother; nor a wise one, even when he can afford it.'

''Tis investment, not speculation. Can ye not see that?' Pat spoke now in a raised voice.

'Far be it for me to affirm anything about investment. Folk have the strangest notions of what is sound and what is more akin to the throw of the dice.'

'Simon, I merely seek a sound home for my precious small capital, as you know well,' Pat replied, his tone growing more irritable.

'There is no call to grow chuff, Pat,' Simon retorted.

'You would have me laid by the lee again,' Pat's vexation and voice deflated: he knew he could not best Simon save in matters nautical where his friend had scarcely the sense of the greenest midshipman.

Simon heard the resignation and proposed, amiably 'What do you say to us scraping a little; a cheering ceilidh tune or two, and perhaps a bottle of your admirable port? Is that trifle of toad in a hole in the dish spare perhaps?'

A suggestion of a little playing customarily brought Pat round to his sociable side. Pat passed the little silver dish. 'Yes, yes, Simon, of course we will; 'tis just that my mind had shifted from the pleasure of being back on board after these past four years to thinking how best we would be fighting the ship once more. Freeman! Freeman! A bottle of my best port, if you will: the seventy-five. And no breakages, d'ye hear me? Of course we have time to improve, and so we will, without sparing the powder. Yes, here you are, I have quite lost my appetite.'

Tuesday 29th July 1823   *Off Sicily*

Stromboli to starboard as *Surprise* approached the Messina Strait at the top of the day presented none of the keenly hoped for signs of eruption. Etna, once through the Strait, displayed only a very little of smoke, to the great disappointment of all on board. Simon customarily passed much time every day on the quarterdeck with Marston, the two of them watching keenly for birdlife, or Simon sometimes trying his hand at painting watercolours in Duncan's expert company, accomplished artist that he was. Despite spring being a far more favourable time to see large scale northbound migration, late July still presented opportunities to see some birds returning early to their African wintering grounds.

'Look there, quickly. No, there: surely that is a Montague harrier, *Circus pygargus*?' shouted Marston, waving his arm.

'No, colleague, I believe it is a fine example of Eleonora's falcon, the bearded vulture, *Falco eleonorae*,' Simon replied, peering intently through Pat's best Dollond five-lens achromatic telescope, it having been loaned solely to Marston with the strictest of instructions as to its care, Pat not wishing to see it in Simon's hands where it had been near lost on several occasions.

The birdwatching was necessarily abandoned after dinner as the great guns exercise resumed each day, every day, as *Surprise* sailed east, holding her course for the Ionians; the times for firing three shots from both sides steadily reducing until Pat pronounced himself satisfied only when this was achieved once again in his self-imposed maximum five minutes. By then, they anticipated arriving in Ionian waters the next day.

Shortly after dawn the heights of Cephalonia came into view from the tops. *Surprise* continued her steady easterly course for several more hours until she eventually turned north to enter the great bay of Argostoli, tacking frequently against an adverse but weak summer north-easterly *Gregale* before heaving to and letting go her anchor in seventy-five feet of water in the roads, Pat preferring to await *Eleanor's* arrival before entering the harbour proper. It was some several hours after dinner, in the late afternoon, that *Eleanor* appeared, anchoring a cable away from *Surprise*. Codrington crossed to *Surprise* by barge on Pat's signal. They had no news of *Hercules*.

In the great cabin, as the hot and breezy day shifted to the relative stillness of early dusk, warmth still plentiful, the port lids being hauled open to capture what cooling breeze might still be had, Pat briefed his officers. 'Gentlemen, we are arrived in Greek waters. Politically however, we are in Ionian waters. That is to say: the United Islands of, principally, Corfu, Cephalonia and Zante, with four lesser ones, Lefkas, Kythira, Ithaka, and Paxos. Together they are a British protectorate, quite independent of Greece, and free of any Turk suzerainty. No Turk ship will venture here. The Governor, Maitland, has placed the islands in a state of quarantine from mainland Greece. No one can cross without incarceration here on account of the plague so prevalent on the mainland. At present we are flying English colours and perfectly welcome. When *Surprise* hoists Greek colours we may expect that to change. For that reason we shall take every possible sounding afore we change our flag. Mr Codrington, *Eleanor* will at all times maintain her English status, and so may come and go as she pleases, save for any contact with mainland Greece. Gentlemen, I anticipate that we will be in Greek service afore many more days have passed. Make your personal preparations, such that they may be.'

Bombard   *J.J. Baugean*

Chapter Five

Must we but weep o'er days more blest?
Must we but blush? — Our fathers bled.
Earth! render back from out thy breast
A remnant of our Spartan dead!
Of the three hundred grant but three,
To make a new Thermopylae!

Saturday 2ⁿᵈ August 1823   *Argostoli, Cephalonia*

In their finest dress attire of starched and pressed white dungarees, blue smocks, black hats, neckerchiefs, and with the most carefully plaited of pigtails, Pat's barge crew, Barton in command, rowed him dry across to the quay of Argostoli accompanied by Simon, Duncan, Pickering, Mower, and Codrington. The captain of the port was standing on the quay as they tied up, a frigate being a most rare arrival in Argostoli. He was a native Cephalonian and an affable man, welcoming Pat's party and introducing himself with neither airs nor formality, 'Teodosio Cazzaitti, at your service, gentlemen.'

After introductions had been completed he readily opined his belief in the imminent arrival of the Greek fleet and his anticipation of its destruction of the Turk. Pat did not think fit to disabuse him of his optimism, 'Captain Cazzaitti, please to introduce us to the Resident if you will.'

The port captain explained, in heavily accented and imperfect English, 'Colonel Napier away: Gone away with General Adam, with Admiral Moore, gone see Turk Pasha. You see secretary, he here.'

'Very well, Captain Cazzaitti, the secretary will serve. Please, if you will, lead on,' said a resigned Pat.

Cazzaiti was pleased to escort Pat's party to the Resident's house, a short walk away, albeit tiring in the blistering heat – though it was only a little after nine in the morning. A servant met them at the door, bidding them wait whilst summoning the maid. After a short while, Pat growing irritable in the intense humidity, the maid brought them to the office of the Resident's secretary.

Captain Kennedy, a very amiable man, seemed genuinely pleased to greet them, his voice warm with the most gentle of Ulster inflections. 'Good morning to you, gentlemen. John Kennedy, captain Royal Engineers and secretary to Colonel Napier. The Colonel is away presently, most likely for a few more days.'

Pat's impatience drained away in a moment, presented with this hospitable aide, and after he had introduced himself and his officers, Kennedy replied, 'Your servant, Captain. Gentlemen, may I offer you tea? Punch perhaps?'

The temperature had been rising steadily since breakfast, and it was now even hotter than Pat could ever recollect experiencing, even when in the West Indies. 'Thank you, Captain Kennedy, punch would be most welcome.' Pat was now sweating heavily in his best dress uniform of a particularly heavy cloth, pressed to perfection that morning by Murphy. It was now bereft of any Royal Navy insignia, save for the Nile medal in his buttonhole, a paucity of official status which Kennedy could scarcely miss.

Kennedy smiled, 'The maid makes a particularly fine punch with green tea. And we may even have a little Trieste ice left in store which we receive with tolerable frequency from Corfu.' As Pat and his officers were seated in the secretary's office the maid promptly returned and served the iced punch. Kennedy continued, 'The Resident will return within a very few days, Captain O'Connor, and will no doubt be pleased to receive you. Until then may I enquire as to the purpose of your visit? We have received no prior notification of your arrival in the Islands.'

With no change of expression Pat looked carefully at Duncan on the opposite side of the table who almost imperceptibly shook his head, just once. It was enough of a signal for Pat who replied cautiously, recalling a now distant briefing from the First Lord. 'Captain Kennedy, *Surprise* is not a Royal Navy vessel as such. Rather she is chartered to engage in hydrographical surveying in the waters of His Majesty's Protectorate. We are here to provide our assistance to Captain Smyth, *HMS Adventure*, whose fine surveys are much appreciated by their Lordships at the Admiralty. Their Lordships are minded that in the present, will I say, *delicate* political circumstances a survey vessel of some, however small, military standing might well be more respected by any belligerents she may encounter in the course of her task.'

Duncan was impressed with Pat's credible polish, added to Melville's strategem. Pat, though no academic, was remarkably quick of thought when pressed in such circumstances, a particularly valuable talent when engaged in and considering of his immediate military options. Pat's lieutenants assumed blank faces.

Whether Kennedy believed or doubted Pat's story, his face did not register either way, and his reply was noncommital, albeit in a tone that suggested he was a little sceptical, 'I *see*, Captain O'Connor. No doubt Colonel Napier will be pleased to discuss that with you on his return. In the meantime, if I may be of any assistance to you and your assignation please do not hesitate to ask of me.'

After the customary pleasantries of leave-taking, Pat and his officers returned to *Surprise*; Pat, Simon and Duncan to take their supper together and to discuss matters further. 'What was I to say, Duncan?' Pat asked of his fellow conspirator.

'An admirable answer, Pat; an' one which will endure tolerably well until such time as we secure oor letter-o'-marque. If ye collect oor briefing from Lowrey in London, in a wee few days ah am to meet wi' his promised contact here in Argostoli, who will make hisself known to me, an' who will have the most recent information on the political an' military situation in the Morea an' in Greece generally. Until then we will seek some accommodation fer the ladies an' assume the task o' surveyin', whate'er that may involve. Ah have nae doot that ye will make a credible fist of it fer the benefit o' any onlookers, fer there will surely be Turk agents in this place. Fer the moment let us take supper an' perhaps we may enjoy a wee hour o' music afterwards, if the lassies an' bairns are comfortably settled? Will ah invite Marston?'

It was during Pat's late second breakfast with Duncan and Simon that Mower reported *Hercules* entering the bay and proceeding slowly towards them, her courses reefed, and approaching the outer anchorage of Argostoli's port.

'Pat, listen will ye now?' said Duncan. 'Ah say this advisedly. Might ah suggest that we maintain just a wee dialogue wi' Lord Byron fer the moment, only that which is necessary; an' perhaps it should be conducted solely through masel' until at least such time as we have secured oor Greek letter o' marque, not wishing fer any association between ye an' such a well known Hellenist to be remarked upon, particularly when ye are here officially fer hydrographical purposes? Brother, wid there be any more o' those tolerably flavoursome kidneys left in that pan?'

'You are truly more suited to these ... these engagements under false colours than ever I will be, Duncan, being just a simple jack tar. Do we, I wonder, ever profit by them?' Pat mused.

'Och, to be sure 'twould all be much simpler were such trickery an' deceit ne'er necessary, dear soul.'

'You may consider of this: would the Greeks ever have taken Troy without the deception of the wooden horse?' Simon interjected.

'Such sharp practice; that is scarcely my line of country, Simon.'

'Forgive me if I am in error, brother, but I do collect our dear *Tenedos* hoisting certain colours on occasion, colours which were never strictly in his Majesty's gift?' Simon failed to conceal his mirth, laughing out loud as he spoke the latter point, which did raise a smile from his captain and loud laughter from Duncan.

Colonel Napier came aboard *Surprise* at eight bells of the Morning watch, being sighted beforehand by Barton as the Resident was being rowed out from the quay, accompanied by Kennedy. Barton alerted Tom Pickering who entered the cabin as Pat was finishing his first breakfast, Duncan with him.

'Sir, we have a visitor approaching the ship, possibly the Resident as he is accompanied by Kennedy.'

'Very well, Tom, I shall come on deck directly. Murphy, light along and ask the Doctor to join me in the cabin in ten minutes. And Murphy, ensure that he is shaved and clothed respectably for our visitors,' said Pat, pleasantly. 'Duncan, I must visit my closet, and then speak with Simon; please to welcome our guests on deck if you will.' Pat stepped out.

'Of course, sir.'

'Napier,' said the visitor simply, introducing himself as he climbed aboard up the accommodation ladder and on to the deck, hand outstretched towards Duncan, Kennedy following.

'Ma pleasure, sir,' Duncan replied, shaking his hand. 'Lieutenant Duncan Macleod. Captain O'Connor invites ye to please step intae the cabin; it will afford a wee shade.'

They entered, and Freeman appeared after a peremptory knock, unbidden but perfectly familiar with Pat's expectations, setting glasses and cups on the table. He whispered to Duncan, 'Doctor coming, massa; he no find wig.'

'Are you associated with the other vessel recently arrived, *Hercules*; Lieutenant Macleod, with Lord Byron aboard?' Napier came straight to the point.

Just at that moment, Duncan's reply hanging in the air, Pat entered the cabin with Simon, having just caught the question. Simon stood quite resplendent, Duncan thought, in clean pressed clothes and freshly shaven, his wig newly-powdered atop his head; a rare sight indeed. Duncan introduced them, 'Colonel, will I present Captain Patrick O'Connor and our surgeon, my particular friend, Doctor Simon Ferguson.'

'Your servant, sir,' said Simon with a slightly theatrical bow.

'Good morning to you both and a grand morning it is, to be sure,' said Pat, shaking hands with Napier and Kennedy, and beaming brightly towards the guests. He was speaking with his usually indistinguishable Irish lilt very much to the fore, Duncan noticed, a little puzzled. Pat continued quickly, leaving no

190

opportunity for anyone to interject. 'To be sure, 'tis a pleasure and a very great honour to meet one of Ireland's most illustrious sons; a veteran of the Peninsula and of the 1812, and a staff officer to His Lordship, Wellington, to boot. Did you know, Lieutenant Macleod?' Pat quite nimbly diverting all thoughts from Napier's unanswered question, but leaving unsaid the other thought on his mind: 'and cousin to Lord Edward Fitzgerald, leader of the United Irishmen and the Rising.' It was a subject Pat was particularly keen to avoid, being a former sympathiser of the brotherhood in his enthusiastic younger days. Pat continued, brooking no interruption, and smiling as he turned to Kennedy, adding, 'Captain Kennedy, you are of the Donegal Kennedy's, I venture?'

'Why, yes indeed, a Donegal man I am, Captain O'Connor. Are you familiar with the County?' Kennedy replied, evidently pleased with Pat's interest.

'Most certainly I am, sir, the glory of the world, so it is. I once hooked a prodigious fine salmon at the leap in Ballyshannon, and I have played cello in the Donegal style with Hugh Doherty in Glencolmcille – I visited in the year Boney was sent to Elba. My colleagues and I are particularly fond of our music, and often tend towards the traditional rather than the classical. Perhaps you would like to attend our playing? We have a fine quartet aboard, with my officers and our assistant surgeon, Michael Marston, who is most melodic with the violin. Excuse me, Colonel, Captain, I blather on inexcusably. Would you care for tea, a glass of Madeira perhaps?'

Pat paused only for long enough to draw breath, but Napier interrupted. 'Thank you, Captain O'Connor,' he said, a little taken aback by Pat's verbosity, 'Doctor Ferguson, are you, perchance, acquainted with our Emerald Isle?'

'I am familiar with the sweet County Clare, having once visited the Burren: a wondrous place for fritillaries you know; the water beetle too, very rare. 'Twas a splendid few months I was there afore I reluctantly bade farewell to return to my position in Plymouth Dock.'

Fortunately just at that moment Freeman entered bearing a tray of Madeira and tea. Duncan could bear his captain's rambling diversion no longer, and, seizing his moment, interjected. 'Thankee Freeman; well done. Colonel, Lord Melville has requested us to assist Captain Smyth, *HMS Adventure*, in his hydrographical surveying o' the Ionian watters an' thereaboots, wi' particular interest in the Corfu Channel. His Majesty's Government is particularly keen to help the economies o' the United Islands prosper, given the Turk blockade o' the Morea an' the merchants o' Corfu wishing to stimulate their olive oil sales, greatly depleted since the end o' the war wi' Boney. An' likewise the local currant producers, their trade also being much doon.'

If Napier and Kennedy were astonished by Pat's blathering and Duncan's subsequent efforts at a plausible explanation for *Surprise* – a warship of some significance - appearing in this emerging place of congregation for foreign supporters of Greek independence, ostensibly to facilitate further the growing principal commerce of the Islands, of which they were perfectly aware, by additional hydrographical surveying, they gave no sign; both their faces remaining blank, as if weighing the truth of Duncan's remarkable statement.

'Colonel, there is one matter in which I might beg your assistance. My family and Lieutenant Macleod's will seek accommodation ashore, *Surprise* being oft away. Will you suggest some suitable place of abode for them, within, shall we say, no more than an hour of the port, and suited to a horse and carriage?' Pat asked, keen to talk about anything other than their mission.

'Of course, Captain O'Connor; if I may offer the assistance of my brother, Charles: he is here on the island and perfectly acquainted with suitable locations,' Napier volunteered, bemused.

After finishing the Madeira and tea Napier stood to leave, bidding farewell and adding pleasantly, 'If we may render any service, however small... Captain Kennedy and I would be delighted to accept your offer to hear your ship's musicians. Captain O'Connor, perhaps you and your officers might join us for dinner in the Residence at your convenience? We must away now to *Hercules,* and attend His Lordship. I bid you all good day, gentlemen,' Napier concluded, and departed with Kennedy.

192

'Duncan, you are indeed a dissimulator of the very first order. That was a tolerably entertaining story: olive oil and currants indeed. How did you conceive of that?' asked Pat, intrigued.

'Och, ah ken noot o' such things, Pat, but Codrington joined us yesterday fer dinner in the Gun-room, an' we discussed *Eleanor*. She is in need o' a deal o' new canvas noo; neither was she refitted when *Surprise* was in Plymouth Dock, 'tis foor years since she was last oot o' the watter. Codrington was explainin', o'er the very finest o' plum duffs fer pudding – wi' fresh raisins which came aboord only yesterday mornin' – that his family had some interests wi' a Venice merchant, one customarily buyin' the olive oil o' Corfu an' the currants o' Cephalonia an' Zante, all near unobtainable fer him 'til the Turk blockade o' the Morea removed the mainland competition from the market. So, ye see, Pat, 'twas nae the fanciful story ye thought it to be,' Duncan concluded, with just the slightest note of triumph.

'My compliments, brother,' said Simon, 'that was a capital invention. Would there be any of that plum pudding left? Tea leaves the strongest of cravings for just a very little morsel of something sweet.'

Pat smiled, 'I venture *Surprise* has a greater prospect of sinking a seventy-four than our duff had of surviving Murphy's return to the galley.'

Thursday 21ˢᵗ August 1823   *Argostoli, Cephalonia*

Some weeks had elapsed since *Surprise's* arrival, and no contact had been received from the provisional Greek government, although Duncan did expect to hear news from Lowrey in due course. A small abode had been found for the O'Connor and the Macleod families in the village of Metaxata, some five miles from the port. The house belonged to a relative of Captain Cazzaitti who had immediately offered to assist their search for accommodation. It offered a fine view of Zante to the south with a distant glimpse of the Morea far beyond. The ladies were very pleased with the location and threw themselves enthusiastically into arranging their accommodation as they wished it to be. Patrick Coghlan, with some half a dozen of *Surprise's* crew – principally those hands who had served in Pat's Claddaghduff household – was tasked with cleaning the house and the fresh painting of its walls, without the slightest delay being brooked by the ladies. Simon had accompanied Pat and Duncan to the house.

'Here we be, Simon; 'tis a plain, honest abode, but wide is the door of a little cottage,' pronounced a delighted Pat.

'Little is what I behold, Pat, and there are many of us. Would there be a room for me? There is a veritable cornucopia of plants and birds about this place which are not familiar to me. There is always a want of time to study such fascinations when we are engaged in your briny world, plants and birds alike all absent, save for the gull.'

'Why, of course there is. Eight bedrooms there be, though in some, small as they are, I would not care to swing the cat out of the bag.'

The twins and Brodie, ashore since some days, the appeal of the voyage having tired, were delighted to explore the environs of their new abode, and they gloried in the unbroken days of fierce heat such that they had never experienced at home.

Pat and Duncan felt obliged to stay and assist in the establishment of the family abode for several days, a handful of Surprises helping out with the moving of all the baggage from the ship. Such enforced domesticity increasingly grated with Pat as he considered the lack of progress with the mission until, to his delight, the morning arrival of Surprises from the port brought welcome news.

'Sinéad, my dear, Duncan awaits a most important letter from London, and the packet from Corfu is expected today,' Pat announced, breakfast having been consumed. 'We will be away directly for the port.' Shortly afterwards they departed for Argostoli, riding two locally purchased, fine Thessalians; it being less than a gentle hour for the horses, carefully favoured in the extreme heat. To Pat and Duncan's great surprise a most familiar old acquaintance awaited them on the quay, sitting outside the port captain's office in the shade.

'Abel Jason, so it is! How it pleases me to see ye again!' exclaimed Duncan, vigorously shaking the hand of his old shipmate and friend, *Tenedos's* former purser.

'I am very happy to see you, Mr Jason,' declared Pat, pressing his hand until Jason near winced.

'It is most pleasing to see you both again, Captain, Lieutenant,' replied Jason, extricating his hand from Pat's steely grip.

After the customary cordialities had been exchanged and enjoyed by all Jason apprised them of his mission, 'I am arrived today from Corfu, having taken a packet there from Falmouth – in some haste – at the bidding of Mr Lowrey, and herewith a letter from him,' he declared.

'Pat, perhaps we should repair to oor dear *Surprise*; here is nae the place to discuss any letter, nor indeed to decipher it. Dootless it will be encoded.'

'Let us go aboard, directly, out of this damn heat; perhaps we will find a cold bottle of Sillery,' said Pat, bathed in sweat.

Once returned to the great cabin and settled, sipping pleasantly cool champagne, fetched from the lower hold by Freeman, he being sent to tell Pat's cook that Jason would join them for dinner, Duncan asked of his old friend, 'Pray, Abel, we hope we see ye well an' will ye tell us o' your activities these past foor years.'

'I am in perfectly good health, dear colleague, thank you.'

'Heartily pleased,' said Pat with evident pleasure.

Jason resumed, 'After our return from the South Atlantic my cousin pressed me to assist him in the further development of the family estates, an occupation of which I had long begun to tire, and so the letter I received from Mr Lowrey, enquiring as to my interest in rendering him some assistance, was manna indeed. I hastened to London, and that is how I am here.'

Duncan looked across to Pat and asked, 'Pat, will ye excuse us, it may take some wee time to extract Lowrey's message from his letter, it no doot being in his code?'

'Why of course, Duncan. I shall be on my quarterdeck. Please to shout for Freeman should you require further refreshment.'

195

Jason brought Lowrey's letter from his inside breast pocket, and pressed it on to the table whilst Duncan shifted the table itself towards the stern windows where the sunlight could aid their deciphering. 'It is in the D3 code wi' one shift ah find,' Duncan pronounced after a few minutes. 'One moment, colleague, ah shall find ma key.' Duncan went down to the gun-room, his customary berth, to search his dunnage, re-emerging after a quarter hour. Near another hour passed. 'It has been some considerable time since I last engaged wi' this task, dear Abel, an' ah find some difficulty wi' all these combinations, however the message has emerged in principle, an' we will bring this to Captain O'Connor's interest wi' nae delay,' Duncan remarked before sending Freeman to find the captain.

Pat appeared after a very few minutes with something akin to worry across his latterly unperturbed face, as he looked at Duncan's grave expression. 'Freeman, we will take coffee now, if you please, and see if cook can find any of those marchpane biscuits.'

Though Freeman was gone, Murphy loitered still by the door. Duncan, well acquainted with Murphy's tendencies, whispered, 'Pat, 'tis clear from those parts o' this letter which we have satisfactorily decoded that the situation in Greece is far worse than we had thought. Internecine strife abounds throughout the provinces an' the government in Nauplia, since January, carries nae sway either in the Morea or elsewhere. So much so that the letter-o'-marque fer *Surprise,* promised by Secretary of State Mavrocordato, cannae safely be brought to us here, wi' the Turk embargo on all marine traffic throughout these watters, save for His Majesty's ships associated wi' the United Islands. The letter will therefore be brought an' entrusted to the Greek government's representative in the western provinces, in Messalonghi, where we are to collect it. However, the town has been besieged by the Turk fleet, under Khosref, since late in July.'

Freeman returned. 'Ain't no biscuits left, massa. Cook bakin' more. Here be coffee, fresh now,' as he put the tray down on the table, 'anythin' else, massa?'

'No, Freeman. Biscuits when ready will be most welcome, thankee,' said Pat, pre-occupied with his contemplation of the letter's contents, and having no intention of enlightening Murphy's self-evident curiosity, he lingering still near the door. 'I dare say there will be some significant Turk ships 'tween Cephalonia and the mainland. We know little of the lagoon and shallows afore Messalonghi, and with no pilot available to us it would be a passage with some hazard. No, we cannot take *Surprise* there. No doubt her arrival would be remarked in Constantinople within a week and Corfu in just a day or two when King Tom... *Maitland* would throw us out of this place directly.' Pat pronounced his assessment rather gloomily before continuing, 'A way must be found, Duncan, to collect the letter when we know it has arrived in Messalonghi. We cannot act without it, for such would be plain piracy, and if taken we would all be hung from the yard, and rightly so. We will send *Eleanor* if necessary to fetch the letter. She can slip over in some fog, and being so much shallower in draught she will better cross the bar and navigate the lagoon approach to the town. Without a local navigator or the finest of charts we could not hazard *Surprise* on such a venture.' A plan began to form in his mind, 'As we are here assisting Captain Smyth in hydrographical surveying, it would not go remarked were we to ask of him the charts for that place. Until we possess the letter we will offer our assistance to Captain Smyth and see what can be done.'

Sunday 31st August 1823   *Argostoli, Cephalonia*

After breakfast, church and divisions had concluded Pat, Simon and Duncan, together with Marston, Jason, Sinéad and Kathleen went ashore in the barge to join Napier and Kennedy for dinner, the musicians taking their instruments. Pickering and Mower accompanied them, Mower desperately keen to meet his poet idol, Byron.

Napier, with his colleague Kennedy, welcomed them all most warmly to the Residence. Lord Byron, having already arrived, greeted them in the friendliest of manners, Mower being rendered tongue-tied as he shook hands with the great man. 'I am, sir, a devoted admirer of your most excellent works,' whispered Mower, in awe.

'Thank you kindly, Mr Mower. Are you a poet yourself?' Byron asked, in an encouraging tone.

'Why, yes sir, indeed I am.'

'Then I hope that we may find occasion to read your own works together,' offered Byron, smiling, 'here in this most pleasant and tranquil place. None finer for any bard could there be. Perhaps we will both enjoy the creation of further works? I will await you. Please call at your convenience.'

'Thank you, sir; it is my most precious hope that we may do so.'

Byron introduced his companion, Count Gamba, who had accompanied him from Genoa. It was a most affable gathering at the Colonel's table, several bottles of a superb Amontillado enjoyed by all as they sat waiting to dine. The chef had excelled himself, serving a most excellent selection of grilled fish accompanied by a local retsina, followed by sofrito – albeit his Lordship demurred in favour of cheese – with a magnificent burgundy, and then baklava puddled in honey; finally, copious local brandy and the strongest of Greek coffee to conclude, a finale wholly to the taste of Pat, Simon and Duncan.

It was with tremendous satisfaction that Pat thanked the Resident. 'A capital dinner, Colonel Napier; we must see how *Surprise* can thank you. If only we were still a commissioned vessel, I think we would assuredly press your cook,' joked Pat in the cordial ambience of after dinner contentment. 'Most assuredly, sir, I have not eaten as well since leaving London,' added Jason.

'And what are your activities and intentions here in Cephalonia, Mr Jason? We are already accompanied by probably the most well known Hellenist of all, here beside me in his Lordship,' Napier said, smiling towards Byron whilst seizing his opportunity for a prescient question, which alerted them all to some caution. 'Would you be another, at all?'

'My dear Colonel, my sympathies lie wholly with the Greeks, of that I make no secret, but I am here merely as linguistic assistant to Captain O'Connor. I have some proficiency in the Greek and Turk languages, which may conceivably be called upon should *Surprise* encounter any of the ships of either side in the current strife. I am come from Corfu on account of attending to pressing family affairs before my Admiralty letter of appointment was delivered to me. It was too late for me to reach Falmouth ere *Surprise* left. Tell, Colonel, how do you anticipate matters developing in this conflict, and how are you affected here in the Islands?' With this question Jason smoothly switched the interest of the ensemble.

For Colonel Napier, a distinguished veteran of the Peninsula and the Hundred Days, such questions held no fear, as all looked to his answer. 'My dear Mr Jason, as an officer of the Crown, and being subordinate to Sir Thomas Maitland, my duty lies in maintaining the avowed neutrality of the United Islands. Sir Thomas, who may fairly be called a rough old despot, is very strict on that, and will brook no infractions of our neutrality, as is rightly so, and my own personal opinions must be subordinate to that. I must tell you all that Sir Thomas insists on a policy of strict quarantine for anyone coming to these islands from the Greek mainland where disease and pestilence is rife. We will brook no traffic at all with Greece.'

Lord Byron interjected. 'It is sure that Maitland's neutrality prevails, even here, for I can find no means to cash my bills of exchange. Both Cariddi and Corgialegno, the richest proprietors and merchants in the island, have refused me, which is a considerable inconvenience.'

'Virtue never has been as respectable as money,' remarked Pickering.

Pickering's comment did not distract Napier, who was assuredly aware that Byron's pro-Hellenic sympathies would not find favour with Maitland, and he continued, 'As a military man it is obvious that the Greeks lack a great deal. Professional officers and a standing army are woefully absent. Their struggles are contingent on little more than militias, who are in reality brigades of bandits, fighting amongst themselves more often than against the Turk. They have no artillery, no cavalry, no training regime, no commissary, and they feed off their impoverished fellow countrymen. Our sources report that the German Legion survivors in Nauplia are starving and subsist only on tortoises! Perhaps not wholly unpalatable to you mariners, accustomed as you are to eating the turtle, but plainly it evidences the woeful lack of money and any kind of proper administration. The Greeks have very few of warships, but no one would doubt their courage, and if that alone can deliver them then delivered they assuredly will be. They have two particular admirals: the Psariote, Canaris; and the Hydriote, Miaoulis. Both have fought the most successful actions against the Turks. Yet, for all that, their fleet lies inactive, their crews in want of money, and so the Turk, Khosref, blockades Messalonghi in impunity with his squadron of fifteen of sail, whilst twenty-thousand Ottoman troops besiege it by land. The Greeks have several generals: in the east, Odysseus; in the Morea, Kolokotrones. Everywhere there abound innumerable politicians, all squabbling amongst themselves; the prominent one being Secretary of State Mavrocordato, who I believe has now fled to Hydra under threat from Kolokotrones.'

At this news, most probably throwing their plans into disarray, Duncan glanced quickly at Pat who had similarly taken it in, and who now seemed sunk in thought.

Napier continued, 'Should the Greeks succeed in uniting their forces by land and securing stronger warships, then they have a prospect of victory. Until then they will always be suppressed, if not controlled, by the Turk who by virtue of his fleet can place his brigades anywhere throughout the Greek communities, in any of the Ottoman provinces. Any seasoned general would relish the task of bringing the disparate Greek forces to a concerted direction, but that seems unlikely to come about on account of their political chaos. They have plentiful foreign volunteers of course, adventurers and dreamers for the most part, and ill-equipped to meet the full force of even the most lamentable Turk brigade. Any capable admiral with but a modicum of sound warships might well intercede with great success in choking off Turk resupply, as there is certainly no Turk Nelson.'

At this, as if prompted, there was a polite but subdued laugh from around the table before Lord Byron interjected, 'Colonel Napier, surely that is too pessimistic? Greek heroes, as worthy as any of their predecessors of antiquity, are dying every day, most recently the brave Marco Botzari. The honourable aspiration for freedom surely beats as firmly in Greek hearts as it did in Napoleon's subject peoples. Even that man of arguably military genius, *as is said by some*, could not hold the tide of freedom at bay. And so are these adventurers, whom you state are so ineffective, not providing a beacon, illuminating the path to follow, for the peoples of Greece to throw off the Turk yoke?'

'Very admirably put, my Lord,' said Napier, 'but it cannot be denied that Bonaparte was beaten only by the most experienced and substantial forces of the Alliance, on land and by sea, and only after very many years of costly struggle - and even then it was a near run thing. No, 'twould not do to underestimate the Greek difficulties, nor the time it may take them. Yet, were I pressed to conjecture, I would have to favour the Greeks.'

Neither Pat nor Duncan wished to pursue the subject of the discussion, and so they politely refrained from comment. A little further time passed before it became apparent to all that no confluence of opinions would be established between Napier the soldier and Byron the poet. It was therefore a moment of some relief when the maid announced the return of the ladies, and so Pat brought the military debate to a timely end, 'Colonel, might we perhaps conclude your most excellent dinner with a piece or two from Corelli, ere it becomes time to depart?'

'A most admirable suggestion, Captain O'Connor; Captain Kennedy and I have been keenly awaiting your concert. We hear so little of the classics here in Cephalonia. Please to continue,' Napier replied, beaming jovially at Pat.

'If your Lordship pleases,' Pat looked towards Lord Byron, 'My colleague, Michael Marston, will precede our Corelli with his version of a most magnificent piece we encountered first in his Lordship's home in Genoa, and by the finest musician it has ever been my good fortune to hear. He will play Signor Paganini's *Caprice Vingt-quatre*, though with Dr Ferguson's viola rather than the violin: we find it adds a pleasing warmth to the piece.'

'Most happy, Captain O'Connor,' Byron replied, 'Please to begin.'

Whilst Marston could not achieve the exquisite perfection of Paganini, his own playing was close to virtuoso, and at the conclusion the small gathering was deeply impressed, thanking him with robust clapping, Duncan, Simon and Pat included. It was then for the quartet to play on for another twenty minutes or so of Corelli, Duncan contributing his own gentle and subtle additions with his whistle, before the convivial occasion came to its end.

Napier and Kennedy were delighted, applauding with gusto as the musicians finished. The Colonel stood, as if in summation of the event, 'Gentlemen, so very invigorating, remarkable; I congratulate you all most profusely. Sadly, there is so little opportunity here for us to enjoy such stirring musical talents. I beg you, please accept my ... *our* invitation to dine with us again, and allow us, if you will, another blessed moment in which to hear such prodigious fine musicians.'

'Most kind, Colonel, and thankee for your hospitality on behalf of all of us,' Pat replied, delighted to establish such good prospects for future dialogue. 'I regret we must now away to our abode, sir, my officers to the ship.'

As they prepared to depart, Lord Byron, being kindly solicitous to the ladies, enquired of them their contentment with life aboard ship, he himself still being accommodated on *Hercules*.

'Thank you, my Lord; we have shifted from *Surprise,* and now reside in a little house in Metaxata on a warm south slope. It is a most pleasant village where we enjoy the vista towards Zante,' Sinéad replied.

'Perhaps that place would suit my own modest needs, for I must very soon quit the ship. I collect that the Colonel's brother may indeed have suggested it,' Byron remarked.

The Colonel thanked them again for their playing, smiling and shaking hands with them all as they left the house, bidding farewell as Captain Kennedy escorted them out to the street.

The afternoon was passing into early evening as Pat, Duncan and their families, Simon with them, set off in jovial spirits to stroll back to their new home ashore, Mower and Pickering to return to the ship.

'The prospects of securing our Greek commission are receding like the tide, Duncan. Will we leave for Hydra, would you think?' asked Pat later, as they sat with Simon in their easy chairs on the terrace in the approaching dusk, the whirring sound of cicadas all around them, the air still warm and scented with wild rosemary.

'In this uncertainty o' political stability ah fear such a move might serve only to prematurely disclose oor intentions, an' would secure little were we to find Mavrocordato absent from Hydra. The close preservation o' oor intentions fer the moment must best serve oor interests, Pat. Better to send *Eleanor*, wi' Jason perhaps, to Hydra, to find oot what is afoot. 'Til then we will persevere with sailing up and doon the coast.'

Simon interjected, 'Indeed, 'tis a pleasant enough prospect, though I marvel that such repetitive contemplation of your watery realm holds such evident interest for you mariners. Is there a shard of that toad in a hole left at all?'

'Surveying, Simon, for us mariners is a most engaging pastime; the understanding of our realm is of prime importance. You are to consider that his Majesty has lost many more ships to rocks and reefs in poorly charted waters than ever struck to Boney's fleet. But I see you jest, old friend. *Adventure* and Smyth will be here afore long, and then we shall meet a surveyor of the very first order. Until then we are in accord: *Eleanor* with Jason will be sent to Hydra tomorrow to see the lie of the land. Freeman! Ah, there you are. The Doctor has set his fancy on another of your admirable toad in a hole rations, if you will; thankee kindly, Freeman. And perhaps we will share another claret, Murphy,' said Pat to his steward, even ashore never far from earshot.

Wednesday 17th September 1823   *Argostoli, Cephalonia*

It was more than two weeks before Captain Smyth and *Adventure* eventually arrived in Argostoli, calling to revictual and to take on fresh water, having spent some weeks off the west coast of the Ionian Islands in assessing modifications to charts made some years previously, the west coast being reckoned generally free of Turk warships and the Greek pirates who still abounded throughout those waters, notwithstanding the risks from Ottoman patrols enforcing the blockade.

'William Smyth, sir, at your service, Captain O'Connor,' said Smyth as he proffered his hand, having climbed the ladder and stepped on to *Surprise's* deck. *Adventure*, with her shallower draught, had tied up to the quay that afternoon, Captain Smyth replying to *Surprise's* signal of invitation. 'It is a great honour to meet you, sir. Your reputation precedes you throughout these waters; indeed, I have no doubt, considerably further. I particularly collect, when I was first surveying these waters in the year sixteen, your sinking of *Iskander* and the taking of *Half Moon*. What an action! What a splendid victory, Captain; an honour sir, an honour indeed to meet you.'

'You are too kind, sir; it was in the most propitious of circumstances,' Pat replied, being pleased by – though unused to – such unreserved praise, his naval colleagues' compliments inevitably being customarily restrained within the conventions of the service. 'Please come into the cabin. May I introduce my surgeon, Doctor Ferguson; my officers: Lieutenants Macleod, Pickering, Mower and Codrington.' All had accompanied Pat into the cabin at his invitation.

'Your servant, sir,' said Simon, preceding similar exchanges between the lieutenants and Smyth who was himself a lieutenant in rank, but rated captain – per the customary Royal Navy courtesy – whilst in command of *HMS Adventure*. This was a convention Pat had laboured to explain to Simon many years previously when they were first at sea together in Pat's original command, the tiny brig-sloop *Starling*. Freeman awaited Pat's instruction as to what to fetch from the selection of bottles now customarily cooled overboard in the net, hung from that side of the ship generally in the shade; Murphy averring, even in the absence of any thermometer, that it made a difference of several degrees.

Being keen to establish a cordial dialogue with the undoubted expert of Mediterranean hydrography they entered the slightly

204

cooler great cabin and settled in the chairs around Pat's table, Smyth delighted to be in the cabin of one of the Royal Navy's most famous naval officers. 'May we offer you a little refreshment, Captain Smyth; a glass of wine with you, sir?' Pat prompted.

'I would not suppose, Captain O'Connor, that you might have a cold bottle of sack?' enquired Smyth.

'Freeman!' shouted Pat, who was through the door before he had uttered the second syllable. 'Check the stocks and see if we have any sack. I collect we may have a few bottles left of the Manzanilla.' It was on such occasions that Freeman excelled, having taken aboard a very few days beforehand a small supply of ice from the Corfu packet, well wrapped in stout hessian, within wooden boxes now deposited low in the ship, melting slowly at the extremities, but from which Freeman was able to chip out just a very little on each occasion to further chill the cooled bottles as they came aboard from the net.

In the cabin all enjoyed hearing their captain exchanging recollections with Smyth of their earlier times in Ionian waters, albeit Pat was also pondering how best to make his intended request for the charts he sought. Freeman returned with two bottles of the Manzanilla and six glasses. Pat was impressed by his steward's success, and all were most happily pleased by the chilled sack. 'Well done Freeman, a colder glass I ne'er had when we were off the Horn, and tolerably welcome in this heat; thankee. Captain Smyth, we are engaged by the First Lord to offer our assistance with your surveying of the Ionian and neighbouring waters, should you have need of it. Lord Melville is most anxious that the charts of the waters 'twixt the United Islands and the mainland be as accurate as can possibly be, so as to avoid, in the current troubled times, any conceivable charge of territorial infraction by the Turk authorities, however unlikely that might be. Their Lordships have sent our ship, though she be only a fifth rate, on account of the very troubled situation with the Greek risings in the Morea and western Greece; anticipating that she may go to waters where any prudent captain would well baulk at any prospective challenge to his ship from the Turk authorities: *Surprise* – well, her predecessor that is – being, as you are aware, from former times a ship known well in these parts. I have been particularly charged by Lord Melville to survey again the waters at the approaches to the Gulf of Patras. I have no doubt, sir, that any such further survey will find no distinction from your own most commendable charts from the year thirteen, excellent as they are. I have always used them myself, and ne'er found fault, but when their Lordships request we find it is oft our unfortunate and thankless lot to obey. Captain Smyth; might I enquire, sir, if you could possibly provide to us - on loan of course - your most recent charts of that particular area? With any additions you may have personally annotated, including the region of the lagoon of Messalonghi. Should we find ourselves disoriented in, say, the most extreme instance of fog or of storm, no pilot being available to us, such charts would be of quite inestimable value,' Pat concluded, with his principal objective, his question, now asked.

Smyth, graciously, and having taken no offence at their Lordships ostensible request, replied without hesitation, 'Of course, Captain O'Connor. I have indeed my own charts with many a marking that never was printed by the Admiralty, and I will be most pleased to loan them to you. If I may have them returned at your conclusion I would be in your debt, sir.'

'And I in yours, Captain Smyth, thank you kindly,' Pat replied, finding Smyth something of a kindred spirit, and having himself plotted a useful chart or two during his voyages. He added, 'As a most proficient hydrographer, it is to be presumed that you have a firm interest too in our celestial aids. Jupiter is prominent these past few nights, and I have an excellent Dollond glass. Would you care to join me aboard this evening for supper and celestial gazing? We are surely blessed here with these wondrous clear skies.'

Smyth was noticeably pleased by Pat's invitation, swiftly according with it, 'Most kind, Captain O'Connor. I shall return after six bells of the Last dog watch. It is a particular interest of mine, since visiting Piazzi and his observatory in Palermo, and I will greatly look forward to our evening.'

'And I too, sir,' replied Pat, smiling broadly as he shook hands with the departing Smyth.

Considerable time had passed aboard *Surprise*, surveying the Ionian waters, with still no news having being received from the provisional Greek government. *Eleanor* had returned from Hydra several weeks previously. Codrington had been unable to provide any further information. Jason remained absent, having failed to meet with Mavrocordato, and had stayed on Hydra in the hope of doing so. *Eleanor* had subsequently been sent again to recover him.

Surprise having recently returned to Argostoli, Pat and Duncan were staying with their families in the Metaxata house, which the ladies had put into admirable order. After supper the two friends sat contentedly on the terrace contemplating the view towards Zante, two bottles of the finest quality Robola finished.

'Will ah tell ye o' the recent news, brother?' said Duncan, 'Oor neighbour Lord Byron has abandoned his plan to go to the seat o' the provisional government at Tripolizza; his Philhellene colleagues, Hamilton Browne and Trelawny, having returned wi' news o' further internecine strife. His Lordship had sent wi' them his personal letter urging an end to this fratricidal insanity, which is jeopardising the London Greek Committee's loan, an' they returned bearing a letter from Mavrocordato seeking an interim loan from his Lordship hisself in order that the wages o' the Hydriot fleet could be paid, withoot which they wilnae sail to relieve Messalonghi.'

Pat set down his glass and turned to his friend, replying only after a long sigh, 'Duncan, had we conducted our affairs like this in the year fifteen, Boney would now be presiding in Westminster, His Majesty would doubtless be left languishing in the Marshalsea to rot, and *Surprise* would be sailing under a French pennant. His Lordship is plainly of a more benevolent mettle than us mere mortals. And what is he to do about it?'

'Admirable man that he is - were there more o' his ilk - he has sent his emissary to Tripolizza affirming his personal commitment to providin' a loan o' foor thousands sterling, or the equivalent in dollars, upon the arrival o' the fleet, an' is now disposed to go directly to Messalonghi to assist the Greek defence there.'

'It is to be hoped that the fleet will bear with them our long awaited letter-of-marque,' said Pat, with more hope than conviction, his dolorous face exhibiting the pessimism he felt at that moment.

Saturday 22ⁿᵈ November 1823   Metaxata, Cephalonia

After breakfast, Pat and Duncan, with Simon who had joined them early that morning from the ship, several men under his treatment, strolled through the village to visit Lord Byron in the hope that perhaps his Lordship, who was most presciently receptive to the political winds blowing from the Morea, and who received many letters from his several emissaries sent throughout Greece, might be able to apprise them of the current circumstances generally and Mavrocordato's situation particularly.

On the first floor of his apartment the poet was gazing from his window as the maid showed them in. 'O'Connor, Macleod, Ferguson, how pleasing to see you all. Look here, I do so enjoy this vista,' declared Byron, looking tired but smiling. He turned again to the window, 'I was admiring it only last night, my daughter only latterly recovered from sickness, and I have myself been sleeping ill. The calm, though cool serenity of a beautiful and transparent moonlight showing the islands, the mountains, the sea; with a distant outline of the Morea traced between the double azure of the waves and skies. These sights, of such beauty, have quieted me enough to be able to write. Look, Zante is there to the south, and in the far distance one can glimpse the hills of the Morea. Here in my modest home, in this blessed landscape and amongst these simple people, I have found tranquillity such that has eluded me for too many of these past years. Do you not find it acts upon you in that way?' Byron turned again to his visitors, 'Excuse me, may I offer you tea?'

Simon was plainly moved by the poet's eloquent words, and before Pat could answer replied softly, 'I am no philosopher, sir, but I find that too often our hearts are oppressed by our minds, and sadly our mind can be oppressed by our heart. When we are fortunate to find that neither is the case we oft know not how to embrace the absence of anguish, and but slowly do we come to rejoice. I give you joy, sir, if that is where you find yourself. Leave that place only with the utmost reluctance. Speaking as a medical man, these thoughts are beyond our gift, but of their recuperative benevolence one may not praise them too highly.'

Byron had listened patiently to Simon, and continued to look at him, as if contemplating the sense, the merit, of his words. He stepped towards Simon, grasped Simon's hand between his own, and murmured, 'Thank you kindly for your words, Ferguson; none finer could come from any poet's lips; would that we had more time together to enjoy such discourse.'

'Sir, I am gratified by your kind words.'

After a few pensive moments, Byron still firmly gripping Simon's hand, each of them silently contemplating the other, Pat intervened, 'Beg pardon, my Lord, by that, do you mean ... is your Lordship leaving this place?'

'My dear O'Connor,' Byron replied, breaking as if reluctantly from his thoughts and his grasp of Simon's hand, 'I have recently received a letter from Secretary of State Mavrocordato, whom I pressed to state the intentions of the Greek government, so as to assist the formulation of my own plans. He reports that President Conduriottis has himself paid the first month's pay for the fleet in Hydra, which is to sail shortly in anticipation that I shall loan their continuing costs. I am minded to do so, and I shall reply urging Mavrocordato to come to Messalonghi, to show himself there, the better to demonstrate some restoration of political unity. I am now resolved to go to that place and assist their efforts. I will go first to Zante to cash my bills. Messrs Barff and Hancock there have offered to do so, and on the most generous of terms. It will surely be a loss to leave this place, but sitting here I can do little for Greece.' Byron sighed, his weary voice reflecting his feelings of dismay with Greek disunity. At that moment the maid returned with tea and announced a further visitor: Colonel Napier had arrived. 'Pray, do come in, Colonel,' shouted Byron with a friendly inflexion. Napier entered the small room, and the maid served all with tea.

'Good day, my Lord. I have called first upon Captain

209

O'Connor; to be told he was here. Captain O'Connor, as I left Argostoli your schooner was approaching the quay. I am sent by the Governor, the packet recently arrived from Corfu, to determine and report the further interests of yourself and Lord Byron, Maitland lamenting that I tell him nothing at all,' the reference to Sir Thomas spoken with a broad smile on his face.

It was Byron who replied, 'Napier, we have known each other for some months, and I will say a respect akin to a friendship has arisen between us in that time. So I will tell you in honesty, I am quitting this tranquil place where I have been pleased to find a home, which I shall sorely miss, and I am going to Messalonghi in some few weeks time. I will presume upon our friendship and ask that you retain that confidence until I have left. I wish, Colonel, that you might accompany me. No more admirable leader of military men could the Greeks aspire to secure. I will gladly write you a letter of introduction to the London Committee to that effect.'

'You are too kind, my Lord,' Napier replied. 'In the first matter, my report to the Governor must be sent by the December packet to Corfu. But I understand that Maitland is not well and has gone to Malta. So it may be some time before he receives my letter, and by then you will have departed Cephalonia. In the second matter I cannot comment, but I thank you for your sentiment. Captain O'Connor, in frankness, may I presume that surveying is not perhaps the sole interest you have in and about these islands?'

The question produced only a pregnant silence for a few moments before Pat replied after evident deliberation. 'Colonel, *Surprise* has completed her work on the *west* coasts of the islands of Cephalonia and Zante, but there remain areas of interest to the *east*.'

It was the most circumspect reply, with everything left unsaid, which Napier could hardly fail to notice, though he did not press further before Pat resumed, 'We must be away, gentlemen, *Eleanor* having returned.' Pat, Simon, and Duncan left after cordial but swift farewells.

The news from Jason, when they reached *Eleanor* at the quay in the early afternoon, was deeply significant. 'Finally I was received by Mavrocordato, he being for some weeks reluctant to confide in me, and he was also, perhaps, uncertain of the intentions of the combined fleet. It consists of nine Hydriot and five Spezziot ships. Quite small for the most part and hardly armed at all in comparison with the guns of *Surprise*. How they will fare against Turk vessels of some size is far outside my province, yet they are intending to sail at the end of the month. Mavrocordato himself will accompany them: not in any official capacity, but as a volunteer; he being no longer in office. They will sail to Messalonghi, and their intention is to break the Turk blockade.'

After the shortest of pauses Pat replied, his officers all gathered about him in *Eleanor's* small cabin, 'Thank you, Mr Jason; that is news of the very first importance. Gentlemen; Doctor Ferguson, Lieutenant Macleod, and I will return to our families in Metaxata this evening to make our arrangements. We will convene on the morrow at eight bells of the Morning watch. Our plans will be revealed after we have mustered to divisions. Mr Mower, please to replenish *Surprise's* water. Mr Pickering, provisions for thirty days. Mr Codrington, the same for *Eleanor*. Mr Reeve, my barge is to be here tomorrow at seven bells, if you please. I bid you all good day.'

The ride back to Metaxata was a little more urgent than usual, the heat of the day slightly cooler than in prior weeks, despite which it was a hot and perspiring Pat who dismounted outside the small house. 'I shall be mightily pleased, Simon, to be astride my quarterdeck once again, in the fresh sea air, salt wind in my face. I tire of many more days astride this horse, willing that he is, on this damned inferno of an island. Praise be we are hauling up our anchor tomorrow. Though when we might see our long awaited letter-of-marque the Lord only knows,' Pat griped.

'In the plainest of speaking, I fear you have been eating rather better here these past months and tending again to obesity, brother. Salt horse and ship's biscuit will serve you well until you can shed at least thirty pounds,' replied Simon, disregarding his friend's personal feelings entirely. 'Will I prescribe a daily purgative to assist you?' The comment was wholly ignored by Pat, and they drifted into a contemplative silence for the remainder of the ride.

At supper, shared with their families, Pat announced to their considerable dismay that *Surprise* and *Eleanor* would depart next morning and be away for some weeks. *Eleanor* would return to apprise them of their circumstances were *Surprise* unable to do so, for such seemed possible once the Governor became aware of any participation by *Surprise* in the conflict, when the strict Ionian neutrality policy would preclude her returning to the Islands without fear of seizure or even forfeiture, the United Islands authorities having no knowledge of her covert appointment.

Sunday 23rd November 1823   *Argostoli, Cephalonia*

The colder morning air was reinforced by a grey cloudy sky, some small drizzle falling, as the barge crew rowed Pat, Duncan and Simon across to *Surprise*.

'Good morning Mr Prosser; beat to divisions, if you please,' said Pat, in a formal, businesslike manner as he stepped on to his deck.

'Aye aye, sir. Beat to divisions,' echoed Prosser to Clumsy Dalby, standing ready on the gun deck.

The rousing drumbeat was hardly necessary, as all crew members of *Surprise* and *Eleanor* were keenly aware of the news and awaiting the Captain's return in no small excitement. They all knew that surveying was never their primary intention, and were despairing of it continuing for many more weeks. They had seen the summer and autumn slip away into the cooling approach of winter when, as they also realised, their prospects for prizes would fade away as surely as the leaves after autumn; the Turk fleet being expected to return to its winter quarters in the Golden Horn. The Surprises and Eleanors were immaculately prepared for Pat's inspection, and awaiting his orders, for Pat was a considerate captain, and always ensured at least a modest briefing for his crew before church.

On this morning Pat's decision to read first from the Articles of War succeeded in his intentions of alerting the crew to their imminent change of circumstances better than any briefing although he felt it incumbent afterwards to add a few words of his own. 'Lads, we are preparing for sea and will leave port at three

212

bells in the Afternoon watch, wind remaining favourable. We shall be sailing in waters where we will encounter Greek and Turk ships of war. We must be ready for any event. We will resume our great guns exercises once we are clear of Ionian waters. I know I can count on you all. Stay alert, remain vigilant; thank you, lads. The Reverend Marston will now read a *short* sermon.'

Marston stepped forward to the sea-chest which was customarily placed on the gun deck for church, and after a hesitant moment began, a little nervously. Crews were not traditionally sympathetic to shipboard clergy, but Marston hoped that at least the Wesleyans might lend their support. 'Good morning all. I would like to read to you this morning a short piece from the Book of Joshua, which we may consider being suited to the circumstances in which we are engaged.' As Marston picked up his bible and began to read, he observed that the crew were unusually attentive on this occasion. He looked at his captain, and Pat simply nodded and smiled; it was a small gesture of encouragement which heartened Marston. He began, '*Be strong in the Lord and in his mighty power. Put on the full armour of God so that you can take your stand against the devil's schemes. For our struggle is not against flesh and blood, but against the rulers, against the authorities, against the powers of this dark world, and against the spiritual forces of evil in the heavenly realms. Therefore put on the full armour of God, so that when the day of evil comes you may be able to stand your ground. Stand firm then, with the belt of truth buckled around your waist, with the breastplate of righteousness in place and with your feet fitted with the readiness that comes from the gospel of peace. In addition to all this, take up the shield of faith, with which you can extinguish all the flaming arrows of the evil one. Take the helmet of salvation and the sword of the Spirit, which is the word of God. And pray in the Spirit on all occasions with all kinds of prayers and requests. With this in mind, be alert and always keep on praying for all the saints.* Thank you.' Marston looked up from his bible and at Pat.

'A most fitting sermon, Mr Marston; well done and thankee.' Pat abruptly brought church to an end, having no intentions of any hymn singing this day, nor any inspection of divisions, and retired with his officers to the great cabin.

The ship's bell had just rung six times in the Morning watch. The weather, being hazy but dry, promised a fine day; or so Pat thought, as he contemplated another uneventful day: nothing of note had happened in the more than two weeks since *Surprise* had left Argostoli, and he picked at his first breakfast. *Surprise* was a few miles off the east coast of Ithaca with a light and following north-westerly wind. 'Another week of cruising up and down this channel, Ithaca to Zante, Zante to Ithaca, ne'er any ship to be seen, and the crew may soon be minded to press us to join the enemy, the only vessel we have seen being that Greek mistico, running the blockade yesterday. Much more of this to'ing and fro'ing and we shall ground on our own beef bones ere we ever see so much as a Turk. And no commission yet in hand neither. We are blighted by delay, infernal delay. I am sorely hipped,' an irritable Pat grumbled to Duncan.

'What news from the captain o' the mistico, brother? Ye hailed an' spoke wi' him, ah collect,' asked Duncan, moderately, reaching for the bacon dish, Pat, unusually, not having consumed much.

'Very rum developments if he can be believed. The captain said that he hailed from Hydra. The Albanian besiegers of Messalonghi have marched away, fearing to starve in the winter no doubt, and the Turk fleet has retired to beyond Patras and sits under the guns of the Little Dardanelles, hence the mistico running in daylight. The Greek fleet has plainly sailed, but the mistico is faster by perhaps a knot or two and will sail at all speed at night, accustomed as they are to running the blockade. The captain said the fleet was but an hour or two behind him as he passed Modon. I think I shall go on deck, a breath of fresh air might serve me well,' replied Pat. With that he took his Dolland glass and stepped up to his quarterdeck.

A slow half hour passed by and then the masthead lookout shouted, 'Sail ho! Two points off the larboard bow.'

Training his glass, Pat, his instincts sparked by the report, could see a brig followed closely by several more sail, too indistinct as yet to clearly make out, the morning mist persevering still. 'Mr Pickering, maintain this course until we close and can see who is there. They are beating close-hauled into this north-westerly, it seems. It will surely be slow progress. Stand by to come about in good time, and then we will keep a parallel course,' said Pat, keen interest having replaced his prior lassitude.

The next half hour passed infuriatingly slowly in growing anticipation as *Surprise* closed on the approaching ships, Pat studying them closely with his glass. Then puffs of smoke were visible from the leading ship and cannon fire could be heard. 'A Turk brig, I fancy. Pursued by four or five Greeks: brigs too, but smaller. Her captain is handling his ship well,' Pat murmured, watching frequent course changes as the quarry sought to use her longer range guns to disable or rake her pursuers. 'Mr Macleod, we will wear ship. Bring her about and maintain our distance at one mile from them, not a cable less.'

The first lieutenant reiterated Pat's order, and the crew, with supreme efficacy, brought *Surprise* gracefully on to her near reversed course. She, like the combatants, now required frequent tacking to make the slowest of progress in the windward direction. The Turk ship and her pursuers gradually approached as *Surprise* still sought to recover speed.

'Mr Macleod, we shall clear for action,' ordered Pat.

The sound of Clumsy Dalby's drum brought every member of the gun crews running to their stations: all gun ports were opened and with the thunderous rumble of the carriages across the deck, their frenzied crews heaving with all their strength and sweating with their exertions, the long guns were swiftly run out on both sides of the ship. The men stood ready, chattering amongst themselves, a great sense of expectation prevailing.

'The Turk is being harried at every tack by two or three Greek brigs, and her escape must be doubtful. Her captain is surely weighing his prospects at this very moment,' said Pat quietly to no one in particular, but heard by all on his quarterdeck; Marston and Simon too, they having stepped up to see what was afoot.

The nearest Greek was on a converging course with *Surprise*, and the distance closing quite rapidly, she having separated from the chasing pack. She was now less than one mile off *Surprise's*

215

starboard beam, but presented no danger to the frigate; it being within *Surprise's* far more considerable fire power and range to destroy the Greek brig before she could even engage.

'Steady, Mr Macleod, he wishes to see who we are; let us steer two points to leeward, and make it slowly,' ordered Pat.

The Greek was now a mere half mile abeam of *Surprise,* and, perhaps content with the identification of her as an English ship – her colours flying prominently at her jack and top in the stiff wind – she turned away towards her compatriots, a mile or more ahead.

'Maintain course, Mr Prosser. Mr Macleod, I think we will see what is about over there,' said Pat, beginning to wonder where the end of this chase might lie – the Greeks being between the Turk and the approach to Patras, and so the Turk being cut off with no prospect now of escape, she plainly could not outrun her Greek pursuers. The sound of cannon fire became louder, more frequent, more vigorous, as *Surprise* gained slightly on the little battle.

'Set topgallants, Mr Macleod.' Pat stared with professional fascination through his glass. 'Look, Duncan, the fox pursued by the hounds, I fancy, and no bolt hole available. The Turk is in a dreadful dilemma, quite damaged I see. Her trysail is shot away and her boom spar shattered. Look, she is steering for Ithaca now. I doubt that she will make the turn into the bay for the port afore the hounds close for the kill.' *Surprise* had closed a little, and the action was no more than a mile ahead. 'The Turk is plainly finished now; she has turned away to leeward, with no sea-room available to her. Her captain must be intent on beaching her to save sinking or capture.'

Another five minutes passed. 'The Turk captain is a most determined man. Look – the brig has struck the rocks. The Greeks are standing off now and lowering boats; 'tis a flagrant breach of Ionian neutrality, and doubtless there will be the devil to pay for someone. Mr Macleod, we will come about and approach no closer; stand down the gunners. Mr Prosser, set course for Messalonghi, if you will. I am set fair for my second breakfast; will you join me, Duncan?' asked Pat.

'Certainly, brother, ah wid like it o' all things, an' ah have a sure cravin' fer a pot o' tea this past hoor. Wid it be wise to approach Messalonghi in *Surprise* rather than in *Eleanor*, do ye suppose, Pat?'

Pat wasted no time in thought, 'Whether or no, we are going. We have seen precious few Turks, and it will be as well to find Mavrocordato ere too many more weeks are gone, I venture.'

The tedium at the start of the day had now gone, and the decisive Pat O'Connor of old was returning, Duncan thought. Some hours elapsed with the crew remaining in a state of excitement, the officers scanning the horizon, and Prosser bringing *Surprise* close to the approach to Messalonghi until he enquired of Pat, 'Shall we stand off sir, and send our cutter to seek a pilot? I have no acquaintance with these shallows.'

'Never fear, Mr Prosser, I have Smyth's personal chart in the cabin. Barton shall fetch it, and we will be assured of safe passage; Smyth is a perfectionist you know,' declared Pat, bouyantly.

Within the hour *Surprise* had threaded her way over the bar, through the outer islands, and cast her anchor inside the lagoon, a mile or so off Messalonghi town. Some two hours later the Greek fleet followed them in, *Surprise* now being surrounded by a dozen or more small brigs, no hostility in evidence. A tumultuous reception, which seemed to consist of the whole population of the town, had gathered to welcome their fleet, firearms discharging and even the odd cannon heard above the good-natured demonstration of the newly relieved residents. The besieging Ottoman army had departed some two weeks previously, and now resupply by sea was once again at hand. Pat was swiftly aboard his barge, and his immaculately dressed bargemen rowed him through the gentle chop to the distant shore. The port captain, once he could be found, declared that there was no quarantine, unlike the Ionian Islands; no papers would be required, and Pat's crew were at liberty to come ashore – indeed would be welcomed for assuredly there would be festivities and celebrations until the dawn.

'I think, Duncan, that we shall remain aboard *Surprise* until the morrow,' Pat declared after short consideration. 'It would not do to be here, the crew ashore and drunk, all kicking up Bob's a-dying,

217

were the Turks to return. No, we shall allow shore parties of no more than two score, from tomorrow and for a few hours only. Let us return to *Surprise*.'

Supper was taken by the crew on deck, watching the distant lights and listening to the festivities of Messalonghi, ruefully wishing that they were ashore, the celebrations continuing all night.

Thursday 11ᵗʰ December 1823   *Messalonghi Town*

It had been very late when Pat had finally turned in, and he was therefore most displeased to be roughly shaken awake shortly after first light by Duncan, shouting directly into his ear, for that is how it seemed. 'Pat, wake up, quickly noo, hurry, ye must come on deck. Wake up. Hurry noo. There is a great deal o' commotion between the Greek ships. What it signifies, we cannae tell.'

Throwing on his cape, Pat hastened up to the quarterdeck. 'Mr Pickering, what's afoot? Why am I shaken awake at this ungodly hour, pray tell?'

Pickering pointed towards several of the Greek ships. 'There seems to be some disturbance between several of the Greek brigs, sir. I think between the Hydriots and the Spezziots, even several have run out their guns and are hoisting anchors. Look, there, sails unfurling now and the crew hauling on a kedge to swing her round. Will we beat to quarters, sir?'

In an instant Pat decided, 'Yes, Tom, beat to quarters, but do not open our gun ports until we grasp what is happening here. We do not want any of the Greeks to see us as a threat. Murphy! Murphy, there! Will we send down your hammock? Rouse up Freeman, and ask him to bring coffee on deck,' this shouted down to Murphy, loitering below the steps to the quarterdeck and chattering to Old Pennington, within Pat's earshot.

'Well, Jesus, bejabers, the water ain't 'ot yet an' Freeman's bin grindin' the bleedin' beans this past half hour,' moaned Murphy, not loud enough for Pat to hear.

Pickering turned to Dalby, 'Dalby; beat to quarters.' The resonant beat swiftly brought bleary-eyed Surprises rushing up from below, slow-matches already lit from the galley, powder boys standing by their guns with reloads. Hammocks were hastily tied into the rigging with many loud curses from men who had but recently been watching the shore festivities before retiring late to their sleep.

'My glass, Murphy, shouted Pat, grasping his coffee gratefully from his steward, Freeman still at the galley, and taking a deep draught of a lukewarm, bitter liquid. 'Murphy!' to the fast receding steward, 'Did you find this vile stuff in the bilges? Toss it over the side and bring fresh.'

'Take my glass, sir,' proferred Pickering, 'here.'

'Well, coffee first, rush, rush, glass next; to be sure, I'll be a'labourin' all bleedin' night afore long,' muttered Murphy, bearing away the coffee pot on its tray.

'Never fret when busy, Murphy; save it for when you are idle,' Pickering remarked, as Murphy passed by.

'Thankee, Tom,' Pat peered through the glass with anxious curiosity. 'What on earth are they doing over there? Anchors hauled up and catted, all sails unfurled with yards all ahoo. What do they know? Is there any news or sightings of Turk ships?'

'None, sir.'

Within a half hour there seemed a general awakening of all the Greek fleet; several had caught their wind, their sails filled with a steady north-easterly off the land, and were departing.

'Mr Codrington, you are to take *Eleanor* in to the quay and see if you can determine what is happening. Mr Mower, take Mr Jason with you in my barge, and approach one of those brigs still anchored. Hail and ask them for an explanation. Mr Macleod, let fall tops'ls and spanker, leave them slack; warp her bow round to the south and prepare to get underway,' Pat ordered.

Murphy returned, holding out Pat's Magellan jacket. 'Well, put it on d'reckly, sorr,' he cried angrily. 'Now you'll catch yer death without it.'

'Are we departing, sir? An' what o' oor purpose here?' asked Duncan, anxiously.

Pat had by now scrambled into his clothes, brought up by

Murphy, and replied, "Tis just a precaution. No ship has fired, though some have run out guns and are leaving so swiftly, sails and rigging all ahoo, that I wondered if they might even cut their cables, but no, it seemed for some minutes like hostilities were about to break out between the Hydriots and the Spezziots. Who is to know what is up; they are foreigners you know. Where is Mr Mower?'

'Over there, sir. He is aboard the near brig.' Another quarter hour passed, and the barge returned alongside, Mower and Jason scrambling swiftly aboard. Pat hastened towards them, anxious to ask their news. Mower revealed the startling story which Jason had gleaned from the captain of the Spezziot brig. 'It seems, sir, that the Hydriots captured a huge booty from the Turk which ran aground on Ithaca yesterday, half a million piastres. They have refused to share it with the Spezziots, and are running away with the lot. The Spezziots are boiling with rage, as might be expected, hence guns being run out. Though her captain said he doubted anyone would actually fire.'

'Such conduct cannot be considered amicable,' remarked Simon, who had appeared on the quarterdeck, barely half dressed.

Pat looked up to the heavens and turned to his first, exasperation plain on his face, 'Tell me Duncan, lest I forget, these are the people we have come here to assist. Running away with the prizes – with no fair distribution – readying to fire upon their brothers! What brings these people to such acts? Will we weigh and return to England directly with no more time wasted here? Stand down the crew, Mr Pickering. I shall take breakfast and then go ashore to see if there is anyone in charge of this house of Bedlam.'

With some exasperation, and followed closely by Duncan, Pat stomped back into the cabin. Murphy was there before he arrived, and, perceiving his ire, announced in the meekest of tones, 'Well, Freeman has yer breakfast ready, sorr.'

'Tell him to bring it in directly, Murphy. And tea if you will, thankee,' Pat replied, tiredness returning to his voice.

Later, in the town the atmosphere remained highly charged: excitement at the fleet's arrival and their delivery from the Turk blockade now mixed with consternation, the Hydriote squadron having left in haste. Pat had gone ashore with a small landing party, and Codrington came striding briskly towards them along the quay, accompanied by Reeve and a Greek civilian, seemingly of some standing, he being surrounded by an entourage of a score or more civilians and militiamen, all cheerfully mingling with half a dozen Eleanors. A somewhat flustered Codrington brought the march to a halt in front of Pat. 'Captain O'Connor, sir. Will I introduce Mr - that is to say - *Prince* Mavrocordato?'

Pat could not have been more surprised had Nelson himself been introduced. The many months of waiting to meet this very man, weeks of surveying, more weeks of fruitless patrolling the Ionian waters off the Greek coast, two successive days of beating to quarters, and now the man was here himself; standing in front of Pat and Duncan. He was, at first glance, an unimpressive man in his early thirties, with unkempt long black hair, a huge drooping moustache, slightly short, a little overweight, and with thick lensed spectacles, though his companions exhibited considerable reverence towards his person.

'Your Maj ... your Highness. It is an honour to make your acquaintance at long last,' Pat extemporised, much taken aback by such an unexpected development, and plainly floundering.

Duncan interjected to save his Captain's embarrassment: 'Prince Mavrocordato; Lieutenant Duncan Macleod at yer service, sir. Ah collect we have some business o' a confidential nature to discuss. Will ye join Captain O'Connor an' masel' aboord oor vessel, *Surprise*, so that we may engage wi' some confidence o' privacy?'

'Captain O'Connor, Lieutenant Macleod, I would be honoured to visit your ship. Let us do so without delay,' Mavrocordato replied with some gravitas. He gave some instructions to his cohorts and turned back to face Pat: 'Captain O'Connor, would that I could have arrived in this place sooner. Alas, the wheels of Greek politics do not turn smoothly, and the consequences are sometimes quite brutal, as perhaps you saw this morning. Let us away to our business before we are overtaken by other necessities. Please, lead on, Captain.'

'Barton, help his Highness into the barge, and row dry back to the ship,' said Pat. His barge crew had mingled with the Eleanors, seeking further explanation of this evidently important Greek about to come aboard. A half hour later and back in the great cabin, coffee having been served, and with a brace of bottles of cooled Amontillado which his Highness seemed to favour, Freeman was sent away to seek something better than biscuit to offer their guest. Pat remained unsure of how to begin, and being no diplomat struggled to find a start, 'Your Highness, it is an honour to welcome you aboard His Maj ... that is, our dear *Surprise*. We have passed the summer in these waters gaining but little understanding of the current political situation. You will readily understand therefore that we are most pleased that we now meet with you.'

'Captain O'Connor; the honour is all mine, sir. It is a very great pleasure to meet such a renowned naval officer. My aides have provided to me the most interesting of information, the quite exceptional account of your prior service in our waters; and an account of your sinking of the Turk ship *Iskander*. It is an exemplary record, doubtless of no equal, Captain.'

A slow but most cordial hour of pleasantries elapsed until Duncan could discern that Pat's reserves of patience and diplomacy, limited as they were even at the best of times, were being sorely tested, and so brought matters to a head. 'If ye will permit me; yer Highness will collect that Captain O'Connor an' his ship arrived here in the Islands since some months past, an' we remain anxious to assist yer struggle for liberation. Yet lackin' any commission we are unable to engage withoot the most serious consequences. Indeed, a charge o' piracy might well be levelled agin us, were we to do so. Does yer Highness possess the letter-o'-marque that we understand has been prepared for oor arrival?'

Mavrocordato beamed genially over a pair of half-spectacles. 'Of course, Lieutenant Macleod; the letter is here with me, signed since some months by President Mavromichalis and by myself as Secretary of State, though it is an office I no longer hold.' Reaching inside his jacket the Prince removed and handed over the long awaited document to Pat, who grasped it eagerly; the cherished key to their endeavours, a start now possible. Mavrocordato continued,

'Perhaps you could study this at your convenience, sir, and if it proves acceptable then the Hellenic Republic will be pleased to consider that you are in her service. Sadly, as I am no longer Secretary of State, and am come here only in the capacity of a simple volunteer, no changes can be made to the terms. However, the President has consulted closely with one of your compatriot officers in our service, one Captain Hastings, in preparing the letter, and trusts that you will find it acceptable. My aide, Monsieur Léli, will come to you in Cephalonia. He will tell you of our priorities and communications when you return there. Captain O'Connor, I must now go ashore else doubtless some other burden will accost us. Thank you for your interest in serving Greece, gentlemen; we are assuredly poor of funds, but do not lack for appreciation of our friends.'

Pat gingerly placed the precious letter inside his table drawer, shook hands with the Prince, and replied cautiously, 'Doubtless the letter will serve, your Highness. It is an honour to commence our service for your country.' Pat paused for a moment before resuming, 'My first here, Lieutenant Macleod, is particularly tasked by our Admiralty with facilitating communication between this ship and your naval colleagues. In the first instance, it is proposed by their Lordships that he shall pass some time with you to gain a familiarity with your procedures.'

'That will serve us well, Captain O'Connor. The Hellenic Republic is obliged to you.' They shook hands.

'My crew will set you both ashore. Good day, sir.'

Duncan hastened away for his sea chest as Pat escorted Mavrocordato to the ladder for the barge. Returning to his quarterdeck after they had disembarked – Duncan with time for only the briefest of farewells to his fellow officers before he departed – Pat stood there, sadness returning to his mind, as he contemplated prior occasions when he had seen off one or the other of Duncan or Simon, but the feelings of loss and anxiety never relented. His attention was restored by Tom Pickering standing in front of him, enquiring of his intentions as the men at the helm looked across, patient enquiry written all over their faces. Pat pondered their new status. Should he now hoist a Greek flag? Should he make any announcement? Instead he simply murmured to Pickering, 'Take us out of this place, Tom. We will return to Argostoli. Keep a very sharp watch for any ships, Turk or Greek.'

Mistico   *J.J. Baugean*

Chapter Six

What, silent still? and silent all?
Ah! No; — the voices of the dead
Sound like a distant torrent's fall,
And answer, 'Let one living head,
But one arise, — we come, we come!'
'Tis but the living who are dumb.

Monday 29th December 1823   *aboard Surprise, Gulf of Patras*

'Can you still see them, Mr Pickering?' asked Pat of his second lieutenant.

'Aye sir, the mistico appears to be going ahead of the bombard, but 'tis now difficult to be sure, with the light failing.'

'Let us pray this wind remains a favourable westerly,' Pat opined, straining his eye into his glass, searching for the two vessels, now near three miles distant and disappearing into the oncoming colder darkness of the night, it now being near 10 p.m. 'Let us pray too that the Turk fleet stays at Patras roads, for that is where it is said to be from our reports obtained in Zante. It is to be hoped that both vessels reach Messalonghi without interception, and without any help from us. I would wish that the Turks did not yet know we had come to the aid of the Greeks, and so I prefer not to be sighted with them. That is why we shall keep our distance from the bombard and the mistico.'

'What are the Doctor and Mr Jason to do, sir, in their company?'

'Mr Jason is to translate, he speaking the Greek and the Turk, should his Lordship be accosted by either side. The Doctor is to aid Count Gamba similarly. Though he speaks but a trifle of the Greek and little of the Turk he will support the Count with his story that they are bound for Calamos. That is, should they be waylaid – let us hope that will not be the case. We will shadow them, principally his Lordship, and interpose *Surprise* between them and any Turk that comes along seeking to stop them. That is, if we can stay in sight of them during the night. They are showing no lights whilst running the blockade,' said Pat, explaining his strategy and adding, 'Will you double the watch men?'

'Aye aye, sir, that we will,' replied Pickering.

Just at that moment Freeman appeared. Since *Surprise* had left Falmouth he had assumed a right to tread Pat's quarterdeck, at least as long as he professed to be bearing any message or refreshment, a presumption that Pat had not thought fit to disabuse him of, the formalities of the whole voyage having become somewhat less than that which the strictest Royal Navy captain might have mandated. 'Stirabout, he spoilt, massa; gone cold. You want fresh?'

It was a welcome reminder to Pat that he had quite forgotten his customary supper in the activity of the departure from Zante, plus the near sleepless crossing from Cephalonia having been made the night before, and Simon, his usual companion for supper, also having transferred to the bombard. In the close following of the two vessels for five or so hours since leaving Zante he had not shifted from his quarterdeck. 'Thankee Freeman, I will come to the cabin shortly. Supper will be most welcome. I am amazing short set. Tom, would you care to take some supper with me? Ask Mr Mower if he will join us too. Freeman, supper for three if you will, and look out a bottle of port from my stores; a bottle of the da Silva of the year fifteen would serve admirably,' Pat said, pleasantly, continuing half in thought and half in speech to his lieutenant, 'Now there is an enterprising man, Tom. I met him in London one year, I collect it was in Black's, Bruno da Silva, would you know? He also had a letter-of-marque to arm his ship, so as to more safely bring his wine to London. He kindly gave me a case of his port wine. I have always bought his wine since, and ne'er opened a spoiled bottle. Come; let us go to the cabin, all this talk reminds me it is time to eat. Mr Prosser, you have the barky.'

Tuesday 30th December 1823, 5 a.m.   *Aboard the bombard*

Simon and Gamba had remained on deck whilst the mistico, which was now lost from their sight, had been in close accompaniment. They had lingered for hours until going below to seek sleep as

3 a.m. approached and the wind freshened to a much colder northerly, progress near stopped. Now returned to near the wheel, Simon spoke to the captain, 'would it be uncivil, sir, to ask of your intentions, your expectations of our landfall?'

'Can we ask the wind of its intentions, Doctor Ferguson? I know not. These are difficult waters for the navigator; shoals and rocks all about us,' Captain Valsamarchi replied, cautiously. He had declined to continue at best speed in the darkest hours, despite the danger from Turk patrols, being concerned for the shallows, and preferring to mark time, to await first light. So, after a cold supper of black bread and cheese with thin red wine, Simon and Gamba had sought uncomfortable sleep for two hours on a huddle of blankets of doubtful provenance. At five o'clock, in the first lightening of the emerging dawn, they had stirred; the motion of the vessel changing and awakening them as it gained speed, when at least some small degree of better visibility was welcomed by the captain. Simon gazed, shivering, at the grey and choppy waves, the wind now having shifted round to the customary north-easterly *Gregale* of those island waters.

'Pray, Captain, are we far now from Messalonghi?' asked Simon.

'We are approaching the Scrofes, the small islands and rocks outlying the lagoon. In several hours we will be in the anchorage some way off from the town. The water will soon become very shallow for all the remaining distance from here to the town. Great care of navigation is now our foremost priority,' Valsamarchi replied, his reservations plain in his voice as well as his words.

Tuesday 30th December 1823, 5 a.m.   *Aboard the mistico*

'Will you take tea with me, Jason?' Lord Byron asked. The two men had enjoyed the most cordial of conversation since losing sight of the bombard around midnight, the two crews having continued firing pistols and carbines for another half hour or so in a fruitless effort to maintain contact. The captain had shortened sail so that the following bombard might keep up with the faster mistico.

'That would be most welcome your Lordship; WAIT!' Jason

exclaimed. 'Look there, look, over there, do you see it? A ship, larger than the bombard, I venture ... just there.'

'Keep silent and do nothing,' ordered the captain, appearing beside them; great anxiety plain in his voice. 'It is a Turk frigate and he will be near alongside in but a very few minutes. We cannot escape him. Our only hope is to pretend we have not seen him for as long as that is credible, and pray we reach the shallows where he cannot follow. Keep silent if you value your life, and pray to your God.'

With a sinking feeling Jason could not take his gaze from the approaching frigate. Indeed all eyes on the mistico were focused upon it, every stitch of her sail now hoisted, the crew urging every last half knot of speed from the vessel as they contemplated two very different destinies; which one would occur would be made plain in the next few minutes. The Turk frigate was plainly bent on their interception, and swiftly approaching, sailing large, wind astern of her, a creaming bow-froth plainly visible as she swiftly closed on them.

Tuesday 30th December 1823, 5 a.m.   *Aboard Surprise*

'Sail ahoy! D'reckly off the starboard bow,' hailed the lookout atop the foremast.

Pat, astride his quarterdeck once more, peered long into his glass before shouting, 'Mr Mower, we will beat to quarters.' Pat bellowed his own commands to all around him, the crew hastening up to the yards with alacrity, the alarm and urgency clear to all in his voice. 'Mr Mower, open gun ports; run out the guns, if you please. All crews to stand by their guns. We will leave our English jack on the staff for now, but prepare to hoist the Greek flag on my command.'

'What do you see, sir?' asked Tom Pickering.

'It is a Turk frigate, I venture, and closing on the mistico, perhaps a league between them,' Pat announced, looking again for a few minutes through his glass. 'The mistico will surely be struggling against this northerly, as are we to close on her. We cannot reach the mistico afore the Turk hauls alongside of her and

228

takes them, but, God speed, we may yet distract him – if he has seen us. He is on a beam reach, a league and a half from us if he is a yard and barely one from the mistico, though he will be sailing with some southing too. It will take us three parts of an hour to close on him,' said Pat, the urgency diminishing in his voice, as he had now calculated the likely time before any action could commence.

Tuesday 30th December 1823, 5:30 a.m.   *Aboard the mistico*

'Pray earnestly to your God, gentlemen, and keep still your silence,' said the captain. All aboard could no longer ignore the hailing from several crew on the quarterdeck of the Turk frigate, which had swiftly crossed their bow a bare fifty yards ahead, firing a gun to reinforce her command. The frigate had now turned, and was running down the mistico's larboard side, perhaps only fifty yards away, the two vessels moving in opposite directions, angry faces visible on the Turk deck, as all aboard the mistico could not fail to notice. The Turk guns were run out, and at such close range, were the frigate to fire, obliteration of the small mistico and all on board her could not fail to be the result.

'I do not understand why he is passing by close-hauled under full canvas with no notice of us,' said the captain to Jason. 'Perhaps he thinks us simply the stupid crew of a stinking fishing boat; we are not dissimilar in size and rig.' After a few more minutes, he added 'We are too close now to the rocks for him to come about, I pray we may be saved, thank God ... thank God,' the captain said, breathing more easily, and with his relief so evident in his voice. The frigate had by now cleared their stern, though she loomed large still with her bulk and presence so close to them.

'Captain, will you now put us close into those rocks, so he cannot possibly reach us again?' asked Lord Byron, with the utmost concern in his voice. 'Never fear for any damage to your vessel for I shall guarantee you any necessary repairs.'

From the deep sigh of relief from the captain, no bidding or any guarantee was necessary at all; no slackening of sail or speed was made, but the little mistico seemed now so close to its destruction from a different means as the shallows were upon them. The captain, knowing the waters intimately, and with a sure touch ordered a swift series of course corrections to bring the vessel through between two islets and to safety from both the frigate and the rocks. 'We can go no further, the wind being so much against us now,' he declared. 'If the Turk so wishes, he may yet launch boats to capture us, and we can do nothing. We have but a very few sidearms, and to use them would be folly, ensuring our certain execution after capture. We must await a change in the wind to continue to Messalonghi, or we may beat for hours into this wind and sail for Dragomestre where we can at least take to the land and away from any Turk pursuit. What is your preference, sir?'

On this sobering note, Jason and Byron paused but briefly to consider their fate before Byron declared, 'To Dragomestre, Captain. We must not be apprehended. Let us proceed as best we may to that place.'

'Yes, my Lord,' nodded the captain, his own relief so evident.

Tuesday 30th December 1823, 5:30 a.m.   *Aboard Surprise*

'The Turk has seen us, Tom, and he has left the mistico alone. He is coming towards us, a full spread o' canvas and at best speed. Another ten minutes and we shall see his mettle,' said Pat, peering through his glass. Within the minute he added: 'No, he is slowing. I venture the light is good enough for him to see our jack and our guns; I doubt that he would wish to challenge an English frigate, even as we are in their claimed territorial waters and off the through channel for the United Islands. I fancy the Turk will be no trouble. He is turning away: yes, he is going about, and so does not fancy engaging with us.'

Tuesday 30th December 1823, 6:30 a.m.   *Aboard the bombard*

'Look, a sail over there, approaching off the starboard beam,' the captain announced, a little more buoyantly, to Gamba and Simon as they peered with straining eyes into the rising but low sun, still barely above the horizon. 'We are still some twelve miles out from Messalonghi, but the Turk fleet is said to be beyond Patras at Lepanto. It will be a Greek warship sent out to ensure that the whereabouts of the Turks remain known. We are hoisting the United Ionian Islands flag. The topman reports he also saw another, a smaller vessel, perhaps our mistico, beyond the Scrofes islets some two leagues ahead.'

'May I borrow your glass, Captain?' asked Simon, being far less sure than the confident Greek captain. 'Thank you,' he added, taking the proffered glass, and after peering intently for a few moments he enquired mildly, 'Would I be correct, Captain, in thinking that a red pennant might signify a Turk?'

At which comment Captain Valsamarchi brusquely snatched back his glass and looked hard at the approaching ship, a frigate as could plainly now be seen, and flying a Turk red flag at the jackstaff. 'Hell and damnation!' he shouted, or the Greek equivalent, for that is how it sounded to Simon, no translation being necessary. The captain and his crew were stunned, in some disbelief that this was happening to them. The Turk fleet was supposedly shut in at Patras, or even beyond the forts of the narrows, the Little Dardanelles as they were called, and at that moment they began to despair. Within what seemed like moments the frigate approached, turning swiftly into the wind to lose way, and came near alongside.

'They are hailing us now,' said Gamba to Simon, gazing at him with the utmost attention and deep concern, 'What should we do?'

'Might I suggest, sir, that were you to have any papers of a confidential nature – confidential that is in the matter of his Lordship's intentions in the Morea and for Greece generally – aboard this vessel, that they would be better for his Lordship's and indeed our own interests and prospects were they consigned over the side, and with the benefit of a large leaden weight?' Simon replied, in a measured tone.

'Of course, of course, I will do so immediately,' said Gamba, and rushed off to his berth to retrieve them.

'What can I say?' asked the captain of Simon. 'God help us! They will surely ask why we, flying an Ionian flag, are so far away from the Islands channel. What conceivable explanation have I to offer? We will be taken as blockade runners, and probably put to death.'

Gamba now having returned, and the papers being held by his servant on the side opposite the Turk frigate, he whispered to Simon, 'my servant shall throw our papers into the deep should any boat put off from the frigate.'

Just at that moment the Turk ship lowered a small boat. The servant panicked and threw the papers into the water where they sank immediately from sight.

'My dear Gamba, do you have anything else of a conceivably incriminating nature?' asked Simon, as the Turk boat drew alongside, and the captain was summoned into it, without any of the pleasantries as are customary between navigators.

'Nothing,' replied Gamba with some relief.

'Then I will join the captain, and go aboard the Turk vessel. We are merely en route for Calamo and have lost our way in the night,' said Simon, with some measure of sang froid.

At that moment there was shouting from the Turk frigate and some pointing of hands to the south-west. All looked about, towards far and approaching sails, in the direction of Zante. Simon could not be sure at this distance, no longer having the benefit of Captain Valsamarchi's glass, but he wondered if it could be *Surprise*, possibly with her consort, *Eleanor*, coming to their aid. The Turks were obviously becoming nervous, the shouting from their quarterdeck becoming shrill and strident. Simon hastened with alacrity to scramble down the net to join Captain Valsamarchi in the barge, and its crew rowed hastily across to the frigate. The Turk captain was shouting to his first officer, now taking charge on the bombard, to bring her behind the frigate and follow its lead. Within a few minutes both vessels were underway, heading north-east towards the Straits, beating slowly into the wind.

Tuesday 30ᵗʰ December 1823, 7 a.m.   *Aboard Surprise*

'It is the bombard, Tom, alongside the same Turk frigate,' said Pat, his spirits sinking, whilst peering through his glass, the morning light still weak, visibility poor. 'They are getting underway, towards Patras; the bombard is captured... and Simon too. Send to *Eleanor*, "follow closely, bombard and Turk together".'

Just then there was a shout from the foremast topman: 'Sails Ho! Two point off the starboard bow... six ships... seven.'

Pat swept his glass to the north-east, pausing to study the horizon for long moments before lowering his glass, 'By Jove, Tom, 'tis a whole fleet of ships,' he exclaimed, looking again through his glass as if to confirm what he knew he had seen, 'and plentiful frigates amongst them. It cannot be the Greeks. It is the Turks come out from their anchorage at Patras. I think we must leave the bombard to the Turk; plainly we cannot prevail against such numbers. We must turn away,' Pat declared, in a tone of deep resignation. 'Well, that surely signifies our departure, gentlemen,' adding, 'Signal again to *Eleanor* "follow closely". Mr Pickering, Helm up! Let her go off, handsomely! We will go west and away, back to Cephalonia. Home, gentlemen; we can do no more here this day, and must await another time afore we try again for Messalonghi.' Pat ordered their turn away with considerable disappointment in his voice, tiredness creeping in after a second night of very little sleep.

Tuesday 30th December 1823, 7 a.m.   *Aboard the Turk frigate*

Simon sat alongside Captain Valsamarchi on the planks of the Turk deck, surrounded by towering, deeply hostile Turk sailors, angry faces prevalent. A frightened Captain Valsamarchi whispered to Simon, 'The Turk captain feared the mistico was a fireship and so left her alone when they espied an approaching ship of war behind it, coming so as to take off its crew when it became ablaze, and then we appeared, and they became concerned that we too were another fireship, set to grapple with and consume them.'

'Are we in extreme peril?' asked Simon, nervously.

Valsamarchi nodded towards a most ferocious Turk, speaking loudly with his captain, who was holding his drawn sword and staring closely at them. 'There, that big fellow, he may be the second officer; he is urging the captain to cut off our heads and throw us over the side, and then sink our vessel.'

'Oh, dear God,' exclaimed Simon, fearing the worst, as the Turk captain stridently shouted something to the crew.

A great babble of vehement exchanges now took place amongst the Turk captain and his officers, Simon growing ever more anxious by each passing minute. Though he could understand only the barest smattering of the Turk language, the exchanges were so fast and furious that nothing could he comprehend, and so he looked with great anxiety to Valsamarchi for translation. The Turk captain, thankfully, appeared to be gaining control of the argument, his officers subsiding yet staring menacingly at their captives. Valsamarchi strained to hear whilst gazing unblinkingly at the Turk captain.

'Put them in irons,' bellowed the captain. Valsamarchi translated for Simon's benefit, whispering uncertainly, 'The captain seems familiar to me.'

The captain himself had shown no such sign of recognition, and shouted his question at them, asking if they were bound for Messalonghi. By now Simon and Valsamarchi were more closely surrounded by a still deeply hostile and gabbling crew, two of them clutching chains, and close enough for Simon to smell their foetid breath, even to see a plethora of rotting teeth, and to observe the hostility in their unwashed faces.

'Be not afraid,' advised Valsamarchi. A bewildered Simon thought it advice of very doubtful validity for rarely had he been in such a perilous predicament, one which seemingly offered only the immediate prospect of chained confinement. Perhaps even death was now close at hand.

'Your advice is doubtless kindly meant, sir, though you will understand why I find myself hesitant to accept it,' whispered Simon, fearful, as four Turk seamen approached closer with rattling chains, glaring viciously at them.

The next development was utterly astonishing to Simon, as his companion stood up, the Turk seamen halting in their intentions, as taken aback as was Simon. Valsamarchi gulped, rose to his full height, and then addressed the Turk captain in a loud and confident voice, 'Will Captain Zachiriá kill the man who saved his life, the man who saved his brother's life, who saved his crew from shipwreck in the Black Sea?'

The Turk captain started with surprise and indignation. One of his impudent captives was addressing *him?* He swivelled swiftly towards them, and stared at Valsamarchi, intense curiosity now in his eyes, peering closely at Valsamarchi's face for some moments, but saying nothing. Slowly, a long minute passed, before uncertainty flickered across the face of the Turk captain, and then, in an instant, a change of demeanour came about; anger giving way to curiosity, concern even. He stepped closer, no more than inches away from Valsamarchi, and said in the most fluent Greek, 'What? That cannot be. Is it you, Spiro?' The Turk captain dropped his still unsheathed sword to the deck, raised both his arms in the air, and without further hesitation, seized and embraced Valsamarchi tightly, as if meeting a returning brother – one long deemed lost, holding him close, as if to prevent any second separation, for clearly that is how he felt. He was now beaming brightly, astonishment and joy both showing on his face, before stepping back, grasping and shaking Valsamarchi's hand vigorously for several minutes more, seemingly lost for words, both of them now smiling at each other. The crew, all tension relieved, relaxed immediately, stepped back; the chains were removed from sight. All hostile babble had ceased at this most unexpected turn of events; a very welcome turn, thought Simon, relief flooding through his every fibre. He marvelled at this swift reversal of fortune, and stood staring at Valsamarchi and Zachiriá in a state of complete disbelief.

'Come Spiro, with your companion to my cabin. We shall have soup and coffee together, my friend,' declared Captain Zachiriá, his demeanour so positively reversed from the frightening moments of their first minutes aboard the frigate. 'Captain Zachiriá at your service sir,' he nodded to Simon when they were in the cabin.

'Please introduce me, and thank the Captain for his attention, Captain Valsamarchi, if you will,' Simon replied, savouring every sip of the proffered Turkish coffee as if it were his last, but grateful relief now near superseded by restored normality in his voice.

For near an hour Valsamarchi and Zachiriá exchanged reminiscences of the intervening fifteen years since they had last met in such extreme circumstances before their conversation turned to recent times and their present situation. Zachiriá explained his particular fear of fireships, having been captain of the Turk admiral's flagship that had been engulfed by a Greek fireship at Chios in the previous year, and swimming from the burning ship to save his life, but the Admiral, Kara Ali Pasha, losing his when struck by a falling, burning spar. A further hour passed as Valsamarchi and Zachiriá continued to reminisce, Simon content to allow his anxieties to further subside as he enjoyed the Turkish coffee, and then it was time for Zachiriá to return to his duties.

'We are to be taken to see the Admiral later. Zachiriá will vouch for us,' Valsamarchi explained. After Zachiriá had left them and returned to his deck, Valsamarchi concluded his scarcely credible story of how, at some risk to himself and his crew, he had rescued Captain Zachiriá, his brother and his crew from their sinking vessel, some fifteen years beforehand. So long ago that mutual recognition had dimmed, but had not, fortunately, been totally extinguished.

Tuesday 30th December 1823, 4 p.m.   *Aboard the bombard at Patras*

Under the close scrutiny of her captor the bombard had reached Patras, and let go her anchor alongside the Turk frigate, amidst the Turk fleet of some fourteen ships. The captain's barge came alongside the bombard, and Gamba crossed to the frigate, summoned by Captain Zachiriá. On boarding he was greeted by a somewhat more relieved looking Captain Valsamarchi, with Simon. Valsamarchi repeated his explanation of the recent turn of events for Gamba's benefit. Gamba listened without interruption until the end of Valsamarchi's story, and he offered only, "'Tis strange but true, for truth is always strange; stranger than fiction. Verse fourteen of his Lordship's poem, *Don Juan*, did you know?'

'Count Gamba,' Captain Zachiriá spoke sternly, 'your captain, Spiro Valsamarchi, has confessed that it is your intention to reach Messalonghi in contravention of the blockade. What say you?' This was translated by an Italian, Captain Francesco, in the service of the Turks as pilot at Patras.

'That is most certainly not the case, Captain. We are bound for Calamos, and merely became lost in the dark of the night. What

236

Valsamarchi has to say is of no worth whatsoever, for I have chartered his vessel for Calamos, as his papers will vouch, and therefore I must remonstrate against our detention and that of our vessel,' Gamba replied valiantly, glaring coldly at Francesco.

Simon then interposed, shrewdly observing more than an intermediary's interest on the part of Francesco – perhaps a pecuniary one, perhaps anticipating a goodly share of the prize, as the eight thousand dollars aboard the bombard had doubtless been remarked. He spoke very seriously, surprising himself with his calmness, 'Captain, respectfully, as one seafaring man to another, and as personal physician to Lord Melville, His Majesty's First Lord of the Royal Navy, I appeal to your undoubted goodwill as a fellow navigator, and to your considered observance of the appropriate diplomatic formalities. Our continued detention will not sit well with his Majesty's ministers at the Court of St. James's. It will no doubt bring the severest remonstrations to the Sublime Porte from his Majesty's ambassador in Constantinople. Will you care to consider of that?' Simon asked, studying Zachiriá's reaction closely.

Captain Zachiriá was by no means an unintelligent man, and the potentially dangerous implications for himself of his arrest of the vessel he readily perceived. He peered closely at Simon, as if in assessment of this unkempt, unimpressive, man before him, and his face broke into a great slow smile. 'Captain Valsamarchi's story was no doubt motivated by fear, Doctor Ferguson. By the grace of God and his Prophet Mahomet I have no doubt that the Admiral will release you and your vessel without delay,' this Zachiriá declared after but the briefest of thought – roundly sinking his interpreter's aspirations for a share of the booty, acceptance of that being visible to all in his countenance. Zachiriá continued, 'I am so sorry to detain you, and perhaps you would be so gracious as to complain to the Admiral of your capture at my hands, so far out beyond the gulf, so far from the forts and many, many leagues beyond the line of blockade, for that will surely be well received on my return to Constantinople, the Greek warships being known to be in those waters. With God's grace and that of his Prophet Mahomet this recommendation will be worth a half million of piastres to me.'

'I will assuredly do so, Captain, thank you kindly, sir,' replied Simon, with great relief, contented by the success of his reference to his somewhat exaggerated credentials, as was Gamba who continued to glare at Francesco with deep hostility for the remaining time of the interview.

Captain Zachiriá continued affably, 'We must all be grateful to God and his Prophet this day, for they have granted me the opportunity to thank again the man that saved my life, Spiro Valsamarchi. He is a good man, and it pleases me that I can repay but a small portion of the debt I owe him. God, in his benevolence, has smiled upon us this day.'

Simon permitted himself a wry smile and replied, simply 'I am of your way of thinking, Captain. All men have need of the Gods, and that, sir, is the opinion of a wiser man than us. Homer it was.'

The mood of the interview now being more cordial, Gamba picked up the bag he had brought across from the bombard. 'Captain, may I present you with my very modest gifts?' he said to Zachiriá, handing over a small cloth-wrapped bundle. 'Here are bottles of rum and porter, and a telescope. The latter may be of some use to you in your capacity as a seafarer and navigator.'

Zachiriá seemed genuinely pleased, particularly with the telescope, and after thanking Gamba he announced, 'Doctor Ferguson, Count Gamba; until tomorrow, when we shall meet the Grand Admiral, his Excellency the Pasha.'

Zachiriá shook their hands, and with that the interview was concluded, Simon and Gamba being escorted to the deck and taken by barge back to the bombard. When they were returned aboard and alone in Valsamarchi's cabin Gamba seized Simon's hand and shook it with both his own, saying, 'A companion's words of persuasion are effective. That too is Homer, Doctor Ferguson. A most fine intervention, you have my thanks, sir. I am greatly in your debt,' his overwhelming feeling of relief so plain in his voice.

'Not at all, Gamba; though the Dear knows it is not a day I would care to repeat. Would there be any prospect of good coffee to be had on this vessel, and perhaps a tot of brandy? For medicinal purposes only, it will relax the fibres.'

'I will press Valsamarchi. Doubtless there will be brandy, perhaps coffee too.'

'And perhaps too a final Homeric quote will serve us well this day?' Simon added, the tension within him near gone.

'By all means,' replied Gamba, curious.

'There is a time for many words and there is also a time for sleep,' said a deeply fatigued Simon, yawning wide.

Wednesday 31ˢᵗ December 1823   *Dragomestre port*

Lord Byron mused aloud about their predicament in a somewhat melancholy review, his words steeped in great sadness consequent to the loss of his friend, Gamba. 'Jason, Gamba has been taken by the Turk frigate yesterday; that was plain to see. My horses all lost, and also some eight thousand dollars of mine all gone, but never mind, we have more left. We had a narrow escape last night, being so close under their stern, and hailed even; and again this morning, the Turks perhaps searching further for us. But here we are, run away once more, with the sun and clearing weather, within a pretty little port, but whether the Turk may seek us again and send in their boats to seize us is another question, especially if we remain long here, since we are blocked out of Messalonghi by the direct entrance.'

Jason searched for some consolation. 'We are at least safe here from the Turks, my Lord. If necessary we can take to the hills and walk to Messalonghi should any of their vessels approach the port,' he offered, seeking to cheer Byron.

'No, Jason, such thoughts had occurred to me also. But the mountains are impassable, the captain of the mistico has explained. So steep that land affords no road to reach Messalonghi; plentiful snow now abounds upon them, we see it here in the wind. And there is too the matter of roaming brigands, Turk and Greek, twixt here and there. It is quite impossible, a desperate resort for us at best. No, we must await Greek ships from Messalonghi to escort us ere we leave this place, and hope that they might arrive before any inquisitive Turks,' Lord Byron concluded.

239

In the mid-morning Simon and Gamba were escorted to meet the Ottoman supreme commander and Governor of the Morea, Yusuf Pasha. The Pasha was lying on a sofa smoking a pipe, and did not rise to greet them. With a wave of his hand he indicated to an adjacent sofa on which they were expected to be seated. Servants brought them strong Turkish coffee and pipes filled with mild but highly aromatic Turkish tobacco. As Simon enjoyed the coffee and Gamba smoked his pipe, the Pasha continued for several minutes to speak with his officers and counsellors seated around him before turning to Gamba and Simon as their conversation ebbed. Smiling broadly he offered greetings – expressed in Turkish and translated into Greek by his secretary, Gamba translating into English for Simon's benefit - before asking them for an explanation of their incursion into the blockaded Greek waters.

Gamba reiterated his story as told to Zachiriá, adding his lamentations concerning the state of the Morea: 'Such turbulent times, Excellency; making the aspirations of the mere traveller utterly difficult. Bandits and brigands abound throughout the Greek provinces, particularly the Morea, and safety to be assured only within your Excellency's military oversight.' Gamba finished with a complaint about his capture by Zachiriá, 'sailing brazenly alone, and taking them so far beyond the line of blockade.' The Pasha, for the most part inscrutable and listening through his interpreter, nodded and appeared mollified with Gamba's additions, satisfied with his explanation, and seemingly pleased to hear of his captain's exploits.

After a brief pause the Pasha conversed again with his advisors before turning to Simon, and asking, 'What does Sir Thomas Maitland think of the Greek brigands pursuing my corvette upon the rocks of neutral Ithaca, and the slaughter of many of its crew, including the captain, my nephew? What of the money lost which was onboard, and which was to pay my troops? Will Maitland not seek revenge for such an outrage by those pirates?'

Slowly Simon stood up, the somewhat theatrical move allowing him a further few moments with which to formulate his reply. He addressed himself directly to the Pasha, speaking with conviction: 'My name is Ferguson, Excellency, physician to the First Lord, Lord Melville. Assuredly, Excellency, His Majesty's Governor, Sir Thomas Maitland ...' Simon paused to let Gamba translate into Greek and the Pasha's secretary to translate into Turkish, '... deplores most strongly the incursion of the Greek pirate ships. Speaking personally and without the least authority ... it seems likely that His Majesty, through the august offices of his Governor ... will make recompense to your Excellency in due course.'

The Pasha nodded gravely, indicating his comprehension, and seemed satisfied with Simon's response, declaring, 'We will detain you and your vessel no longer, your passports will be returned to you, and you may continue your travels.' After an imperial wave of his hand in dismissal he turned again to his secretary to dictate his orders for their release. Gamba and Simon rose as one and thanked the Pasha, both offering a diplomatic bow before retiring from the room.

'My dear Doctor Ferguson,' said a very grateful Gamba when they were finally outside the Pasha's residence, 'you were most convincing in your statement, and well received it was too, but is such recompense likely to be forthcoming?'

'Oh, I have not the slightest idea, Gamba, yet it would not surprise me. The Governor, Maitland, is reputedly a man of the strictest demeanour, and would doubtless have been outraged by the Greek incursion on his Imperial coastal periphery. Such minds customarily tend towards rigour and rectitude. Some clever mechanism for recompense may likely emerge from it, given time. What do you say to a perambulation along the coast whilst we are here and awaiting our passports? The marshy nature of the landscape suggests we will find a goodly population of waders, and perhaps raptors too, I dare say.'

'By all means, Doctor Ferguson, I will bring a fowling piece, and I believe I still have a few bottles of porter,' Gamba replied, relief still evident in his voice.

Prince Mavrocordato was volubly grateful for the return of *Surprise*, the frigate having dropped anchor that morning a mile off from Messalonghi, in the nearest deep water anchorage. Some little way off were the five Spezziot brigs, as had been there during *Surprise's* last visit, but of their crew very few were visible about their decks. Pat had gone ashore, rowed in his barge to the town, and they were seated in a small house in which Mavrocordato held court.

'Thank you most kindly for your valued escort of his Lordship from Cephalonia, Captain O'Connor. No doubt it was the appearance of your ship which drove off the Turk frigate, allowing Lord Byron to escape. I have word from my agents of the encounter, and that he is in Dragomestre, a small port along the coast to the north-west. I have sent a squadron of our gunboats and the brigantine *Leonidas* to fetch his lordship from that place. He will be quite safe in the waters behind the offshore islands. I have asked our fleet to go to sea to find the Turk fleet, so that no similar event can recur. The Turk frigate with Dr Ferguson is gone to Patras. The English consul there, Mr Green, will doubtless make representations for his release. I would speak with you about our situation in the Morea, and also in Candia, where the assistance of your own frigate will now be so beneficial.'

'May I ask, sir, where is the rest of your fleet, the ships that captured the Turk brig on the shore of Ithaca?' asked Pat.

'Sadly, the Hydriots, with nine ships, have gone home to Hydra, their month of pay from the government having run out, and Lord Byron having declined to provide funds for further months to such mercenary crews. The five Spezziot crews are also ashore for want of pay. Lord Byron possesses of an understandable, if not wholly accurate, perception of our mariners, I fear. Whilst it is true that they will not sail without pay in advance, such pay is certainly meagre, and they do not hesitate to place their lives at risk in the service of our embryonic state, though doubtless the prospect of prizes is not entirely absent from their considerations. The Pasha has already called upon the Ionian government for compensation for his loss of half a million of piastres; in turn the Ionian government has called upon ours, but there is nothing to be done. There is no money, and even were there money to be found doubtless it would never be paid over to the Turks. No, we are now indeed in bad grace with the Ionian government, and the money seized from the Pasha's brig all gone to Hydra. The Spezziot crews, when their Hydriot compatriots departed, left their five ships anchored out there and came ashore, refusing to continue to serve without further pay being received. My own interventions between them may have prevented a worse debacle, one which would have been to the lasting shame of all Greeks. I find I am now appointed head of the provincial government here, and no longer a simple volunteer. Our resources remain meagre, our equipment but little, troops few, and money nil. This is common knowledge, and will certainly find your ear during your stay. I hope that you will not be so dismayed as to leave us too, Captain O'Connor?'

'Your Highness, we are presently well equipped, and want for nothing other than direction,' Pat replied, more positively than he felt at that moment, the loss of Simon, for that is how it seemed, weighing heavily on his spirits. 'My jack tars waited for many months, a year or more, for their pay when fighting Boney; a bare few months late is of little moment to them. Now that we have our letter-of-marque and can begin seeking Turk prizes our prospects will doubtless change for the better.'

'Thank you, that is most heartening. We await the arrival of Lord Byron, which will assuredly change our circumstances here in Messalonghi for the better, and I believe will be so very favourable for all of Greece.' Mavrocordato continued, 'However our situation in Candia is far from favourable, deteriorating in fact, and I have been asked by my government to convey to you the ever more urgent need for succour for our forces there, so very severely oppressed by the Turks. We are at our last throw on the island; men and arms dwindling. One more victory for Hussein Pasha there and we are done for. In the matter of interdiction of Turk resupply ships, your frigate could be most profitably engaged. Our commander in Candia is also a Hydriote, Manolis Tombazes, and he has but recently been sore pressed by plentiful Turk reinforcement. It is conceivable that in some very few weeks to come he may require to evacuate his remaining combatants from the island. In this too your ship will be invaluable. Will you therefore, Captain O'Connor, accept our direction for your service as guard ship here until our need becomes greater in Candia, when you will sail to help us there? It will give me grave concern to lose your frigate from here, where it may serve the protection of Messalonghi, our own fleet having left us and the Turk squadron still here in Patras, but the needs of our compatriots in Candia may become more urgent still.'

'We will replenish our water tomorrow, your Highness, and with that we may stand ready to depart on your order for Candia without delay. Are you able to gain any news of Doctor Ferguson and Count Gamba through your sources in Patras?' Pat asked, a little anxiously.

'My agents will bring news within a very few days, Captain. Of that you can be assured,' replied Mavrocordato, as positively as he could put it.

Outside and once again at the quay, a disconsolate Pat stood in the pale winter sunlight, the warmth of the day ebbing with the onset of the early evening, and a cooling easterly wind coming off the hills. The prospects for Simon, captured and helpless in the fiercely hostile midst of the plainly untrustworthy foreigners, filled his mind with a chilling dread. He contemplated his immediate plan, standing silently and looking rather distantly across to *Surprise*, moored a mile off in the lagoon, for some long minutes, his small band of shipmates standing ready about him.

A few more minutes passed by, Pat still absorbed in his private deliberations, until he became aware of his men staring at him, and his attention returned to them. 'Mr Pickering, we will allow a rota for crew leave ashore this evening. Not less than half the crew to remain aboard *Surprise*, in case of any eventuality. Tomorrow after church we will water the ship, my barge to be used to carry our barrels to and fro. Barton, look about for a clean water supply. I believe I will return to *Surprise*,' Pat concluded.

With half of his crew and officers ashore in Messalonghi, their leave reinforcing Pat's painful awareness of the absence of his close friend, it was all Freeman could do to try to bring some cheer to his captain's gloomy face by ensuring the very first quality of his toad in a hole for supper. He was accompanied by Murphy, bearing a bottle of the finest red that Pat had ever had in his stores, a Romanée-Conti burgundy of 1817, supplies of which in only the tiniest quantities had become available after the demise of Bonaparte. It was a bottle long previously secreted away by Murphy, who had wholly unfounded pretensions of wine knowledge, but more real aspirations of usurping Freeman's role as butler, the bottle put by for no reason other than his vague and indiscernible feeling that some prime reason would come up. Murphy was sadly disappointed, the savoury aroma of the freshly roasted toad in a hole and the taste of the exceptional red being scarcely noticed, producing no more than a grunt from Pat who was seated at his table studying his Admiralty charts of the Aegean.

Murphy persevered 'Well, sorr, now yer supper will be a'ruined if it ain't eaten up hot.' This producing no response from Pat he added, 'Mr Marston is asking of you, and would you care to see him in the cabin this evening?' adding almost as an afterthought, 'sorr.'

The question broke Pat's train of thought. He seemed to welcome the disturbance of his morose mood and looked up, 'Why yes, thankee Murphy; please pass my compliments to Mr Marston, and if he should care for a little music I am at his service. Freeman, could you kindly bring extra toad in a hole and a glass for him? This is a prime wine, Murphy,' said Pat, noticing the bottle for the first time. 'I collect that you said we had none left. Was it in Gibraltar, or Mahon?'

'Well, it was in the wrong case, in with the claret,' Murphy explained, unconvincingly. 'The extra toad in a hole and glass will be here d'reckly ... sorr.' Murphy hastened away before he could be asked further questions by his grumpy captain.

'Ah, Mr Marston, there you are, come in. Please, take a seat, over there near the window; we have still a little light. You have brought your violin, excellent.' Freeman bustled in and set down the glass and toad in a hole for Marston, Murphy hovering at his elbow with cutlery and napkin. 'Allow me to pour you a glass of this most excellent burgundy, perhaps near my last one, and we are certainly favoured to enjoy it,' said Pat, his voice flat, toneless.

'Thank you, sir, most kind,' Marston was slightly anxious, wondering if he might somehow stand in bad grace with his captain. He took a large gulp, 'An excellent wine. Never have I tasted better.' A sideways glance afforded him the impression that his captain, who was pacing slowly and repetitively up and down the cabin, was far from contented.

'Murphy there, we will have this bottle's fellow to follow if you will.' Pat turned to look at his guest, and Marston could plainly see Pat's face betraying his unhappiness.

'Sir, should it be even the smallest concern, I feel sure that the sick bay presents no difficulties at all until such time as Doctor Ferguson returns,' offered Marston, perceiving that his captain looked worried, depressed even.

'Well, this is the last one,' declared a bouyant Murphy, returning within a few minutes, and triumphantly clutching the famous burgundy.

'Thankee, Murphy. Mr Marston, please, the toad in a hole is cooling. This surely is the very finest of wines. You will allow me to refill your glass,' Pat striving to brighten, to observe the civilities. 'Now, what would you care to play, as we lack our viola?'

'Perhaps a little *Vivaldi* might bring some cheering warmth to our playing, sir? What do you say to the *Four Seasons*? I have oft heard it played in this cabin. *La Primavera*, if you will?'

'An excellent choice, Mr Marston; Dr Ferguson and I do enjoy playing that most wonderful first movement. Why 'tis not more popular these days is a mystery to us all.' With a determined effort to entertain his visitor, the toad in a hole and burgundy having been enjoyed by both of them, Pat set to with his cello, but played diffidently for half an hour before setting it down on his knee and looking across towards Marston. His guest had winced at Pat's sometimes flat and occasionally shrill notes, had become uneasy, but held his tongue; no words were necessary: it was plain that

246

Pat's heart was not in his playing. Marston had patiently held in check his observations of Pat's errors, his captain's gloomy mood so evident despite his best efforts to play and to entertain his visitor, and so he had doggedly persevered, he much wishing to cheer his captain, but all to no avail. Pat sat quite still, his cello on his lap, his face devoid of any expression, his indeterminate gaze void of any focus, his clenched fist slowly and repeatedly tapping on his chair.

'Captain O'Connor, it pains me that you may consider me to be presumptuous, yet I find my observations and leanings, that is to say my inclination in our Lord's service, necessitate my enquiry. Pray tell, sir, if you are not equal to company... are you well?' said Marston, gently.

'There is no need like the lack of a friend,' whispered Pat, with something akin to despair in his voice.

Marston became aware of a growing, perhaps necessary, shift in his own position, from shipmate to chaplain. 'Perhaps, sir, I should leave you alone to your thoughts... or could I be of some small service to you at this time? I have some little experience in my capacity as a man of God at such difficult times. Pray forgive me if I presume too much,' said Marston, quietly.

'Why, Mr Marston, I believe that you may.' Pat looked up and peered closely at his companion, and whispered his explanation, 'I am tolerably uncomfortable since Simon was taken by the Turks. We have served together since the year three, and I have loved that man as a brother for so long, more than twenty years, that I can scarcely believe what my life would be like were he never to play his viola again in this cabin. I have fought in many a battle, lost many a fellow crew member, yet never have I felt such a loss, no, let us say a *potential* loss so personally. Some months ago, you may collect, my new cox'n, Barton, joined us, and reminded me so powerfully of our loss of his brother in the year thirteen. So many years have passed by since then yet he is oft still in my thoughts.'

Marston looked into his captain's troubled face for long moments before replying, summoning every vestige of the authority he considered vested within him by his calling into his voice. 'It is surely a great compliment to you, sir, that in all your years at sea, and doubtless many other men having been lost serving with you, that you have retained your compassion for your fellow man. Your humanity is plainly preserved, as all can see, and no one could ask more than that. Though doubtless at such moments it surely seems a heavy burden.'

'Scores, perhaps a hundred or more men have been lost on those vessels I have commanded, Mr Marston. It is a burden I am oft reminded of. A sleepless night and some of them are there, in and out of my dreams. Old comrades such as Brannan Barton often, and others that are too many to remember; many of their names I can no longer collect, I regret to say.'

'Sir, your mind is doubtless much disturbed by the thought of the possibility, *the mere possibility* that you may lose more men in this venture. You have gained many victories in His Majesty's service. No more celebrated captain ever commanded any English ship, even Nelson included – I doubt that anyone would dispute that – and in so doing are we not now very much safer in our English homeland - Bonaparte's invasion never having departed? Do we not sleep safer in our beds: surely so?'

'I would never wish to boast away about my own service, Mr Marston, but there are times when I contemplate whether 'tis finally time to tie up, for good, the end of my sea-going days, a life ashore. No more loyal and good men would I lose,' Pat stopped, the strain and distress so evident in his ashen face, and he looked to Marston.

It was the prospect of losing Simon that had brought this despair pressing to the forefront of his captain's mind, Marston now realised, and he replied softly, but with firm conviction in his voice, 'Captain O'Connor, you are to consider that Doctor Ferguson has not been killed in conflict. He was not injured nor taken in the heat of battle. He is reportedly now in the custody of the most senior officials of the Turk regime in Patras, officials who will certainly accept their diplomatic responsibilities and the requests of British consular officials to see him. He will stand well with the protection of his British passport and the standing of his companion, Count Gamba. I think therefore, sir, that we may safely place our confidence for his well-being and ultimate return in diplomatic conventions.' Marston looked at a silent Pat O'Connor and persevered, 'We may most assuredly also place our confidence in our Lord. Let us take comfort in the words of psalm thirty: *Weeping may endure for a night, but joy cometh in the morning.* Doubtless soon we will have news of Doctor Ferguson,' Marston concluded.

Pat looked up directly at Marston with an affinity he had never formerly felt for him, and said quietly, 'I would never have countenanced a chaplain aboard any of my ships but for the persuasion of Doctor Ferguson. It is he that we both have to thank for you being here. I thank you kindly, Mr Marston.' It was all that he felt able to say, but he rose to his feet and shook Marston's hand with an iron grip, a further half minute passing until Pat released it. 'Thank you: you have been most kind, listening to the dreary woes of an old salt. I take comfort from what you have said. Please excuse me, I find my mind ails me; I believe I must retire. I bid you good night.'

Sunday 4ᵗʰ January 1824   *aboard Surprise, Messalonghi*

'Good morning, Murphy, Freeman,' said Pat, in pleasant surprise, gazing at the silver tray as his breakfast was brought in by his steward, a plethora of fried bacon, eggs, mushrooms, tomatoes, and toast; Murphy bringing cutlery and napkins.

'Well, it is, to be sure, sorr,' said Murphy before Freeman could speak, and noticing his captain's tone of approval, a change very much for the better in comparison with the prior evening.

'Pass the word for Mr Pickering and Mr Marston. I will inspect divisions at four bells, and we will rig church for six bells,' Pat ordered, 'and Murphy, be so good as to check our stocks in case of any further bottles stored in the wrong cases,' Pat added in the lightest of tones.

'Aye aye, sorr, d'reckly,' replied Murphy, his spirits lifting as he felt the improvement in his captain's mood.

At divisions many a thick head was evident, the crew having enjoyed a very rare run ashore in the prior evening amidst the best that Messalonghi had to offer. Yet all were present, which was testimony enough to Pat that he had a prime, keen crew; obviously not a pressed man amongst them. He doubted that any of them would have been other than volunteers, even were the press still to be a recruiting force. 'The Press,' he mused, 'where would his Majesty's fleet have been without it?' And yet on his own ships during the war he seldom employed pressed men. *Tenedos* in particular had long been known as a happy ship, and its crew favoured with plentiful prizes; prizes which had substantially enriched those crew from Falmouth, and indeed the town generally.

'Dalby, have you had a fall?' asked Pat, looking at a very swollen black eye and heavily bruised cheek. 'What have you to say for yourself?'

'Climbing back on deck, sir,' replied Clumsy Dalby; it was a fiction no one aboard believed, least of all Pat, knowing Dalby's temperament well of old. 'Hmmm,' said Pat, moving on.

'Mr Tizard, are you with us fully this morning?' asked Pat, the ship's carpenter favoured with his title as a non-commissioned officer, as was his rightful due, but seemingly striving with some little difficulty to appear fully awake. Pat did not wait for his reply, but passed on to the crew of *Axeman,* all of whom seemed considerably worse for wear. 'Hartley, Johnston. Do I see you both Bristol fashion this morning?' asked Pat, pleasantly, although to everyone the answer could hardly be in the affirmative.

''Twas the ouzo brandy, sir; they said it should be drunk with plentiful water, but Barton said the water supply wasn't greatly clean, so we left it out,' explained an amiable but somewhat emboldened Hartley, obviously to all still suffering from the ouzo influence.

'I see,' said Pat, concealing his smile as best he could. 'Perhaps you need to see the Doc ...' Pat's words tailed off as the recollection of Simon's absence returned to him.

Hartley, with surprising mental agility, quickly redeemed himself, replying with firm conviction, 'As soon as he is back aboard, sir.'

It was a consoling belief that Pat clung to in his thoughts during the remainder of his inspection, much abbreviated due to the evident fatigue of his crew. 'Very good, Mr Pickering,' said Pat, when he had finished, although "very good" it would most certainly not have been described as by any of his peer captains during the French war. Pat had more important things on his mind, and their status as a letter-of-marque had slowly changed his perceptions of what was strictly *de rigeur* aboard *Surprise*. The long layoff since his command of *Tenedos* had, to his own reluctant admission, taken the edge off even his own demands of his crew, but not his expectations; his confidence in them being diminished not one jot. 'Mr Marston, we will hold church a little earlier this morning if you will,' said Pat, the ship's bell striking five bells. *Surprise* held steady in the very mildest of swells, hardly a breath of wind evident, and the sails, left hanging in case of any urgent necessity to shift, hung loosely from the yards, but still the sharpest of eyes remained at the tops, gazing seawards. The morning was warming with the sun's progression towards noon, and remained dry, with not a cloud in sight except over the far peaks of the Morea to the south.

'I am quite ready, sir.' Marston stepped forward to the sea-chest, customarily used as the pulpit, on the deck, and began the service with the reading of the Covenant prayer. '*Christ has many services to be done. Some are easy, others are difficult. Some bring honour, others bring reproach. Some are suitable to our natural inclinations and temporal interests, others are contrary to both. Yet the power to do all these things is given to us in Christ, who strengthens us. I am no longer my own but yours. Put me to what you will, rank me with whom you will; put me to doing, put me to suffering; let me be employed for you or laid aside for you, exalted for you or brought low for you; let me be full, let me be empty, let me have all things, let me have nothing; I freely and wholeheartedly yield all things to your pleasure and disposal.*'

Marston concluded by calling on the crew to join him in a hymn, thinking that perhaps the more jaded of them might be revived by the singing, but plainly this was not the case – as was evident by the many for whom song remained beyond their powers this morning, after the prior evening's indulgences – and so he moved swiftly, with no urging from Pat, to the last piece of the

251

service, his oration. His reference, as he commenced, to their missing shipmate, the Doctor, did bring about a resurgence of concentration and a shuffling of feet, the torpor sloughing off the grossly indulgent of the prior evening, a change that was particularly noticed by Pat, now listening intently to his chaplain. Marston swiftly moved on to his conclusion, one on which he had determined as most appropriate to his captain's mind after Pat's confiding in him of the prior evening. 'I will finish our service this morning with the very shortest of quotations, words from psalm one hundred and twenty-one: *I will lift up mine eyes unto the hills, from whence cometh my help. My help cometh from the Lord, which made heaven and earth ...*' Marston paused, looking up from his bible as a widespread murmuring became evident within his audience.

Before Marston could utter a further word there came a loud shout from the lookout on the main mast, 'Ship ahoy, larboard beam.' All eyes stared directly out to sea.

'Murphy, quickly now, my glass,' shouted Pat.

'It is a small ship, sir, shifting very slowly against the north wind – well, the breeze – hardly any way on her at all, and it may take her some hours yet to get in,' said Pickering.

Murphy returned with the glass, and Pat continued to study the approaching ship very carefully, and for some minutes, it being barely visible amidst the haze and the sparkling light refractions over the water. The lookout had done well. Clarity improved steadily as she gained a mile in the next hour; all aboard *Surprise* gazing at her approach, Marston's service quite forgotten.

'My God, Tom, could it be? Could it be? It is the bombard, it is Gamba's bombard!' shouted Pat to his second officer standing alongside him, and, quite uncharacteristically, slapping him on the back, great joy and excitement welling within him. 'Barton, go aloft, quickly now, signal to her,' Pat ordered his cox'n.

'Aye aye, sir,' replied an excited Barton, the lingering effects of the prior night falling away in an instant, and he clambered up the ratlines at a speed never exceeded by the fastest of the young midshipmen of all Pat's prior commands. A half hour passed, but no reply came from the approaching ship in response to Barton's signal. Apart from the men aloft, all aboard *Surprise* were now leaning on the larboard hammock netting and staring intently at the distant vessel, still moving very slowly, tacking every twenty minutes or so to make any headway at all, but closing inexorably.

'I think we can be sure she is the bombard, sir,' said Tom Pickering with growing conviction. The ship was now not more than one mile off, and her hull form and sails becoming ever clearer. A great hubbub of excitement was growing amongst the crew on the deck, preparations for dinner quite forgotten, the cook indignant as he emerged from below, but soon taken up in the suspense and anticipation, the dinner burning and remaining quite ignored by all as it ruined in the galley as a further half hour passed. The bombard, for all were now sure that was what she was, was now barely a half mile away, and all could perceive two waving figures on her prow, identities still obscured. The effects of the haze were now considerably diminished, the sun higher, and the late morning much warmer. Pat studied the ship with his glass, tears beginning to well from his eyes, as it became clear that Simon was one of the two figures waving back vigorously.

''Tis he, the Doctor; Tom, Mr Marston; 'tis Simon, and Gamba, returned to us. Thank God... thank God, Mr Marston,' Pat pronounced, wiping his eyes on his shirt sleeve as unobtrusively as he could, thinking perhaps it was not good form for his crew to see their captain shedding tears. But all were looking away towards the bombard, cheering and frantically waving now; shouting and laughing, pointing towards the returnee; joy endemic to all.

Another half hour and the bombard came near alongside *Surprise*, her anchor let go, and her jollyboat was lowered. Simon, together with Gamba, was rowed across to *Surprise*, willing and jubilant hands swiftly hauling them up the accommodation ladder without ceremony, Pat standing close by. Royal Navy convention quite forgotten, the crew pressed forward to greet Simon, who staggered under the onslaught of much backslapping whilst edging slowly through the throng towards Pat, smiling at all and greeting many with a handshake, 'Good day, shipmates. I am most sensible of this prodigious fine welcome.'

Without any ado Pat embraced his friend in both arms; hugging him fiercely, finding himself quite unable to speak; beaming with delight, and finding it impossible to halt the tears of relief that streamed down his face, a flood-tide of joy, now quite unashamedly visible to all. The euphoric ensemble of Pat and Simon shuffled through the impromptu crew assembly with the aid of Pat's officers clearing a passage towards the cabin. Pickering and Marston led Gamba down to the gun-room, rightly perceiving that Pat would wish some time to speak with Simon alone. After several minutes of pushing through their jubilant throng of shipmates Pat was able to close the great cabin door behind them, their ears ringing with the cheers of the crew behind them still. Not a one had taken the slightest notice of Mower's calls for 'silence, silence there,' half-hearted that they were. On deck, the ship's officers now swiftly brought to an end all pretence that the crew inspection was "very good", and a series of commands were barked out by Mower to the still excited crew; half going below for a belated and ruined dinner whilst the others were pressed to a myriad of ship housekeeping tasks which they minded not the least.

'Simon,' said Pat, seizing his hand. That the single word was all that a moved Pat O'Connor could utter, and that he was overwhelmed, was plain for Simon to see.

'Pat, oh you are a good hearted soul. Stand firm, brother,' said Simon gently.

Pat had now recovered his composure, but still could find no words, and simply stood there; gripping Simon's hand in a vice-like embrace, his strength overwhelming any intention Simon may have had to step back. A near minute more passed, Pat searching for the right words to greet his friend until the status quo was broken by the voice of Murphy, insistent and whining in its usual tone, but cheering and warming too by its very familiarity.

'Well, there is one last bottle been found o' that Roman burgundy, sorr, and will dinner now be convenient?'

'That exquisite elixir? The seventeen? Murphy, you are a fine fellow. That is exceedingly handsome in you,' remarked Simon.

'Yes, yes, Murphy, thankee,' croaked Pat, finding his voice at last. 'I rejoice to see you, Simon. You look quite famished, thin. Come straight to my table, I have asked Wilkins to cook the best he has in his store, and a glass or two of good wine will answer the case.'

'And I am so pleased to see you again, Pat; for a moment after we were taken I thought my time had come. The Turk crew were as hostile as could be.'

They settled at Pat's table, and Freeman arrived within a very few minutes with a steaming dish of swordfish soup and fresh baked bread – normally a rare delicacy, but the proximity to Argostoli affording Wilkins welcome scope to practice his art.

'Please, Simon, eat up, you look fair clemmed.'

'Thank you Pat; rations, though edible at best, have been short and infrequent these past days. At many a meal did I have a hankering for some morsel more nearly resembling food. Though perhaps we are too accustomed to our good fare in these recent times?'

Pat smiled, his customary good spirit returning, and he refilled their glasses. 'I collect the County Clare in that dreadful year seventeen. A visit to the Burren to see old acquaintances; no food to be found, nor a potato to be had anywhere; Mrs O'Rafferty's cow killed, nothing to feed it; her son leaving the land for America, for Boston. Lord, we are well blessed these days, to be sure, though I do not need to tell you that. Here, we have nothing finer on this ship, drink the last bottle with me. I can think of no better occasion.'

Between mouthfuls of bread and spoonfuls of soup Simon recounted the story of his capture and subsequent release. A smiling Freeman brought a huge dish of stewed boar, cooked with plentiful bacon and mushrooms, accompanied by a mound of steaming rice. Simon resumed his tale between gorging on the food. One incongruous but seemingly important recollection of Simon's, which bemused Pat, was his days before release studying the wading birds of the coastal marshes; herons, plovers, cormorants and many others being mentioned, and raptors too, including harriers, ospreys and eagles of several variants. It all passed over Pat, he merely nodded with pleasure, spoke but little, and contented himself with refilling their glasses, his returned friend's presence giving him immense pleasure, and he called to Freeman for several more bottles as they enjoyed their reunion dinner together.

'We departed at 4 a.m.,' said Simon, 'unfavourable winds held us back until then, and even whilst we sailed they were scarcely less of an impediment. We had waited with a deal of anxiety for our passports, as ships arrived from Cephalonia; fearing that Turk agents might speak with the Pasha of our intentions to go to Messalonghi and assist the Greeks; hence, fearing too that we might be detained further; but what news of Lord Byron and Abel Jason?' Simon asked.

'Safely hereabouts, along the coast, and they will be with us presently,' said Pat. 'Pray tell, have you considered further of the Turk fleet?'

Simon hesitated, the question not one for his personal province, he thought, a little perplexed. 'Not as often as I might or, perhaps, should have done,' he replied, cautiously.

'But what Turk ships did you see in their squadron whilst you were there? Did you count frigates, brigs, and the like?' Pat raised his voice in emphasis.

'I did not. I am ashamed to say such enquiry was far from my mind, brother,' Simon replied. 'I dare say there were a score or more, all with several masts, guns aplenty, and the associated plethora of sails and nautical accoutrements so familiar to you mariners. Mind, it was only a general impression; I do not commit myself to the precise number. As to what form of vessels they were, that I cannot say. Doubtless there were both frigates and brigs. Shall we say a dozen of each? Let us not split hairs, for all love.'

'Simon, 'tis a matter of some interest for our prospects.'

'I dare say, but I never paid it any attention.'

'Can you remember of the number of vessels at least?'

'I should have to consider of it.'

'Pray do, if you will.'

'The Pasha asked me of the prospects for compensation from

256

Maitland for the very considerable specie wrecked on his coast and stolen by the Greeks, and 'twas only the mention of Melville as my patron, that is to say in a medical capacity, which secured our release. That seems sure to me.'

'Lord, what a fellow you are, Simon,' Pat smiled cheerfully.

Tom Pickering looked in to announce that Gamba had gone ashore in the barge, and took the moment to shake Simon's hand again. Two pints of coffee followed their dinner until they simply sat back in the deep satisfaction of their mutual company. It was Marston, a full hour and a half later, that eventually interrupted a quiet reverie that had turned to slumber, knocking persistently and admitting himself to find them both emerging from a semi-sleep state. 'Would the gentlemen wish to join me and play for the crew on deck this evening? Our playing has been requested,' he asked.

'What say you, Simon?' asked Pat.

'With infinite pleasure; after supper, if that is convenient for the operation of this vessel,' Simon replied, with particular satisfaction, looking closely at his friend's wide smile.

'Brother... may the hinges of our friendship never grow rusty.'

Some hours later the trio, Pat and Simon more awake, emerged on the quarterdeck; the crew were sitting patiently along the gangways and on the forecastle, conversing in little more than whispers. The wintery evening was fine and dry, but the temperature was cooling noticeably, and all on deck were dressed for warmth. From far across the lagoon Messalonghi remained very visible, the lights from houses now beginning to be seen as dusk set in, weak shimmering reflections on the flat, still water. The trio began with an old favourite, the third movement of Mozart's third violin concerto; the light and delicate playing accompanied by the crew tapping their heels on the deck; the music now almost as familiar to them as it was to the musicians. As the piece closed, a general round of applause came from the crew, and the musicians nodded their heads in appreciation. Then came music from Bach, Boccherini and Corelli, all received by increasing applause until they reached their finale, the wonderful solo *Caprice Twenty-Four* from Paganini, played by Marston. Although he could not approach the genius of Paganini, never did any of the assembly enjoy hearing a piece so much as they did that evening. It was a memorable occasion, the crew in great heart, the joyous satisfaction of all with Simon's return so obviously endemic. The music had been played far into the night with such heartfelt vibrancy and zest, and a memory of those moments would be cherished by all for the rest of their lives. At the end the crew clapped until their hands were sore, and stamped their feet until the officers became concerned for the deck – unwarranted concern as almost all were barefoot. The trio looked at each other with wide smiles, in deep satisfaction, then stood and took their bow before retiring to the cabin.

'A wonderful day, brother, to be sure,' whispered a very emotional Pat to Simon.

Monday 5th January 1824   *aboard Surprise, Messalonghi*

In the early hours of the dawn, with thin shafts of light permeating the darkness from behind low cloud towards the Morea, Pat awoke and stepped briskly to his quarterdeck to look about at the sea state, the weather, and for sight or report of any ships. Far visibility remained obscured by mists arising from the sea surface, and *Surprise* rocked gently in the slight swell. Pat, bereft of anything save his shirt and breeches, shivered in the cold northerly wind. To his astonishment, anchored a bare fifty yards off from *Surprise*, was the mistico on which Lord Byron and Abel Jason had embarked in Cephalonia, and later sailed from Zante. He spoke quietly with a descending watchman who declared that the mistico had arrived, according to their fellows previously atop, at six bells of the First watch, and that no one had thought that its arrival warranted waking their captain from his slumbers. The master, Mr Prosser, had been on duty when it arrived, and declared that, 'The Captain needed more his rest than an awakening with news of a boat that was scarcely bigger than a fishing boat; even one on which Lord Byron might or might not be travelling; and the news could be revealed when the Captain awakened.'

A growing number of Surprises gazed over towards the mistico, though little activity could be seen on her deck until, at seven bells of the Morning watch, the mistico's boat sheered off from her side. It was bringing back Abel Jason to *Surprise*. By now many more of *Surprise's* crew had emerged on deck, including Simon, and whilst Jason's welcome could scarcely resemble that displayed for Simon, he was nevertheless very warmly greeted by all present as he stepped aboard, particularly Simon, before being hastened off to the cabin for breakfast with Pat, Simon and Tom Pickering.

As they settled at Pat's table, Jason began his account to an eager audience. 'We had remained three days in Dragomestre after our escape from the Turk frigate until a Greek gunboat, sent by Mavrocordato from Messalonghi, arrived to take us there. However, his Lordship declined the offer and determined to reach Messalonghi, free of obligation in his own vessel, and so we set off again in the mistico. We later stranded on the Scrofes rocks, his Lordship urging his attendants into the water to push us off whilst the Greek crew did nothing but fluster and lament their ill fortune. Fletcher, his Lordship's valet, and three or four servants struggled valiantly, and shamed the Greek crew into assistance until we were off. More Greek gunboats arrived the next morning, and in their company we have been beating all the way against the wind until we arrived yesterday evening: too late to navigate the shoals into Messalonghi, but we espied *Surprise* and tied up as near alongside her as we dared in the darkness.' Jason concluded his story, but added as an afterthought, 'His Lordship is undaunted by his near capture and demise. He remains in good heart for this venture. I admire him greatly.'

'And rightly so, his Lordship is a pearl amongst a bed of thorns,' Pat opined, muddling his metaphors, as his close companions had oft come to expect of him. 'What are his Lordship's plans, Jason?'

'I believe that he is preparing even now to go ashore, leaving at about ten o'clock.'

'Well,' said Pat, 'we will postpone our own sailing for one day, and accompany his Lordship ashore. His Lordship is deserving of our escort. Tom, prepare my barge and its crew, as best dressed as they can muster, if you will, and the barge is to be priddied particularly well today; fit for a Lord, for a Lord it is we will be carrying.'

'Aye aye, sir,' said Pickering, nodding.

At 10 a.m., Pat's barge came alongside the mistico, and Barton with great care assisted Lord Byron down the side and into the seat alongside Pat, Simon and Jason sitting in the seat ahead of and facing them. The crew had plainly done their best, Pat noted. All of the old *Tenedos* hands had retrieved, from the depths of their dunnage, and donned, their old watchet-blue jackets, which had never been seen on *Surprise*, and they had buffed the brass buttons until they shone brightly. Others without jackets of their own had begged the loan of them from their shipmates. All were attired in clean, starched and pressed white duck trousers, and little shoes highly polished to gleaming black, and wore low-crowned hats with the customary ribbon with the ship's name to the fore – run up by Whitaker, a mainmast hand who had been a tailor before being pressed in the year eleven. The barge crew's long pigtails had plainly all been combed out before being tidily replaited, and a better turned out barge crew Pat had never seen. 'Very creditable, lads, well done,' he said, beaming with pleasure, and reflecting that his crew did justice to the old saying: *You can always tell a ship by her boats.*

Byron himself was attired in a clean and freshly pressed red cloak, undoubtedly of military origin. He was wearing a golden metal helmet resembling something of ancient origin.

'Ancient Greek perhaps?' wondered Simon. He looked closely at Byron for a moment or two before speaking, Byron noticing his gaze. 'My Lord, I am but recently become an admirer, and speaking with the greatest presumption, a friend, for I hope that is how you may consider of me, and if you will forgive my remarks, your arrival in this place is of the very deepest significance. Might I say therefore, with infinite respect; that your cloak is most symbolically suited to your purpose this day, though perhaps the helmet less so? We may consider that the Greek need is for modern arms, and such a helmet may strike the observer as a relic.'

260

Byron considered the comment for a few seconds before leaning forward to grasp Simon's hand and replying, 'Thank you, Ferguson; that is a most prescient thought. I venture you are too polite to say what you really meant; that I look like a buffoon. It would please me were you to keep the helmet, as some small memento of my friendship for you too, for indeed that is my sincerest perception of you,' and with that he removed the helmet and placed it in the bottom of the barge.

'Welcome, my Lord,' said Pat, warmly, marvelling at the spirit and generosity of the man, his humanity so evident, yet preserving a humility that oft escaped others elevated to such heights.

'Thank you, O'Connor,' Byron replied, taking and shaking Pat's hand, smiling all about him; to Pat's scrutinising eye, the barge crew all plainly feeling honoured to be there in his presence.

'Barge away, Mr Pickering... row dry, Barton,' ordered Pat.

The sun was now free of the south-eastern cloud and shining brightly as they rowed across the calm, still waters of the lagoon, the winter day warming as the morning passed. Byron's arrival had been observed by the Greek ships anchored off the town, which fired their guns in salute as he passed by within Pat's barge. Word had also reached the town itself because the fortress began to echo the gunfire of the ships. Another twenty minutes steady rowing by the crew, none wishing to splash their most honoured passenger ever, and the barge pulled up on the beach of the town. Pat sprang ashore, helping Byron from the barge. Huge cheers broke out from the waiting crowd, which surged around the arrivals. Duncan, Pat was pleased to see, was standing alongside Mavrocordato. The Prince in all his ceremonial finery, stepped forward to welcome Byron, grasping his hand as the rest of the barge crew scrambled to the beach, the crowd cheering still, and the guns of the town continuing to fire their loud welcome in the background: fully a twenty-one gun salute.

Chapter Seven

In vain — in vain: strike other chords;
Fill high the cup with Samian wine!
Leave battles to the Turkish hordes,
And shed the blood of Scio's vine!
Hark! rising to the ignoble call —
How answers each bold Bacchanal!

Friday 23ʳᵈ April 1824   *aboard Surprise, off Candia*

The dawn had been quite exceptional, spectacular even; a glowing red orb rising above the haze, throwing a pink blanket over a sea quite devoid of any ripple, slowly turning orange, and finally yellow whilst burning through the few wispy cloud remnants lingering over the clearing mountain extremities of Candia off the larboard bow, the summit of Mount Ida prominent. With barely the slightest zephyr of wind to disturb the flaccid sails, the temperature being already so hot, the deep blue sky promising much greater warmth to come later, and with no respite of a cooling breeze in prospect, all aboard anticipated another scorching day.

Surprise had sailed southbound for nine days since leaving Argostoli, fighting to make only the slowest of progress, tacking frequently to make headway against strong southerly winds, but now she barely moved. The sound of creaking rigging was the solitary noise breaking the rare silence, with only the exception of an occasional bird call. Even so early in the day the windsails, rigged to provide a little relief to those below, could do nothing against the heat. Overnight, *Surprise* had glided with infinite slowness, and across the calmest of flat seas towards Candia, royals hoisted up and stuns'ls all boomed out, but all making no difference, arriving within distant sight of the islands' peaks shortly after the dawn, and scarcely closing since then.

The ship's bell, rung by Clumsy Dalby – who had seized the role with alacrity, and who struck the bell with unequalled vigour –

tolled eight bells. *Surprise's* officers stood on the quarterdeck, Duncan now returned and with them, all anxiously sweeping the horizon in every direction with their glasses, the crew on watch washing the decks: wholly unnecessarily so they thought, having done it every day for as long as anyone could remember, and scarcely a speck of anything necessitating cleaning could be found on them. The crew laboured with a sense of expectancy, an awareness of events about to happen; a sense of, if not foreboding, keenly felt anticipation. Of what they knew not, but every one of them had picked up the discreet signals, the frequent conferences of Pat's officers, their alertness with their glasses, and their urgings to the topmen to stay vigilant.

'How far off Candia are we would you think, Mr Prosser?'

'To pass Cape Vouxa, perhaps another four leagues, sir,' the master replied.

'What does the line signify, Mr Mower?'

'Barely half of one knot, sir: we may as well be anchored.'

'Very well; Mr Pickering, let us pipe the hands to breakfast while we are becalmed.' Pat descended the steps to the gun deck. 'Ah, Mr Marston, there you are, will you take a bite with me, I think there is still some bacon, if it ain't gone off, or sausage.' They entered the cabin together, Pat calling to his steward, 'Freeman, a fresh pot of tea, bacon if we have it, or sausages, eggs, soft tack; and enough for Mr Marston too.'

Murphy was also present, keenly aware of the sense of anticipation pervading the ship, and hastened as quickly as he could to the galley with Freeman to fetch Pat's breakfast so as to ensure no time was lost and his ear was returned as close to Pat's door as he dared without precipitating admonishment from his captain, who was, fortunately for both of them, long inured to Murphy's foibles and irritating shortcomings.

'Should we sight any Turks, Mr Marston, you may yet find some wet work below. I pray we do not, with Dr Ferguson remaining on Cephalonia to care for Sinéad,' Pat said, adding, 'Please take a seat, I doubt that Freeman will be long.'

'How was your wife, sir, when we departed Argostoli?'

263

'Oh, tolerably comfortable, and no more in danger, Dr Ferguson did assure me, though the prior days were as anxious as any I ever found at sea. The fever was thankfully broken. Sinéad remonstrated with me to sail when I declared that I would wait another day afore sailing on Mavrocordato's request to guard the flight of Tombazes from Candia. She quieted herself after accepting my promise to depart directly only if she would accept that Dr Ferguson remained to care for her. Nine days have passed since then, and with *Surprise* now almost becalmed whether we reach Candia afore the Egyptian regiments are there to seize Tombazes must be doubtful. Oddly, we have seen ne'er a one of the Greek fleet, which Mavrocordato assured me was bound for Candia too. There is no relying on your foreigner, Mr Marston, and this Greek enterprise is a damned fine pickle of fish.'

Marston did not dare to correct his captain's muddle, and just at that moment Freeman returned with their breakfast: a huge pan of coddle, highly spiced and peppered so as to disguise the advancing term and doubtful flavour of the sausages; coffee, toasted soft farl, baked fresh by Wilkins, a rare treat, offered as if in compensation for the ageing sausages; and one of the few remaining pots of Falmouth marmalade, though the butter, beyond rancid at the end, was long gone. Freeman set it on the cabin table, bowed his head, and withdrew to return to his station outside Pat's door. Pat nodded his thanks to Freeman and peered at the sausage dish, sniffing, as if to verify or assuage his doubts over the desirability of Wilkin's efforts, 'Allow me to help you to a little of this coddle.' He continued quickly as if to preclude any objection, 'I fancy Dr Ferguson will doubtless be following us in *Eleanor* by now. Reeve is a prodigious fine master of her, and with Codrington to spell him there will be no speedier vessel on God's ocean - if you will forgive my reference to our Lord?' Pat added hastily.

'No matter, sir, I imagine our Lord would wholly concur with your opinion,' Marston replied, smiling. 'Is the Greek cause now lost in Candia, sir?'

Pat looked up from ladling coddle into his guest's bowl. 'Sadly, it seems so. The Porte has sent its Egyptian vassal's army to subdue the rebellion. The Hydriot commander, Tombazes, has struggled unsuccessfully against the invasion for more than a year. He has now retreated to Loutro where he and his few remaining men are to be taken off by the Greek fleet afore they are overwhelmed. It seems that the Greek fleet has other matters to deal with, for we are here alone, but with this absence of wind neither *Surprise* nor any other ship, Greek or Turk, is likely to fetch Candia. Tombazes's men may soon find themselves sorely pressed, if they are not already,' Pat opined, gloomily, adding, 'We may yet have to employ sweeps.'

'Where is Loutro, sir? My knowledge of the geography of these parts is weak.'

'Oh, it is near Sfakia, on the south-west coast of the island; the province of some or other Greek band of brigands.'

'What conceivably could have happened to the Greek fleet, sir?'

'Without doubt they have a difficult task. The Turk is unfettered to arrive at any part of their coast and all their islands, to sack and plunder any of the Greek port towns. Perhaps they are already engaged in evacuation elsewhere? Perhaps their admirals have received reports of the Turk fleet movements, and sent their ships away to find them? Perhaps the crews have again refused to sail for want of pay? Certainly they have fine admirals in Miaoulis, Canaris, and others, and they do not lack for bravery. In the year twenty-two at Chios they defeated a Turk fleet, much larger than their own, with the deployment of fireships; the Turks being terrified of them. Even the Turk admiral was killed in the engagement after running his ship aground seeking an escape from the bourlotas, as the Greeks term them. No, 'tis far from sure who will win this war, but the advantage must still lie with the Greeks, for it is they who are defending their homes and their families. If only they would agree a consensus of government and military command, for the want of such is the Turk's greatest weapon, and we will be here for many a year yet until the Greeks can speak with one voice, of that I have no doubt. That is unless our lads develop the Greek approach, for want of pay.' Pat laughed out loud with great mirth at this thought. Marston smiled, pleased to see his captain in good spirits. The prior months of naval inactivity

265

following the distressing period of Simon's capture and release, and most recently his wife's severe illness, had taken its toll on him he thought. Now, as a first mission of some importance was developing, the becalmed state of *Surprise* was distinctly unhelpful. A sociable near hour passed until breakfast was finished; Pat looked to his companion, 'Come, let us go up and see what we are about.'

The studdingsails and royals had made little difference, *Surprise* was sailing, near drifting, with every stitch of canvas she possessed aloft, and made barely a knot. Three more dreary hours passed, and Pat had long returned to the shade of his cabin, when from the tops an excited shout was heard; indistinct, but clearly audible, as the cabin doors through to the gun deck remained open to catch the tiniest scrap of cooling breeze, but the words remained unrecognisable nevertheless. Pat let fall his cutlery on his plate, and abandoning his barely half-eaten second breakfast hastened up the steps to his quarterdeck.

'Mr Pickering, what's afoot?' he asked. 'Ships? Where away?'

Pickering indicated to larboard, towards the east, into the still lingering haze, 'Over there, sir. The topman thinks he sighted a ship, perhaps two, hull-down on the horizon, but I see nothing.'

Pat stared hard into his glass; the sun had climbed away from the horizon, and it no longer hurt his eyes to stare carefully, for long, tense moments, before he finally exclaimed, 'There! Four points off the bow. Look hard, Mr Pickering, they come and go. Damn that haze. Mr Mower, we will beat to quarters.'

'Clear for action, Mr Prosser,' Mower ordered the master.

Prosser shouted down to the deck, 'Beat to quarters.' *Surprise* having no marines aboard, the task was carried out by Clumsy Dalby.

Pat remained all the time peering into his glass, and then declared at last, 'I see no sails...., no sails. Why, they must be galleys, sails still furled. Turks! That is why we could not see them! Galleys! Have you ever seen such a vessel, Mr Mower? Well done that lookout. Half an hour more and the galleys would never have been sighted with the Candia headlands behind them. Who saw them, Mr Macleod?' Pat asked.

'Young Pennington, sir.'

'By God, that fellow has the very best of eyes,' said Pat, lowering the telescope, cleaning it with the briefest of wipes with his handkerchief before peering again through the indistinct, early morning haze, a thin wispy mist rising from the warmer waters into the colder air. 'Two galleys: we will be sore pressed, there is no doubt. There's a guinea in my purse for him, a capital hand. Well done Young Pennington.' Several more minutes passed; all the time Pat continued to gaze through his glass at the approaching galleys. Finally he spoke, very quietly, as if he did not wish his words to carry, 'Mr Macleod, we may shortly find ourselves in some difficulty. No wind to shift, nor manoeuvre; no means of training our guns to bear if they come for'ard or astern of *Surprise*, save our chasers. As galleys their bow and stern guns can fire only fore and aft. Most likely they have twenty-four-pounders, or even thirty-two's, which will outrange our guns, and they can row into any position to their advantage. They can stand off all day and beat us to a pulp. However, need teaches a plan. We must confuse them, as best we may. We will hoist a Turk pennant, and below it a yellow jack.'

'Would that be entirely regular, sir?' came the unexpected interjection from Marston, looking on, aghast, and with the most anxious of voice; eyebrows being raised by all on deck within earshot.

The interruption was such a gross breach of protocol that Pat himself was utterly taken aback, his mind solely focussed on the imminent threat from the galleys. He simply stared at Marston without expression for a bare few moments, his look becoming very cold, before turning back to his first. 'Mr Macleod, I want the Turks to see no one on deck. Every gunner is to crouch behind the ports, and not to show even the top of their head around them. Send a man to the heads, to lie there as if dead. Set everything aloft all ahoo, our royals and tops'ls all a'fluttering - and her courses too - everything all loose and flapping. We will look like Bedlam. Mr Mower, leave the gun ports closed but unshackled; prime the flashpans; send half a dozen shot to be heated in the galley stove, and run it hot so we see no smoke. We will let them come close, our deception will reel 'em in. Remember, Mr Mower, be sure to tell the captains of those two guns a'side firing red hot shot to load only reduced charges. It will serve us well if their balls do not break out of the Turk hulls, and so the better to start fires burning inside. Remind all other captains, of the eighteens that is, load reduced charges too; they will break scores more of splinters as they strike, and so better to kill their men. We will load both shot and canister for the first broadside: one hundred and forty iron balls from each of fourteen guns will quickly disable the rowers. For the second and thereafter we will load shot and grape too: much the better to cut up their rigging. For the carronades, load shot only for three, and aim low, so that they may smash holes in their hull, perhaps below their waterline, and then shot and grape to follow. We shall clear our quarterdeck from Turk sight.' Pat now turned to his cox'n, 'Barton, put the strongest twelve lads we have in my barge and eight more into the cutter. You are to command them both from the barge. Make fast the boats to *Surprise* at her bow, with short lines, thirty yards only, no more. Stay behind *Surprise,* close by her hull at the starboard beam, so the barge and cutter will not be seen by the Turks, and Barton,' Pat spoke gravely to his cox'n, 'it will be for you and your lads to haul her round by the bow when we signal, so that we may fire our guns; 'tis our only chance.'

'Aye aye, sir, twenty men into the boats, hide, and haul her round on your signal,' Barton repeated his instructions and hastened away to gather his men.

As the boats, filled with the chosen men, were being tied to *Surprise's* bow, Pat looked back at the galleys, still far distant, but clearly approaching. 'Mr Marston,' said Pat, quietly, to his immediate companion, 'You may care to make your preparations below.'

Marston appeared quite unprepared for Pat's prompt at that moment, the responsibility of ship's surgeon now thrust upon him, and the prospect of an engagement looming large. 'Those galleys, sir, will it be necessary to engage them? Perhaps flight would better serve our cause if we are to reach Candia and without hindrance to our purpose in that place?' The helmsmen and the master near the wheel exchanged shocked glances.

Pat's reply was infused with only the mildest of indignation. 'Do not think me a warmonger, Mr Marston, a death-or-glory merchant. I assure you I had rather see a brace of fine ships burnt and sunk than lose a single man of my crew killed or wounded. We have no wind, no means of flight. Those galleys will soon be upon us, before we know it, and to fight presents our only prospect for salvation.'

'Certainly, sir; pray forgive my doubtless ill-considered notion, but can we not fly His Majesty's colours, as *His Majesty's Hired Vessel Surprise*, as we were when charting the Ionian waters? And would they not then pass us by?' he pressed, a little nervously.

Pat looked again at his assistant surgeon and chaplain with mild astonishment and not least a modicum of irritation, and he replied with as much impassivity and formality as he could find. 'Why certainly we could, Mr Marston, until they asked our papers. And then we would be treated as pirates. Since we received our Greek letter-of-marque, to be taken with any other flag at our staff would condemn us to be hanged. No, we must either fight as a Greek or strike our colours as a Greek. We may hope that the Turks may not yet know of any frigate in Greek service, and that small thing may yet set things in our favour.' The latter point said more confidently than Pat felt.

Marston, now realising from Pat's tone of gentle rebuke that he had overstepped the mark, anxiously sought to make amends, 'I have expressed myself badly, sir: plainly I am not to teach you your trade; I beg you will forgive my impertinence, please accept my apologies, if you will.'

'Oh, I think we may overlook it this once, Mr Marston,' Pat relented, smiling, bearing no ill-will towards his chaplain, and his recollection of Marston's kindly words in the cabin before Simon's release and return so firmly registered in his mind, his respect for Marston undiminished. 'Mr Macleod, all sails loose to a bowline. We will likely need to shift away quickly, and at best speed. There will be no time to make sail. All canvas flapping will doubtless aid our deception.'

'Aye aye, sir.'

'Mr Mower,' said Pat, 'Prepare our marksmen. They are to stay out of sight, and on my mark to climb into the tops to fire down on the Turk officers only, *officers only*; make that plain to them, and were they to clear the Turk quarterdeck then gun captains next, but only *after* they have swept the galley quarterdecks clear. Each man is to carry two muskets, ready to fire, with powder and shot for six reloads. I doubt this business will last longer.'

'Very good, sir; we have ten men to send aloft with some competency with the musket.'

'Keep them all close below the bulwark 'til I shout,' Pat reiterated. 'Mr Pickering, all hands to keep silent as the Turks near, pass the word.'

An anxious half hour slipped by with infinite slowness until the nearing galleys became clearly visible without a glass. On *Surprise* not a soul could be seen, neither about the gun ports, nor on the quarterdeck where Pat and his companions crouched low, so as to remain out of sight. He turned to Marston, alongside him, and whispered 'God between us and all harm.' The chaplain only stared. All of Jemmy Ducks' brood had been taken below, and at the heads a very convincingly dead seaman lay over the prow. Barton and his men were waiting patiently, lashed alongside in the boats. Pat, lying on his chest on the deck, peered through his glass through a gun port wedged just ajar, scrutinising the approaching Turks.

'Mr Marston, will ye go below, sir? Ye may be needed in the cockpit presently. Afore ye ken the shot an' splinters will be a'flyin' aboot,' whispered Duncan, Marston lingering still on the quarterdeck and looking very dismayed.

'The wind is freshening, sir,' said Pickering quietly, as the loosened topsails began to flap, the southerly blowing once again.

'Aye, Mr Pickering, that may yet be our saviour,' Pat replied, adding, 'They are diverging now, the first heading to come at our bow, and the second to hold back, near on the line of our stern, as would I were I their captain. Doubtless they intend to position so as to rake us, one after the other. They are half a mile away now, no more. Our guns are all double-shotted?'

'Yes sir.'

'We will hold our fire for short range when our shot will smash straight through both sides, even double-shotted, and with grape or canister too.' More tense minutes passed. The only noises that could be heard were the loosened sails gently flapping and the creak of timbers, *Surprise* rocking with the most gentle of motion. The crouching crew held their silence, anxiously awaiting their orders. From the nearest Turk galley, closing from ahead of *Surprise*, came a hail. Her oars were raised, and the galley, a mere hundred yards or so away, began to slow perceptibly. From the Turk the shouts came louder, and more frequently. The second galley was some hundred yards or so behind her companion, but coasting to position herself at *Surprise's* stern; losing way as she too slowed, her oars raised. The moment was eerily quiet, merely the slap of wave against hull breaking near total silence, as the vessels converged. Time, to Pat's mind, seemed to be standing still. He looked again at his watch, mentally noting the time. Never before had the closing seconds to an engagement ever passed so slowly. Within a few further minutes Pat judged the critical moment had arrived, and leapt to his feet to shout his orders. 'Note down the time, Mr Pickering, and give the order to our boats - to row as if all our lives depend on it, for they surely do.'

Pickering leaned over the side and bellowed to the men below in the boats, 'ROW, lads, ROW for all ye are worth!'

'Mr Prosser, strike the Turk flag and the yellow jack; hoist Greek colours. Swiftly, gentlemen, to your guns; go below, if you will,' this to Pickering and Mower. As they hastened to the companionway Pat rushed forward to look down over the waist rail to his gunners on the gun deck below. 'Now lads!' he shouted through his speaking trumpet, 'Pull those guns out, swiftly now!'

The change aboard *Surprise* was instant: up sprang sixty men on the quarterdeck, and gun port lids were hauled up. On the gun deck a hundred more hastened to run out their guns. The eighteens

271

on each side began to be hauled out; at each six men were heaving and sweating to shift their near two tons weight until the gun mouths protruded through their ports. At the two guns held back their crews waited. From the galley came four men carrying two red hot shot in tongs which they hurriedly loaded into the two remaining guns, numbers seven and nine, *Hurricane* and *Delilah*, of the larboard side. The unfamiliar Greek flag, blue stripes bold on white, fluttered lively at the jack-staff in the strengthening wind, as if with its own vitality. No one aboard *Surprise* had time to notice or consider the strange flag. The startled Turk galley had also sprung into life, and resumed rowing. Urgent shouting of orders and whips cracking could plainly be heard by all on *Surprise* before the galley's bow guns spoke with a fearsome thunder, blasting roundshot and flames from their barrels. Great clouds of bilious smoke thrust out, enveloping the gap between *Surprise* and the galley, near off her bow, the two vessels just a mere fifty yards apart. Fortunately, the galley shot flew high, making a sound like tearing silk in passing twelve feet or more over *Surprise's* quarterdeck.

'Greek slave gunners amongst the galley crew perhaps sighting their country's flag at *Surprise's* jack and firing high?' was the thought that struck Pat. The swell too was noticeably increased in the past hour, and the galley's bow alternatively rose and fell as she approached. Pat pondered on this as he looked about the sails and rigging. Little damage was evident on *Surprise* save for some holes and tears in her main course and foresail – which had not been furled as they would normally be in an engagement, they being left loosely hung as part of Pat's deception – and a section of rigging had been torn away. *Surprise's* marksmen were sent hurrying up the shrouds, their burden of two muskets being no weight at all in their haste. Pat leaned far over the side and shouted encouragement, 'Haul hard, lads!' to the men in the barge and the cutter, the twelve and the eight, who were now pulling frantically, as they had never rowed before, and gradually, in agonisingly slow progress, *Surprise* began to come round by her bow.

'Hold fire! Hold fire! Not yet! Not yet!' shouted Pat over the rail and down to his officers and gunners; Pickering and Mower standing just below the boat stations, forward of the quarterdeck, repeated his orders. A further long minute passed, Pat near biting through his tongue, looking about and behind him, studying the approaching second galley with some anxiety for a long, long ten seconds, a lifetime in such desperate moments. From aloft on *Surprise* a ragged musket fire was opened upon the Turk quarterdeck, and several figures on it fell down, stricken.

'The Turks will be reloading, sir,' remarked Prosser unnecessarily, he being more than a little nervous, adding, 'The second galley nears our stern quarter.' *Surprise* had now been hauled further round, and although no more than a little way past half way to parallel with the forward galley all her guns could just be brought to bear, their shouting captains having driven their sweating crews to haul the gun carriages round to their very limit.

'FIRE! FIRE!' shouted Pat with all his voice, waving his hat, and the ear-shattering crescendo of noise was near instantly reached as all of *Surprise's* larboard battery opened fire almost simultaneously, great flashes of orange fire and smoke belching out from the guns and the smashers; two red hot shot amongst the missiles; the deck shaking violently and the masts quivering. *Surprise's* crew had not missed, could not possibly miss, the distance now no more than forty yards. Along the galley side from the seventeen shot strikes great gaping holes could be seen by Pat and all his larboard crew; many of her oars being smashed and many more missing; much of her bulwark was battered clean away; her bow guns thrown aside by shot strikes. From the two thousands of canister shot projectiles the effects at such short range were horrifying: dead and dying men lay strewn across her deck, not an officer could be identified, and no shouting of any further orders could be heard amidst the carnage aboard her.

On *Surprise* the gun crews had no time to stare; amidst the shouts of 'Hurrah! Hurrah!' the most frantic reloading was taking place, and the frenetic activity on the decks was spurred by the orders and curses of the gun captains, the powder monkeys rushing as fast as they could shift to bring fresh charges. All along the larboard side the guns were being wormed, sponged, charges and wads rammed home, shot and grape reloaded, and guns run out as fast as any crew had ever managed to do so before. With *Surprise* turning as the desperate rowers hauled her round, the second galley was near directly off *Surprise's* stern, still one hundred yards off, and none of *Surprise's* ready starboard guns could yet bear on her. The barge and cutter crews were still rowing frantically, not yet tiring, Barton's shouts of encouragement hardly audible. Few could still hear with any clarity, the noise of the guns drowning out all else. *Surprise* was coming round further each minute by the head yet it did not look to Pat as if *Surprise* could fire before the second Turk fired, and so all attention remained on the first galley, clearly stricken very badly and aflame too, black smoke rising from amidships. She was plainly shearing off, some semblance of command restored, and a very desultory rowing could be seen at her beam. *Surprise,* larboard guns swiftly reloaded, fired again, delivering another fiery series of hammer blows on the first galley, and this time firing grape too. The one hundred and forty missiles inflicted the severest carnage on the galley crew, still reeling from the roundshot and canister of the first broadside. It seemed as if the deck had been swept clean, barely a man was left standing, or sitting; scores lay dead athwart her deck and on her benches; dozens of corpses had already been thrown into the water. The first galley was clearly in great distress, presenting little danger, and so could be relegated from Pat's attention. He turned away to consider the second, less than sixty yards or so away, and her guns, he thought, bar a miracle could not possibly miss *Surprise*.

'Lie down, lads. Lie down!' shouted Pat, 'Flat as you can, lie down,' and, convention abandoned, he threw himself on to his chest on the quarterdeck. Instantly, BOOM, BOOM thundered, as the second galley fired. The near shots, so close, did not miss their target. The sound of shot ripping through the air was heard, as it tore across *Surprise's* deck, cutting rigging, rising and tearing foremast sails. Pat's command to his men to throw themselves down to the deck had probably saved several of their lives. He turned his head and looked about him whilst still prone, seeing anxious faces staring back towards him from the quarterdeck gunners. Within minutes the galley's guns roared again. This time the shot entered *Surprise* below them, striking and smashing through planking, breaking the companionway and its steps from the quarterdeck to the gun deck into kindling, having entered through the great cabin, shattering much of the glass in its windows. One shot smashed into the capstan and the second struck one of the guns amidships before ricocheting off into the heavens.

'UP lads, UP now!' shouted Pat, leaping to his feet. 'Mr Pickering,' he leaned over the rail and shouted down to the gun deck, 'send the larbowlins to the braces and set every yard and sail all a-tanto, topgallants and all. We will need to catch every breath of wind if we are to survive this day.'

'Aye aye, sir: larbowlins to make all sail.'

On *Surprise*'s gun deck, even as many of their comrades of the larboard gun crews swarmed to their task, the starboard gun crews waited anxiously for the command to fire their guns. Double red hot shot had been loaded in those two nearest the ship's galley, *Pure Poison* and *Old Nick*, numbers eight and ten. On the barge and the cutter the crews were tiring, drenched in their own sweat, breathing heavily, and strength near gone. Yet still they valiantly pulled at their oars, but very feebly now. Fortunately, their efforts were no longer necessary, as the second galley was now near abeam *Surprise*, to starboard, but backing her oars frantically. The first, to larboard, had plainly had enough, had broken off any intent of further action: command had been restored to her, and her few remaining unwounded oarsmen were plainly striving to shift her away from *Surprise* as best they could. *Surprise*'s starboard gun crews now had the second galley in their sights, the galley being a bare forty yards off her quarter. A few shots still rang out from the tops, as the last of the marksmen's powder and shot was fired, seeking officer victims aboard the second galley, although the still-billowing smoke much obscured any targets.

Pat looked about him, seeing many a gun captain's enquiring face looking towards him, and in that same moment he observed with a near overwhelming surge of grateful relief – which welled up from deep within him, suppressing momentarily his anxiety –

275

that there seemed fortunately few casualties. He raised his arm, and sensing the roll of the ship being at the precise position to unleash the cannonade in an instant brought it sweeping down, his cap in hand, with a concurrent shout of 'FIRE!' to his starboard crews, his shout echoed by Pickering and Mower. All guns, it seemed, fired together instantly, with a cacophony of deafening, roaring, thunderous sound, the deck pulsating and the masts shivering violently under the great strain: vast long orange flames belched out, the guns sending their deadly missiles on their way, for *Surprise* too, at this range, could not possibly miss. Frantically the crews rushed to reload their guns, the anxious captains urging their sweating men to haste amidst more shouts of 'Hurrah!' The powder boys were running amidst the frenetic activity of guns recoiling and men heaving them out again to bring their fresh charges from below, shot together with grape being rammed into the barrels. As each gun was run out it was fired again without delay or any order being given, and a second ragged barrage erupted again from *Surprise's* starboard side, hurling more death and destruction at the galley. Thick, sulphurous smoke enveloped all on deck in its bitter, choking maw. In moments, as it began to clear, blown off to larboard by the still freshening wind, all aboard *Surprise* could see that the galley was utterly destroyed. Its larboard side was near crushed along its length by the heavy blows from the great guns, the carronades in particular firing a very heavy ball and doing frightful damage. Barely a solitary intact oar remained, and a huge list was now remarked upon. Of the galley's boats, wheel, capstan, and binnacle there was no trace left; her mainmast had been shot away, its sail half in and half out of the water; alongside it floated great swathes of timber jetsam, many dead bodies visible all about it; smoke rose from the galley midships, as the embedded, red hot shot did its work.

On the galley, all was in chaos: oarsmen struggled to rise from their positions; a very few men at her ends were striving still to ready their guns; shouts of command could still be heard from determined officers, urging shocked and stricken men to action. At that moment, *Surprise* fired again, the third volley not nearly concurrent as each gun crew reloaded and fired as soon as the grapeshot could be rammed into the muzzle and the gun run out again through its port. At a bare forty yards distance the carnage on the galley was immense, the shocked survivors of the first and second discharges were swept away as if by a hurricane. The devastation wreaked by the shrieking hail of grape left not a single man standing, or sitting; bodies upon mangled bodies lay prostrate all over her deck; blood ran in small streams across the deck, and out from the scuppers. Shrill, shrieking wails of agony could plainly be heard from men who would never be whole again.

Pat averted his gaze from the galley, the ghastly, gory business being done. The horror unleashed from his guns had removed all danger to *Surprise* with just five broadsides. He shouted, 'Cease fire. Cease fire. All hands to the braces.' He shouted down to his second, 'Mr Pickering, recover our lads from the boats. Swiftly now, afore the galleys turn about; we are still vulnerable to an enterprising captain, and one against two; though I doubt they have still any spirit for a fight. Mr Prosser, luff up and touch her; south as best you can.'

'Aye aye, sir; are they finished, would you think?'

'Were I their captain I would be hastening towards land at best speed, so as to beach and save what may. Let us capitalise on this freshening wind, and be away as quick as we can. We have still to embark Tombazes and his men,' ordered Pat, huge physical tremors of relief shaking his body; his thoughts mixed: anxious feelings of caution tempering the momentary jubilation he felt at a near miraculous victory, for assuredly that it was.

The Turks would not fight again, and might not even make any beach, let alone reach home, the damage they had suffered being so extreme. The attention of all aboard *Surprise* now turned to gaining as much speed as she could achieve in the stiffening breeze, for it was still no more than that. Topgallant yards and slings were lashed tight to their masts, all the yards were braced at their extremes to harvest what they could, and studdingsails were rigged again on their booms. The Greek flag now streamed vigorously at the jack. The barge and cutter crews had been recovered, utterly exhausted and dripping, so little strength left that they were barely able to clamber up the ship's side, as the boats were left in tow, bobbing far astern on lengthened ropes. All the rowers collapsed on the deck, the ship's boys bringing them water which all gulped gratefully; pint after welcome pint, speech quite beyond them.

'Well done, lads. Well done,' Pat found a moment for a grateful shout of praise and a wave of his hat from his quarterdeck before returning to gaze on the galleys, for they were now three hundred yards or more astern of *Surprise*, not moving in the water, and more smoke visibly rising from both of them. Pickering and Mower had now joined him on the quarterdeck. Of Duncan, who had shifted below to the gun deck at the beginning of the battle, at Pat's bequest to help his other lieutenants, *Surprise* having no midshipmen, there was no sign. 'Mr Mower, go below and ask Mr Marston of our casualties, if you will,' said Pat softly, through dry lips; great fatigue now clearly evident in his face, and sweat having streaked the black powder smoke particles engrained in every pore of his skin; a bloody gash evident above his eye, and blood running down the side of his face.

'Aye aye, sir,' Mower replied, wearily, tension releasing as the adrenalin rush subsided and exhaustion set in.

'Water, massa?' asked Freeman, emerging beside Pat, and proffering a cloth and the ladle from a bucket he was carrying.

'Thankee Freeman, thankee; obliged,' was all a grateful Pat could say, gulping greedily, the water gushing from the ladle into and out of his parched mouth as he swallowed the warm pints, pausing to spit to wash away the foul and acrid flavour of the great guns' smoke whilst an anxious Murphy strived to mop the blood from his face even as Pat waved him away.

The galleys were still watched closely until they had been left some five hundred yards in *Surprise's* wake as a very weary crew settled to recover from their exertions, the ship's boys bringing water buckets along the deck to quench the thirst of the crew, for the sun had yet to reach its zenith and the air temperature was measured already at eighty-seven degrees on the Fahrenheit scale.

'I think they will have their hands full for some hours or more,

Tom,' Pat said to Tom Pickering, relief now awash in his voice, and formality slipping away. Mower had returned to the quarterdeck. 'How many men have we lost, James? God, how I wish the Doctor was here with us.'

Mower wiped smoke from his eyes and sweat from his brow, and with the barest smile of relief reported, 'I am pleased to say, sir, that we have suffered no deaths, though Mr Macleod has been knocked down. He is below, unconscious; Mr Marston is tending him. Ten more men are being treated: eight with splinters, two of them severe. One of the new gunners has a crushed foot, as he did not move swiftly enough when his gun recoiled. The last has a severe burn on his leg from the red hot shot; I know not yet how it came about,' Mower concluded.

'A cheap victory,' said Pickering, adding, 'Here, sir; take my scarf, for you are bleeding well from above your eye.'

'Yes, indeed it was, Tom; thankee; 'tis but a scratch. I thought we surely would be dished that time. I find I care little for the taste of this victory. Perhaps I find I am becoming old?' said Pat, wiping a renewed small stream of blood away from the side of his face.

'And only twenty minutes since the first galley opened upon us,' Mower added.

Pat looked his third squarely in the face for a few moments, as if collecting his thoughts from far away before replying, very quietly, 'Would anyone wish such horror to last longer, James? I collect that *Chesapeake* struck to *Shannon* after just fifteen minutes, only eleven of them firing. I was there, and that was a bloody affair: Captain Broke severely wounded and poor Lawrence of *Chesapeake* - he lingered so - losing his life. No, twenty minutes is plenty enough for me: such bloody butchery. I venture the Turks have lost scores of men, and most likely many Greeks amongst them; galley slaves, poor souls. Now they will know there is a frigate in Greek service, and our next engagement will afford us no surprise.'

The aft companionway being smashed to pieces by a ball strike, Pat walked forward to the waist, and descended the steps to the gun deck. He paced very slowly amongst his weary gunners and crew, looking at each of them as he passed by, staring about him and assessing the damage, exchanging a word here and there, passing many a compliment, and asking of many an old shipmate until he returned to the point amidships where his men could congregate about him and hear his words. He halted and the animated discussions amongst the crew faded slowly as all became aware he waited to speak. The hubbub had now ceased, and the slap of the bow wave along the hull was again audible, *Surprise's* speed increasing with strengthening wind. The sound of cut shrouds slapping against halliards, against yards and masts, intermittently interrupted Pat's words to his men, spoken with great pride, as he stood amongst them. 'Well done, lads. Well done, every one of you. A bloody business, but never better gun handling did I ever see on *Tenedos* in all our actions, and you have my compliments and my thanks.' There was a growl of appreciation from scores of voices before Pat continued, 'Lads, we cannot tarry here to take prizes, nor to sink those galleys, for we have still to reach Candia where our mission is to relieve the Greeks awaiting embarkation and fleeing the Turk forces nearing Loutro, for they will assuredly be lost without our help should any Turk ships encounter their barkys. Let us eat now, rest a while, afore we clean guns and ship, but remain vigilant, for the Turk has many more ships and we are but one. Mr Tizard, it seems that you have much work to do,' smiled Pat, waving to the smashed planking and the quarterdeck steps.

'D'reckly, sir,' replied the carpenter, cheerfully.

Pat continued his tour, stepping down to the lower deck where a still busy Marston laboured amongst the injured, helped by three assistants, including Mrs Boswell, the gunner's wife; one of the few women permitted to sail with them by long convention. Fortunately, the generous dispensing of laudanum had quieted the agonies of the four most badly wounded seamen: one with a foot quite crushed by the recoiling gun carriage of *Hell's Mouth*, amputation being at the forefront of Marston's deliberations, but inexperience and doubt staying his hand; a second who had taken a deep splinter right through his thigh, fortunately missing all the major blood vessels. It was a large splinter which Marston had struggled to remove, and he had succeeded only with the man strapped to the gun room table, with two assistants to hold his struggles, and one to quieten his screams; the injured man biting down on a block held in his mouth to safeguard his tongue, as the splinter was drawn back and out in two agonising minutes. The third casualty had taken a significant splinter into his chest, penetrating his lung, and his life expectancy was now short, draining away like the red froth bubbling from his mouth and nose, Marston finding the wound far beyond his limited competency to treat. The fourth, a man burned by the red hot shot, William Currie, had also been given plentiful laudanum, and now slept a deep sleep, his pain temporarily suppressed for some hours whilst his brother sat by him. Six others were awake and talking amongst themselves, their smaller and less critical splinter wounds all cleaned and dressed by Marston. All would, bar any infection, recover completely.

'How ... how is it, Mr Marston?' asked Pat, anxiously, his concern very evident in his voice, low and wavering.

Marston looked up, wiping the sweat from his brow with the back of his bloody hand before replying to his captain, quietly but with firm conviction in his voice. 'Sir, I believe I may answer for all but one of these men. I am very fearful for Symes here, who I am not competent to treat. I doubt that even the finest surgeon could preserve him. I shall keep him as comfortable as can be until he is gone. He will be with God this day. He has an hour, perhaps two; I doubt more.'

Pat stooped down to the cot, and looked at his stricken shipmate, great anxiety plain in Pat's face. He stared for some moments at the unconscious Symes, whose breathing was greatly laboured, gently taking his hand, and he whispered, 'Ye are not alone, Symes. Your shipmates are here, with ye. All are hereabouts.'

Marston, determined to return his own attentions to his patients, interrupted Pat's gaze and silent thoughts after a long minute, 'Mason should recover, given time. It will be some weeks at least, perhaps months, afore he will be fit and about on the leg that took the splinter. Edwards here may lose his foot, but I will defer to

Doctor Ferguson on that, and I will keep him tolerably comfortable until then. The six men over there will be fit within a few weeks,' he concluded, waving his hand towards the more fortunate half a dozen of the wounded.

'How is Mr Macleod? Where is he?' The question whispered.

'Freeman and Old Jim Lamb have taken him to his cot. His head was struck hard, a splinter most likely; fortunately its force was surely spent when it struck him for there is no wound, save a scratch or two. He is unconscious, a great swelling on his head. Freeman remains with him, attending, should he awake.'

'When will he recover?' Pat asked, nervously.

'Sir, I can saw, cut, stitch, and dress wounds. His wound is far beyond my skills. Our Lord may preserve him, but I can do nothing. Rest is the only remedy. We must leave him be, sir; silence will be beneficial. We will pray for him.'

'Thank you, Mr Marston,' murmured Pat, looking back at Symes, his relief at so small a butcher's bill tempered by the impending loss of one of his crew, Symes, a long-serving Tenedos and a Wesleyan elder too, if Pat's memory served him; and Duncan's uncertain, perhaps critical, status.

'I must see that wound above your eye.'

'Oh, 'tis nothing, a scratch.'

'That's as may be, but an inch lower and you would have required Nelson's patch. I will attend you later.'

'Thank you … *Michael*,' Pat repeated his thanks very quietly, and left Marston to his ministrations. He walked aft, to Macleod's cot, and looked at his unconscious friend for some minutes until he nodded to Freeman and walked slowly and disconsolately back the length of the deck, to and up the for'ard steps, looking again in assessment at the treated casualties. He paced aft along the gun deck, nodding to his men in passing; though the after-battle exhaustion, the onrushing severe debilitation of his energy which came every time with the release of tension, and the great shock of finding his friend so dangerously wounded left him unable to speak with any of them. He nodded to several enquiring faces staring at him as he paced the length of the gun deck, his thinking frozen, and he scarcely noticed the blood oozing all down the side of his face.

Back in the great cabin a very tired Pat sat alone at his table, deeply unhappy, his head in his cupped hands, his chair amidst hundreds of glass shards scattered all over the deck from his shattered cabin lights, barely a pane remaining intact, the adrenalin rush of the battle near gone, and exhaustion draining his every fibre as its successor. Gratefully, he sipped a large tot of fiery Greek brandy accompanied by strong black coffee, freshly brewed by Freeman. Pat was reflecting on the engagement and the casualties when Murphy entered, together with his chum, Old Jim Lamb, another long-serving veteran of *Tenedos*'s many voyages, and these days still serving as cook's assistant and Murphy's dogsbody.

'Well, Jim here will clean up the cabin, sorr, an' Freeman will fetch yer dinner d'reckly. Will I take a look at that scratch on yer 'ead, sorr? 'Tis still all a'bleedin' o'er your collar?' asked Murphy, concern in his voice.

Pat slowly raised his head, his reply very quiet, near despair, 'Oh! Thankee, Murphy, a wet cloth will serve: 'tis nothing. And dinner will be welcome, I am fair clemmed. Would you ask Mr Pickering and Mr Mower if they would care to join me? Pass the word for the carpenter. Perhaps Mr Tizard could board over some of these broken windows later?'

Murphy was gone when Pat looked up again, but within, it seemed, bare moments his officers had joined him; and Freeman had returned with a large pot of lobscouse, bowls and all, Old Jim Lamb clutching two bottles of claret and glasses. Murphy fussed about his captain, wiping the still flowing blood from his forehead and the side of his face, and would have pressed on to clean the shirt with Pat in it had Pat not waved him off with a softly murmured, 'Thankee Murphy, thankee Jim,' as Lamb was affectionately addressed by all aboard, the captain included. 'Gentlemen, we shall not stand on ceremony this day. Please, allow me to help you to this food whilst 'tis still hot,' said a very muted Pat, as he ladled out generous bowls, and pushed them to his officers, realising in that moment that he was very hungry, and had eaten nothing since leaving his breakfast uneaten. Mower poured the wine, and for a few minutes all three said nothing and ate hungrily, the lobscouse soon devoured, yet the wine remainder still lingered in the bottle.

When they had finished eating none spoke; all looked to the others as if seeking to avoid any inappropriate comment as Murphy busied about them, collecting the plates. Pat looked up to his steward as Murphy's hand hovered about the bottle; he could not shake from his mind the sight of Duncan lying unconscious in his cot. 'Murphy, will you kindly take the cold ham and a jug of ale, and set it alongside Mr Macleod? Mr Marston will be busy for many an hour, and I would not care for Mr Macleod to come round in the night with thirst and no bite at hand.'

'Well, sorr; I will be taking turn and turn about with Freeman; sitting with Mr Macleod, until he does,' Murphy replied, no trace of the curmudgeon in his voice.

'Thankee, Murphy.... thankee kindly,' whispered Pat, nodding gratefully to his steward.

It was Mower who spoke first, seeking to lift the gloomy ambience in the cabin, and in breach of the custom that the officers did not speak except to reply to their captain. 'A bloody business, sir: there must have been scores and scores of dead and wounded on the second galley from the close firing, and after our grape I could not see a soul sitting or standing on her deck.'

Pickering too had sensed the mood, and seeking to lift his captain's spirits added his own observation. 'The first galley took a pounding too. I doubt either will see the Golden Horn again.'

Pat looked up at his officers for a few moments and settled his glass on the table. He licked away the blood from his lips, trickling still from the gash above his eye, and his quietly spoken words seemed to struggle from afar, a long way back; pulled from deep down in his memory, 'At Trafalgar, I collect when *Colossus* took *Swiftsure* – the Frenchie that is – I was serving on her as third for a few months in those days, we had inflicted near five hundred casualties in her crew of seven hundred, and her sides ran red. It was said that *Victory's* first broadside, fired at Villeneuve's flagship,

Bucentaure, inflicted four hundred casualties and smashed or shifted twenty guns on her decks. It is assuredly a bloody business we are engaged in, gentlemen. We may take small comfort from the thought that the Greek cause is just ... and our very few casualties.' Pat took another draught from his glass and, no one else caring to speak further, he resumed, his voice revealing his sorrow, his fatigue. 'We will lose another old shipmate this day. Poor John Symes: for many a year he made his way, with me, with us; I think since the year six. I collect he was with us, alongside of me, when we captured *Half Moon*, seven long years ago or more. To be sure, our lease on this life is short.'

Saturday 24th April 1824   off Sfakia, Candia

'Good morning, Mr Pickering,' said Pat as he stepped up to the quarterdeck shortly after dawn. 'Anything sighted?'

'An hour ago, sir: a schooner, over there,' Pickering replied, waving towards the larboard bow. 'About two leagues off when sighted, tacking out from Lautro. She is making heavy weather of it with this south-westerly directly against her. Nothing else have we seen these past three hours.'

Pat peered through his glass for a few minutes, looking at the mast tops of the far distant schooner before declaring, 'Let us come about, Mr Pickering. We will shift in towards her: slowly now. It may be our man, though precious few troops could he carry in such a small vessel.' A near hour of steady convergence passed, and the schooner came within hailing distance. *Surprise* was flying her Greek flag. It was fluttering proudly at the top and very visible in the strong south-westerly wind. Pat turned to his second who stood alongside him; Marston and Jason had come up to the quarterdeck too. 'Let us edge closer; Mr Prosser, port the helm and bring us to thirty yards off her beam.' The distance narrowed slowly, and all standing on the schooner's deck became plainly visible. Of troops there was little sign, perhaps a score or so of men on her larboard bulwark, all staring at *Surprise*, but of recognition of her presence from the schooner there was none. Near her wheel her captain stared stonily ahead, as did his companion, better garbed than the

285

typical seaman. 'Mr Jason, were you to hail them in the Greek tongue, friendly-like, we may discover if they carry the man we are seeking to escort to the Morea, to Monemvasia,' a very weary Pat suggested.

'Of course, sir,' Jason replied, pleased to be of some small service. He took up Pat's speaking tube and leant over the fife rail. 'We are here to escort the Harmost,' Jason bellowed in Greek, his words carried with clarity by the wind, adding, '*Surprise:* from Messalonghi, from Mavrocordato.'

This latter hail produced a reaction on the schooner. The well-garbed man standing alongside the captain entered into conversation with him, and after a few minutes both waved across to *Surprise.* The schooner shifted closer until they were separated by a bare thirty yards or so when her captain entered into rapid dialogue with Jason, the words plain across the short gap.

'It is Manolis Tombazes, sir; bound for Monemvasia in the Morea. He thanks us for our guardian presence and bids us accompany him there,' Jason reported after his exchange.

'Tell him we will stay close by him all the way.' The rendezvous and brief greeting satisfactorily concluded, Pat turned to his men, 'Let us now enjoy our breakfast. Mr Marston, Mr Jason; will you join me in the cabin? Mr Pickering, we will keep this wind on her larboard bow, keep her close-hauled and northbound. Once we have passed the cape bear away for Cerigo, and away from this place as swiftly as we can. There may be many more Turks about this island.'

Sunday 25ᵗʰ April 1824   *south of Cerigo*

Surprise, sailing large; with topgallants and royals all filled; and flying along at nine knots with studdingsails boomed out, encountered the Greek fleet shortly after dawn. The fleet had evacuated many hundreds of refugees, thousands even from Candia to Monemvasia, but hauled off after the arrival of a powerful Turk squadron patrolling the north coast of Candia to intercept Greek seaborne reinforcement, or evacuation; the army of Ibrahim now having seized virtually all the island.

The task of escorting Tombazes was handed over to the Greek fleet, *Surprise* parting with a single gun salute and setting a north-westerly course to return to Cephalonia. Pat was keenly mindful of his wife's illness, and although she was recovering he remained anxious to see her. He was also keen to secure Simon's attention to Edward's crushed foot, and its probable necessary amputation. Duncan remained unconscious. The seaman with the lung splinter, Symes, had fought hard for his life and lingered, but he had died shortly after midnight, and, it being Sunday, Marston was to speak of him before burial and the customary Sunday service.

After breakfast, the crew mustered to divisions. They gathered on the gun deck; so many that some stood as far forward as the galley, the majority standing fore and aft of the mainmast. Pat and his officers shifted down to the gun deck as the crew assembled. The topmen remained aloft, ever alert, and the only other men not present were the men at the helm and the injured, who remained below. The Wesleyans, four score or more of them, had turned out in their best white attire, washed and starched; every man adorned with a purple scarf, their customary colour for funerals; in due deference and respect to their deceased comrade, Symes having been one of their number. At six bells of the Forenoon watch the temperature had risen steadily to a baking hot eighty-five degrees, but the still strong south-westerly wind did little to cool the assembled crew. Marston waited to begin the service. Behind him, Pat and his officers stood, hats removed, looking silently forward at the gathered crew, the Wesleyans prominent at the front. With a sharp tap of a fid on the repaired capstan, Mr Prosser captured the hands' attention, and the assembly came to order.

Pat stared at his men for some moments in silent contemplation, his gaze roving across them, picking out near faces he long remembered from his earliest commands; nearly all he could see were old *Tenedos* hands. The crew quietened, as all became aware he was waiting to speak. Pat was, of course, oft acquainted with death and funerals at sea, but the first such in many years struck hard at his mind's equilibrium; and it was some minutes, the crew holding their silence, not a single whisper uttered, before he was able to begin, the bleak significance of the moment weighing heavily in his thoughts. He removed his hat, tucked it under his arm, and began. 'Lads, we are gathered this day to respect our old shipmate, John Symes, who has sadly lost the number of his mess: long-serving with us these many years on our dear *Tenedos,* and now *Surprise;* 'tis assuredly a loss to us all.' There was a general murmur of accord in the briefest of pauses before Pat continued, finding difficulty with his words, 'Our friend, John Symes, has crossed the bar for the final time, but let us remember him, today and long in our future.' Pat looked about him again for a few moments, as if seeking guidance in this, the most painful of his duties, and then resumed, speaking slowly and softly, 'I have asked Mr Marston to speak a few words... afore we bury our shipmate.'

Pat stepped back, to the side of the smashed companionway, and Marston stepped forward to the makeshift lectern. The chaplain began to speak, a little slowly at first yet with the assurance of deep conviction, his words steady, 'I am mindful of a prior eulogy, a very famous one by Pericles, at the end of a previous Greek war, long past. I could never do better than to borrow just a few words of that most magnificent speech, so famous in Greek history.' Marston paused for a few moments to gaze upon his audience, all silent, all reflecting on their past acquaintanceship with their lost shipmate, John Symes. From all about them, from the air, and from *Surprise* herself, the customary sounds of their sea-going routine, of gulls calling, of the bow wave slapping on the hull, of the creaking rigging, all pressed on them with particular clarity as Marston took a deep breath and resumed, 'Pericles said this: *In doing good we are unlike others; we make our friends by conferring not by receiving favours. Such a man may benefit his country or his cause whatever the obscurity of his condition. On the battlefield their feet stand fast in the confidence of freedom, and in a frank and fearless spirit, and in an instant, at the height of their fortune, they passed away from the scene, not of their fear, but of their glory.*' Marston paused again to look up, sweeping his gaze across the gathering. All remained silent, quite still. In the reverential silence he continued, '*The value of such a spirit is not to be expressed in words, but in foreign lands there dwells also an unwritten memorial of them, graven not on stone, but in the hearts of men. Make them your examples, and esteeming courage to be freedom and freedom to be happiness, do not weigh too nicely the perils of war.* We bid our farewell to our comrade, our friend, our brother, John Symes; may he rest in peace.' Marston's short reading found favour with all his listeners, grave nods and murmurs of 'hear him' signalling their accord with the deep sentiments expressed in Pericles' eulogy. Marston took another deep breath, looked about him again, and resumed speaking. 'We will conclude this sad day with but a fragment of Psalm one hundred and seven: *They that go down to the sea in ships: and occupy their business in great waters; these men see the works of the Lord: and his wonders in the deep.'* As Marston finally concluded and raised his head to gaze at his audience Pat looked to the four sombre Wesleyans holding the bier on which John Symes lay, bound in his hammock, two eighteen-pound shot at his feet, and at Pat's sad and silent nod they tilted the bier through the open gun port and John Symes slid overboard to his watery grave.

Tuesday 27ᵗʰ April 1824   *approaching Argostoli*

In the last flickering moments of the fading light in the dusk, little wind also remaining, *Surprise* slowly came about in the approach channel into Argostoli, no Greek flag in evidence on *Surprise* on this occasion; Pat being mindful of the necessity for diplomatic conventions not to be breached, as would be the case were the Ionian government to be made officially aware of her real duties in Greek service. Whether the government was now actually aware at all of her duties, officially or otherwise, Pat knew not, but the hastily repaired battle damage along her sides could not be concealed from even the most inexpert eye, particularly the smashed windows of the great cabin. Although the carpenter had done his best to patch the worst of the splintered planking along the gun deck (fortunately no shot had penetrated *Surprise's* hull below the waterline), and had replaced, after a fashion, the disintegrated companionway steps to the quarterdeck, lacking suitable materials and with so little time available much of the repairs could at best only be described as jury-rigged.

'We will lay a little farther off from the harbour this time, Tom, and perhaps a kedge might keep her damaged stern lying away from prying eyes on the shore?' Pat suggested to his second lieutenant as the crew prepared to drop anchor, *Surprise* moored a little over three-quarters of a mile off from the quay.

'Aye aye, sir.' Within a few minutes Pickering reported, 'The lads are lowering the cutter now to get you quickly ashore.' As *Surprise* steadied on her anchor Pat clambered down into the cutter, helped aboard by Barton who had stowed Pat's small bag under the prow. Marston remained aboard ship to tend the wounded, and so Jason joined Pat as companion for the ride to Metaxata. The row for the most discreet landing place at the far end of the harbour quay was swiftly accomplished. *Eleanor* was tied up alongside the quay, but of her crew only a watchman could be seen. It being past 11 p.m. the port office was closed, and so there was no customs agent at hand to delay them. The horses were rapidly procured from Pat's agent at the fringe of the town, and in the cool of the very late evening they made light of the familiar road at a slow pace; slowed only by Jason, he being unaccustomed to horses, and so most uncomfortably served by his poor riding proficiency. At midnight they reached the little house at Metaxata, candles now burning and visible through the windows. The horses were tethered at the trough, and without any ado, Pat, anxious to enquire of Sinéad's health, swept through the door and into the small living room. To his very great relief, Sinéad sat talking to Kathleen and Simon, all of whom leapt to their feet with great pleasure to greet the arrivals. Pat stood hugging Sinéad tightly for several minutes, their private exchanges whispered between them after initial exclamations of mutual joy. It fell to Jason to greet Simon, Kathleen hastening to the kitchen to procure refreshment for the arrivals.

'Is that coffee I smell? By God that is welcome,' said Pat. Sinéad was now free of his embrace, and the two of them were seated opposite Simon and Jason, Sinéad tightly clutching Pat's hand.

'Here it is, and there is brandy too, warmed bread, olives and local cheese,' said Kathleen, placing all on the small adjacent table, her rising feeling of anxiety plainly evident to all in her voice as she wondered why Duncan was absent, though she did not ask, and awaited Pat's explanation.

'Thankee kindly, my dear,' said Pat, beaming with happiness to see his wife, but wondering too how best to explain Duncan's absence.

'Pat, what is that fresh wound I see, by your eye? What has happened, tell?' asked Simon, with rising concern in his voice. With Sinéad now near completely recovered from her illness the most unsettled man present was Simon, plainly fretting about his absence from *Surprise*, away without him, his fears aroused by the sight of Pat's healing head wound, small as it was. 'Pray be good enough to tell me of your voyage, brother. I have languished anxiously in this place since your departure, my proper place being aboard our dear *Surprise*. Did you engage in any conflict, pray tell; and were any of our crew stricken? Am I needed now aboard?' he asked, perhaps with some premonition, and in his anxiety forgetting the presence of the ladies, waiting only until after Pat had gulped a great draught of his coffee.

'Perhaps the ladies might wish to retire?' Pat volunteered, cautiously, though his suggestion was completely ignored by both. Accepting that, he recounted his story. 'Even afore we reached Candia we were assailed by two Turk galleys. Though we saw 'em off with little but a few of our spars knocked away and some broken windows in the cabin, Symes was killed by a splinter into his lung. Sadly, there was nothing that Marston could do for him. Mason too, took a tolerably sizeable splinter in his upper leg, which Marston took out with some difficulty: it will be some months afore he can reach the tops again. There is Edwards, one of the new gunners: his foot was crushed by *Hell's Mouth*; he did not mind the recoil. He is in some pain, though Marston did not care to amputate the foot, and awaits your opinion. Another of our gunners, Old Tom Currie's younger brother, William, is mightily burned on his leg from hot shot; Marston can keep him comfortable only with plentiful laudanum. Half a dozen others have lesser splinter wounds, but will recover within a week or two.'

'Dear Lord, I was not there in their need,' Simon gasped.

Pat, unsure of how to put it, Kathleen being present, had kept mention of Duncan to the last. With great trepidation he returned to his story. 'Duncan was struck down by a splinter, a blow to the head, and he ain't woken up since; Marston is caring for him,' Pat concluded the grim list.

Kathleen screamed, rose from her chair, dropping her cup, and stood stock still. Sinéad gasped and rushed to embrace her sister. After a few moments the two ladies turned to stare at Pat. They looked horrified, but said nothing, the shock so great, even as Simon sprang to his feet. 'Hell and death. If only I had accompanied you. I will be away directly, at all speed for the ship to help Marston,' Simon replied.

'I am sure the morrow will serve,' Pat suggested, 'Marston is with him.'

'I need not tell you brother, that there are occasions when there is not a moment to be lost. I am leaving now.'

'I will ride with you,' Kathleen declared, and strong-willed woman that she was would brook no protest.

'Take our horses. They are outside, and though not fresh will not mind another hour. William Codrington on *Eleanor* will take you across in his cutter. I will return in the morning,' said Pat, realising any further effort to dissuade his friend from leaving until the morning would be fruitless. Realising too that Sinéad would never release him until many more hours had passed.

Wednesday 28th April 1824   *aboard* Surprise, *Argostoli*

Late-morning brought Pat, somewhat restored in spirit, back aboard *Surprise* to check on his wounded crew members. A bruised Jason could not agreeably contemplate the immediate return ride to Argostoli and so remained at the house in Metaxata, intending to walk back in the cool of the evening. Brodie and the twins had left the house together, earlier in the morning to walk to the port. Looking about him, Pat noted agreeably that repairs were underway to the planking, several of his crew busy painting over previously damaged and repaired timbers. Before lingering further to inspect his ship Pat went below to visit his severely wounded

292

shipmates; all had now been accommodated in the tiny cabins off the gun room, previously occupied by Sinéad, Kathleen and Marston on the voyage out from Falmouth, the lesser wounded having been discharged for light duties. There was no sign of his surgeons, and so he looked in first to Duncan's cabin. Brodie was sitting at the side of his cot on a small stool, gripping his hand, the evidence of plentiful tears streaked down her face. She looked up as Pat entered, her face so very pale. In answer to Pat's unasked question she shook her head, all the while her wide, liquid green eyes seeming to bore into his face, questioning, imploring, her physical stillness at odds with the frantic racing of her thoughts, the deep, deep pain racing, tearing, through her mind.

'Courage, child... he is in the best of care. Dr Ferguson will set him to rights. Where is your mother, lamb? Where are the Doctor and Marston?'

'Mother has stepped out for a moment. The doctors have both been here, sharing the watch over father, all night, looking too to their other patients, and retired but an hour ago.'

'I will return in but a minute or two, my dear. Will I send Murphy with some tea, with a sandwich perhaps?'

Brodie shook her head, could say no more, and turned back to her father. Pat moved along to look in at the next cabin.

'How goes it with your brother?' he asked of Old Tom Currie.

'Mending slowly sir, thankee. He has taken some burgoo today, and the Doctor has given him laudanum agin' the pain, so he is a'sleepin' still.'

''Tis the ramrod for him next time. No more hot shot for him,' Pat joked, weakly.

'Aye sir, that's sure,' smiled Old Tom, pleased with his captain's interest for his brother.

'Mason; how goes it?' asked Pat of the patient in the next cabin.

'Toppin', sir; stitched up better'n the wife's sewin', thankee,' came the cheerful response from Mason.

'Good man. Ye'll soon be back to my barge crew,' Pat replied, encouragingly. The last patient was Edwards with his crushed left foot. Happily no infection had set in although the foot was swollen to the monstrous size of twice normal, and was deep blue, black and yellow in colour. 'Ye won't be at the Maypole on Saturday, Edwards,' smiled Pat to the obviously pained sailor.

To his credit, Edwards returned a sickly grin, and in a laudanum-slurred voice, answered his captain anxiously, 'Will oi keep the foot, sir? To be sure, oi won't be any use in the riggin' if 'tis gone.' To which Pat could only reply, 'If anyone will heal it, Edwards, it is Doctor Ferguson, of that you can be sure.'

After Edwards pained 'Thankee, sir' Pat headed to the great cabin, intending to speak with Simon and Marston. 'Freeman. Freeman there; ask the Doctor and Mr Marston to step into the cabin at their convenience.'

Within a few minutes the surgeons entered, both looking extremely tired. Freeman, needing no bidding, brought in a great pot of steaming coffee, and withdrew from the cabin. In Pat's absence overnight Murphy, with Old Jim Lamb, had removed the last of the shattered glass and timber shards whilst the carpenter had boarded over many of the gaping holes, the window remnants; and the cabin, though much darker, was no longer so exposed to the elements.

'How are the wounded, Simon?'

'All are tolerably comfortable, Pat. No small thanks to my colleague here who has served them as well as ever I could.'

'How is Duncan?' Pat asked, anxiously.

'He is still unconscious. The blow to his head must have been very great, the swelling is receding but slowly. It would not be erroneous to believe he may not come round for some time. I have known such cases to last many days, weeks even. You are to consider that generally such injuries do heal, in time, though we must pray that his intellectuals are not impaired.'

'Will Edwards keep his foot?' asked Pat when all were seated.

'With the blessing, we have some small hope of that. Thank the Lord, there is no infection - no smell of the gangrene - and no cut vessels, it seems. When the swelling recedes the prospect will be plainer to see though in any event I cannot see him ever running again, for the damage to bone must be so very severe. He may retain a club foot, with luck. 'Tis Marston to thank for that, the foot cleaned and set as neat as ever it could be, as are the splinter cases. No better a job could I have done.'

Pat turned to Marston and spoke slowly whilst nodding as if in confirmation, 'Mr Marston ... *Michael*, you have my most particular thanks for your excellent service helping those men. For sure they are in good heart because of it.'

Marston's heart swelled and his eyes watered: never before had Pat referred to him in company as Michael. This was recognition as a friend and comrade of the very first order, and his pleasure ran deep. It was all he could do to reply with the briefest of words, 'Thank you sir. It was no more than any other man of medicine would do.'

Pat would have none of this, and spoke further, deep conviction in his voice, 'No, that is not true. I am informed that you have barely slept these five days past; never leaving your patients, and tending to them as they have recovered; ministering too with words of support and comfort all these days and nights. They, and I, are surely in your debt. There is no doubt.'

'Thank you sir,' was all that Marston, quite overcome by his captain's thanks, could manage to mumble.

'Most excellent work, Michael; I could not do better. Neither could I have saved Symes, for his wound was so very severe,' Simon added, which was some small comfort to his friend.

Murphy entered the cabin to announce, 'Well, the dinner is in half an hour,' adding, 'there is plenty enough sea pie for three, sorr, fresh tunny it is.'

Pat, when such thoughts occurred to him – which was very infrequently – marvelled at Murphy's efforts to manage the minor details of his life. The implied invitation to the two medical men – who were generally held in the very highest esteem by the crew, after the captain that is, Mr Marston now having joined those Olympian heights of crew respect after his treatment of their wounded comrades – could never have been respectfully delivered by anyone else aboard other than Murphy. 'Thankee, Murphy. Sea pie for three it is, in half an hour, and a bottle or two of the best wine in my stores, if you will,' Pat bellowed after his steward who, despite the boldness of his suggestion, had departed in haste before any unwelcome rejoinder could come from his captain. 'I trust you will tarry for dinner, gentlemen?' asked Pat, to observe the proprieties, the answer assured.

Within mere moments, Murphy hastened back into the cabin, quite breathless, and without ceremony or invitation gabbled out his message. 'Mr Macleod, sorr... Mr Macleod... he's a... a...'

All shot up from the table, fearing the worst, Pat shouting at his steward, 'Calm yourself, Murphy. Mr Macleod; what of him? Spit it out man!'

'Well, he's a stirrin', maybe a'comin' round, sorr.' Murphy was near shoved aside as Pat and his surgeons pushed round him and out the cabin door, hastening to the companionway and below to the gun-room, to Duncan's tiny cabin berth, the illumination so poor after the light of the cabin that they could barely see the pale face, the lips quavering, nor hear the murmurings which were so indistinct, his eyes still closed. A very nervous Freeman stood outside the door, his customary cheer quite absent; Kathleen was now seated alongside Duncan's cot, holding a cloth with which she had been wiping Duncan's brow; Brodie stood in the corner, silent, weeping.

'Stand aside, Pat,' ordered Simon, stooping to listen closely to the barely audible words, and to feel the pulse; steady, constant, unwavering, stronger; his breathing near normal once again. 'Duncan, you are awakening, tell?' the words laden with relief.

'Aye, these past few minutes,' came back the very faintest of whisper. 'A glass o' watter wid be the grandest thing.'

Pat's own sigh of relief was audible to all. He stooped and seized Duncan's hand, but did not speak as Simon resumed. 'Listen, brother, do not speak further or call out; rest, do not agitate yourself: Freeman is here with the water, and will attend you until you can sit up. You have had a very severe knock on the head and must stay here some days more.'

But Duncan had slipped back into sleep. Pat stared at him for a few moments before turning his gaze to Simon, his questions unsaid, his face saying all, blessed relief combined with concern.

'He will do well, Pat, with the blessing. Time and rest will serve him now,' Simon opined, nodding, his quiet words bringing a tidal wave of release to all pressed into the tiny space, the palpable fear and tension diminishing.

With great relief they exited to return to the cabin, leaving Kathleen and Freeman hovering near Duncan, she gently wiping his brow and face and he very quietly resuming his quiet singing of a low African song as they left.

Seated once again around the table, they sipped sweet Greek white wine, Santorin Vino Santo, Pat's original cellar so very substantially diminished, and nibbled on stale Captains' Thins, brought by Murphy, until he served the sea pie within a quarter hour. 'What of you, in our absence, Simon? I am pleased to see Sinéad now so well,' asked Pat, his relief at Duncan's recovery still so very evident in his voice.

Simon set down his cup, and replied in the gravest of voices, his tone strong in emphasis of his disapproval. 'My ministrations to Sinéad were comforting only and not strictly necessary, Pat. As I said, Sinéad was mending ere you departed. I beg of you, I must never be left behind again. My place is on this ship, alongside of all who sail in her.'

'On that, dear friend, you have my solemn word,' pledged Pat, Simon's tone setting an alarm bell ringing loud in his mind. 'Let us leave that matter and set dear Sinéad aside for the moment; did you receive any news of note?'

Simon resumed, his voice sinking to little more than a whisper, 'A few days after you sailed, at near midnight of the seventeenth, the Saturday, if my recollection serves me, I was, as was everyone else in the house, awoken from my slumbers by the most intemperate hammering on the house door. I hastened to see what was afoot. There in the teeming rain, amidst a veritable hurricane, at our door stood William Codrington, utterly sodden. He had received a summons of the utmost urgency from Prince

Mavrocordato, delivered by his ship *Leonidas* that night from Messalonghi, and asking for my immediate attendance on Lord Byron. William had ridden through the most foul of nights to deliver it personally, so as no time would be lost. *Leonidas* had striven into the teeth of the hurricane to get out from Messalonghi to reach Cephalonia, and Mavrocordato had sent her speculatively, not knowing whether we might still be found here. Only by the smallest of chance it was that I remained, being left ashore when you departed.'

Astonishment and fear were the expressions that Simon could see passing across the faces of Pat and Marston though neither interrupted his story. As Freeman entered with the dinner tray, setting it down on Pat's table, Murphy bringing the wine and glasses, Simon resumed, 'Without further ado I seized my medicine bag and hastened with William to the port, and upon our boarding *Eleanor* we departed for Messalonghi: the crew, even in the full force of the gale and the utter blackness of the night, hoisting as much canvas as she would bear without it tearing away. Even I, no longer now such a lubber as ever sailed upon a ship, feared greatly for our sails – and our souls – yet William simply urged the crew to lash them tighter. How we crossed that channel and then cleared the islets and traversed the shallows approaching Messalonghi in the vilest of seas I have ever had the misfortune to experience will ever remain a mystery to me. Mr Reeve excelled himself with his navigation. Now brother, I digress. We reached Messalonghi in the late afternoon of the eighteenth, Sunday, and I hastened to Lord Byron's house where I arrived at five o'clock. His Lordship was asleep. His doctors, Dr Bruno and Dr Millingen, were there, and had bled him vigorously beforehand; twenty ounces on the sixteenth, and thrice twenty ounces on the seventeenth. I feared this was greatly excessive, being some four tenths of his blood, and such a loss would not help his Lordship to fight any fever. At three o'clock in that afternoon his Lordship had retired to his bed, and at four o'clock his physicians had administered a draught of claret, opium and bark, with mustard blisters applied to his legs, Lord Byron refusing their application to his feet, being shy of showing his club foot. When I arrived on Easter Sunday I was tolerably distressed that I could neither suggest, nor do anything for him; merely observe their ministrations from the door.'

With a considerable and rising feeling of fear Pat and Marston patiently held their tongues as Simon continued, 'He had awakened at five thirty or so, shortly after my arrival, and his clarity of mind was failing him as I watched, and his speech rambled. His servants kept his head raised as his breathing became difficult. At six o'clock he declared *"I wish to sleep now"* and slipped back to the unconscious state. Those were his last words. His doctors sought to lessen the blood fever, as they thought, and applied dozens of leeches to his temples though I said I greatly doubted they would now assist him at all. Quite the opposite was likely to be the case, yet they would not take any heed, and so he bled copiously all night. I remained at hand all through the next day until finally, amidst the greatest of thunderstorms, his Lordship departed this life at six o'clock in the evening of the nineteenth, Monday, no longer any heartbeat evident; may God rest his soul.'

Simon's despairing tale ended, his low voice quite failing him. He looked up and across to his friends, horror plainly astride their faces as they strove to comprehend the loss of a man they had come to know and admire so much in such a short time. A minute or more passed, their dinner left untouched on the table. The silence prompted Murphy to enter the cabin. How much of Simon's tale he had heard would never be revealed, but without a word he placed a full bottle of brandy on the table and swept the plates away for warming in the galley. Freeman had followed him in with the large coffee jug.

'Simon,' Pat prompted his friend gently, 'pray continue.'

'Nothing more of any importance can I add; save that we stayed in Messalonghi for much of the next day in case we might render any service, but the town simply closed, as if in shock. On that day at sunrise the Grand Battery fired thirty-seven guns in salute to his Lordship's thirty-seven years, and at the end of the day we departed, returning here with the seas greatly abated. On our return Sinéad had by then fully recovered.'

Silence returned to the cabin, none knowing what to say, and Pat poured them all a sizeable measure of the brandy which was swiftly swallowed down. For once Murphy's rare knock on Pat's door was welcome, and he entered again bearing plates for the warmed dinner. 'Well, cook says it will be ruined if left any longer,' he said, Freeman entering immediately behind him, and placing the pie on the table, both leaving with Pat's mumbled, 'Thankee, Murphy, Freeman.' With feelings of great sadness, they picked at the sea pie, but could not do it justice, and steadily consumed the brandy instead until, after a decent further hour of halting conversation, Simon and Marston felt obliged to return to their patients, and a now disconsolate Pat determined to return to Sinéad, leaving the cabin for the deck whence he hailed Barton to row him to shore in the cutter.

A deep feeling of sadness and loss descended upon him as his crew rowed him across the choppy three-quarter mile to the quay in silence, all of them cold and windswept. Grey water splashed over the cutter, soaking them all, but quite ignored by Pat, and not a word passed his lips, his crew remaining in silence, none of them wishing to disturb his obviously distressing thoughts.

* * *

In the still lingering warmth of the evening, Pat arrived home and sat with Sinéad on their terrace, high on the south-western flank of the island's premier peak, their small supper slowly consumed with few words said. Pat sipped his brandy and held hands with Sinéad as he contemplated the southward vista of the gently descending terrain of small farmsteads, irregularly shaped fields, and green copses leading down to the coast; the scent of rosemary so prevalent in the air; the constant chirrup of cicadas the only sound in the tranquillity of the moment. He gazed across the calm, still waters of the channel between Cephalonia and the low gentle hills of Zante in the distance, a far glimpse of the hills of the Morea still just visible as the light began to fail; Pat reflecting that it was the very same view that Byron had enjoyed so much.

'Will I tell you about poor Duncan?' he asked, gently breaking the contemplative quietude of the past hour.

'How is he?'

'He is mending. He has awakened for a moment or two before settling again to sleep. Simon is tending him. He will be well, with the blessing.'

'Thank God and Saint Patrick,' said Sinéad, and then fell back into silence. Another quarter of an hour elapsed before Sinéad spoke again. 'Pat, was Lord Byron a good man?'

'Why, my love, I knew him only this past year, since we met in Genoa, and I know little of his prior life. Certainly there were stories, of which I paid little heed. He came to this country with some expectations of great substance, and generally found the Greeks wanting. Yet, he did not let this dissuade him from his perseverance and his exertions in their cause. Perhaps his expectations were really within himself? He was a man willing to expend every last sou he had for the Greek cause, in which he so much believed, and no man can surely find fault with him for that. The tree remains, but not now the hand that planted it.'

'Will he be missed? Will *you* miss him?' Sinéad pressed.

'My dear, doubtless his is a great loss to Greece. His fame was the perfect promotion for their cause, and that cannot be exaggerated. As a man, I am less sure. It seems, in the main, that he was always surrounded by admirers, but doubtless too he enjoyed many sincere friendships. He was, to be sure, a great man in the... in the *philosophical* line. Such men have something we mere mortals do not possess. It is a subject on which Simon will speak better than I. Will I miss him? I found joy in his company. He carried himself well, in a manner that rose above the doubts of the rest of us. We have lost someone of significance, for sure. In all my years of service, I have lost many comrades, yet for the most part they were losses that we seafarers are accustomed to; in engagements it is a commonplace, yet they pain me increasingly. You may collect that my cox'n, Brannan Barton, was lost in the year thirteen. Barton was so good with the twins in Claddaghduff. Do you remember of him?'

'The twins and I were all very fond of him,' Sinéad replied, uncertain as to how best to deal with this hitherto un-revealed Pat O'Connor.

301

Pat continued, 'His twin brother joined us. He came aboard in Plymouth, brought by Mr Prosser, the master. God's life - excuse me my dear - never have I been so shocked to see anyone. All those memories of Barton came back, as if on a flood tide. Sinéad, my love, something in my mind has changed since that day; I know not what. Some months ago, when we crossed to Messalonghi for the first time, Simon was captured by the Turks. The uncertainty of his return created very great anxiety for me, and for the first time ever in my life as a ship's captain I spoke of my mind with our chaplain, Mr Marston. He was tolerably encouraging, and to my great joy Simon returned within a very short time. Never was I so relieved as that day.' Pat sighed as he stopped speaking, and then drained his brandy.

Sinéad gazed at her husband, the tears in her eyes now beginning to stream down her cheeks, 'Pat, my love, these thoughts are natural to all of us. Captain O'Connor is getting older and perhaps becoming more like us *ordinary* mortals. Would you wish us all to return to Claddaghduff? Perhaps it is time to enjoy retirement there. No one would deny you have earned it.' Sinéad was now weeping and struggled to add 'We have no longer any want of money; you have no need to fight any more battles.'

Pat embraced his wife gently. 'Here, take my cloth,' he offered, wiping the tears from his wife's face.

'Give me hope Pat... hold me... please. I cannot endure much longer. Promise me we will leave these struggles; poor Duncan.' Sinéad was now sobbing profusely, shaking uncontrollably in Pat's arms.

A long and pensive pause followed, as Pat considered his wife's pleas. Finally, some few minutes later, whilst now holding her tightly about him, he answered her, 'Sinéad, my love; I am sensible of your sound thoughts, and that is where we will set our course. Yet I am now here, with many all about me, old comrades and new; all of us are engaged in Greek service. We will return to Connemara together, though afore that we will finish this undertaking in the service of Greece. Many have died here already, Lord Byron but one whom we knew. We shall see this task through to its bitter end.

After that it is my hearth and horse for me, at home in Claddaghduff, my love. No more voyages, neither for King nor foreigner, no more battles, no more deaths. I have seen plenty enough. Thank you, my dear, for your kind words. Be assured, we will enjoy retirement together, afore all of our time has slipped by.'

Brig hove-to   *J.J. Baugean*

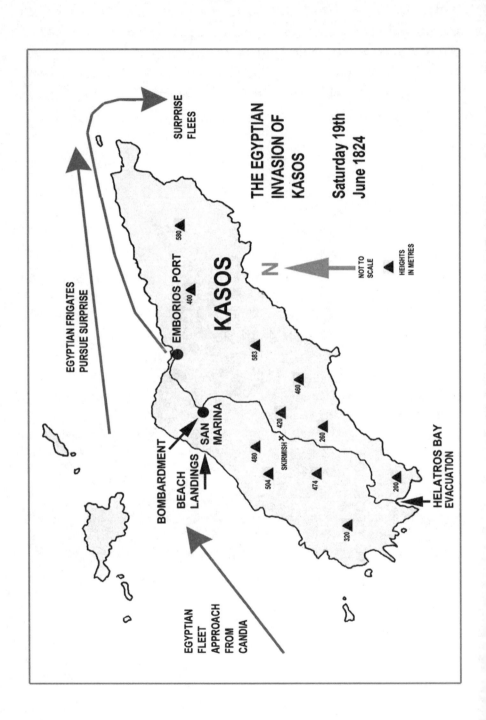

THE EGYPTIAN
INVASION OF
KASOS

Saturday 19th
June 1824

N

NOT TO
SCALE

HEIGHTS
IN METRES

KASOS

EMBORIOS PORT

SURPRISE
FLEES

EGYPTIAN FRIGATES
PURSUE SURPRISE

SAN
MARINA

BOMBARDMENT

BEACH
LANDINGS

SKIRMISH

HELATROS BAY
EVACUATION

EGYPTIAN
FLEET
APPROACH
FROM
CANDIA

580

400

583

460

420

260

480

504

474

200

320

Chapter Eight

Trust not for freedom to the Franks —
They have a king who buys and sells;
In native swords, and native ranks,
The only hope of courage dwells;
But Turkish force, and Latin fraud,
Would break your shield, however broad.

Wednesday 16th June 1824   *approaching Kasos Island*

With a steady north-westerly behind her, *Surprise*, with *Eleanor* astern, glided slowly across the bay towards the port of Emborios in the gentle wind of the late afternoon. On his quarterdeck Pat gazed towards the small harbour, peering with keen curiosity through his glass before he turned to the Kasiot standing next to him, the captain of a brig they had encountered en route, and who had left his command in the hands of his first officer, transferring to *Surprise* on hearing of her destination. 'Captain Zouvelekis, there seems to be precious little room in your harbour. I see a dozen or more square rigged vessels, brigs for the most part; and perhaps two score smaller ones, schooners and the like. I venture there is no room for *Surprise* in there?'

'No, sir; our fleet has been tied up in there for many months, and the port is full, but here in the bay the ground is firm and your anchor will not drag, save in the full force of the *Meltemi*,' Zouvelekis replied with conviction.

'Mr Pickering, we are on a lee shore. Bring her about and let go best and small bowers, veer long cables for both,' Pat ordered his second, not completely trusting in his Greek shipmate's advice. 'Mr Mower, prepare my barge, I will go ashore with Captain Zouvelekis directly. Mr Prosser, signal *Eleanor* for Mr Codrington to come aboard.' Duncan, recovering slowly, had been left behind in the house in Metaxata to convalesce, Simon unwilling to allow him to return to duty and insisting on further rest.

Simon, Marston, and Jason had all now joined Pat in his cabin as Pickering organised *Surprise's* mooring. They discussed their plans. 'Pat, dear, this small and barren island will assuredly have great colonies of sea birds of every distinction. If we are not hurrying from this place, would there be any objection at all, that is to say, it would please Marston and I greatly, were we to enjoy some time ashore to explore the high cliffs and crags we have seen approaching this island. For they are ideal habitat for gulls and others of many and varied species – were you not minded to depart in great haste,' Simon enquired tentatively, mindful of the very many places in past years where there had been no time at all to contemplate the natural flora and fauna before *Tenedos* had departed without any unnecessary, even fleeting, moment of delay.

Pat considered the request for a moment, wishing to oblige his friend, but mindful of the possible return of some enemy squadron at any time and so replied cautiously, 'I shall accompany Captain Zouvelekis to the Magistrate today to see what might be done here. It pains me to see those ships tied up. Perhaps tomorrow I will go aboard some of them, or meet with their owners. The addition of such a squadron would doubtless be valuable to the Greek cause. Mind, Simon, we will soon leave this island, Friday being very likely. You must collect that we may depart this place in great haste, with no time to dwell on your pleasure. Be sure to return to *Surprise* for supper time tomorrow or earlier should we fire the signal gun.'

'Thank you kindly, brother.'

'Mr Jason, I would be grateful if you would join me ashore, I may need your services to speak the Greek, if you will.'

'Of course, sir.'

Simon and Marston still beamed with pleasure at Pat's consent to their absence of leave, short though it was, and hastened below to make their preparations.

William Codrington had by now been rowed across to *Surprise*, and came up the undamaged fo'c'sle steps, and aft to the quarterdeck.

Pat, though pleased to see his friend, wasted no words on pleasantries, 'William, keep *Eleanor* out, she will be our eyes. You will circle this island all the time *Surprise* is here, so that you may watch for any Turk approaching on either side. I do not care for our situation: we are near a lee shore, and with this constant *Etesian* north-westerly leaving this place may present some difficulty, should we require to depart, to claw off in haste. You will fire a signal gun should you see any ship at all, and hasten back.'

Codrington nodded his comprehension, 'Aye aye, sir,' and swiftly departed back to *Eleanor*.

With *Surprise* now anchored a half mile out, Pat's barge crew pulled hard through the gentle swell to bring them to the shore. As they entered the harbour Pat gazed at the ships within, fifty or more of them, all self-evidently long tied up at their moorings. He continued to study the Kasiot squadron even as he spoke to Zouvelekis, 'I see perhaps a dozen or more brigs and corvettes. Such a squadron might have saved you from the Egyptian bombardment on the second of this month, which is why we are sent here. Why did they not go out to drive them off? Oh, I see now, none have sails, all have been struck down! Here's a pretty kettle of fish. Captain Zouvelekis, pray, why are those ships not now being readied for duty?' asked Pat, incredulously.

With a sigh of great despondency the Kasiot sought to explain the inexplicable. 'Our fleet was formerly engaged in blockading Candia, but the Hydriot Admiral Tombazes transferred those duties to the Hydriot squadron, and so our ship owners claim they are forced to economies. Now that the Egyptians control Candia and the waters hereabout as far as Rhodes the owners will no longer risk their ships with Ismael Gibraltar's fleet so strong. All have been laid up since many months, even three in build left unfinished, though they have just been floated off the stocks. After the Egyptians bombarded the island on the second the people were in great alarm and distress, and so pressed the Primates to urge the ship owners to ready their brigs so as to defend us. Yet the owners would not heed their pleas, and so we are left with but three brigs and one corvette still in service, my own included. I was sent on the fourth of this month to seek help from Hydra. With the *Meltemi* of last week so strong I could sail no faster against it, and hence, as

307

you know, it was but four days ago that I reached Thira, and with good fortune met with you and your frigate patrolling there. I pray that my own brig has now reached Hydra and more help is coming,' the Kasiot concluded, the shock and fear created by the recent bombardment of his home island still so very evident in his voice, face and demeanour.

Pat was perplexed; the inactivity so far beyond his comprehension that he could say nothing more until they reached the quay and all clambered ashore. 'Simon, Michael,' he said to them with some little anxiety, 'Pray, do not forget, return tomorrow by supper time, no later. Our stay in this place will be short.'

With smiles they assured Pat of their timely return, and set off with a jaunty step along the coastal road, Simon burdened with his canvas and easel and Marston carrying a large bag on his back.

The arrival of *Surprise*, a frigate flying Greek colours, was most unexpected, Greece having none in her service, as all believed; none knowing of *Surprise's* engagement as a letter-of-marque, so the harbour quayside had already begun to fill with seamen, ship's officers, ship owners, and the dignitaries of the island; all volubly curious about her. Most of the Primates and even the island's Magistrate had arrived at the harbour within an hour of *Surprise* being observed at anchor. Captain Zouvelekis struggled to keep up with the flood of questions thrown at them from all and sundry. Jason translating at best speed could not hope to keep Pat apprised of every question, and after a near hour of Bedlam or so it seemed to Pat, sweating profusely in the heat of the sun, he stepped up upon the deck of a small caique laid up out of the water nearby, threw up his hands into the air, and shouted as loud as he could, 'SILENCE!' The babble ceased and Pat spoke, 'Mr Jason, would you kindly ask the Magistrate, the Primates, Captain Zouvelekis, and any ship owners and captains present to attend me in that taverna over there without delay. All others are to wait outside. Thank you.'

With that Pat strode off to the small taverna behind the quay, waiting for no man. He ducked as he entered, blinking as his eyes adjusted to the gloom, gratefully welcoming the cooler air inside. By now, his patience exhausted, and neither Jason nor Zouvelekis having caught up with him, and the babble behind having resumed even louder, Pat requested a cold drink. Having no Greek he simply pointed and shouted, 'Cerveza, cerveza, por favor,' which was all he could think of to say. The barkeeper fortunately rose to the occasion, and the lukewarm frothing drink came quickly, to Pat's great satisfaction, and was consumed in one draught just as Jason and Zouvelekis, accompanied by the island's dignitaries and senior ships' captains and owners, bustled through the door and filled the small room. 'Mr Jason,' said Pat, fuming still, 'this is a rum affair. There is a tolerably sizeable squadron sitting out there, idling, all in ordinary. The island has been bombarded by the Egyptians these two weeks past, and yet there is not a man working to restore those ships to service. What ails these excitable people? Damn foreigners.'

The situation and any conceivable explanation were utterly beyond Jason's comprehension too and he made no answer. Zouvelekis, perceiving Pat's anxiety, hammered hard on the servery, bringing the assembly to near silence. He turned to Pat, shouting above the rekindled low plethora of continuing conversations in the room, 'Captain O'Connor, sir, would you speak to the room? Would you declare your plans?'

'Plans? Plans! I have none!' Pat shouted back angrily, and then rapped his empty glass hard three times on the servery, bringing the room to near silence. Just one man continued to speak until Pat finally shouted at him, 'You, sir, keep your silence or leave this place.' It was instantly translated by Zouvelekis, and the miscreant halted. Pat waited no further, and seizing the moment, allowed his sentiments full voice as he shouted across the room, niceties wholly absent from his address. 'What in God's name are you about? The Egyptians have bombarded your homes and gone away. Do you not think they will return? Do you think they have satisfied themselves? Do you think they have not seen your ships laid up? Do you care so little for your wives … and your children that you leave those ships sitting idle? Why is not every man jack of you out there now, restoring their sails, laying in their stocks; water, powder and shot? Do you think the Hydriot squadron will reach you in time to save you all when the Egyptian ships return?'

309

Jason struggled to keep pace with his translation of Pat's questions. Pat paused for breath and looked around the room. The prevalence of glum faces seemed to suggest that his questions had struck the right chord. He continued, 'You will collect that 'tis four days sailing from Hydra – that is with a fair wind – and but two from Rhodes, or one from Candia. Who will get here first? Plainly it will not be the Hydriots. I am told your ships are laid up as an economy ... *an economy!* When the enemy arrives your homes will be plundered, your sons killed, your wives and children taken as slaves. This is as happened on Chios. Have you forgotten? What foolish economy is this? Get out your money, engage your seamen. *Hurry!* Rig your ships as fast as ever you can, afore it is too late. There is not a moment to be lost!' Pat finished, wiping the perspiration from his face, as Zouvelekis concluded his translation. Jason, proving quite incapable of keeping pace with the rapid barrage from Pat, had been overwhelmed and given up. The room erupted into loud discussion, a dozen or more conversations being simultaneously conducted; the noise rising until Pat could barely hear himself asking Jason, 'What do they say? Can you tell?'

Zouvelekis himself was now engaged in animated and loud discussion with an elder. Jason admitted he could not readily follow anything of the discussions, explaining that the Kasiot accent or dialect was somewhat removed from the demotic language form with which he was familiar. Some ten minutes later Zouvelekis pushed his way through the throng back to Pat, leaving the elder with whom he had been speaking. 'Captain O'Connor, sir, we are indebted to you for your plain words; words which many have spoken, but words on which no one has yet acted. That lamentable situation will now change. Here today are the leading sea captains of the island including ...' Zouvelekis referred to the slip of paper he clutched in his hand, '... Kantartzis, Maliarakis, Makris, Ioulios, Grigoriadis, Manolis, Koulokoundis, Papadakis, Nikolaou, Rethimnis, Markakis, and Diakakis. I have been speaking with the Magistrate, and he is now engaged with those twelve ship owners. All have pledged to restore their ships to service, and many more are now expected to do so. Work will commence on the morrow.'

310

Pat began to feel very tired; his emotive address to the Kasiots and the extreme heat having left him drained, and so he resolved to return to *Surprise* for his supper. To Zouvelekis he announced, 'I will come ashore in the morning, Captain. If *Surprise* can be of any assistance, doubtless we can speak further of it on the morrow.' With that Pat left the taverna, accompanied by Jason, weary but relieved that his address had seemingly moved many to action.

Thursday 17ᵗʰ June 1824   *in the Kasos hinterland*

'Marston; there, over there, beyond that rock, no, the very large one, do you see it? The gull, I swear I have never seen the like,' exclaimed Simon.

'Why, 'tis just a Herring gull,' Marston retorted, dismissively.

At times his friend's occasional boorishness exasperated him, and so Simon did not reply, not taking his eyes from the gull; instead groping for Pat's best Dollond glass from within his satchel, which he had taken to borrowing surreptitiously, rightly fearing Pat's refusal as he had once left it high aloft on *Surprise*, quite forgotten until Pat remarked upon its absence when Murphy, to his great disgust, was sent in haste to retrieve it. Simon focused on the gull, barely thirty paces away from them and sitting within its nest on a rocky cliff ledge. Simon now murmured to his companion, 'Look closely, Marston. Can you see its short red bill, not yellow? No Herring ever had a red bill. There is a black tip on the bill, but 'tis not a band, so 'tis not the common Mediterranean, which in any event is a smaller bird.'

He passed the glass to Marston. Marston raised it to his eye and looked hard towards the gull, 'Why, I beg pardon, I do believe there is something in what you say. 'Tis much plainer with the glass, and there is no possible confusion. There is a significantly less prominent forehead, and it is certainly lighter in grey on the upper parts than the Herring,' he conceded, his interest now growing. 'Perchance you have found a new species?'

'I have a copy of Willughby aboard ship,' Simon replied, adding, 'and perhaps a Tunstall too. We will consult them later. Is there anything left of the sandwiches to eat?'

'Sadly not, colleague, the last of the bread and cheese we consumed at two o'clock.'

'Oh, how I crave for a prime beefsteak, fat and blood red.'

'Should we not soon return, before the Captain frets?'

'Wait, wait, look there; do you see the falcon? Michael, there he is. He flies in circles, near above our gull, catching insects in flight I venture. I have not seen his like. What a splendid day this is, colleague. Look closely; see his dark underwing coverts over the pale wingtip flight feathers. I have never seen that combination before. Slowly now, let us see if we can get just a little closer.' Simon stepped forward, but after a few paces stumbled heavily, his foot twisting under him, and he fell, crying out in some pain. A few anxious moments passed as Marston scrambled to catch up with him, the stony ground being extremely uneven. As Marston sat next to his friend, Simon, in great pain now, removed his boot, his ankle already swelling significantly. 'A twistle for sure; a severe sprain, I fear. Thank God the glass did not break in the fall; Pat would be mightily vexed, would never forgive me.'

'Can I help you stand?' asked Marston, anxiously, for the swelling was large indeed, and the whole foot from above the ankle to the toes was bright pink.

'No, it is too painful. I must rest it a little before we try to get back,' Simon concluded, dismayingly adding, 'Perhaps you might find some stick on which I might ease my weight when we start?'

Marston looked at his friend with concern, 'Here, take the satchel, there is some water left. I shall search out a stick and return as quickly as can be.' He set off to retrace their path, picking his way now more cautiously amidst the rough grass and rocks. An hour and a half later he returned with a dismal report. 'There is not a single tree that I can see on this barren rock of an island. No fence, nor any construction that would serve to provide a stick or crutch. We will have to struggle back as best we can, and I will carry you.'

Simon looked with some hesitation at his friend's slight physique, wholly unaccustomed to physical exertions of any form save for the gentlest of walking, and that for short duration. Their trek on the hills of Kasos had proven to be a struggle for Marston, even before they stopped to eat their sandwich dinner at two o'clock, having left their simple accommodation in San Marina after an early breakfast. 'Well, if you can support my side a little that may answer tolerably well and we will shift along slowly. I will assuredly be crankie, and if we make but little progress then you will leave me and fetch help,' Simon declared, fearing for his friend, should he overly exert himself, as surely would be the case were he to try to carry Simon some four or so miles back to the village, unaided. 'What o'clock is it?' he asked, his prize Breguet having been forgotten in their haste to set out on their rare expedition.

'It is approaching six o'clock, colleague,' Marston replied.

'Pat will be mightily displeased,' Simon pronounced, gloomily.

* * *

At 8 p.m. and sunset near, Pat was pacing the quay with rising frustration, and was indeed mightily displeased. Despite his strictest of cautions to his friend, of Simon there had been no sign, nor any report all day. It had been a very busy day in which he had gone aboard all the laid up Kasiot ships, assessing their degree of readiness for restoration to service, and listing, with the aid of his lieutenants, the many and varied matters needing attention, the missing necessaries for a return to sea, and calculating the likely time all these things might require. Whilst there had been a start on the renovation of many of the ships it was by no means a start to all, and the work seemed to him, founded on his own experiences of ship refitting, to be moving exceedingly slowly, insufficient men being present, and so he believed that a week or more might pass by before even a part of the potential Kasiot squadron could be fit for service, and that plainly was not fast enough, would not be anywhere near fast enough with a hostile Egyptian squadron within a few days sailing time of the island.

Pat remarked to Pickering, 'This is a dangerous time, Tom. Though they have plainly started to prepare those ships, without their men will spread a deal more canvas it will plainly take too long. We, and they, must hope for the arrival of a Hydriot squadron, and I fear it will come too late. There are plainly enough summer months left for any expedition or invasion; they can come at their leisure. To have failed to have prepared those ships is folly of the highest order. I hope they are not asked to pay the price, for surely it will be very high. We, by ourselves, will be able to do little, likely nothing, should the enemy return as a squadron. It would grieve me to flee before it, but that will be our only choice. And what are we to do now? The Blue Peter hoisted through all the Afternoon watch, and the Doctor and Marston have failed to return. Come; let us return to *Surprise* for our supper, we can do no more today, darkness approaches. In the morning, at first light, we will send two score of men to scour this rock and seek them out.'

Friday 18th June 1824   *Kasos*

In the cooler air of the early morning, and with no sign of the absentees, Pat had despatched men towards all parts of the island, each party of half a dozen accompanied by a Greek with a grasp of English to translate for them anything that might be learnt from speaking with the populace. All parties were briefed to hurry back to *Surprise* were she to fire her signal gun.

* * *

Simon and Marston, with yesterday's onset of darkness making further movement impossible over the rock strewn Kasiot landscape, canvas and easel long abandoned, had rested overnight on a hillside some two miles south of San Marina. Marston, unable to shift his friend further, though the lights of the village had been tantalisingly visible below throughout the night, had refused to leave Simon. Now wearily awake after fitful sleep on the hillside, they contemplated their situation.

'Michael, listen well. We cannot linger here without water when the sun rises higher. Go now; I will rest near this summit where you will, God willing, find me without difficulty when you return with help. Perhaps a mule might be found in that village?' a very tired Simon pressed Marston.

'Of course, I will be away but a very short time, and assuredly will return with help and water. Pray do not move one step until my return, dear colleague,' Marston replied, anxiously, and set off.

* * *

314

'Tom, there is no news from our searchers,' Pat lamented to his lieutenant, as he entered into the shade of the harbour taverna where they had retired for refreshment in the fierce heat. 'Will you sit and take some of this coffee with me? It is pleasing at least that more men are arriving by the hour to restore those ships,' Pat remarked, nodding towards the window, 'though I have a dark foreboding about this place which I cannot shake. Why would the Turk, now so strong in Candia and in Rhodes, leave this squadron untouched in their midst, astride their route between the two? Surely this island has been a thorn in their side in the past year, and its fleet enjoys a reputation of little more than pirates. The squadron is plainly laid up, as the Egyptian ships would doubtless have observed on the second.'

'They are toiling in haste on some of the ships, sir. Though on others there is still not a man to be seen aboard,' Pickering replied.

'We can do no more for them, Tom. Let us return to *Surprise* and await the return of our lads with news of Simon and Marston. I venture there can be few places on this island that our lads cannot reach ere midday. Come, we will return aboard.'

* * *

A near exhausted Marston had now scrambled down the hill and staggered the two miles or so to reach the village of San Marina, in such haste that several tumbles had left him with bruised shins and a badly scratched face, his clothes torn in two places and all caked with grime and dust. On entering the village taverna, lacking any Greek, he could not make himself understood. It was whilst exchanging mutually unintelligible words with the innkeeper that he was found by the ship's party of searchers, in pursuit of news of any sightings and of refreshment too, the day getting hotter as the morning progressed. Clumsy Dalby it was that recognised him, a mutually welcome and heartening event for them both for Dalby was the friend of Mason, the casualty from whose leg Marston had extracted the serious splinter after the battle with the galleys.

'Dalby it is, Mr Marston, tie-mate of Mason. How are you, sir? Where be the Doctor? We have scoured this place some hours for you,' Dalby announced in his booming voice.

'Ah, Dalby; I am so pleased to see you,' said Marston, huge relief plain in his voice, adding, 'The Doctor has injured his foot and cannot walk. Please let us see if a mule can be found to carry him down from the hill.' The Greek accompanying the search party, Grigorios, hastened out from the taverna in search of a mule whilst a grateful and very thirsty Marston greedily gulped down water provided by a now anxious to help innkeeper. Twenty minutes later Grigorios returned, and Marston was invited to ride the mule, which had readily been procured, to locate Simon, still waiting on a now scorching-hot hillside. All set off at the best pace the mule deigned to make, scarcely more than the slowest amble, and despite much hearty encouragement from the six seamen to shift along faster, faster he would not go.

* * *

On the quay at Emborios, Pat and Pickering were about to board Pat's barge for the return to *Surprise* when the very faintest of deep notes, the most discordant of sounds he dreaded hearing, reached Pat's ears from the west. 'Hark, Tom, did you hear that?' Pat's mood instantly switched to an anxious alert. 'Row swiftly, lads, as fast as ye can, to the barky. Quickly now, there is no time to lose,' he commanded, the urgency very audible in the timbre of his voice, and quickly communicated to his barge crew who began to row as if their lives depended on it, great splashes of water coming aboard, soaking all to the skin. 'I fear that was *Eleanor's* gun, Tom, though I cannot see her.'

Pickering too was straining his eyes, and standing now, swaying with the roll of the barge; looking at the far west headland of the island. 'Nothing in sight yet, sir, wait ... yes, I think I see her tops now.'

At that moment the distant *Eleanor* fired her gun again, the sound now more plainly evident to all in the barge. The rowers redoubled their efforts to reach *Surprise*, all realising their worst fears that something of the very utmost urgency was imminently looming upon them. Ten more minutes of desperate rowing brought the barge alongside *Surprise*, and Pat scrambled swiftly up her side, hastening into the great cabin in search of his glass,

316

fruitlessly as it happened, it being in Simon's bag. The barge crew were a bare moment behind him, the last coming aboard as Pat reached his quarterdeck to gaze at *Eleanor*, closing from a league off, so greatly hard-a-lee and with a square topsail straining so on its yard that her gunwhale near touched the water. 'She is in haste, Tom. Prepare our own signal gun. We must get our men back aboard. Hand me your glass,' said Pat, in some little trepidation.

'Aye aye, sir. Mason, prepare the signal gun,' Pickering reiterated.

Pat's attention remained fixed on their approaching consort. '*Eleanor* is signalling now ... Turk ... squadron ... thirteen ... ships ... five ... leagues. My God, they are returning as I feared, and are near upon us,' Pat gasped, lowering the glass and turning to his officers. 'Tom, fire the gun to recall our men. Send a fresh crew ashore in the barge and the cutter too, to collect them. Mr Jason, you will go ashore with them. Find Captain Zouvelekis quickly, and tell him the Turks - the Egyptians from Candia most likely it is - are returning and will be here within a very few hours. Two hours, perhaps three and they will be here. Ask of Simon and Marston, and return swiftly with our men in the boats, we will be away from this place directly all are aboard.' It was now noon and *Surprise* erupted into activity, fresh men hastening into the barge and cutter, rowing strongly for the shore; gun captains busied about their charges, men set about readying shot at hand, topmen swarmed aloft to rig top-gallant yards struck down. Every man aboard sensed the urgency of their situation and busied themselves with preparations for rapid departure and possible battle.

'Hoist white ensign at the jack, Mr Mower. Doubtless with that and our Nelson chequer they will take us to be Englishmen. Haul down our Greek colours,' ordered Pat. 'We must hope to stay their guns for as long as we can ... and Melville ain't here to fret,' he added to himself in a whisper.

* * *

On the island, every member of *Surprise's* crew who were ashore looking for Simon and Marston had heard her signal gun, and the search parties, wherever they were, hastened to return to Emborios.

317

'Dalby; was that a shot from one of our guns I heard?' asked Marston, uncomfortable astride the mule, now a mile and a half out from San Marina. 'What does it signify?'

It was plain to Dalby and his five companions that it was the recall signal. The seamen looked at each other, unspeaking, and then to Dalby who was their natural leader. Dalby looked down at the mule's head, thinking hard, and then looked to the men walking alongside before replying, "'Tis but a custom when *Eleanor* returns, sir, that is all. Now how far away would the Doctor be, sir?'

'Oh, perhaps another half mile.'

'We will shift along, sir, at all speed. The Doctor will be in pressing need of water. This heat will quickly tire the strongest of men,' Dalby added, his companions nodding their agreement.

Another forty minutes of laborious uphill walking towards the hilltop which Marston remembered from the morning brought them in distant sight of a small figure, lying in the short grass of a boulder-strewn hollow, and surrounded by half a dozen curious goats, all chewing the coarse vegetation. 'Doctor, Doctor,' shouted Dalby, leaving the mule and his companions, and running with leaps and bounds over the uneven terrain. He reached the prone man after a frenetic two or three minutes and in a lather of sweat; gasping to regain his breath. From the still figure, huddled in a very dishevelled old cape, face shrouded by a pulled down cap, there was no movement at all. Dalby shook the man's shoulder, all the time repeating, 'Doctor, Doctor.' The man slowly stirred, to Dalby's immense joy and relief. The Doctor struggled to fully awaken.

'Ah, Dalby, is it you? Would you kindly spare me a glass of water? Is there some emergency? Why are you shouting?' asked Simon, dozily, pulling himself into a seated position and looking about him. 'Why, Marston too is returned, and a mule. That is most helpful, this foot pains me still.'

Dalby, now most anxious and mindful of the signal gun, which they had ignored, pleaded, 'Doctor, sir, Doctor, listen, listen well, *Surprise* has fired the recall gun, and we are now an hour past returning to the ship. We could not, in good conscience, leave you here, we must hurry; can you stand?'

Simon had gathered his senses and some comprehension of Dalby's urgency. He struggled but failed to gain his feet. Without ado, Dalby swept him up over his shoulder and started to carry him down the hillside until, after a bare five minutes, they met with the others approaching with the mule. Marston had already dismounted, and Simon was lifted astride the mule, firmly held, one seaman each side of him as they started down, Simon drinking copiously from the water bottle for a hundred yards or more. Steadily, they retraced their steps, descending as fast as the mule would shift. Another hour of slow going, Marston struggling hard and assisted by two of the crew, one on each of his arms, brought the party to within a mile of San Marina. It was 2 p.m.

* * *

On *Surprise* the ship's bell tolled four bells as the barge and cutter pulled alongside, and the men scrambled aboard, Jason too, but no Captain Zouvelekis amongst them.

'All hands on deck, Mr Pickering,' ordered Pat. The order was relayed to the bosun whose pipe swiftly brought up the men. 'Up anchor! All hands: up anchor. Look alive there,' shouted Pat, adding to his lieutenants, 'We cannot tarry here longer, the Turks will soon be here, and we will not be caught on a lee shore with a dozen or more ships agin us.'

Pat looked all about him, gazing through his glass to the west, the Turks had rounded Cape Pounta and were in sight, less than a league away. Pickering rattled out the orders: 'Rig the capstan... bring to the messenger... man the bars... heave round... fresh and dry... fleet the messenger... surge-ho!'

The first cable was taken in and stowed, the second swiftly hove short. 'Loose jib and spanker! Helm hard a-starboard,' barked Pickering; Pat staring through his glass at the oncoming vanguard of the Turk squadron; on they came, closer by each passing minute, two miles away now, perhaps a little more.

To his ears there came the welcome shout of 'Up and down,' from the forecastle. The topmen had hastened aloft and were ready as Pickering resumed, 'Haul on the spanker!' Almost imperceptibly *Surprise*, drifting slightly astern, began to cast away from her remaining larboard anchor, her bow swinging until the north-westerly wind was blowing abeam.

'Anchor's aweigh!' came the shout from the forecastle. The men on the capstan were working furiously.

'Haul up the jib,' Pickering's commands were pouring forth as quickly as he dared, 'Helm amidships!' The anchors were swiftly catted and fished. 'Man the tops'l sheets and halliards... tend the braces!' Pat looked about his ship in assessment, little time left.

Pickering shouted again, 'Loose tops'ls,' the crew letting go the clewlines, and at the order 'Sheet home... hoist!' the topmen quickly followed, sheeting the topsails very swiftly.

'Haul taut, brace up!' and *Surprise* began to move off. Infinitely slowly at first on a north-easterly beam reach, for with the wind being the prevailing *Meltemi* north-westerly she could do no other to escape the island and the looming Turks. All the detail of the leading ships of the Turk squadron, the leading frigates which had rounded Cape Pounta to the west some ten minutes before, were plainly visible to all aboard, no further need for a glass. Through his glass Pat could see that their guns were run out, their courses double-reefed and clewed up. The forerunners of the thirteen ships, as *Eleanor* had reported, were upon them! *Eleanor* herself had been signalled to haul away to the north-east, and she was half a league ahead of *Surprise*, making headway, sailing swiftly.

On *Surprise* Pat was considering his lack of options, and spoke ernestly to his officers, 'Gentlemen, we will shift very slow for at least the next mile. Within the hour we will round that north-east cape, when we will run south afore the wind and likely escape those frigates. Until then, nip and tuck it will be, and they will surely catch us if they chase.'

* * *

Half an hour's more plodding descent, now they were on gentler ground, brought Dalby's shore party of Surprises to just above the village edge of San Marina. The Emborios harbour and *Surprise* herself, some two miles distant, were plainly visible. 'The barky is underway, a'leavin' us,' shouted Hartley. *Surprise* was clearly now in full sail; though even from the far hill the experienced seamen could plainly see she was struggling to make way against the *Meltemi*.

Simon, recovering after consuming further deep draughts of water and eating bread and olives, was looking through Pat's glass, at the waters even more distant than where *Surprise* was toiling near straight into the wind, or so it seemed, and in a low voice he remarked, 'Hell and death! She is sailing away from a Turk fleet; look beyond her, to the east.'

'West, sir,' replied Dalby.

'Yes, *west*, as I said, but you did not attend. Some miles off, see there,' an irritable Simon pointed, but all had already clearly seen the full sails, perhaps only half a league beyond and behind *Surprise*, thirteen ships approaching her, three frigates to the fore.

* * *

Aboard *Surprise* the mood was tense. Could *Surprise* gain speed and haul away before being caught by the approaching Turk frigates; of which there were now three in pursuit, followed by ten brigs, as could plainly be seen? They were together far more than a match for the very best of any single frigate crew, and *Surprise* could not hope to emerge from any encounter with three of them – as Pat and all his crew knew very well. 'Mr Mower, haul the line, if you will,' he ordered.

'Three knots,' came back the steady shout from Wright, the linesman. Five minutes had passed.

'Three knots, three knots, 'twill be a close run thing,' Pat whispered quietly so no one else would hear. He turned to Tom Pickering, 'Do not open our gun ports until my command.'

Pickering passed the order to the silent gun captains, all keen to know their captain's intentions. Linstocks had already been lit at every gun, as standby for the gunlocks, no gun captain being happy without a slow-match as backup in case of a misfire. Five more minutes had passed; the Turks were now little more than a mile off, and their courses were converging. 'The line, Mr Mower?' said Pat, as evenly as he could.

'Four knots,' shouted Wright.

'Steady as she goes,' Pat ordered. His officers and the helmsmen, Barton included, stared at him, anxiety rising and visible in their faces. Five more minutes passed. *Surprise* was continuing to gain speed, but the distance now closed to three quarters of a mile between her and the leading Turk frigate, approaching abeam of *Surprise*.

'Five knots,' Wright shouted again. With time seemingly frozen, another five minutes crept by until the linesman shouted again, 'Six knots.' The nearest Turk frigate was now three-quarters of a mile off *Surprise's* beam, and Pat was aware that he was being scrutinised by the Turk captain through his glass.

'She is making six knots too, I fancy,' remarked Pat, quietly; to himself. Twenty more tense minutes passed and the Turk had closed to a half mile abeam *Surprise*, the Turk gun ports now open and her guns all run out. The Turk frigate had been signalling *Surprise* to heave-to for the past mile, and now fired a signal gun to reinforce her demand. 'For inspection of His Majesty's papers no doubt. I think not. Can he not see our white ensign?' Pat remarked, now in better humour as the other two Turk frigates were trailing some way behind their compatriot, and so the odds were improving a very little. A further fifteen minutes and *Surprise* was just clearing the rocky islets on the north-east point of the island, and Pat measured his tactics in his mind. 'We will clear the point and turn south quickly, leaving the two trailing frigates far in the wake of the first,' he said, loudly to all at the helm. 'Stand by to come about.'

Pat looked to the rocks of the cape off her starboard quarter; the first Turk, most likely Egyptian, frigate was barely a hundred yard behind her. If *Surprise* maintained her lead as she rounded the point she would have a chance; as long as she did not strike rocks which, Jack knew, might well populate the shoal water between the point and the islets. Despite their acute peril, Jack would not, and the Turk frigate similarly could not, shave the corner of their sharp turn about the north-east point of the island and its outlying rocks, for no sane captain would hazard his deep-drafted ship any closer.

'We will wear ship. Mr Pickering, put the helm up... swiftly now!' Pat shouted his orders with a confidence that greatly heartened his men, all being aware of the frigate closing their stern with two of her fellows behind her. 'Barton!' Pat shouted across to the wheel, 'Hard over!' Barton and his three mates, though keenly mindful of the rocks to starboard, pulled harder down on the wheel, and *Surprise* heeled as she turned sharply, men everywhere hauling hard to brace her yards to the new, southerly course, *Surprise* gaining speed swiftly as she began to run near directly before the wind. As she turned, the Turk, so very close, seventy yards behind and no more, turned too, her captain dicing with the outermost rocks of the tiny islands off Cape Akti. She turned within *Surprise's* turn, which brought her a bare two hundred yards off *Surprise's* starboard quarter.

'He is surely seeking promotion, that captain, Tom. I would not hazard *Surprise* so close to those rocks, though I doubt he will care to fire on His Majesty's ship. I fancy we will soon show him a clean pair of heels,' said Pat, grinning broadly. 'Mr Mower, the log, if you please. I fancy we may be close on ten knots.'

Surprise, now sailing large, swiftly picked up speed, quickly reaching the anticipated, indeed the prayed-for, ten knots. Everything that could be done aboard *Surprise* to speed her escape had been done, even her studding sails had been boomed out. She raced ahead of the Turk, the two frigates tearing through the warm lee waters of the island in the still bright sunlight, near parallel. Steadily *Surprise* hauled away, and Pat's prediction proved accurate, the Turk frigate broke off the pursuit after another mile, and there was a palpable gasp of relief from all on the quarterdeck.

'I venture he has been recalled to his squadron; other more pressing matters, no doubt,' Pat opined to his officers, as relief visibly spread throughout the rest of the ship, the danger fading. 'Mr Jason, please to come up to my quarterdeck, if you will,' shouted Pat to Jason, who had watched the chase from near the mainmast with some considerable anxiety, though he had not uttered a word throughout the drama. 'Did you receive any news of the Doctor and Marston when you were ashore?' asked Pat.

'None, sir.'

'What of Captain Zouvelekis, where is he?'

'Captain Zouvelekis was determined to stay and protect his family. However, he did assure me that he would personally look for Doctor Ferguson, and when he was found, as he assuredly felt he would be, they all would go to the south of the island and hide from any Turk invasion, which he said would be a very bloody affair. He said that there is a small bay, Helatros, on the southernmost point where it is possible to reach the beach via a goat track, and where the water is deep enough for a small vessel to shelter, to take off any persons from the beach. He suggested we go there, to await his arrival with Doctor Ferguson and Marston.'

'Mr Pickering, you have the command,' Pat went below to examine his charts.

* * *

In the San Marina taverna where Simon, Marston, Dalby, and the other Surprises were now resting, there came the distinct dull, thudding booms of naval gunfire. Dalby, with his shipmates, quickly left the taverna to investigate. 'What are we to do, colleague?' asked a very weary Marston, exhausted from his double trek on the hillside. 'You cannot walk, *Surprise* has left without us, and now there is a Turk bombardment,' he added, as the first crashing noises of falling shells could distinctly be heard outside.

'Is there anything to eat in these premises, do you suppose?' Simon asked. 'A man could waste away here for want of refreshment, and perhaps a very little wine too would be agreeable. After such a trial a man's soul cries out for succour.'

An hour passed in which the bewildered old innkeeper's wine, bread, and olives were consumed, his wine being especially savoured. Then the Surprises returned. The mood in the taverna was extremely tense. 'The Kasiot batteries are firing agin the Turk ships, sir, though the Turks are getting the best of it. There is damage to plenty o' houses already,' Dalby announced.

The bombardment continued in a desultory fashion for hour after hour until the onset of twilight when firing died down. Dalby returned again after further investigation to report, 'The Turks have anchored and plainly will fire again in the morning. Scores of houses in this village have now been damaged.'

324

The Turk cannonade opened again upon the small town shortly after first light, and quickly became very heavy, several hundred shells falling every hour, and severe damage was soon evident. In contrast, the Kasiot batteries firing back at the Turk ships anchored some two miles to the north, near the islet of Makra, enjoyed little or no success, accuracy being so very difficult for their eighteen-pounder guns at that range. Hour after hour the bombardment continued. In the village, many people, fearful, had decided to leave, and a stream of villagers now trekked away towards the three smaller villages of the island. The taverna had filled with the local old men, the ones least able to contemplate a long hike, and they engaged in a babble of discussion about the bombardment. The younger ones were presumably at the batteries and any other defences that existed, the remaining women and children still in their homes. Slowly the day passed into early evening when Simon and Marston were pleased to greet a most welcome arrival at the taverna; Captain Zouvelekis accompanied by his wife and two young sons entered as dusk fell. 'Doctor Ferguson, Mr Marston, I have searched all the villages of this island for you. I am so pleased to find you. Why are you still here?' he asked, incomprehension plain in his voice.

'Captain Zouvelekis, thank you for your courtesy and attentions, sir. I find myself quite incapacitated, having injured my foot and ankle on the hill. My profuse thanks are no compensation to Mr Marston here and these gentlemen of our crew, who extricated me from the hill and brought me here, where, to our considerable dismay, we find ourselves under a Turk cannonade. Pray tell, what is your own intention?' Simon asked.

Zouvelekis explained his instructions given to Jason, adding, 'A Turk emissary has come ashore at Emborios and demanded that the island surrender. The smaller villages are minded to do so though the Primates here in San Marina are undecided. Our batteries may inflict damage and casualties were the Turk ships to approach closer, and so there are many minded to resist, and hope for Hydriot and Spetziot help. I fear, as Captain O'Connor explained in

Emborios, such help, were it to come, would be too late, and the island will be sacked before we can expect help. I fear for my wife and sons, and so I intend to walk to Helatros with my own confidence and hopes placed in your comrade, Captain O'Connor. I am sure he will come to take us off. I urge you to prepare now to come with me, with us, without delay. The Turks, having come this far, having expended some eight thousand shells on this town, will surely not return home without a landing, and that must be soon. Their launches have been sighted, filled with troops, moving along the coast. It will not be long before they come.'

Simon hesitated for a moment only before replying, 'Alas, I am no military strategist, but of the veracity of your predictions I have no doubt. No admiral could countenance such prodigious expenditure of powder and shot without some defined purpose, some eminently sizeable return, in prospect, and it is sure that sailing away would not deliver any such reward. I am entirely of your way of thinking; we must hasten from this place. The way to this Helatros, is it perilous? For I have already lost the use of one foot and cannot consider of walking far.'

'It is no more than two leagues, and there is a goat track which presents little difficulty.'

Simon turned to the Surprises and asked, 'Dalby, be a darling and endeavour to engage that fellow Grigorios with his mule.'

* * *

Beyond the south of the island, all day Pat had been careful to keep *Surprise* some distance off the land and with plenty of sea-room, at least a league off the island at all times in case any Turk ship be sighted. During the previous dusk until nightfall *Surprise* and *Eleanor* had loitered several leagues off the south-west coast, sometimes venturing west to observe the Turk squadron at a comfortable distance, hearing the bombardment from the guns and observing the gun flashes from the ships at anchor in the channel between Kasos and its satellite islets off the island's west coast. In the morning, *Eleanor*, a fleeter sailer than *Surprise* and drawing much less water, had been sent in to Helatros Bay, which was scarcely a bay, being no larger than an inlet amongst the steep cliffs.

Aboard *Surprise*, Pat, in conference with his officers after breakfast, declared, 'Here we wait. Let us hope that Zouvelekis brings Simon and the others to that bay, to *Eleanor*. If they are coming then they cannot be long, for the Turks will surely soon be all over the island.'

The hours passed with no sign of *Eleanor* coming out. The sun rose to its zenith and time passed by very slowly as it began its descent, the hot temperatures baking all on deck and creating a stifling humidity below. In the great cabin Pat contemplated his position, his dear friend once again missing. As the sunset faded, Pat's anxiety and uncertainty got the better of his caution, and he decided to take *Surprise* as close to the mouth of Helatros Bay as he dared, and to take his barge into the narrow bay and across to *Eleanor*. 'Tom, I want twenty good lads with me, in my barge and in the cutter; pistols and cutlasses for all; ten muskets and three lanterns. If we are not returned at dawn you are to take *Surprise* out two leagues and patrol there until *Eleanor* comes out. If she is not out and we are not returned tomorrow then I venture we may be in some difficulty. Likely in Turk hands or worse, and you will return to Cephalonia.' Pickering's protestations that he should accompany Pat and his landing party were overruled with finality, '*Surprise* has greater need of you, Tom; were we not to return. Though that is far from my intention, be assured.'

* * *

In the San Marina taverna, Simon, Marston, Zouvelekis and his family prepared to leave for the trek south. Grigorios and the mule had been located. Grigorios was feeding the mule behind the tavern, and they waited only for Dalby who, with the other Surprises, had gone to see what was happening on the western or coast side of the town, for the cannonade had ceased again as darkness fell.

'What is that commotion I can hear; shouting, screaming, the discharge of firearms? Would that Dalby was returned,' said Simon, anxiously, the noise of clamour wholly audible despite being some little way off, and the nervous, waiting ambience of the tavern escalating instantly to extreme anxiety; Captain Zouvelekis's wife was beginning to plead with him with a desperation in her voice that needed no translation.

'Where can Dalby be?' asked Marston.

At that moment Dalby burst through the door with his companions, blood streaming from a head wound down his face, his shirt red, sodden. 'Quickly now, the Turks are here, in the town, killing. We cannot stay longer,' Dalby shouted. A great commotion was now audible in the street outside, and Dalby and his men hastened to drag a heavy table across the door. 'Is there another way out?' he shouted.

Zouvelekis translated to the innkeeper who hastened to pull Zouvelekis's wife to the internal door, beckoning and shouting unintelligibly, at least to the Surprises, though the meaning was plain. At that instant there was a great crash against the door; Dalby and his men pushed the table hard against it. Captain Zouvelekis with two Surprises near carried Simon out into the backyard, and heaved him without ceremony on to the mule. Grigorios needed no instruction, and swiftly followed the old innkeeper out from the yard, tugging the mule into a narrow and deserted small alley leading up towards the outskirts of the town. Three of the Surprises were with them, Dalby and two still within the taverna. Zouvelekis and his family were now shuffling alongside the mule which had swiftly learned haste, departing from his prior slow gait as the urgency of their situation now transcended human communication. Loud, shrill screams and pistol shots plainly could be heard all about them. Fifty yards on and they stared back in the near darkness to see Dalby and one companion helping the other, who looked to be suffering from a gunshot wound or sword slash to his leg; at that distance and the light near gone it could not be determined. Grigorios whipped the mule to a canter, and all ran alongside, save the three Surprises who went back to assist their fellows, four seizing up the wounded man by his arms and legs, Dalby behind them watching their exit from the taverna. Two Turks appeared, fortunately with only swords and no firearms; they glanced at the fleeing party, now a hundred yards away, before turning back into the taverna.

From adjoining houses women, children, and old men spilled into the alley, and all joined the growing throng in a rush towards the hills, shouting and screaming, pandemonium having become endemic. Behind them appeared more Turk soldiers, cutting down the stragglers and shooting the old men. The villagers were running in blind panic, some fifty or more fleeing around the mule party. Dalby had caught up with his companions, the strong seamen making light of carrying their wounded comrade. The manic throng left the town, still running, along a stony track that led towards the south-west, rising gradually between two hills. After a near half mile the elderly were too tired to run further, and the flight slowed. Many looked back to see the roaring flames from houses set afire; all could hear the continuing screams and shots, still plainly audible even at that distance. Simon, though a proficient rider, had no saddle, and gripped the mule tightly by its mane until its exertions diminished and it slowed to its customary gentle plodding. Marston, still quite breathless, struggled to enquire of Dalby's wound and that of the wounded seaman, still carried by four Surprises, who had caught up with the mule.

Dalby replied to Marston, 'Oh, mine, sir; 'tis but a scratch. They were in the village afore we could reach the tavern, and one swung at me with a sword; 'twas only the pommel that caught me afore I put my knife into his chest. They were in the taverna too, pushing agin the door, and the table pushed aside as we left. Poor old Hartley here took a ball in the leg. We stopped 'em with chairs over their heads, and cut 'em up with broken bottles. If they get home, their wives won't want 'em anymore,' explained Dalby, whilst breathing hard, his bloody face bright red with exertion.

There were by now some sixty or more Kasiot civilians accompanying them as they stumbled at best speed along the track, midnight now long past, and their only light a near half-moon in a cloudless sky, bright star formations all about it. 'Hurry, hurry,' Zouvelekis urged, a mile on from the village, 'I think we may have pursuers.' His words produced another bout of screams from the women present, many of whom were barefoot and bloodied from leaving their homes in haste as they gathered up their children even

329

as the Turks burst in upon them, slaughtering their menfolk. 'Keep silent,' shouted Zouvelekis, 'and keep moving,' as he picked up a child aged no more than five whose mother could now carry only her youngest. The Surprises were all heavily burdened; four still carrying Hartley, and Dalby clutching young children, their mothers not letting them from their sight and struggling bravely with infants all about them.

* * *

At Helatros, Pat's barge had reached *Eleanor* a half hour before midnight, and with still no arrivals at the waterside Pat determined upon making the landing he had contemplated aboard *Surprise*. With ten more men from *Eleanor* they reached the shore at midnight and set off up the hill from their beach landing. Pat's barge and *Eleanor's* cutter remained at the shore, guarded by four Eleanors. Pat led the way up the steep and winding hillside track, Barton at his side with a lantern. Apprehensive but at best speed they trudged along the winding track towards the north of the island.

* * *

After their mile in fearful haste out of the village the refugees of San Marina were slowing as more bare feet were cut on the rocky surface of the path. The children were crying, their mothers failing to console them, and deep, weary fatigue was setting in with the old men and women. Looking back, it was possible to make out in silhouette their pursuers, backlit by the orange and red glow of the fires now raging in the town. An occasional musket shot boomed out, rekindling the fear and desperation in the hearts of the villagers. Captain Zouvelekis urged them to greater haste, but such was long past their capability, and their pace was little faster than a crawl, the oldest of the villagers now struggling to move at all. The Surprises would not leave the civilians, and loitered at the rear of the party, though with little more than pocket knives, there was likely nothing that they would be able to do were their pursuers to catch them. Slowly the Turks came on, and it seemed that they must soon catch up. At two miles from the village and the time near 2 a.m. a small house loomed in the distance on a tiny plain alongside the track.

330

'We must take shelter there; we cannot endure on this hillside when the Turk catches us. Perhaps we may be able to keep them out?' said Marston, hope failing in his heart. Their pursuers were now a bare hundred yards behind, and could be made out as a score of soldiers, firing muskets at them, but from far beyond any effective range, the sound more frightening than dangerous.

* * *

'Quickly, lads,' urged Pat, now just a little to the south of the refugees; 'I hear muskets.' The Surprises had walked through the darkness on the unfamiliar track near four miles from Helatros, and, burdened that they were with muskets, shot, and water flasks hastened on towards the converging refugees.

* * *

The Turks had closed to a bare hundred yards behind the refugees who had reached the small house, scarcely big enough for the sixty odd people now clamouring to enter. The occupants, a bewildered old goatherd and his wife, simply stood aside, uncomprehending, but greatly anxious, having heard the shots. Outside, the Surprises helped the infirm towards the door. Simon was still astride the mule, Marston and Grigorios alongside. 'Dalby, 'tis a desperate affair, to be sure; perhaps you and your men should leave us? We will barricade the door, and hope to keep them out until morning when there may be some prospect of help or Turk bloodlusts be spent. We are a prize of little value to them and perhaps they will return to better pickings in the town?' suggested Simon.

'We ain't a leavin' you, Doctor. Best get inside, quickly now, they are but moments away,' declared Dalby; Simon greatly warming to him in his moment of decision. The Greek civilians were now all within the house; Marston, near despair, at the door; and the Surprises, anxious, outside.

'Oh dear Lord, please grant our salvation,' prayed Marston in a low murmur, his spirits swiftly sinking.

'Marston, will you help me off this mule?' asked Simon.

Just as the Turk pursuers approached the house, now just thirty or fewer yards away, shouting in full voice, a ragged fire of muskets opened upon them from beyond the house to the south; three Turks falling, and bringing the others to an immediate halt. From out of the darkness came the shrieks of Pat's thirty Surprises and Eleanors, running, shouting, discharging pistols, screaming, and waving cutlasses, as loud as ever they were in any ship boarding. The Turks turned about and fled, bolting as fast as they could, leaving their wounded behind.

'Pat! Praise the Lord! A more timely arrival I could not conceive of. Marston, steady this mule if you will, an irascible fellow, that he is. Oh for a Sheltie! I do most humbly beg your pardon for failing to rejoin the ship,' shouted Simon from the skittish mule, as Pat and the pursuing Surprises came back to greet their fellows, the Turks in full flight back down the track towards the town. The Surprises gently brought all out from the house, and passed round their water bottles, which were eagerly appreciated and quickly emptied by the exhausted refugees.

'Come; there is not a moment to lose. We must return to *Surprise*,' ordered Pat, gasping for breath after his exertions, running the last half mile, now lost for words for his dear friend, and mightily relieved to see him. The Surprises helped the civilians to their feet, picking up children and the most infirm of the elders. 'Marston, there you are; be so good as to start that mule,' remarked Pat, looking about him for any further sign of Turk pursuers, urgency foremost in his tongue. 'Quickly now, all haste to the south. Dalby, you are bleeding heavy, and that is a deep cut for sure. What has happened to Hartley?'

'Thankee, sir. You have saved us, for sure. Hartley has took a ball in the bum, sir. 'Tis nothin' the Doctor will fret about. It looks bad on account o' all the blood. We'll get 'im to the ship, sir,' Dalby replied cheerfully, the desperate anxiety of the past few hours now subsiding.

'Step along there at the back; lively now. Lads, collect those children there, hiding behind the rock, quickly does it,' Pat shouted.

The refugees, now bolstered in numbers and in spirits, set off again to the south, and though the pace still remained painfully slow the wailing and sobbing of beforehand had ceased with the passing of imminent danger of death. A deep feeling of relief spread through Pat's mind, as he walked beside the mule, alongside his close friend of twenty-one years, his frustration at Simon and Marston's non-appearance at the appointed time at the quay fading.

'Pray tell, Simon, what has happened?'

'Tolerably exciting, brother, 'Twas a gull and a falcon we had ne'er seen before,' Simon began.

Pat interrupted, 'A gull? *A gull!* The island aflame, the Turks back, and you ramble about a ... a *gull*. Have you had a knock on the head, Simon?'

'Not perhaps of great significance to you folk of a less inquisitive mind, I grant you,' Simon resumed, 'but in shifting for a closer look at the gull and the falcon, my ankle lodged in a crevice, turning wickedly and throwing me to the ground. Alas, I could no longer walk; the sprain was so very severe. Marston there went for help, and Dalby, it was, bless him, came with the mule to fetch me off the hill. Before we could do more the Turks were upon us in the town, and 'twas a mighty close thing that we escaped as they burst in. Dalby here, with Hartley and Fisher, held them back for the minute we needed to get away. Without him and his lads, Marston and I would be likely a'lying dead back there.'

The enormity of the narrow escape from near certain death sank in slowly with Simon, and with Pat too. For the next five minutes or so neither spoke as they plodded along, their slow progress dictated by the slowest of the exhausted refugees. Three more hours went by, and all of the party had long since fallen into the silence of exhaustion when the faintest glimmer in the eastern sky heralded the imminence of dawn as they stumbled the final yards down the steep track to the horseshoe bay of Helatros; *Eleanor* being the most welcoming sight the Surprises had seen for years, and the refugees greatly heartened that their painful trek was over.

Sunday 20th June 1824   *Helatros Bay, Kasos*

The horizon brightened just as the refugees slumped down on the pebble beach, relief satiating their fatigue with the realisation that they would walk no further. The Eleanors had come ashore amongst them bringing water and bread which all gulped gratefully and munched hungrily. For Simon a makeshift crutch had quickly been procured, and he attended the wounded Hartley, bandaging his posterior and leg tightly to stem the blood that soaked his trousers and boots.

'Mr Mower, the women and children away to *Eleanor* first, if you will,' Pat organised the evacuation. 'Barton, up that hill with three lads with muskets, let fly if you see so much as a scout.'

Since attending to Hartley an exhausted Simon had fallen deeply asleep, and Pat could not speak with him, and so, unable to converse with any of the Greeks and Zouvelekis gently chiding the civilians in turn into the boats, he contented himself with checking with each of his men in turn. A deeply tired Marston busied himself bandaging the villagers' torn feet as all recuperated as best they could whilst waiting to board the cutter. The chilling realisation of their personal losses was returned amongst them, and wives were once more sobbing for their husbands, daughters for their fathers, all utterly disconsolate in their grief. Steadily, as the sun escaped from the horizon, the refugees were all transferred to *Eleanor;* Pat's barge and *Eleanor's* boat conveying them the short passage to her in the midst of the bay; *Eleanor's* crew carefully helping the aged and injured up her side until all were aboard; the Surprises coming last from the beach.

Grigorios elected to remain on Kasos; his concern for his family, somewhere on the island, being paramount. Marston and an awakened Simon thanked him profusely for his help before they boarded the barge, Grigorios remaining with the mule on the beach, continuing to wave his farewell as they crossed to *Eleanor*.

'Let us away swiftly, Mr Codrington, to *Surprise* ere we sight any Turk again,' Pat urged. A quarter hour out from the bay and *Surprise* was near. Pat decided to bring *Eleanor* alongside, lashing her together with *Surprise* to facilitate the transfer of the refugees, some sixty of them, between the two vessels, *Eleanor* being too small to accommodate them for a voyage of some days to another of the Greek islands. 'Mr Pickering, I will be in the cabin. We shall beat north-west to return to Santorin. Let us first make several leagues to the west so as to keep away from the Turk squadron on the north side of the island. You have the command,' Pat ordered his second; Pickering quite failing to disguise his relief at their return, 'Aye aye, sir, west, then north-west at best speed it is.'

Never was Simon more pleased to see Freeman, entering the cabin quite unbidden, and bearing a silver tray laden with coffee, Greek brandy and lobscouse, the aroma of which was most welcome.

'Coffee, massa, an' food,' Freeman pronounced, setting it down with glasses for three just as Marston joined them, bringing Simon's bag so as to surreptitiously return the appropriated Dollond glass.

'Thankee, Freeman. Bear a hand with the refugees on deck. See cook and Wilkins too, and ensure that all are fed and watered. Nothing more to drink this day other than grog for the women and goat's milk for the children,' said Pat wearily, adding, 'and please to enquire of Hartley. How is he, Simon?'

'He will be well in a week, with the blessing. The ball passed through his upper leg near his posterior. He will not sit comfortably for a month I venture, but there is no danger. I will clean and dress the wound again in a very few moments,' Simon replied, biting hungrily into the lobscouse without further ado.

'That is a mercy,' said Pat and turned to Marston. 'Michael, please to describe your time since Simon was injured. Will I pour you a glass of brandy?'

Marston had begun to recover a little only after coming aboard *Surprise,* and to Pat's eye still looked utterly exhausted. Plainly it would be a few hours before he would become an effective assistant surgeon again. Slowly Marston described the whole time of their escape, beginning with his trek off the hill, his return to fetch Simon accompanied by the Surprises, the sound of the signal gun, Dalby pressing on to find Simon, their return to the town, the Turk bombardment and invasion, the sack of the town, and their close run escape amidst the pandemonium in the taverna as the Turks burst in – Dalby, Hartley, and Fishley holding them back to make time for the others to get away – and finally the trek south across the island until they were saved by Pat's timely arrival.

335

'Hell and death! That is a desperate tale, Michael,' exclaimed Pat at the end of Marston's story. 'Simon, would it be of any use my suggesting you give up these ramblings in search of birds; gulls or any other kind?'

'None whatsoever,' Simon replied, pausing from his coffee. 'You are to consider that there is nothing finer to warm the soul than to discover a new species, gull or any other creature. I must consult Willughby after supper.'

'I ain't fit enough to be running about these islands at my age, I can tell you; that last furlong till we found you, I was running faster than a yearling at the Curragh; mortally fagged, I was,' said Pat.

'Plainly a modicum of more exercise would serve you well, brother.'

'I hope you gentlemen will give me the pleasure of dining in the cabin later? Now, I must see about the islanders and speak with Dalby and his men,' Pat said, setting down his glass.

The *Meltemi* provided a pleasing cooling wind in the rising heat of the late morning, near noon, as *Surprise* ploughed her wake, beating close-hauled, now nine leagues west of Kasos and Candia looming off the larboard beam. Simon and Marston had gone below to treat the injured, Hartley the most serious, but scores suffering with cut soles and muscle strains, unaccustomed to the strenuous trek that had been their flight. On deck the women coddled the children, exhausted and generally all sleeping, as were the elderly. Dalby and his companions were sitting below the hoisted boats, backs to an opened larboard gun port, enjoying the wind and the shade. All sprang to their feet as Pat approached.

'Dalby, lads, do I see you well?' Pat smiled in greeting, his men relaxing to stand at ease, and all replying simultaneously with a brief, 'Aye, Cap'n, thankee.'

'I am grateful to you all for fetching the Doctor off the hill; that was very well done, bravely done indeed, holding the Turks back in the taverna. Mr Marston has told me the story. Should I flog you all for ignoring the signal gun?' Pat asked, smiling broadly and clearly in jest, continuing quickly as Dalby's face registered confusion. 'Give me your hand, Dalby,' said Pat, proferring his own and seizing firmly and shaking Dalby's hand. 'I thank you most heartily. That was a handsome action. Well done, well done, all of you. I will send Freeman to you with a bottle later this day. Thank you, lads,' and Pat moved off to look about the Greek passengers on his deck, Dalby and his companions mightily pleased by their captain's very personal words of thanks and remembering not least the mention of a bottle to appear later.

Within a short time Pat went below to check on Hartley, who was lying uncomfortably face down on the table. Simon had opened his dressing and was cleaning the wounds made by the pistol ball; the exit wound looking particularly red, ragged, swollen and painful. Hartley, sweat pouring from his brow, struggled to bear the pain of Simon's attention, even with the heavy dose of laudanum given him. Half conscious, his senses drifting, his face covered in sweat, it was all he could do to nod at his captain's greeting. Pat persevered, 'Hartley; that was a brave thing you did back there in that taverna.' He paused to see if Hartley had understood. His half nod suggesting he had, Pat continued, 'I thank you kindly, Hartley, well done.' Pat grasped his hand, hanging down towards the deck, and squeezed it gently; Hartley now with a just discernible smile on his pained face as Pat spoke again, 'We are greatly in your debt; thankee. Rest as best ye can.'

In the cooler hours of the evening after supper, Pat and Simon convened in the cabin, settled in an ambience of relaxation. Freeman fussed about them like an old mother hen, bringing the toad in a hole, then coffee and brandy, proferring tiny marchpane slices, until Pat sent him away with instructions to take out two bottles of Greek brandy for Dalby and his mates, resting still on the gun deck – the air remaining too warm for the liking of many of the crew, and the hammocks below on the lower deck occupied for the most part by sleeping Kasiot women and children.

'Brother, that was a timely arrival, to be sure,' said Simon, slumped back in the chair, his toad in a hole eaten up, and gulping all the remainder from his glass of his favourite Tempranillo. His chin was greasy with the fat which had escaped his meal, his shirt and coat sleeves showing ingrained signs of the oft-repeated ordeal.

'You would not care for a hand of cards, chess perhaps, I suppose?' said Pat.

'I could not play either,' said Simon. 'My mind is burdened with other thoughts.'

'You have more than the nine lives of Cerberus, Simon, escaping yet again entering into Hell,' a still relieved Pat joked, trying to lift his friend's spirits.

'Three heads, brother,' Simon murmured, savouring his second large glass of Tempranillo, Freeman refilling with not a moment lost, and equally pleased to see him returned. 'Three heads it was he had, not nine lives, and keeping souls in it was, not out. And who is to say I will be going down there? Indeed, I think not.'

Wednesday 23rd June 1824   *approaching Santorin*

The north-west voyage to Santorin was arduously slow, requiring of constant tacking into the teeth of the exceptionally strong *Etesian* wind, and *Surprise* rarely exceeded one and a half knots, the crew having to work hard to achieve even that. The presence of some sixty-plus Kasiot refugees on board was a sobering, even depressing influence on the crew, all of whom did their utmost to lift the spirits of grieving wives and children who had left behind husbands and fathers, certainly many of them dead and others missing. The gunner's wife fussed about the children unceasingly. The ship's cook strived to provide the best food possible from the ship's limited provisions, plain and unfamiliar as they were to the recuperating Kasiots. The refugees never grumbled at eating ship's biscuit and salt beef that had very probably been in cask for two years or longer, accustomed as they were to only the freshest of food, and *Surprise* not encountering any fishermen to reprovision with the plentiful tunny to be found in those waters. The Kasiot children, painfully remembering the horror of their recent days, rarely left the side of their mothers, and it was two days before they began to engage with the Surprises, emerging only slowly from the shock and horror of their escape from their homes. It was therefore a great relief to all aboard when Santorin was reached, mid-morning, and the Kasiots disembarked, Captain Zouvelekis bidding

Simon, Marston, and Pat a subdued farewell before going ashore in the barge. Only a solitary wave was espied from one of the small children, to Mrs Boswell, who was sobbing floods as the barge pulled away from *Surprise's* side on its seventh trip.

The final return of the barge surprisingly brought back a joyful Duncan Macleod. 'Ah am come back, Pat. Ah am sent wi' this letter fer ye. It originated from Hydra an' ah received it in Argostoli, an agent of Mavrocordato presentin' it.'

'Why, Duncan, come in, come in; give you joy of your recovery,' exclaimed a delighted Pat, seizing and shaking his hand vigorously, the pleasure being so much more in the unexpected sight of his friend.

Murphy had marched directly into the cabin with Duncan, and now spoke up, 'Well, this gentleman, that is to say Captain Zouvelekis, is returned, sorr.'

'Thankee, Murphy. Would you ask Captain Zouvelekis to wait just a moment? Compliments of course; I shall attend him in but a few minutes; and please ask Mr Jason to come to the cabin directly.'

'Ah see ye cannae manage wi'oot me, Jack,' joked Duncan, gazing at the still evident damage in the great cabin, many of the lights remaining boarded over, and the evidence of the Candia destruction lingering still.

'So very dull the cabin has been without you. How well you look. We will surely enjoy our bottle this night; so much to hear.'

Jason entered within a few moments and shook hands with Duncan, the two exchanging warm greetings.

'Mr Jason, I am in need of your services,' Pat announced. 'I find this letter awaiting our arrival and it is written in the Greek. Can you kindly read it for me? Freeman! Freeman: a bottle of something red if you will, afore dinner, perhaps the Margaux? Is it pork for dinner? Light along and ask of Wilkins.'

The writing on the folded letter being in the Greek script, Jason picked it up and broke the seal. He began to translate, slowly, '*Dear Captain O'Connor, I hope Lieutenant Macleod and this letter will find you in Thira. All Greek squadrons being engaged, the Hellenic government requests that you sail immediately north to the vicinity of Lesbos and Limnos so as to search the approaches to the Dardanelles, with your priority being to locate the Turk fleet of Admiral Khosref. It is reported to us that Khosref and his fleet departed the Golden Horn on the twentieth of April, and as yet their whereabouts are unknown. Should winds be favourable, you are to approach as close as can be, without endangering your ship, to Mitylene, where it is believed the Turk fleet may lie. Should you locate the fleet you are to proceed directly to Hydra to report. Captain Zouvelekis, should he still accompany you, has, by this order, been requested to remain on board your ship, as your liaison officer with the Hellenic Navy, and we trust that you will accommodate him as such. Signed, Andreas Vokos, Admiral, Hydra, dated the twentieth of June,'* Jason concluded his translation.

Pat asked, 'Who is this Vokos? I have never heard of this man. Murphy, light along and fetch Captain Zouvelekis to the cabin.'

Zouvelekis entered the cabin within a minute, smiled to Jason, nodded to Duncan, and waited for Pat to speak. During the voyage from Santorin to Kasos he had noted and assumed the custom of the Royal Navy that the captain always spoke first, his officers only replying.

'Captain Zouvelekis,' Pat started, 'pray tell me, are you acquainted with an Admiral Vokos?'

'Most certainly, sir; Admiral Vokos is customarily and better known by the name Miaoulis. Surely you have heard of him?' Zouvelekis replied.

Clarity struck Pat immediately, 'Ah! Yes, of course, Miaoulis; a most famous fighting officer indeed. Why, his customary name had escaped me for just a moment. Miaoulis, so it is. No braver man ever served aboard any ship. Captain Zouvelekis, are you aware of his request of us? His request that you serve aboard this ship, in the capacity of liaison officer between this ship and the Hellenic Navy,' Pat enquired, looking hard at Zouvelekis, as did Duncan and Jason.

'It has been communicated to me, sir. In which capacity it would be an honour to serve with you, if you will have me? I have the strongest of respect for this ship and all its crew,' Zouvelekis replied, his back stiffening, his voice firming, as he answered.

340

Pat stepped towards Zouvelekis as he replied, offering his hand, his voice lowered, 'You honour us with your compliments, Captain Zouvelekis. Thank you. You will honour us more by shifting aboard,' whilst shaking Zouvelekis' hand.

At that, Duncan and Jason shook hands in turn with Zouvelekis who appeared to be both pleased and surprised by the turn of events, saying only, 'Thank you, Captain. Thank you,' in very quiet voice.

'Murphy: a cot in the gun-room for Captain Zouvelekis. Look lively now,' said Pat, affably.

In the quietude of evening, after supper, Pat and Simon sat in the cabin playing chess. The atmosphere, thought Pat between moves, seemed strange. Their usual jocularity was absent; an undefined, small tension hung in the air, a restraint, their communication mechanical, Simon seemingly pre-occupied, his very being almost absent, their thoughts seemingly staying on parallel tracks, never converging, their short exchanges never reaching any meeting of minds. Whilst waiting for Pat's moves, he being a slow player, Simon studied his Willughby, contemplating the gull observed on Kasos, and musing to himself, 'No; I cannot find any red-billed gull with a black wing tip, and the falcon will have to await the morrow. Perhaps I shall write to Latreille at the Muséum d'Histoire Naturelle; perhaps I will go there? I have refused his invitation in the past, pleasing though it was. I feel sure these new species, if I am in the right of it, will warrant his comment. Though in truth his interest is more in arthropods; without doubt he is an entomologist of the first order. I collect he may have a colleague more in the ornithological line. Now what was his name? Payraudeau! Yes, that is it, Charles Payraudeau.'

'Checkmate!' exclaimed Pat, who did not give a stuff for gulls of any colour beak, though he was far too polite to say so. 'Arthurpods? Ento ... ento-molists ... orthologicals? Simon, why your mind ain't been in this game at all.'

Casting his book aside, Simon replied, his voice low, trembling, 'Bah! How many games have we played in this cabin, Pat? Has not the same sixteen pieces a'side brought tedium long ago? The same

341

opening moves, the same sequences. Is there a move we have ne'er seen? Don't the game tire you now?'

Pat looked at his companion in some surprise and with concern. 'You do look miserably hipped,' he said, staring at him, his attention and deep concern for his friend rising. 'I have been so engaged in this damn business on Kasos that I have not been minded to consider of you. I am so sorry, Simon. Is there something troubling you, old friend? If anything is amiss... can I be of some use?'

Simon sighed before replying, his voice low and shaking, 'All the world's oceans we have travelled: Sickness, death and destruction a'plenty we have seen, and ne'er is there enough time to pass a day in pursuit of our gentler interests. 'Twas but a few days ago when Marston and I espied that red-billed gull; a falcon too that was not familiar to me; and then we are plunged again into bloodshed and killing, into days of darkness. I have seen enough of it. It brings me to the deepest despair… I doubt I can endure more.'

'Brother, though you may say it don't amount to much - I am no Plato, I never set up for a philosopher - I will say this one thing: you and I, our shipmates all, we have saved many lives these past days, and there is surely something to be said for that.'

'Indeed there is, but how high is the price we are asked to pay? I am at a stand. I do not know where my mind leads me. Oh, how I miss my dear Agnes: she is so much in my dreams these past weeks. I fancy I can still smell the lingering ghost of her sweet scent. I find I long to see the green of the Isles, to glimpse the sea eagles of Rhum, to walk again on the Cuillins of Skye and the peaks of Hirta. I so much wish to be at my hearth and home again in Tobermory, that precious sanctuary. In those black moments of waking from such dreams I despair of ever seeing them again. *Will* I ever see them again, Pat? Will we ever leave this bloody strife and return home?'

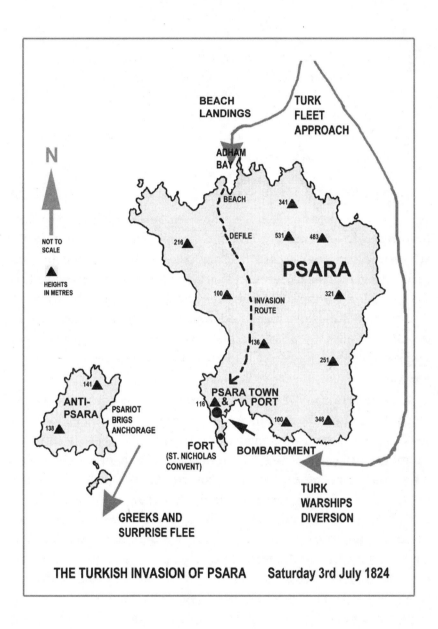

THE TURKISH INVASION OF PSARA   Saturday 3rd July 1824

Chapter Nine

Fill high the bowl with Samian wine!
Our virgins dance beneath the shade —
I see their glorious black eyes shine;
But gazing on each glowing maid,
My own the burning tear-drop laves,
To think such breasts must suckle slaves

Wednesday 30ᵗʰ June 1824   *Psara Island*

A week had passed as *Surprise* slowly tacked north from Santorin, the northerly *Meltemi* still blowing strong and allowing only the slowest of progress. At noon Psara came into sight, and *Surprise* reached the roadstead between Psara and Anti-Psara at two bells of the First dog watch in the late afternoon, passing by the fringe of more than a hundred sail, all tied up yet few sailors visible on their decks and yards. *Surprise* continued east beyond the fort peninsula and then north in the lee of it to drop anchor within a short row of the town.

Pat had, unusually, dined and breakfasted without Simon for all of the past week, with many an hour spent in contemplation of his dear friend, and he remained puzzled by his absence from the cabin. Pat had scarcely seen anything at all of Simon, who had eaten with the other officers in the gun-room, and had also never appeared in the cabin for any of their customary evenings fiddling, Pat playing on two occasions with Marston alone, who had not cared to comment on Simon's absence. Pat had not asked, but had contented himself with letting things lie, leaving Simon to his own considerations, Simon's momentary exhibition of profound unhappiness still a shock to him; and Simon's thoughts of returning home laying ill on Pat's mind. He felt that the matter was best left to Simon to work out, to reach his own conclusion, and so Pat had wondered all week whether the dismaying sentiments still prevailed in Simon's thoughts. As the barge was lowered alongside he was mightily pleased to see Simon emerge from below and step up to his quarterdeck, still hobbling in evident discomfort and with the aid of a stick. They were joined by all of Pat's lieutenants and Captain Zouvelekis.

The quarterdeck party gazed across the narrow isthmus between the town and the fort to the masts of the armada of anchored Psariot ships. As *Surprise* swung on her anchor, Barton and his men busied themselves into the barge for Pat's trip ashore. Simon stood alongside his captain, and spoke quietly to Pat as all studied the town and fort, 'Pat, I spoke intemperately to you when last in the cabin. I ask your pardon.'

'I hope you are no longer in such ill humour. I collect that you have been low, out of spirits, since we fetched you off that wretched island.'

'For shame I have not come to the cabin this week, Pat. I find myself in better humour this morning. I regret my black mood and sharp tongue of last week. I owe you a thousand apologies.'

Pat found the words very heartening, and turning to his friend replied softly, 'That pleases me greatly, brother. Black days ... they afflict us all. To return to such bloody events as you found on Kasos, after four years ashore and in tranquility at home, will always be shocking. That is not to say that we should ever wish to become accustomed to them, far from it. That is our very purpose here, to do what we can, to stop such horrors. We are weak, the Greeks are weak, yet the Turk is strong, and so we will surely fail more times than we will succeed. To continue, with the great odds against us as we and the Greek admirals do, is only to hold the line in the fragile, *the very fragile*, hope of better days, of more and bigger Greek ships. Alas, alone we with our dear *Surprise* cannot achieve much: the Greeks lack proper government, their organisation or lack of it fails them; yet it may not always be so. They do not lack for brave men: Miaoulis has struck the Turk hard in the past and doubtless will do so again.'

'War is the business of barbarians, Pat. I hated the tyrant, Bonaparte, but he was surely right in that.'

Pat placed his hand on Simon's arm, 'And there are times,

Simon, when men of conscience cannot run away. We must choose to fight or perish. We surely saved sixty souls from the hell that was Kasos. That is why we are here. Be in no doubt, Simon, we all aboard *Surprise* need you: there will surely be more bloody days yet. Never be so put about, it will not serve you well. I urge you, if these feelings ail you again, speak with me. Never forget, a friend's eye is a good mirror, and doubtless is an ear too, so it is. How is your foot? How is Hartley?'

'Thank you, Pat. I am sensible of your kind words. Hartley? He is recovering well, the wound has healed over. He walks but does not care to sit. I doubt he will row in the barge for some months, but as a gunner he can return to duty, I dare say. My foot is healing, 'tis of no consequence,' Simon replied, his spirits lifted just a little by Pat's words.

'The barge is ready, sir,' announced Barton at that moment.

'Very good, Barton; Captain Zouvelekis, Mr Macleod, Dr Ferguson, Mr Jason, we will go ashore directly. Mr Mower, you will accompany us in the cutter, and see about finding fresh water. Mr Pickering, you will remain in command until our return,' Pat ordered.

Psara town lay astride a tiny peninsula at the south-west corner of the small island. At the very tip of the peninsula was the fort of Saint Nicholas. It was a short row to the town. On the town quay, on the eastern coast of the peninsula, a welcome party had gathered, the principal of which was Vice-Admiral Canaris; himself a Psariot. Zouvelekis made the introductions. Canaris seemed particularly pleased to greet them, and invited them all to a quayside taverna, adopted as his ad hoc headquarters. When they were seated and enjoying the welcome shade, Zouvelekis translated the exchanges between Pat and Canaris.

'Welcome, Captain O'Connor. Welcome to Psara. You have a most handsome ship, nothing of her like have we had in our navy before. She is a fast sailer, I venture? And her guns, eighteen-pounders? We do not have her like in all Greece. Your fame precedes you. It is a pleasure to meet you, and your service in our cause does us great honour. Pray tell, whereabouts have you been these past few months? What have you seen of Turk ships? The news from Hydra has made no mention of your ship since she was at Messalonghi accompanying Lord Byron.' As Canaris paused for Zouvelekis to catch up, Pat did not know where to start, the questions were so many and so varied. Canaris resumed, 'Captain O'Connor, would you do me the very great honour of accompanying me to the island's council of war, which is to convene on the morrow to discuss our position and response in reply to emissaries sent by the Turk Admiral Khosref, demanding our surrender in return for an amnesty?'

Pat was quite taken aback, but replied as best he thought fit, 'Sir, I am no politician. I have been sent by Admiral Miaoulis of Hydra to locate Khosref's fleet. We have stopped here merely to enquire of any sightings, before continuing to Mitylene in search of him. Tell, are his whereabouts known to you?'

Admiral Canaris answered, 'Captain O'Connor; no reliable sightings of his ships have been received these past two weeks. There are of course rumours, plentiful and varied: that he has gone south-west to attack Volos on the mainland, that he has passed Chios and is preparing to land on Samos, and also that his ships remain still at Mitylene. But these are rumours expounded by fishermen, and generally fishermen who have not been to sea in fear of his fleet. There is no certain news of his whereabouts. Though, were I Khosref, and given his recent demands of surrender, and even his sending of the Bishop of Mitylene to demand it, I venture here is his interest, Psara itself. I am striving to persuade our council of Primates to recommission all those ships out there in the roads; for only with them will we have any prospect of defending this island. Whilst they sit there with no crew, we have, in my opinion, no hope whatsoever. We sit here like a plum ripe for the plucking. Khosref cannot be a fool; our circumstances cannot be unknown to him: on every Greek island, in every Greek province, there are Turk spies. Captain O'Connor, can I press you to support me tomorrow? It is of the very first importance to all my people living on this island, as well as the five thousands more of Chiots who have already fled before the Turk monsters, their own

347

island being sacked but two years ago – twenty thousand deaths and forty-one thousand souls taken as slaves from that island. The numbers are exactly known to us because a Turk customs certificate was given for every one of them: five thousand of enslaved Chiots being sent to Constantinople alone; so our agents reported. I am so desperate to prevent the same occurring here. With those ships I can fight; without them I am helpless. I beg of you, will you give me your help, Captain?'

The emotive plea from Canaris struck chords in Pat's heart though his own responsibilities to his crew and his orders left reservations in his mind. He replied cautiously, 'Sir, there is indeed a squadron out there in the roads capable of defending this island against a sizeable Turk fleet, but why, pray, is it not in readiness now to do so? I fear *Surprise*, a small frigate in these days of forty-fours, can do little against a Turk fleet by herself. Certainly, I will do all I can to help you. I will of course attend you and your council on the morrow. A very small delay of some hours only is of little consequence, but we must sail after the council meeting.'

Canaris was greatly relieved to hear this and replied, 'Sir, our primates have ordered the ships guns to be brought on land to reinforce our batteries, and that is where they lie. Our ships can do nothing without them.'

'What!' Pat exploded, 'What madness is this? Ships guns taken ashore! They may as well be spiked for all the good that will do when the Turk fleet arrives: folly and madness, for sure; and the crews too, also ashore?' He stared at Canaris in disbelief.

'Yes. The gunners are at the batteries, and all others pressed as infantrymen,' a despairing Canaris replied, bleakly, adding after a few moments, 'The Primates intend to order that rudders be unshipped to salve the fears of our Roumeliot brigade, who fear they will be left behind to face the Turks alone.'

'Hell and damnation! Is there no grain of sense within your council?' Pat said, with great vehemence, adding, 'I fear we shall never repulse the Turk when I find these ... these ...'

'Calamities may suit, Pat,' Simon interposed before his friend could say worse.

'*Calamities*... that is the word I was seeking. Thank you, Simon. Admiral, you may count on my support tomorrow. I will come ashore after breakfast, at eight bells of the Morning watch, and perhaps you will then kindly escort me to your council?' said Pat, adding, 'Would there be water to replenish my stores, Admiral?'

'We have but four wells, all brackish, on the whole island, but you are welcome to replenish from them, Captain O'Connor. I will send ten of my men to assist yours immediately,' Canaris replied.

'Thank you, sir.'

In the barge returning to *Surprise* Pat's spirits sank even as his voice rose, 'Good God; many fine ships tied up, sails all a'reefed, guns removed ashore, gunners ashore, seamen pressed as infantry. Is there no end to this damn stupidity? First Kasos, their squadron laid up in ordinary because of economies. Economies! We are at war, and they concern themselves with economies. Doubtless all those Kasiot ships were lost and the island sacked. Now Psara, and I find a second squadron sitting idle. Hell and damnation!'

'You are objectionably intemperate this afternoon, Pat,' remarked Simon, mildly.

'God help us, Simon, for that is all the help we may now have. What ails these people? Is it a necessity to lack all sense when in government? For that seems the case in these islands. Damn foreigners. Have they no notion they are condemning their people to death and slavery?' Neither Simon nor an equally mortified Duncan could find any answer.

Thursday 1ˢᵗ July 1824   *Psara Town*

The Psariot council discussion proved nigh on impossible for Pat to follow, despite speedy and whispered translations of the important snippets by Zouvelekis in his ear, Jason adding his own gleanings in Pat's other ear. From several of the Primates there was the wish to settle with Khosref, to send an emissary signalling compliance with the Turk suzereignty over the island; yet such voices were a minority. From other members came bellicose statements professing the island's significance to the Greek cause: fight, fight for independence from the Porte! From a majority came a

349

confidence in the impregnability of the island, the batteries now substantially reinforced by the ships' guns, and the fortress well provisioned with powder and shot.

After near two hours of deep frustration, and the gathering moving towards a consensus supporting the status quo, Canaris rose to speak. Softly spoken at first, despair perhaps influencing his voice, he began, 'Gentlemen, I am a Psariot. I heartily commended this island when, in the year twenty-one, Psara declared its commitment to fight against the Turk yoke. I hastened back from Odessa to assist my island and its people in any way I could. With ships from this island I sailed to strike back for the sack of Chios. I laid my own fireship alongside the flagship of Kara Ali and burned it and killed him.' Canaris's voice began to rise as he continued, extreme anxiety now shaping its tone, 'You must believe that only with ships can we fight the Turk. We must have those ships out there returned to service *without delay;* else we all on this island are doomed when the Turk comes. Those ships are our guardians. *We must have those ships!*' His desperate conclusion brought about a voluble discussion, all in the room seemingly speaking at once, shouting even, so as to be heard above the hubbub.

After some minutes had elapsed, the Magistrate banged hard upon his table with his gavel, bringing near order back to the meeting, though some still babbled on. He rose to speak in reply, 'Admiral Canaris. Your service on behalf of this island and of Greece is of the highest order. We, the Primates, acknowledge and thank you for it. Whether the Turk will attack our small island or pass by for larger prizes we cannot know. Yet it remains our conviction that our ships cannot sail whilst the whereabouts of the Turk fleet is unknown. Let us suppose our ships were to sail and the Turk fleet to arrive in their absence: how could we defend our island in the absence of our ships and with so few guns? The commander of our infantry brigade of Roumeliot compatriots has assured us that with those guns our island can be defended. Yet without them his men can do little. His men are frightened that our ships, with guns restored and with many islanders aboard, were the Turk to appear, would flee, leaving his men to their mercy. He has therefore asked for our assurance that all ship's guns will remain ashore; and also that all the ships' rudders will be dismounted, so that a flight from the island, abandoning his men, cannot occur. We have decided to comply with his requests.'

At this verdict, demonstrating such devastating military ignorance, Canaris, still standing after his own plea, sat down, disheartened and defeated. Pat too, when the conclusion had been translated for him, was aghast. He looked for some signal to Canaris, seated on the other side of Zouvelekis, but the Admiral sat staring blankly at the Primates, wringing his hands in great discomfit until he turned towards Pat, raising his arms but quite unable to speak, his lips quivering and his brow furrowed. Pat, in grave disgust, raged loudly to all nearby at the decision of the Magistrate. 'Damned fools and poltroons they are. How can they leave their island and homes so ill-defended? How, on God's earth, can they expect to resist the Turks after they have landed? There is no doubt; the massacre of innocents is sure to result. God damn them, God damn their souls.'

Help came from a quite unexpected source. Simon rose from his chair alongside Jason, to whom he said, 'Abel, swiftly now, follow me, if you will.' Simon moved quickly to the front of the room, to the table where the Primates were sitting and stood alongside the now-seated Magistrate. The Primates stared at him, this untidy and nondescript man, unknown to them all. The hubbub in the room died down as the gathering focused on Simon, his very lack of stature bringing about a curiosity with his presence. Simon raised both arms high, lowering them only as near silence descended upon the room, and he spoke, loudly and authoritatively, directing his voice at the Magistrate. 'Sir, my name is Ferguson. I am come here to Greece with Lord Byron.' Jason translated and the residual hubbub of conversation throughout the room died to silence at this, all present staring as if mesmerised at this badly dressed and unshaven man in their presence. Simon drew a deep breath and continued, his voice faltering yet his determination showing through, 'I am sorely dismayed ... I have failed Greece once. It has long preyed on my mind ... I was with Lord Byron at his death ... he

351

had become my friend and ... I was unable to save him.' There was a collective gasp from the room and but the shortest of pauses before Simon resumed, his voice steadying, 'Many more will die afore this bloody business comes to its end. I am merely a doctor and have no knowledge of military matters, but I beseech you, hear out one man who does. Hear out Captain O'Connor, who came with me and with Lord Byron to help you.' At that, Simon pointed to an astonished Pat who rose slowly from his seat and came forward to the Magistrate's table, Zouvelekis hastily following him.

With Zouvelekis translating, Pat now addressed the room in loud voice, 'My name is O'Connor. I fought against the French and Bonaparte for near twenty years. I am here with my frigate and men to aid your cause as best we can. I too was with Lord Byron when he came to Messalonghi. Two weeks ago, I was in Kasos. On that island also their ships were tied up when the Turks arrived: *for economies*, so they said. No number of shore batteries could prevent the Turks landing on that island. They came in the night when no gunner could aim his piece with any prospect of success. Their host overran the island, killing all afore them; men, women and children. The ships of Kasos were tied up and quite useless. Those ships might have held the Turk at bay. We will never know; the dead will never know. You have amongst you a captain of great experience and immense courage; no finer captain ever put to sea; Admiral Canaris is here with you. I urge you. I implore you. Put your faith in him, please listen to him. Put your ships in order. With their great guns returned to them they may save you when the Turk comes, for surely he will. Your ships have been a thorn in his side since this war began. He cannot pass you by. Be assured, he is coming. Make ready your ships. There is not a moment to be lost.'

At Pat's conclusion the Magistrate stood again and thanked him, even as the meeting returned to a loud clamour of voices, shouting widespread as the discussion volubly re-opened. The Surprises took their leave of Canaris, who thanked Simon and Pat with endearing gratitude, his evident dejection so clear and painful to them all.

They walked in despondent silence back to the quay until Pat

352

asked Simon, 'There was nothing you could do for his Lordship, I collect. Have you now a different opinion?'

Simon sighed deeply, his answer seemingly dug deep from within him, 'His doctors bled him too much by far, but that was the day afore I arrived. I watched him decline, in anguish with my impotence to help him. Had I arrived but one day earlier perhaps they would have listened and drawn less blood? Perhaps I could have argued more to prevent them fixing the leeches about his head? For near an hour I argued with them. I beseeched them. Damn them, they would not listen. He bled copiously from them, the leeches, until he was gone. Ne'er afore was I so set back by anyone dying before my eyes as that man. So much given, so generously, by one man; and not even for his own country. That brave spirit struck down, so young, and when so much was promised. It has left black turmoil in my soul, and I cannot shake it.'

It suddenly became clear to Pat that it was indeed several factors which had oppressed the mind of his friend in the recent weeks. Pat had not realised that the loss of Byron had struck Simon so hard, and the bloodbath of Kasos had only added to his torment. He was at a loss for any suitable words of consolation, and so, his Irish upbringing in the words of his grandmother delivering the memory, said simply, 'There is no sorrow like the loss of friends. Come, brother, let us return swiftly to *Surprise*. We must away from here to seek Khosref's fleet. I fancy Wilkins might run up a Strasburg Pie, and Murphy, the rascal, has doubtless hidden away a bottle or two of our favourite, the Haut Brion. We shall enjoy a fine dinner and then be gone from this place.'

The row back to *Surprise* in such beautiful surroundings – the sun now almost oppressive in its fierce heat at the top of the day – seemed deeply incongruous and saddening to them all. They had come from Kasos, from the sight of one squadron of ships lying idle and the island being sacked, to the sight of a second squadron and island seemingly poised for a similar eventuality. Yet they could not make the islanders shift from what was plainly, to these deeply experienced, fighting seafarers, the gravest of errors. Would these ships still be idle when the Turk arrived? Would the islanders be butchered and enslaved in their thousands? Would the town be burned about them? These likelihoods pressed on all their minds as they climbed the ladder to *Surprise's* deck.

The barge and cutter crews resumed their trips to the quay, still fetching water as Pat sat down to his dinner. Simon had returned to the great cabin to join him and Duncan for the first time in a week. Marston, Jason, Pickering, Mower and Zouvelekis were also present. Wilkins, Pat's cook, had excelled himself, Freeman delivering the most magnificent of Strasburg pies, greatly enjoyed by all at Pat's table, and the gloomy prognosis for Psara faded just a little from their thoughts as they ate.

'Simon,' said Pat, smiling across his table. 'You brought them all up as if in irons, with your speaking of Lord Byron.'

'Would that they had listened to Canaris, not I: my words were of no importance,' Simon replied, looking up gloomily.

Zouvelekis added his own thoughts, 'His Lordship was dearly loved in this country. Our mercantile shipping had spread the story of him throughout all these islands. He is deeply mourned, even in such far places as Psara.'

'What is our plan, sir?' asked Marston, emboldened to ask questions in the cabin by his much improved relationship with Pat.

'We are bound first for Mitylene, the principal port of Lesbos. Khosref was last reported there. We will be careful and mind our approach so as not to be caught without wind in our sails, were his fleet to be there. So, we will sail up the west of the island, keeping plenty of sea-room, and run speedily before the wind from the north, down the east side channel, past Mitylene, with a full press of sail, showing any of his ships leaving port a clean pair of heels.'

As Dalby rang eight bells of the Afternoon watch *Surprise* hauled up her anchor and set her topsails, jibs, and spanker to sail south-east to clear the island, so as to begin her tacking north towards Lesbos, Duncan in command, as Pat remained talking to Simon in the cabin, the other officers all gone to the quarterdeck.

'I have been a poor friend to you this past week,' said Pat, setting down his cup. 'I did not see what ailed you and left you alone to bear your torments.'

354

'I did not wish to inflict my black thoughts on you, brother. 'Tis I that has been the poor friend, when after all these years I should have confided in you, but did not, keeping my own company.'

'We are getting older, Simon, and what we could carry twenty, or even ten years ago without breaking wind, we struggle with now.'

'Stride, brother, not wind. Heaven forbid,' laughed Simon, Pat laughing now with him.

Friday 2nd July 1824   *north of Psara Island*

During the quietude of the night, *Surprise* had tacked close-hauled into the northerly wind, making slow progress, and by dawn had sailed just five leagues past Cape Korakiat. She was making no more than three knots. An hour or so later, there came a hail from the topman to the quarterdeck, 'Sails ahoy! Four points off the starboard bow.' Mower, on duty and without ceremony, shouted back immediately, 'How many?' There was a long pause during which Pat, now wide awake, his sleep disturbed by the shout, came up from his cabin, scarcely dressed, but anxious to find out himself what might be about to accost them.

'Good morning, Mr Mower. I heard the shout. Here, take my glass,' he said, presenting it to Mower. 'Climb up and look.'

'Aye aye, sir,' nodded Mower, grasping the glass and stepping towards the shrouds.

'Who is up there, Tom?' asked Pat.

''Tis Watson, sir,' Pickering replied.

'Watson, how many sail?' shouted Pat. A few moments passed by with no reply from the top, and so Pat shouted again, 'Watson, would you care for your hammock? *How many sail?*'

Watson now answered, though it seemed to the listeners on deck that he shouted down almost in disbelief, 'Fifty sail, sir. Eighty sail ... a hundred!'

Pat could bear such apparent nonsense no longer, and hastened to the shrouds himself, swiftly clambering up the ratlines and out up the futtock shrouds to swing himself over and into the main crosstree, some one hundred and ten feet above the quarterdeck. By then he was minded to throw Watson overboard had his report not been true. Instead, gazing through his glass, taken back from Mower as his third came through the lubber's hole, he gasped in disbelief. Describing the sight to Mower alongside him, the far ships shimmering, indistinct still in the haze, 'Forty, fifty, sixty ... eighty, one hundred ... more! One hundred and fifty or even more ... I see a seventy-four, a razee, half a dozen frigates, a score of corvettes, scores of brigs and schooners. My God! It is the whole of the Turk fleet!'

'How far, sir, would you say?' asked a now nervous Mower.

'Not more than four leagues, I fancy.'

Pat hastily scrambled back down to his quarterdeck. He wasted not a moment, 'Prepare to bring her about, Mr Pickering; back to Psara as fast as she will fly. We will hoist every scrap of our sail, stuns'ls and all. Dalby there! Beat to quarters!'

Pat rattled out his commands, and *Surprise* near instantly became a hive of frenetic activity as men swarmed up the ratlines to run out studdingsail booms.

'Bring her about, Mr Prosser,' ordered Pickering.

'Prepare to come about,' shouted Prosser. 'Stand by to come about, Barton. Hold fast, lads, we are coming about!' Prosser shouted to the tops, and 'Port your helm, Barton, handsomely now.' *Surprise* responded fleetly to the wheel, coming round quickly at the bow, her yards braced to her new course, and gaining speed as the sails filled with the full force of the north-westerly.

'Haul the line,' shouted Pat, echoed by Prosser to Johnston.

'Eight and a half knots,' came back after a few minutes, and 'Ten knots,' after five minutes on *Surprise's* new southerly course.

Pat stared back, but from his much lower quarterdeck he could no longer see the Turks. 'Mr Prosser, maintain course. You have the command. I will be in my cabin. Watch those ships carefully, and report any change of course. He turned to his lieutenants, all awaiting his orders: 'Mr Macleod, Mr Pickering, Mr Mower, would you care to join me for breakfast, gentlemen?'

In the cabin, Freeman awaited Pat, 'Tea ready, massa.'

'Very good, Freeman; you are to bring breakfast for five. My compliments and will you ask Captain Zouvelekis to join us,' Pat ordered. 'Gentlemen,' Pat began when Zouvelekis and all his lieutenants were seated and drinking his tea, 'It is not a pretty picture; above a hundred sail approaching us, approaching Psara. At the least there is a seventy-four, a razee and six other frigates, and above a score of other fighting ships – corvettes, brigs and the like. With them at least four score of transports. It is an invasion, there can be no doubt. Likely Psara, for that is their course. I would think they are sailing together at the speed of the slowest, likely no more than six knots, and will reach Psara town in perhaps seven hours. We can press on at ten knots and be there in three hours, at worst four, by noon perhaps. It is likely that the Turk fleet is already seen from the heights of Psara. From there they can assuredly see much further than we from the masthead. So, gentlemen, what should we do? We cannot fight against a fleet of this size,' Pat left the question hanging in the air.

Mower was the first to reply, 'Sir, our orders are to find this fleet and report to Hydra, to Admiral Miaoulis. Surely that is our course, we can do nothing here?'

Pat nodded, 'Mr Macleod, your thoughts?'

'Mr Mower is right, sir. 'Tis plain we cannae tarry wi' so many o' these Turk ships. We surely will be lost. Though 'twill cost us noot to reach Psara town wi' the news, an' then away at all speed.'

Pat turned to his Greek officer, 'Captain Zouvelekis. You are familiar with Psara. Were you Khosref, where would you land your men? How would you invade? What use are all those warships here?' Pat pressed for information, striving to find something, anything, to shape a plan, any kind of plan, in preference to simply running away.

Zouvelekis gathered his thoughts momentarily before replying, 'Assuredly the Turk has enough ships to come down both sides of the island. There are a few small coves with beaches on the northern half where the coast is steep cliffs and poor anchorage for his ships were any troops to go ashore there. He will most likely land his

357

men either on the western beaches, though doubtless the Psariots will have batteries there, or on the south of the island, approaching the harbour, for there is also the sandy beach we have seen when we left the island, though that place is well in range of the town and fort's batteries. I would land on the western beaches, sir. The Turk fleet will also close more quickly on the Psariot fleet in the roads between Psara and Anti-Psara if coming down the west side. Perhaps I would send my frigates down the east side, to the southern beaches as a decoy, and from there cannonade the town and fort whilst my men landed to the west.'

Pat looked closely at Zouvelekis with respect in his eyes, 'A fine strategy, Captain Zouvelekis; 'pon my word, a strategy worthy of any admiral; my compliments, sir. We will assume that is the Turk plan. Captain Zouvelekis; what, sir, will the Psariots do with their ships when the horde approaches?'

Zouvelekis replied with conviction and without need of any further consideration, 'It will likely be too late to do much, if anything. Their guns are ashore. Their crews are, for the most part, also ashore. When the Turk opens fire on the town, and his men are known to be landing on the beaches, there will assuredly be panic. No town or fort can stand against that number of guns. Many will run for the ships, though reaching them will be difficult, the boats can carry but few men. The men on the ships will panic too. Doubtless many will cut their cables and seek to flee, though with no rudder shipped, as may be the case, their progress will be uncertain and slow. They will be easy prey for the Turk brigs and schooners. Not many will escape for sure,' Zouvelekis completed his gloomy prognosis.

Pat ruminated on the options available to him, eventually declaring, 'After we have returned to the town we will linger downwind and south of the Psariot ships. If they leave, we will strive as best we might to protect their escape until such time as the Turk takes too much interest in us. If Khosref approaches from the north of the Psariot ships we may be obscured by them, and perhaps the Turk may have little interest in us for some time. That, gentlemen, is what we will do,' Pat concluded his conference.

Sailing large, *Surprise* swiftly made the return passage to Psara town, and it was clear from the activity that could be observed ashore that news of the Turk approach had already reached the islanders. Well-laden boats of all sizes were leaving the quay, empty ones returning. An exodus it was, readily apparent from Pat's quarterdeck where he studied the quay through his glass as they approached to drop anchor. Within twenty minutes Pat, Zouvelekis, and Jason were swiftly rowed to the town, and Admiral Canaris speedily located, issuing orders to his men from the same quayside taverna he had adopted as his headquarters; dozens of men coming and going as Pat's party arrived. It was half an hour after noon.

Canaris rose and came to greet them as they entered, 'Captain O'Connor, it pleases me to see you. Why are you returned?' offering Pat his hand, his words translated by Zouvelekis.

'Admiral, we have sighted the Turk fleet; it was near ten leagues off the north-east of the island when we turned back. They will be here afore nightfall,' Pat replied, shaking hands with Canaris.

'Yes, our lookout sighted them at about five o'clock yesterday afternoon. We have a watch post at the church atop Mount Ilias; it is the highest point of the island. I am doing what I can to restore rudders, and bringing as many seamen as I can locate back to our ships. I have no time to recover any guns, but sail we can. That is were I to have enough men. Many remain at the batteries all round the island, and the Roumeliots will not permit them to leave. The Primates have now panicked, and requested I provide passage for them away from the island!'

Zouvelekis could not conceal his feelings, and spat on the floor, speaking in his native tongue to no one in particular 'Damn fools, leave the bastards behind.' Jason whispered the translation to Pat, though it was hardly needed, Pat's sentiments concurring wholly with those of Zouvelekis. Canaris, diplomatically, said nothing.

Pat described his plan, 'Sir, *Surprise* will remain with you as long as we can. Perhaps we can hold back any Turk that comes close to your ships as they leave, though we are but one and they

359

are many, more than a hundred sail, including a seventy-four; more than six frigates, scores of lesser ships, and transports for an army too.'

A deeply fatigued Canaris stared at Pat momentarily, as if in assessment of his words, as if gauging the measure of the man, and said simply, 'Thank you, Captain O'Connor. Now I must return to my men, few that they are. We have much to do if we are to get any ships away before the Turk arrives.'

'Sir, we will bring *Surprise* as close as can be to the quay, directly. My men and boats will greatly aid yours, and *Surprise* can shift much more aboard her to your brigs than your boats will carry all day,' said Pat.

'O'Connor, you are surely a good friend of Greece. Thank you, thank you,' Canaris replied quietly, grasping Pat's hand again in both his own whilst staring full into his eyes for some moments. No further words were needed and Pat simply waved his companions out with him. They rowed swiftly back to *Surprise,* and Pat ordered her move closer to the quay. She near drifted in on topsails alone, backing them as she came to her anchorage a mere two hundred yards off the quay just as Dalby rang two bells of the Afternoon watch.

'Lads,' said Pat to his crew as they assembled on deck, 'We have but two hours to bring aboard this ship all that is on the quay and shift it out to the Psariot ships in the roads. Use all our boats and work swiftly now, we have not a moment to lose.' The *Surprises*, once they arrived at the quay, were joined immediately by fifty men sent by Canaris, and the loading began, a hundred and ninety *Surprises* toiling hard in the blistering heat. As time passed there grew a great press of Psariot civilians all about the quay, refugees fleeing from the coming strife, women and children for the most part. The *Surprises* sought to work round them, but the crowd grew in number and volume, near all the frightened refugees sobbing, wailing, and shouting loud pleas to their compatriots loading the boats. The *Surprises* themselves became more concerned and distressed as several hours slipped by.

The time available for loading the stores on the quay was far too short, and as Dalby rang six bells the empty boats had returned once more from *Surprise*. Pat shouted to Pickering over the incessant sounds of wailing and pleas, 'Enough! These must be our last loads, we must be away.' Unexpectedly, and before Pickering could reiterate any of Pat's orders, the press of voluble civilians gathered on the quay surged forward, direct to where the boats were tied alongside, and all came flooding about Pat, Pickering and Zouvelekis; a human tide of fear, panic, and alarm. Near all the *Surprises* from the shore loading party had gone back aboard the ship, in preparation for departure, and those few crew members still standing on the quay to load and bring back the boats were swept aside as the women pressed about them; a hundred, two hundred and more. They sought to prevent the boats from being loaded or leaving, they stood about the stores on the quay, they pleaded with the men standing ready to load, in desperate supplication, plainly panic-stricken. Pat, from ten yards away had strived for the past hour to shut the refugees from his mind, and had not anticipated that they would rush towards his boats. A red veil of exasperation, of frustration, descended before his eyes; time was running out. No amount of pleas from Zouvelekis could persuade the women to shift. They demanded that *Surprise* embark them. They flatly refused to move back even when Zouvelekis explained to them that *Surprise* was a ship of war and expected to engage Turk ships before many more hours, and could not fight her guns with such a press of passengers aboard, yet they would not budge. Canaris was called to help, and hastened from the taverna, but even his impassioned pleas to the women changed nothing. They would not step back. The day was quickly passing. It was now four o'clock, there was so little time left. The Turks might be here in another hour, and all the loaded material on *Surprise* had yet to be transported out to the roads, and then transferred to the Psariot ships. Without her boats, *Surprise* could not shift. Pat would not, could not, contemplate violence to move the frightened Psariot women and children. Exasperated, he pushed his way through to where the majority of the Psariots were sitting on the quay edge, edging through the press to stand in their midst. Zouvelekis translated his words for the women, 'Ladies, hear me well. In but two hours the decks of our ship will likely be swept with Turk shot, and all aboard may be injured or killed. Your children will be quite unprotected. Our space below will be filled with wounded, and our surgeon will fill bloody buckets with body parts cut off to save lives. Is that what you wish for your children?' From the screams and exclamations of the women it was plain it was not, yet they still would not shift. Pat stared about him, utterly perplexed, perspiration drenching his shirt, his hat band soaked, consternation rising within him as he considered the precious little time available to him, and how he might fight his ship with the unwelcome throng all about his guns and the lower deck; with no space for casualties.

Zouvelekis, considerable anxiety in his voice, explained to Pat what he had gleaned from the more composed of the women, 'Sir, they may be killed on your ship, but were they to remain here they will surely be killed, and their children enslaved by the Turk. Would you choose differently for *your* wife, for *your* children? Can we not help them, sir?' the plea made with considerable feeling, Zouvelekis himself plainly most uncomfortable, his own desperation so clear in his voice and plain in his face.

There was not the slightest possibility of Pat refusing the heart-rending request after such a stark and fundamental remark, and he accepted the futility, indeed the undesirability, of further efforts to dissuade the refugees from embarking. 'Captain Zouvelekis, this is a pretty pickle. I cannot leave them ashore, God help them. There is no time left to stand here.' He paused in thought for a further few minutes, looking slowly all around him, gazing all about the quay at the panic-stricken refugees, fear and despair showing in all their faces; many women and children wailing and sobbing, infants clutched closely by their mothers. Scores of frightened faces were looking anxiously towards him, as if in silent supplication, their tear-filled, dark eyes seeming to bore into his very soul, and his heart moved in that moment. Pat faced his officers, all of whom were looking to him for his decision; he sighed deeply and turned to Zouvelekis before pronouncing his verdict: 'We may consider that all of us, when we find ourselves in our very bleakest of hours, do live in one another's shelter, and so we will not turn our backs, gentlemen; we will, with good grace, take them aboard and away. Captain Zouvelekis, will you ask them - will they shift to the Psariot brigs, which will be leaving within the hour, when we transfer these stores to them?'

Zouvelekis's face registered his comprehension, his overwhelming relief radiating from his face, and he gulped hard, nodded his understanding, further words seemingly beyond him, before hastening away to speak with the refugees. Pat's proposition appeared to be readily accepted, and so without ado the Surprises assisted the Psariots into the boats. Five trips were necessary to transport them all to the ship, fresh stragglers joining the exodus even as the boats returned for the last time to the quay. Canaris waved as they departed, standing before the discarded stores with his men and looking gravely disconsolate.

Surprise cast off; the kedge dropped by Barton from the barge bringing her bow quickly round, and her spanker and jib shifting her further away from her near quay anchorage until, the kedge hauled up, she turned with the wind, her topsails filling, gaining speed for the bay. Half an hour more saw *Surprise* lying near alongside the nearest Psariot brig, Pat ensuring he had selected one with a rudder affixed. Zouvelekis cajoled the Psariots to transfer to the brig, the women and all the children shifting across within a busy hour in the boats, the Surprises taking over much of the stores embarked at the quay. The Psariot captain was pleased to embark his compatriots, pleased too for the provisions, and he swiftly made off after the barest exchanges with Zouvelekis once all the refugees were aboard his brig; Pat mightily relieved to shed his passengers.

'We have such little time left. To the next Psariot, swiftly now,' urged Pat, and *Surprise* near drifted towards the next, so close were they in the roadstead. Her boats passed over stores as quickly as they could be manhandled, food and water for the most part, and for two hours this task kept them busy. A steady stream of boats continued to come out from Psara town, bringing more seamen returning to their ships. A brig came out as Dalby rang seven bells of the Last dog watch, and passed directly by *Surprise*, no more than thirty yards off her beam, the Primates of the island visible on her deck. The brig sailed swiftly west, not stopping by any of the other Psariot ships.

Zouvelekis, standing next to Pat and Simon on the quarterdeck, spat overboard in their direction, 'There go the rats.'

'Fleeing like the Gabardine swine,' Pat scowled.

'Or even the Gadarene ones,' added Simon.

'I dare say.'

In the dwindling light of the evening the precious time passed by with *Surprise* distributing the last of the stores to the Psariot brigs, and sunset neared with no sighting of any Turk ship, though the lookouts claimed to hear distant cannon fire to the north. *Surprise* had now shifted all the embarked stores to more than a score of Psariot brigs. As the sun began its final slip below the horizon, the fierce heat of the day giving way to a more comfortable warmth, a last brig came out from the town, approaching *Surprise,* backing her sails near alongside her. Admiral Canaris it was, with a hundred more sailors to transfer to the Psariots. Canaris crossed to *Surprise,* and Pat invited him to the cabin. Freeman, unbidden, brought fresh, highly aromatic coffee and a bottle of brandy.

A plainly very tired Canaris reported his news, 'Our telegraphs report the Turks off the north and the south-east capes of the island. It seems they are anchored and awaiting the dawn before they commence their attack. We must use the time to re-affix ships' rudders so as to take off more refugees in the morning. I have a hundred men to help do so. We may have a score of ships able to steer and sail by the morrow.'

'*Surprise* will be here to help you tomorrow for as long as we can until we are engaged, Admiral,' said Pat, for he held Canaris in the highest esteem.

Surprise's barge and cutter were sent to distribute Canaris's men to more Psariot ships. Canaris appeared to have recovered somewhat from the despond of the council meeting, and after a half hour more of discussing what they might do in the morning left for his own brig.

At supper, taken much later than usual, Pat was joined by

364

Duncan, Simon and Marston, though all felt disinclined to play their instruments. Pat was pressed by Marston to play chess, Duncan demurring with 'Not that tedious game again, nae, ah wilnae play,' and Simon had his head in a book.

At 10 p.m., Pat having lost his second bishop and the game with it to Marston, he decided to take a turn about the decks. He was not surprised that most of the crew were sitting and standing about, talking in low voices, some sharpening knives and cutlasses, others cleaning again the gun locks, all of the mast cross trees populated by men striving to see anything at all in the gloom. The night, though clear, afforded only a thin moon, offering little visibility. It remained warm, pleasant even after the fierce heat of the day, and the men, a little weary for their efforts shifting stores, seemed to Pat to be in good cheer. He exchanged a few words here and there as he passed amongst them, purposefully, the opportunity for such before an anticipated action next day rarely presenting itself, and Pat used such few occasions to take fleeting soundings of his crew's morale. All was well. Though the atmosphere on board remained tense throughout, all the Surprises well aware of the near certain prospect of action in the morning, their confidence, bouyed by their success against the two Turk galleys, remained high.

At 11 p.m. he returned to his cabin and cot, the day's events proving impossible to get out of his mind, and his thoughts keeping him awake for hours, the only noise to his keen ear being the usual creaking of the ship at her anchor.

Saturday 3ʳᵈ July 1824, dawn   *Psara roads*

Everyone aboard *Surprise* was awake and on deck well before daybreak, which came at 6 a.m., heralded by the sound of cannon fire from beyond the town. Pat climbed to the main crosstree with his glass, and could see masts on the far side of Psara Bay. Turk ships, including the seventy-four and the razee, had opened their cannonade of the town. The town and fort batteries returned fire until, within a half hour, a great cloud of gunsmoke filled the bay, enveloping the town and fort, and nothing more could Pat see. As yet, no Turks were visible to the north beyond the Psariot ships.

Returning swiftly to deck Pat gave his orders, 'Mr Pickering, leave courses reefed in case of an engagement. Let tops'ls, jibs and spanker stay unfurled but slack; there is barely any wind this morning. Such as there is, though it may drag our anchor south, we will see better of the Turk ships firing on the town.'

The people in the town had realised all was lost. Pickering remarked upon the renewed exodus, 'Over there, sir, a score or more boats being launched from the beach 'twixt the town and fort, pulling our way.'

'Double the men aloft. Half to watch strictly north, the others the town; we cannot let ourselves be enveloped from two sides.'

Within a very few minutes there came a hail from the tops, 'Sails north, sixty ships or more.' Once again Pat climbed to the crosstree, sweating heavily in the heat, and looked beyond the Psariot ships. Six miles or so afar Pat watched a second Turk squadron, a mixture of frigates, brigs and merchantmen. Contrary to the plan described by Zouvelekis he could see no laden boats crossing to the beach with soldiers. As he watched, the frigates opened their fire upon the island's western batteries. He returned quickly to his quarterdeck. 'Tom, within an hour either or both the Turk squadrons could be upon us. It is of the very first importance that our topmen signal any change in their position. Both squadrons appear to be anchored and cannonading. If they haul their cables, we must know in minutes, no more, so our sails can be readied to take us away. Until then we shall stay here, hiding behind the Psariot squadron. In all this smoke I doubt we will be seen. Our men must watch the Turks for the slightest of signs.'

'Aye aye, sir,' replied Tom Pickering, calmly. He had fought alongside Pat on many occasions. Pat had saved his life in one boarding action. He had the utmost confidence in his captain's command of what, to any sea officer and doubtless most seamen, seemed a position of the utmost risk, requiring of the most precise comprehension of their relative position to the Turks and all their movement capabilities if *Surprise* was to survive this day.

The boats from the town began to reach the Psariot ships, and the passengers, women and children for the most part, were quickly brought aboard and the boats sent back. The sun began to rise, warming the morning, and the cannonade of the town continued, more boats coming continually out from the town. At 7 a.m. a huge red Turk flag was sighted, hoisted on the summit of the hill a quarter mile to the north of the town. A landing elsewhere had occurred, as Zouvelekis had predicted, but not on the western beaches. The bombardment continued as the morning approached noon, the sun at its zenith baking a town now burning in many places. The refugee boats continued to ply between the town beach and the Psariot ships, many of which now seemed ready to sail, their rudders shipped, sails let fall but flapping, and their crews eagerly helping aboard their frightened compatriots. In the early afternoon the boats still came out, the rowers exchanged for fresh men, the exhausted men resting aboard the Psariot brigs. By 2 p.m., from *Surprise*, the town appeared to be overrun, no more boats now left the beach; instead there were swimmers in the water, struggling, driven by desperation to reach the Psariot ships.

'We will launch our cutter and barge, Mr Mower. Take them out and rescue those swimmers. The crews must take pistols and cutlasses in case of any Turk boats interfering,' Pat quickly ordered. The boats were swiftly launched, and their crews pulled away strongly towards the beach. Within a half hour a score of struggling swimmers had been taken aboard, women for the most part, some with children, and the boats, heavily laden and water lapping over their gunwales, had returned to bring the panic-stricken refugees to *Surprise*, returning again to seek more in the water. This rescue continued for three hours or more until, as the sun fell rapidly below the red, western horizon, the firing from both sides became desultory as dusk turned into darkness, save for the town which was illuminated by a myriad of fires, dozens of houses ablaze, the thick bilious smoke drifting across the water to *Surprise*.

'It seems we are here another night,' said Pat, wearily, to all on his quarterdeck. 'I doubt the Turks will shift in darkness. They are now behind the town, and must have several thousand men even now plundering the houses. There may be a very few Psariot survivors left to come out in the morning. What a catastrophe. What a tragedy. Why did they not prepare those ships? What folly. Mr Macleod, a sharp watch at all times, we will not move this night.'

On the lower deck Simon and Marston were busy tending the rescued swimmers, many of whom had swallowed great quantities of saltwater and were vomiting profusely all over the deck, Simon and his men helping them sip freshwater. Two older women had quite exhausted themselves and expired after being brought down from the gun deck. Zouvelekis went below amongst the sick and tired Psariots, seeking to garner news of what was happening in the town. He reported to Pat a story of utter horror. The Turks had landed somewhere in the north of the island, in the region of a bay known as Adham, where a tiny beach afforded access to a small area of relatively flat land amidst the cliffs, and gave access to a path alongside a creek which rose through a defile in the hills, and so to the interior and the heights above Psara town. From whence the Turks had descended and entered the town itself, overrunning the Greek batteries en route, and putting all to the sword. It was a cunning refinement of Zouvelekis's prediction. The Roumeliots had been tasked to guard that defile in the north, a position to which no Psariot had expected any Turk approach, the northern side of the island being almost wholly cliffs rising direct from the sea. All thought it impregnable to any landing, and so there the Roumeliots had been stationed, as their loyalty had been feared suspect. They had seemingly surrendered as soon as the Turks came ashore. Survivor's reports continued to be recounted. Many more women had fled to the beach from the town, but finding no boats had sought to swim out, their young children and babies clutched to them until they drowned together. The surviving Roumeliot soldiers had fled into the fort where they had repulsed several Turk attacks, and then came the night, the burning and killing raging unchecked in the town.

Freeman brought coffee up to the quarterdeck. Pat and his officers could not sleep. The boats had been sent out again, even in the darkness, to seek and pluck any last surviving refugees from the water, a very few swimmers visible within the wavelets over a near-flat sea which was illuminated by the reflections of fires in the

368

town. The gunners stood by their guns all night, sleeping fitfully on deck.

'Sir, the Psariot ships are hauling, some cutting even, their cables, and slipping away,' announced Pickering as midnight came, 'Doubtless taking advantage of the darkness.'

'Yes Tom, I see them now, a near score drifting by, a few with tops'ls rigged, hardly a course unfurled. They have so few crew; they cannot stand to be seen shifting by the Turk frigates who have left the Psariot ships alone thus far,' Pat ruminated. 'Perhaps the Turks knew their crews were gone, their rudders unshipped? Perhaps they thought they were left simply for the taking after the town had fallen? Perhaps a spy or a traitor may have told them so?'

At this comment Zouvelekis interjected, 'I have heard it said below, from a young woman the boats collected this day, that Costas, the Roumeliot leader, was said to have betrayed the Psariots to the Turks. She had heard it as gossip and knew no more.'

'That would explain their lack of interest so far in the Psariot ships. No rudders, no crews. How could they leave?' Pat said, though he doubted the explanation, more likely it was simply one of the unexplained events of every battle. 'The fog of war, more like,' he thought to himself.

Sunday 4ᵗʰ July 1824, dawn   *Psara roads*

Surprise's boats had been in the water between the ship and the town beach all night, and had collected a further dozen swimmers, all brought gently below, exhausted for the most part, to Simon's ministrations. At dawn the boats were sent out once more as the firing resumed. 'A tragedy afore oor eyes, sir,' said a gloomy Duncan, alongside Pat on his quarterdeck.

'The fort holds out still,' reported Mower, down from the main crosstree, the day's early firing not yet having enveloped the town in smoke. Still there was no movement from any of the Turk ships. None of the remaining crewed Psariot ships, of which there were half a dozen, had shifted either.

'Perhaps these ones are better crewed and hoping for survivors from the fort?' Pat speculated to his officers. 'They all have rudders.

Keep our boats out, Mr Pickering; and our best eyes on the Turks. We will stay as long as we can.'

The day passed its noisy course, the wind freshening in the afternoon as was usual with the *Meltemi*, blowing the smoke away from the town, many of its houses now visible as burned out ruins, but still the fort held out. The boats were now collecting only the occasional single swimmer. As Dalby rang seven bells of the Afternoon watch the lookout hailed down, 'Two frigates a'moving.'

'It seems we are now of interest to the Turk,' said Pat to his fatigued officers. 'It is time to leave this place. We can do no more here. Mr Pickering, we will sail directly south with the wind full. Let us make haste afore those two frigates round the fort peninsula and come upon us.'

'Aye aye, sir, south at all speed,' Pickering and Prosser acknowledged, and reiterated Pat's orders to the men aloft and a dozen in readiness on the capstan. Those dozen men as they tired were quickly replaced by fresh men, and the anchor was hauled up, catted, and fished in record time as the Turk frigates now passed the point. All firing had now stopped, from both the fort and the Turk ships. An eerie silence hung in the air, contrasting strikingly with the great clouds of smoke arising from all over the town. Pat gazed at the fort through his glass, shifting to the two frigates intermittently, though they seemed in no haste yet.

'There are six Psariots moving off, sir, in our company. Heading south, off our starboard beam,' Pickering reported.

Pat did not shift his glass from the fort. 'They have hoisted a flag now. Not the Greek one. What does it signify?' Pat mused, and passed the glass to Zouvelekis. 'What do you make of that?'

Zouvelekis brought the glass to bear on the fort, and stared for a full minute before exclaiming loudly, '*Freedom or Death*; that is the message on the flag.'

Pat took back his glass and looked hard again at the fort. He was about to reply when the fort simply disintegrated before his eyes, flames surging skywards and rubble hurled a hundred feet or more into the air, all then becoming enveloped in thick black smoke. 'My God, the magazine has exploded!' Pat shouted. At that moment, BO ... OO ... OM, the loudest noise he had ever heard in his life assailed his ears; it was followed by a warm rush of air passing over the ship. The sails backed momentarily, the masts quivered, the ship even heeled slightly before all returned to as it was after but a moment. Pat turned his attention to the Turk frigates. They had been much closer to the fort when it exploded, and seemed to have been hit by some of the debris as they had plainly slowed to a near stop. 'So much the better for us,' he thought, shouting now, his ears not seeming to be working properly. 'Cast the line, Mr Prosser.' Prosser evidently had not heard, and so Pat shouted louder, 'Mr Prosser!' but with no result. Pat stepped forward and hauled on his shoulder, 'What is the matter, Mr Prosser?'

Prosser pointed to his ears and shouted back at the top of his voice, 'I cannot hear anything, sir.'

Pat could barely hear him from only two feet away. Realisation dawned, the explosion, so loud, had deafened them all. Pat looked about him; the effect seemed to be experienced by all he could see, everyone looking to their fellows, waving their hands, rubbing their ears, all to no avail. 'Mr Pickering. I am going below to consult Doctor Ferguson,' shouted Pat. He hastened below to the gundeck to seek Simon out. The effect had been much lessened below by *Surprise's* thick, oak hull, and Simon and Marston conversed as normal, though Pat could not hear them. 'Simon!' Pat shouted, and all looked round.

Quickly grasping the nature of the problem as Pat, becoming highly irritable, shouted louder and louder, 'How long 'til I can hear?' Simon took quill pen to paper and scrawled *'temporary deafness, several hours perhaps'*, presenting it to Pat.

Pat hastened back to his quarterdeck. *Surprise* had now shown the two Turk frigates a clean pair of heels, leaving them still seemingly in irons and a league behind. The line had been cast in his absence and *Surprise's* speed measured at ten knots, a speed which would swiftly shift her away from the island and the Turks. The Psariot ships were struggling to stay with her, and all were now trailing a mile in her wake, though in no obvious danger. Five leagues south of Psara and no Turk ships in sight from the tops, Pat brought her about to a south-westerly course, the Psariots changing course to match her. 'We shall make for Hydra, Mr Pickering,' Pat announced, shouting, as all on deck still struggled to hear.

As the sun began its descent to the horizon off the starboard bow, the six Psariots all following astern, Pat and Simon settled for supper in the cabin. Pat's temporary deafness lingered on, and it was quite impossible to contemplate any fiddling.

'How are the rescued Psariots, Simon?' asked Pat, striving consciously to avoid shouting, though he could barely hear himself.

Simon shifted closer before he replied, 'All well. There will be no more deaths, with the blessing, though all remain weak. Two miles of swimming; it is sure many did not prevail and drowned afore our boats could find them. Their stories are heart-breaking, Pat. Turks breaking down house doors, setting homes alight, killing the fleeing, a desperate flight for the water; many reporting drownings alongside them but a few yards from the shore - old women, children, young women with infants on their backs, in their arms; a tragedy for sure.'

'That it is. And that explosion; the fort gone in an instant: so shocking. I was minded of that bloody day at Trafalgar; the end of the battle marked by *Achille* blowing up. 'Twas said it was heard even in Cadiz.' With conversation so difficult with Pat's deafness, they settled to eat their supper, and eventually the accumulated fatigue of the past few days overcame them both, and they fell asleep in their chairs. Murphy, not wishing to wake them, returned the treacle-dowdy to the galley where he enjoyed it himself.

Tuesday 6ᵗʰ July 1824   *just north of Andros*

At two bells Pat paced his quarterdeck, staring at the approaching strait between Andros and the mainland. The mid-morning wind blew gently from the north, and the sea state was calm. One of the accompanying Psariot brigs had signalled, and was slowly catching *Surprise*. After a half hour she was a mere hundred yards off *Surprise's* beam and edging closer. Pat ordered the sails backed, and the frigate quickly lost way, the Psariot brig coming near alongside as they both slowed to a stop, their hulls rocking gently in the small swell. The Psariot cutter came across, and it was Canaris himself that stepped aboard. Pat hastened to greet him and they shook hands warmly.

'O'Connor, good morning to you,' Zouvelekis translated the Admiral's greeting and Pat's reply.

'And to you, Admiral; we did not know it was you with us from Psara. We have near four score of your compatriots aboard.'

Canaris continued, 'With your permission, sir, perhaps I will visit my Psariot brothers whom you have rescued. They may wish to cross to my brig?'

'Of course, sir; Doctor Ferguson will be pleased to show you,' said Pat, his deafness now near gone, and waving to the steps.

Simon had joined them already, and so led the Admiral, Pat and Zouvelekis following, down to the makeshift sick bay on the lower deck. In the gloom, the rank stench of vomit prevalent in the foetid air, as eyes adjusted, they could make out seventy or more people lying or sitting on blankets on the deck; no Psariot wishing to avail themselves of a hammock. Marston was passing amongst them with water and a thin gruel, their wretched stomachs incapable of more. Simon led the way, Canaris with him, the Admiral pausing and stooping to greet his fellow Psariots with a few gentle words to each in turn as he moved slowly from one to the next, his concern for his fellow islanders evident, occasionally draping a slipped blanket back over the shoulders of those too weak or distraught to do so, and speaking softly for a few moments with others, a gentle hand on the heads or shoulders of children, his kindly words bringing a weak smile from some of them, tears from others. He moved down the line, his face more grim with every step, his own voice now faltering, and as he neared the last of his fellow Psariots the Admiral unexpectedly fell to the deck, to his knees, with a low shriek of exclamation, and seized into his arms a slight woman of about fifty who had been sitting up on her blanket, rocking from side to side, crying to herself. He hugged her tightly, the two sharing quiet and emotional words of mutual surprise, of greeting, and of desperate consolation; the woman now wailing loudly, and Canaris in silence, still holding her close, her head buried in his chest; her body was wracked with shaking and her distress was audible throughout the length of the deck.

Pat and his companions held back, a respectful few yards away, staring at this unexpected and tearful reunion. 'It is his aunt,' Marston whispered. 'She was pulled from the water by Barton, in the barge, after swimming out two miles or more.'

Several minutes passed, neither Pat nor any of his officers moving, all remained standing quite still in respectful silence, until the Admiral rose slowly and with some difficulty to his feet. He turned towards Pat, plainly trembling with emotion, great floods of tears evident on his cheeks. Without a word, Canaris stepped forward and simply grasped Pat, without ceremony, enveloping him in a fierce bear hug, his voice quite failing him, though no words were necessary: his gratitude so obvious. For a near minute he stood in tight embrace before gathering his composure and stepping back, nodding silently to Pat, still quite unable to speak.

'Come, sir,' said Pat gently. 'We will take coffee in the cabin. My officers will arrange the transfer of your compatriots directly.'

Within a short time, discussion proving beyond his capabilities, his distress prevailing and so evident, Canaris had departed. Pat and Simon returned to the cabin after bidding farewell. The Admiral's spirits had been restored a very little as his aunt and the stronger refugees transferred to his brig.

'It is a heavy burden that man is carrying, for sure,' remarked Pat. 'His island sacked; doubtless he has lost many of his family. It is not surprising that he was brought to tears on finding his aunt; 'tis to be hoped that he will persevere.'

'The busy have no time for tears. I collect Lord Byron spoke that,' Simon murmured. 'He is a great loss, Pat. I am sure of it.'

In the afternoon, with the strong following *Meltemi* wind now speeding their voyage, a Greek squadron was espied from the tops, tacking hard from the south-west, from the direction of Hydra. Two hours passed and *Surprise* closed on the Greeks until they joined together, all vessels backing sails and slowing to a stop. It was Admiral Miaoulis, striving to reach Psara from Hydra, unknowing

374

of its fall and sack, of the destruction of the fort and its last defenders. Pat crossed in his barge to the Greek flagship. Canaris's brig was now a league behind *Surprise*. Pat and Zouvelekis convened with Admiral Miaoulis in his cabin, his steward serving strong Greek coffee, much to Pat's liking, and fiery ouzo. The Greek admiral, a man who had pledged his three ships and his fortune to the Greek struggle, a legend amongst his men and widely heard of much further afield in all knowledgeable naval circles - when captured by the Royal Navy off Cadiz when running the British blockade he had secured his unexpected release after charming Nelson himself - was short and portly, in his mid-fifties, his hair slipping from black to grey, clean shaven except for a bushy moustache, and with neither airs nor graces. He exuded warmth and a quiet confidence even whilst responding to the reported catastrophe of Psara. Pat took to him instantly.

Zouvelekis translated Miaoulis's report, 'Thirty-three Psariot vessels reached Hydra yesterday evening, being the ones that slipped in the night before we left Psara ourselves. On the news of their disaster all of the Hydriot populace gathered at the port and went to the convent, the place of government of the Primates of Hydra, where they demanded that the fleet sail without delay. The Primates immediately made funds available to the ship owners and their crews, and the Hydriots set off this morning to relieve Psara. They did not know all was lost, of the fort exploding, and that all resistance had ceased,' Zouvelekis concluded Miaoulis's gloomy report.

Pat lamented that the Hydriots were now too late to help Psara, and explained to the Admiral their rescue of many Psariots from the water, their long delayed departure, pursued by two Turk frigates until the fort blew up, the end of any prospect for Hydriot relief arriving in any time to save further survivors. All to the Admiral's growing dismay and evident distress, until, when Pat had finished his story, Miaoulis concluded their meeting. 'Captain O'Connor, I thank you with all my heart, sir. Please convey any Psariot refugees you may still have aboard and escort your companion Psariot ships to Hydra. My squadron will continue to Psara and see if there remains anything we can do there, if there may be any remaining souls we might rescue.'

'Of course, sir. I pray we may next meet in more favourable circumstances.' The Surprises departed.

As the afternoon slipped into evening *Surprise* closed on Hydra, and as Dalby rang six bells she let go her anchor in the outer roads of the island, the harbour being filled with Hydriot merchant vessels and thirty-three refugee Psariots. Also in the roads was the French frigate *Isis*, near alongside *Surprise* at her anchorage. The barge and cutter were lowered, and Barton with his men began to transfer the remaining Psariot refugees to the shore, where gentle Hydriot welcomers took them into their care. From *Isis* came help in the shape of her boats, her captain sending his compliments to the captain of *Surprise* with an invitation to dinner next day.

'That is mighty civil of the Frenchie,' said Pat to Duncan. 'Are they fashionable coves with the clock; dinner at what hour, tell?'

The frenetic activity and tension of the past days now caught up with them all, and within an hour after supper near all aboard were fast asleep, their exhaustion overtaking them. Pat, grateful to be in his cot at long last, and seeking to blot out from his mind the horror of recent events, focussed his fatigued mind on pleasurable recollections of his native Claddaghduff, of long summer days on the beach as a youngster, of stealing away at low tide to Iomaidh to visit his grandmother's grave, and gathering crabs and shellfish which abounded around its shores. Eventually he became drowzy, began to doze, and dreamed of happy days on boat trips with his father to Inishturk and Inishbofin, of fishing for the plentiful pollack and mackerel, until slowly he slipped into a deep, deep torpor: merciful oblivion had finally claimed him.

Wednesday 7th July 1824   *Hydra*

Pat, yawning and not long awakened, stepped up to his quarterdeck, greeting Barton, Pickering and Duncan who were standing near the stern and looking over to the outer anchorage. Pat blinked in the bright light; he shivered, the warmth of the day not yet arrived, and he smiled pleasantly towards his companions.

'Good morning, gentlemen. Why, 'tis *Alacrity* over there. Charles Yorke, I collect,' he remarked, nodding in the direction of the Royal Navy brig. 'She must have arrived in the night. I did not see her last night, though I was fast gone by four bells and nothing would have wakened me, save perhaps the barky catching a'fire.'

Some hours later Pat, Duncan, and Pickering were rowed across to *Isis* in Pat's barge. 'Larboard, sir?' asked Barton.

'Larboard, Barton, if you will,' said Pat as they approached her, boarding by the larboard side by Royal Navy convention demanding no welcoming ceremony from the crew, though whether such custom prevailed in the French navy Pat had no idea. Indeed, it was doubtful that the crew of *Isis* could have mounted any reception at all as the deck of the frigate was filled with the saddest collection of refugees that Pat could ever remember. Scores of poor wretches in the most dishevelled state, women clutching their children, old ladies sobbing, and just a very few young lads and fewer old men, Isis's second explaining that they were too weak to shift ashore. Captain de Bargemont was with his surgeon below decks where several distressed refugees were being treated. His lieutenant escorted them to the cabin, to await him. Pat was pleasantly surprised to find there an old Portsmouth acquaintance, the young captain of *Alacrity*.

Captain Yorke sprang from his chair and seized Pat's hand immediately, and with the friendliest of greetings, 'Captain O'Connor, sir. I hope I see you well.'

'Prime, Charles: thankee. I did not know *Alacrity* was in these waters. May I introduce my first, my dear friend, Duncan Macleod? And my second: Tom Pickering? Duncan, Tom: my friend, Charles Yorke. We have shared many a bottle together in Pompey, reminiscing about our *Leanders*. Mine the old *Leander* and Charles's the new fifty-eight. We were both lieutenants aboard our *Leanders*, you know. I served on her in the Toulon blockade in ninety-eight, just afore she was captured by the Frenchies. Though she came back to us the next year, recaptured and returned by our then friends the Turks. Ain't that strange? And Charles was third on the new ship when we were in South America.'

'Your servant, sir,' said Duncan, shaking Yorke's hand.

Yorke explained that he too had returned from Psara, arriving some hours after darkness, anchoring some way outwith of *Surprise*, de Bargemont sending his dinner invitation at six bells that morning.

At that moment Captain de Bargemont entered his cabin, apologising for his failure to greet them personally, and more formally welcomed Yorke, Pat, and Duncan aboard his ship, proferring the most cordial amity to both captains and a great respect for Pat in particular. He explained that he had heard all about the exploits of 'the famous *Capitaine de Vaisseau* O'Connor' from his second cousin, Admiral Christy-Pallière, who was also in the Mediterranean accompanying Admiral Henri de Rigny with a large French squadron. They sat in de Bargemont's cabin as they awaited dinner, enjoying the very best of his cellar, several bottles of a magnificent Chateau Margeaux of the year sixteen being consumed before the dinner arrived, and de Bargemont talking of *Isis* and Psara with great sadness in his voice. 'We approached Psara town behind the Turk fleet. The water around my ship was full of bodies of women and children, scores of them, perhaps hundreds. We rescued survivors from the massacre, and brought them here only yesterday, taking them out of the water where they were struggling to reach us, and also off the remoter beaches of the island before they were found by the invader. Terrible, terrible, mon Dieu. We leave for Nauplia with one hundred and fifty-six of them in the morning.'

Captain Yorke then spoke, 'I arrived at Psara on the fifth and espied a sight of the utmost devastation, the fort quite disappeared and smoke arising from the town, Turk ships everywhere. Afore leaving, I met with Ishmael Pasha aboard Admiral Khosref's flagship, going aboard to pay my respects to the Admiral and to enquire of his intentions, the Turks having subdued the island. The fortress had exploded some time afore, and all resistance on the island had been overcome. The janissaries were rounding up all the remaining elders of the island, perhaps for ransom, and they were in chains aboard Khosref's ship. As to the other captives of no significance, poor souls, a future as slaves was the most that they might anticipate. Hundreds and thousands of others were slaughtered. The Admiral did not grant me an audience and I saw Ishmael in his stead. He pretended to be sorry for the loss of Greek life. He showed me a plan of the island, given to him, and explained that it had been prepared by the prior reconnaissance in June which identified the tiny beach where their troops had landed in the north. "Are you going to Hydra? I love the Hydriots," he asked me, the crafty old dog, and then he was called away by Khosref. In his absence I ventured out on deck and saw his men counting the chopped off heads of prisoners. When he returned, I demanded of Ishmael what he was about, with such barbaric acts. He asked me if I would like to see what he was about, and then he left the cabin again. Within a few minutes he returned accompanied by one of his men clutching the head of a Greek, a priest it was, said Ishmael, dripping fresh blood all o'er his deck. I was near sick o'er his deck too, and then he refused me leave to go ashore to see what was happening on the island and so I returned to *Alacrity*. We fired a twenty-gun salute in respect of Khosref as we departed whilst the Turks were setting the town aflame, and so sailed here directly,' Yorke concluded his gruesome account. To his horrific story neither Pat nor Duncan could find adequate words to comment, both quitting *Isis* shortly afterwards with Pickering and Yorke.

'We thought ill of Boney, Duncan, yet never did he sink to such depths as the Turk,' remarked Pat as they were rowed towards *Surprise* in his barge.

'That's as may be, Pat, but ne'er forget that the vile Corsican tyrant's oppression claimed many hundreds o' thousands more lives. Perhaps his victims may be numbered even in the millions? Such prodigious waste: such folly; will we ne'er learn, brother?'

'At such times we may lament that Noah did not miss his tide,' murmured Pickering.

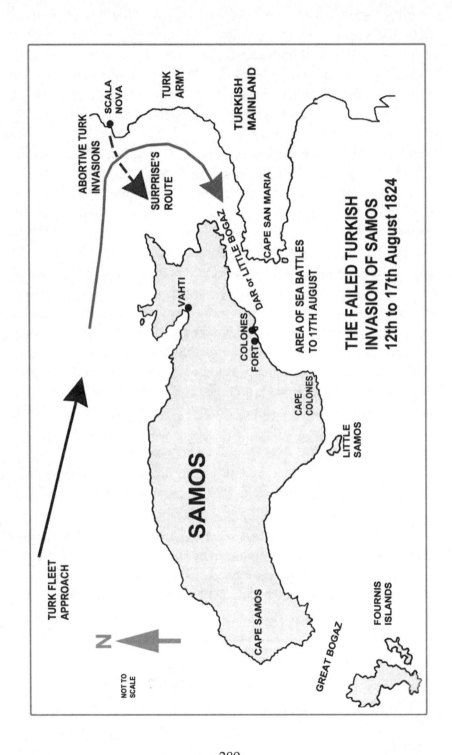

THE FAILED TURKISH
INVASION OF SAMOS
12th to 17th August 1824

Chapter Ten

Place me on Sunium's marbled steep,
Where nothing, save the waves and I,
May hear our mutual murmurs sweep;
There, swan-like, let me sing and die:
A land of slaves shall ne'er be mine –
Dash down yon cup of Samian wine!

Wednesday 11th August 1824, 7 a.m.   *north of Samos*

'Thirty sail, larboard beam!' The shout came from the watch atop the main, the distant ships just visible as small specks, and not yet distinct enough to count from the ship's deck against the still hazy north-west horizon. The sky was still streaked with wispy thin cloud, yet to burn off as the sun had not long begun its climb through the morning and seemed suspended, hovering only a little above the mountains on the eastern horizon, the Turk mainland remaining in black silhouette. The far fleet had been seen by the eagle eyes of *Surprise's* topman, now shouting again, 'Forty sail!'

Pat looked uneasily about his quarterdeck and beyond, to all the far realms of his vision. To the south was Samos which offered no security for his ship; to the east the hostile Turk mainland with its port of Scala Nova. The wind filling the sails was blowing a moderate south-easterly, coming off the mainland mountains, and *Surprise* was reaching north of east, running no more than three or four knots; *Eleanor*, her companion, in her wake.

'Could that be Admiral Sakhtouri, Captain Zouvelekis?' asked Pat, not really believing the possibility himself, a trace of anxiety creeping into his voice.

'I think not, sir. I doubt that he commands forty sail, and most likely he will approach Samos from a more south-westerly direction, from Icaria, as we did. He cannot be more than a half-day behind us, perhaps less. I fear that is the Turk fleet from Mitylene,' Zouvelekis replied, sombrely, resignation plain in his voice.

'Put your helm up, Mr Pickering,' Pat ordered. 'Let us close a little and see what we can of those ships.'

'Aye aye, sir,' Pickering replied, echoing the command to Barton at the wheel, the master shouting to the now attentive crew, who began hauling hard on the braces as the rudder forced her head round to a near northerly course.

'What can we do, sir, against forty sail?' asked Mower, his apprehension plain in his voice.

'Precious little, save to know their strength, and flee before them to Samos. Though first it will serve us well were we to know what vessels wait at Scala Nova, for it is there that the Turk army will surely embark within those ships for any landing on Samos.'

A slow half hour passed, and the far fleet now became identifiable, Pat gazing through his glass to study it, 'I see frigates, perhaps a half dozen, and one line-of-battle ship; a dozen of brigs or corvettes, a dozen of transports too. It is the Turks, there is no doubt. We have seen enough. Mr Pickering, bring her back, course north-east, we will look into Scala Nova afore we turn south. Mr Mower, signal to *Eleanor* to return to Hydra with news of this fleet.'

Surprise returned to her beam reach, the north-easterly course, her progress steady, but faster than it was for the Turks some six miles or so to the north-west of them. Pat mentally calculated how far *Surprise* could go without the Turks closing on them. Their fleet was working hard to make the slowest of progress, tacking alternately south and east against the stiff south-easterly, unusual as it was. Of the customarily prevalent *Meltemi* there was no sign. Zouvelekis had predicted it for the next day, at dawn remarking on the small and scattered high clouds and the absence of the usual early morning dew on *Surprise's* deck; a sure sign, he said, of the *Meltemi* on the morrow. With her few crew waving farewell from her deck, every Surprise answering, *Eleanor* began her turn about, swiftly wearing to reverse her course, and within a half hour she had diminished to a bare speck, flying on her south-westerly track.

'What are your intentions, sir?' asked Zouvelekis as the morning wore on towards noon, bringing them closer to the Turk coast and the port of Scala Nova, the Turks in their wake.

'We must run before them, and pass through the Little Boghaz Strait to Colones. The Spezziots must be there now, leaving Hydra the day afore we left. I think we have enough time to espy Scala Nova first, to see if there are more Turk ships there, before we turn into the Strait,' Pat replied. 'Though this south-easterly gives us precious little margin. Let us take a meal whilst we can. Mr Pickering, Mr Mower, please take a little time for your dinner whilst Mr Macleod and I will remain on deck.' His lieutenants disappeared below.

For his own dinner taken a half hour later Pat was joined by Duncan and Simon. Their meal was eaten in near silence over the table as Pat considered their situation until they had finished when Simon, his curiosity pressing, spoke first, 'Do not suppose that this is more than a general observation, Pat, but there are forty Turk sail close behind us. Is that cause for alarm, would you think?' As Freeman left with their empty plates, Simon added, 'Is there some plan, some nautical strategy, forming in your mind?'

Pat took a deep draught of his coffee before replying, 'Ne'er before did we face such odds, Simon. I could not consider of fighting this fleet without we were accompanied by at least a brace of seventy-fours or half a dozen frigates, forty-fours or their like. There are a dozen Spezziots ahead of us and a dozen Hydriots astern of us. If all act together then assuredly we have a chance. The Turk plainly intends to land on Samos, and, as we have seen at Kasos and Psara, these islands all have beaches which no number of Greek batteries can defend. Unless the Turk can be defeated at sea Samos too will surely be lost. Any landing will require of plentiful transport vessels – schooners, barges, caiques and the like. The Turk fleet is lacking of such numbers, as can plainly be seen, and so many more must be elsewhere in readiness. They are likely in Scala Nova, no other port being close enough for this fleet to support. We shall see Scala Nova afore we enter the narrows of the Strait, which is but a mile across to the Turk side. Over there are mountains, and so any Turk army must embark at Scala Nova; or perhaps from the beaches to the south of it. That is, unless more are coming from the far south. Yet no Turk sail have been reported there: so I was told by Admiral Sakhtouri. It is to be hoped that he is not far behind us. Mind, I am concerned the Turk fleet now separates the Hydriots and the Spezziots, unless Sakhtouri comes around the south of the island, not the north as we did. Doubtless Sakhtouri too will wish to have sight of Scala Nova, and so 'tis likely he will follow our course on the north side.'

'I beg pardon but is there some consideration, some concern, pressing on your thoughts, soul?' asked Simon, watching Pat closely as he plainly continued to ruminate on the situation.

'Yes... 'tis a fine pickle, Simon. If this fleet joins with its transports in Scala Nova so as to protect them, then likely Samos will be lost, and so I am considering of what can be done? Murphy!' Pat shouted, unnecessarily as his ear was closely behind the door. 'Murphy, light along, and ask my officers to join me, Captain Zouvelekis too.'

When they had all assembled, seated around his table, Pat, his thinking done, began. 'Gentlemen, the Turk is but two or so leagues behind us; Scala Nova a little more than two leagues ahead. We are flying His Majesty's colours, and so the Turk shows no interest in us at present. I have been considering of the lame-duck caper.' As only blank faces registered around the table in response, Pat continued, 'Come, gentlemen. We will play a little game: starting the sheets a trifle, steering a point or two off her best; and we will send half the lads below so they don't suspect our trick. Mr Mower, please prepare to hoist all the Greek colours you are able to find, a pennant too if you will, at the jack, the mizzen, and the main. We will engage his attention, but hold for my command.'

'Aye aye, sir,' Mower replied doubtfully, for who in such circumstances would wish to attract such unwelcome attention, though he left to find the flags without question.

'You do not intend to fight, so?' asked Simon, even though he could hardly conceive Pat's reply would be in the affirmative, the odds being so very greatly against them.

'Good Lord, Simon, what a fellow you are! We are but one, and they a dozen at least. That would surely be biting off more tongue than we could chew. We are the fox fleeing before the hounds, yet we will lead them a merry dance, for sure we will. Mr Pickering, the Turk has gained not a cable on us these past two hours; I should like to change that just a little, and without him knowing it is of our choosing. We will drag a sail behind us in the water and shed a knot or so. Lose not a moment; cast one over the starboard side so he will not see it, for he will be looking closely at us when our true colours are flying. I think we will hold Mr Mower's change to Greek colours until the sail is in place and we are slowed.'

Pickering nodded, knowing his captain's agile tactical mind of old, though he too was confounded by Pat's seemingly incomprehensible instructions. Their sea-room was dwindling as they closed on the Turkish coast, and Scala Nova now very near, but the Turk fleet a mere five miles or so behind them.

'Aye aye, sir,' he found himself uttering, though the words did not feel like they came from his conscious thoughts.

'Let us go up, gentlemen,' said Pat, adding nothing more, neither Duncan, Simon nor Zouvelekis caring to ask. On the quarterdeck all looked back to the Turks. Was there now a fresh impetus behind them? Were they carrying more sail? Was their course now converging on *Surprise* more swiftly? These questions and more passed through all their minds, though the still strong south-easterly continued to make their easterly progress very slow, for *Surprise* and the Turks too, the dragging sail now slowing *Surprise* to no more than two knots at best. At last, with their glasses they could see Scala Nova with clarity, and the harbour was indeed filled, as Pat had predicted, with transports of all sizes; scores of masts readily visible over the long north-south harbour mole. He spoke to his officers, 'They cannot escape the harbour in this prevailing wind, fierce as it is. The south end of the mole at the harbour entrance curves back towards the land, and so their departure would be directly into this near gale with no sea-room to tack ship. No, they must await the return of the *Meltemi* on the morrow to escape the harbour. Mr Mower, we will hoist all our Greek colours now, if you please.' Within minutes the ragged, torn, old white ensign was hauled down and the main-royal truck, the jack-staff, and the mizzen-peak boasted huge Greek flags, streaming vigorously in the stiff south-easterly, flying wild and vibrant in the stiff wind, blue stripes on white, and shouting out to all who watched: *Greece!* The display so exhilarant and proud: *freedom!*

As Dalby rang six bells Pat looked again at the Turk fleet. It was undeniably a mile closer now than before. It was time to explain his plan to his officers. Mr Prosser stood alongside him, looking a little nervously at the closing gap between *Surprise* and the Turks, the distance closing too between *Surprise* and the mainland, probably now no more than three miles ahead. Pat began, 'Gentlemen, if the Turk fleet stays here to protect those transports in Scala Nova, nothing on this earth will stop them approaching the Straits together and landing their troops on the Samos beaches when the wind changes round, as it surely will. However, if we are able to draw their warships after us, into the Strait, then the transports may choose not to leave Scala Nova until they return. In short, we can but seek to gain time until Sakhtouri comes up behind us. If we can go through the Strait with those Turks behind us, though they may strike us hard if they close up to us, by themselves they can do little or nothing against the island.'

'How do ye propose to attain this end, sir?' asked Duncan, very quietly, his mind registering all kinds of unwelcome prospects, the other lieutenants too all still dwelling on Pat's words, particularly his mention of entering the Strait with a score of Turk warships astern of them.

Pat continued, 'That is why we have slowed and are flying Greek colours, for now we surely have their attention. It will not be long, I fancy, afore some keen Turk is firing his bow chasers. If Admiral Sakhtouri is behind us, behind the Turks, and their transports do leave Scala Nova without escort of this fleet, should it pursue us, then so much the better; Sakhtouri can wreak grave damage on their transports without let or hindrance, and that may yet save this island. We must bring on those frigates and draw them away from the transports. Mr Macleod, we shall come about, turn towards the Strait. We shall bring her round, but do so very slowly so that we will miss stays and fall in irons. Let us give the Turk some encouragement; that will answer very well.'

Duncan, with considerable fortitude, said nothing, but there was a collective gasp from everyone else within earshot as they heard this. The helmsmen stared at each other, though no word passed their lips. A most high risk plan it was: to deliberately lose way and come to a stop with a whole fleet now in close pursuit of a solitary frigate was simply inconceivable. Who but a madman or Pat O'Connor would choose to do such a thing?

'Perilous, would it be?' whispered Simon.

'Mr Mower, it is time to cut away the trailing sail. Mr Pickering, bring her about,' prompted Pat, cold determination resonating from his voice.

'Aye aye, sir, come about, slowly, and let her fall in irons,' Pickering responded, his voice dropping an octave before reiterating the order to the master. 'Mr Prosser, come about, into the wind; but slowly it is; it would never do were Johnny Turk to smoke our plan.'

Mr Prosser passed the word to Barton at the wheel, 'Bring her to the wind! Keep her full!' coming automatically from his lips before he reminded himself of their plan, and then he shouted, 'Helm down, luff and touch her,' to the helmsmen, all now anxiously gazing at the Turk ships, at *Surprise's* diminishing sea-room, at *Surprise's* Greek flags flying strongly in the stiff wind, and wondering what calamity the next hour might bring them; for surely that is how things looked.

'Mr Pickering,' said Pat. 'If you will, tell the men we will find ourselves in irons in a few minutes, and it will be of our making. Tell them plain so there is no panic, and tell them too that we will need every man jack of them to back the sails as swiftly as they have ever worked afore so as to get underway again. There will not be a moment to lose. Mr Mower, we will double-reef the mainsail, swiftly now. I would not wish her to go aback with it all unfurled. We will favour her rudder fastenings.'

'Aye aye, sir; mains'l to be reefed.'

'Gently does it, Mr Prosser, Barton; helm down,' Pat murmured to his cox'n at the wheel, to Prosser as a courtesy, 'We will miss stays, but not so slowly as the Turk will see that is our intention.'

'Aye aye, sir, gently it is,' Barton reiterated, guiding the firm pull on the wheel together with his mates as they hauled her round, slowly, ever so slowly, much more slowly than usual, feeling her speed fall away as she came up into the wind, the pressure slipping away on her rudder as she slowed, slowed more, and then there was no longer any bite at the wheel, and the ship began to shudder, the mizzen-topsail shivering.

'Helm a-starboard, hard over, Mr Pickering,' ordered Pat, the command quickly reiterated to the helmsmen. All looked aloft to see that the sails now flapped uselessly as *Surprise* floundered with no forward momentum. Imperceptibly, as she now faced directly into the south-easterly, the sails all ahoo, edges flapping, the shuddering ceasing with the crews slackening of the yards' braces, she began to slip back. Scores of puzzled faces gazed back to the quarterdeck, all staring anxiously at Pat; some, the nervous and the newcomers, wondering if he had bitten off a deal more than anyone could hope to chew, and willing some command, anything, from their captain, to start their escape from this perilous situation.

Within a few moments, Pat spoke again to Mower, 'Let out the jibs,' the command quickly echoed forward. Men rushed to obey. Two minutes passed slowly by, a mental agony for all on deck, before the bow began to swing, barely perceptibly at first, round to the south, shifting out from the direct line of the approaching wind, though *Surprise* was now plainly drifting backwards. The horrified crew gazed in anxious hope at the jibs fluttering, willing them to fill as they strived to collect the wind.

'Quickly now!' Pat shouted, 'Mr Mower, brace full the yards,' the order passed immediately to the anxious men. 'Haul hard, back, back!' His commands were echoed by his officers, and every man of the crew now raced as they had never before, hauling hard on the braces, the yards swinging to their maximum of swivel. The crew anxiously looked to the Turk fleet now filling their vista and within the past thirty minutes closing to within two miles, nervous glances towards it reminding them of their urgency and peril, for the Turk warships, eleven of them, had now split from their fellows, the larger ships plainly in pursuit of *Surprise,* and only the smaller of them with their accompanying transports were still bound for Scala Nova.

'Your plan is working, Pat,' murmured Simon, standing alongside his captain, let us pray to all the saints that we will be blessed with the second part,' he added softly and out of earshot of all on the quarterdeck except for Pat.

'Eh? The second part?' Pat blinked.

'For that our escape would answer tolerably well. That is your second part, Pat, or am I much astray?'

'Helm hard a-port!' Pat bellowed the order.

'Tell me, will we escape the Turk host?' Simon anxious now.

'I do not like to show away, Simon, but if we don't you may call me Jack Pudding.' This said with the thinnest of smile.

The crew were still working in feverish haste. *Surprise's* sails had begun to fill, and the yards were now tight braced to harvest the wind off her larboard bow which now faced two points west of south. Slowly at first she began running ahead once again, two more minutes passing with no discernible bow wave.

'Let fall mains'l,' Pat shouted to the men aloft. A further long minute passed, but now her progress was demonstrated by the smallest of bow ripples, the wind captured by the topsails and main course powering her forward again, and all sails were once more straining on their yards. Half a knot; one knot; *Surprise* was at last moving cleanly through the water, sailing south-south-west. Anxious faces all about willed her to greater speed.

'They are closing us, sir. Perhaps making seven or eight knots, and they will be alongside of us within the half hour,' observed Pickering.

'Will we succeed in running clear, would you say?' asked Simon.

'The wind is shifting,' Pat pronounced, sniffing the air. 'Now 'tis a more easterly wind. That will help us.' Pat stepped to the forward rail of his quarterdeck, and shouted cheerfully to all who might hear him, 'We must crack on, like smoke and oakum, me lads. Let us make her fly!'

It was a refreshing sentiment, welcome to all on his quarterdeck and to every member of the crew within earshot, as no one else felt in the least cheerful at that moment; the leading Turk frigates had all tacked to near directly south and were a bare one mile off *Surprise's* beam and on a converging course. If she could not gain more speed quickly then it was likely that she would be brought to action within the next quarter hour, and with such a huge Turk superiority in numbers snapping at her heels she was surely doomed. It was a consideration that escaped none of the crew.

'Mr Macleod, set all topgallants if you please,' Pat ordered.

The anxious crew sprang aloft as swiftly as squirrels up a tree with a fox in pursuit. Five more minutes passed. *Surprise* was fast picking up speed as the wind had shifted further round to the east-north-east. She was making six knots, and gaining speed all the time, every stitch of sail including her studdingsails all run out, and she was now sailing large with every mast under great strain, but the nearest Turk just a half-mile off her starboard quarter.

Marston and Jason too had stepped up to the quarterdeck, in some trepidation, and gazed about them, absorbing the great sense of urgency of all present; immediately sensing the finely balanced prospect of escape or capture, perhaps even destruction. Neither spoke, but both scanned the faces of their fellows for an indication, any indication, of confidence, none being visible. Pat alone seemed to be sure of their situation.

'The Turks are closing, brother. As I dare say you remarked. Are we in peril, Pat? Could we go a little faster would you think? Is there something more we can do, tell?' enquired Simon; Marston and Jason standing next to him, both looking aghast at their obvious peril.

'Oh, I am sure something will come to mind.'

'Could we gain just a little greater celerity with a more favourable arrangement of the sails, at all? Perhaps we could shift to a more advantageous course?'

Pat turned to his friend, Simon's questions breaking his train of thought, 'A more advantageous course? Which do you suggest?'

'Why, is that not a customary tactic of you navigators?'

'Why, certainly it is, though the choice of which course would suit better does escape me for the moment.'

'Perhaps there is some ... some more efficient adoption of the bowlines or the gumbrils? Perhaps we could clap on, or implement some similar scheme familiar to you mariners?'

'Simon, I venture you are close to poaching on my province. Will you see me put out? Vexed? Pray cease barking about the bush.'

'Beg pardon, brother. Can we not do something so as to draw away? I am merely wondering,' asked Simon as he gazed with some apprehension upon the slowly closing Turk frigates; an orange flash coming from the bow of the nearest, quickly followed by the BOOM thundering from the Turk's cannon.

'A hopeful shot,' Pat pronounced, watching the splash of the shot falling short still a hundred yards off and plunging into the chop of the grey sea. He turned to his friend, and stared with mild disbelief, 'Gumbrils? Clap on and draw away? What do you mean?'

'Why, is that not a commonplace term oft used by you navigators?'

Pat, accustomed for long years as he was to his friend's often incredible references to ship handling, could find no answer for a moment. He whispered, as if to prevent his words carrying to the ears of the helmsmen, 'I am sure of it. Though I do not recall it at present, but a most suitable phrase it is.'

'Is there a prospect they may catch us, would you think? I only throw out the enquiry. Doubtless ill-considered it is.'

'Oh, I should never say anything as unlucky as that.'

'You mean that we might yet escape?' Simon brightened.

'Never be so concerned, Simon. The Turk will not catch us now. The barky is sailing large, she has a clean bottom, and 'twill not be long afore she hauls away.'

'That was my very same thought, though I did not care to be so presumptious as to remark it,' Simon replied, blessed relief rushing as if on a flood tide back to his mind, dampening its turmoil, his breathing slowing with the realisation of his hopes.

Still the Turk ships doggedly followed, a frigate leading; the line-of-battle ship, a heavy frigate and eight more in line astern of her. 'A razee, I venture,' said Pat to no one in particular, and now enjoying the coffee that Freeman had brought to his quarterdeck amidst an emerging inkling of escape that had begun to develop throughout the ship. The leading Turk frigate, running at her best speed and closing to within a quarter mile, off *Surprise's* quarter, continued to fire her bow chasers, though no shot had struck *Surprise*, and Pat remained unperturbed.

'Would it be indecently curious to wonder what happens next?' asked Simon, his anxieties only partially mollified, Jason and Marston hanging on his every word.

'Were she off our beam, Simon, then we might well fret. At this range, her twelve-pound balls – or worse she may have eighteen-pounders – would break holes through our hull, but her six, or perhaps even nine-pound chasers can do little damage. My cabin windows are already gone, shot away.'

'Allow me to commend your strategem, Pat; you have confounded the Turk; most impressive, upon my word,' murmured Simon.

'Congratulations, sir. Your plan has worked splendidly. The Turk ships are all astern,' said Pickering, spirits everywhere within earshot lifting, though not yet reaching that pinnacle of relief.

'I collect your better plans, Pat, in the past. Ones less sure to strain the heart,' said Simon, very relieved, but his pulse racing even now. 'I think I may take a tint just now, it will relax the fibres.'

Within a further hour of sailing, *Surprise*, now making nine knots with the following wind, had pulled away a little from her pursuers, and the entrance to the Little Boghaz strait loomed. Off the larboard beam, on the Turk beaches and on the hillsides, could be seen thousands upon thousands of tents, the Turk troops waiting for their moment to cross the strait to Samos. Within a half hour they entered the narrows and Zouvelekis took on the navigation, standing alongside Prosser, he being familiar with the strait and the approach to Colones. The Turks had slipped back to near three-quarters of a mile astern of *Surprise*, but the leading frigate continued firing her bow chasers, bringing excitement to all watching from the shore from both sides of the strait narrows, Turk and Greek alike.

'Colones, sir, off the starboard bow. Perhaps a league now,' reported Zouvelekis.

'Ahead sir, eleven sail. It must be the Spezziots. They have come out of Colones. Why, they are leaving!' exclaimed Pickering, gazing through his glass.

Pat raised his own and stared hard at them, 'Doubtless some watcher ashore has told them of the Turk fleet and its approach. Perhaps with this wind they do not care to fight, with the Turk holding the weather gauge? Their fireships would be of no use at all, and a brig against a frigate, properly served, is a certain defeat, that is for sure,' Pat mused aloud. 'We will follow them. It will serve no purpose to be bottled up over there in Colones. Bear away for the Spezziots, Mr Macleod.'

Colones town was now off the starboard bow, and within the next half hour they swiftly passed by, the Turks' larger ships slowing behind them and opening a bombardment upon the town, which was answered by the cannon of the new fort near alongside of it, until the strait echoed with continuous firing from hundreds of guns.

'The Turk is standing too far off to wreak havoc upon the town. From that distance many of his shot will fall short, and there can be little accuracy at such long range,' Pat observed, looking back at the firing.

Inexorably Colones was left far behind, *Surprise* staying in the wake of the Spezziots who were running at nine knots or more. Four Turk frigates continued the pursuit for near three hours until Patmos came in sight as the sun accelerated its descent in the last hour of the day when, at seven bells, the Turks broke off and began to haul away to the east. As the sun's rays were slowly extinguished into the western horizon, the light swiftly fading, darkness descended upon them. The very distant sound of the Samos cannonade ceased, and everyone slowly sensed the return to the relative silence of shipboard normality: the sounds of the wind in the rigging and the creak of spars and masts. 'What a day, sir,' said Mower with some relief.

Pat looked about him before replying, 'It ain't over yet, Mr Mower. We must now return to Colones and see if Admiral Sakhtouri has arrived; but first, supper for all hands. Captain Zouvelekis, sir; I beg you will cross to the Spezziots, and offer my compliments to Admiral Androutzo. We are returning to Colones after supper, and I trust he will accompany us.'

Pat rattled out his instructions to his officers before descending to the cabin with Duncan; Freeman hastening in with plates and cutlery, his mate Old Jim Lamb carrying a tray with wine and goblets. Within a very few minutes they returned with a steaming dish of steak and kidney pudding, served with bashed neeps, and, miraculously, a rare wedge of butter melting over them. 'By God, Freeman, that is a most welcome sight. My compliments to Wilkins,' said Pat as the dish was set before him and Duncan.

'A glass wi' ye, Pat. A close run thing it was, o' that there is nae doot. Praise oor Lord this day, whispered a deeply tired Duncan, mostly to himself, an exhausted Pat near asleep in his chair.

'I cannot collect this feeling of enduring exhaustion in all our past years, Duncan,' whispered Pat.

'Ah am nae doctor, that is plain, but 'tis the long weeks o' strain, the lack o' sleep, the constant watchin'; wi' ne'er any respite.'

As they laboured slowly over the food, hungry as they were, yet in a silence brought on by sustained deep fatigue, Duncan marvelled at his friend's decision making, his willingness to commit *Surprise* to the most dangerous of tactical manouevres whilst weighing their prospects for a successful outcome; taking *Surprise* into circumstances that few, if any other, captains would contemplate; and carrying his crew with him; for assuredly there were many that would not have cared for his ruse and the danger it presented, little margin for error had there been. He looked up from his dish to pour himself more wine. Pat was fast asleep.

The near full moon, bright in a cloudless and star-speckled sky, had given them adequate light for their slow tacking back to Colones, though the wind had lessened considerably. The Spezziots' intentions remained unknown, Zouvelekis failing to secure a pledge that they would follow in *Surprise's* train. Shortly before dawn they dropped anchor just outside of the port, alongside the Hydriots, who had also now arrived. For all of the return passage Pat had slept in a deep stupor, exhaustion taking its toll on him, the warmth of the day enduring all through the summer night and facilitating his sleep. He had been spelled by his officers and Zouvelekis on his quarterdeck, until at dawn he re-emerged, refreshed, up the steps to gaze upon the gathered Greek squadron, Hydriots and some Psariots too. A boat from Sakhtouri's brig brought an invitation to Pat to a conference of the Greek captains, and he crossed in his barge, accompanied by Zouvelekis and Duncan. They gathered in the brig's cabin, twenty or so captains, drinking thick Greek coffee, as a great exchange of stories passed round, unintelligible to Pat though Zouvelekis told him of anything of note.

When all were present Sakhtouri banged his hand hard on the table and brought the gathering to order. He graciously described first to Pat, Zouvelekis translating, their own experiences of the prior day. They had heard the Turk firing as they approached from Ithaca, and hastened, as Pat suspected they would, along the north side of Samos towards the mouth of the strait. There they had fallen upon the Turk invasion transports attempting the crossing, laden with thousands of troops, but guarded relatively lightly by a handful of brigs, which they had engaged, capturing one, and sending the Turk transports fleeing back to the mainland; killing and wounding thousands with sustained grape firing, and many of the Turk barges running themselves aground on the shore, thousands more of the Turk troops spilling out of their boats into the white, foaming surf and scrambling onto the beaches in desperate attempts to escape. It had been a rout, the guardian Turk brigs fleeing south through the strait, hugging the mainland, and abandoning the transports.

As Sakhtouri ended his story Zouvelekis interjected to explain Pat's ruse, his plan to draw the Turk warships away from their transport charges, and its now readily apparent great success to the gathering. The background babble of the Greeks slowly dwindled, the captains absorbing the story, and eventually ceased completely at his description of Pat's deliberate missing of stays so as to bring *Surprise* to a dead stop in the water as a near dozen Turk frigates, even a seventy-four, speedily gained on her, so as to entice the warships into the Strait and away from Scala Nova. From the naturally voluble and loud Greeks there came now not the smallest of whisper until Zouvelekis had finished his story. Then pandemonium erupted as it seemed as if every single Greek wished to congratulate Pat and thank him personally, until he was immersed in the press of all seeking to shake his hand and say a few words, but still not a one could he understand, though the message was plain in its fervour.

Zouvelekis struggled to keep pace with translating the Greek captains' messages of thanks for Pat; who was plainly overwhelmed and struggling to reply to each in turn with a few words, having no grasp of the Greek tongue. Sakhtouri looked on with benevolent keen interest as Zouvelekis foundered under the volume of goodwill and thanks, until Pat raised his arms in the air in a plea for silence, when Sakhtouri called all to order. Speaking through Zouvelekis translating he thanked Pat on behalf of them all, 'Captain O'Connor, you have rendered us the greatest of service yesterday. Had the Turk warships you describe accompanied the barges, my ships could have done but little, and those Turk troops would now be fighting in Colones. Samos may likely have been saved by your efforts, sir. I thank you. Samos thanks you. We all here do. After Chios, after Kasos and Psara, Greece cannot afford to lose another island. I can speak on behalf of all Greeks and say we are profoundly grateful to you.'

'Why I take that as mighty civil, sir. I am obliged,' said Pat as Zouvelekis's translation faltered, the Greek captains shouting loud and exuberant confirmations of Sakhtouri's words.

Sakhtouri continued, 'The Turks have been sighted but two

hours ago. They are behind Cape San Maria to the south-east, in the Gulf of Karena, so our scouts say, and coming north. Their transports cannot cross in safety to Samos without their escort, and so will remain in Scala Nova, and their barges on the beaches south of there. Our task, gentlemen, is to keep the Turk fleet out of the strait and separate from their transports in the north. The *Meltemi* is now blowing hard, and it will be an hour or more before Khosref's fleet can be here. Gentlemen, to your ships now and make ready.'

Back on *Surprise* once more, breakfast finished, officers and men alike all stood on deck, looking to the south, awaiting the Turk fleet which must surely soon come. Within a half hour the topman shouted down 'Eighteen sail.' Khosref's fleet had rounded Cape San Maria, and was approaching, though struggling hard against the very strong northerly, a gale indeed, their progress tortoise-like against the return of the vigorous *Meltemi*. *Surprise* lay at anchor behind a screen of Greek brigs, and there seemed little prospect of any immediate action, the wind holding the Turks to a near standstill, and their leading frigates making long tacks to and fro to gain but a very few yards.

'This is astonishing good fortune, this splendid wind,' shouted Pat at the top of his voice to all in earshot on his quarterdeck. 'It is doubtful the Turk could make the strait against this wind, even were we not here to fight him. It blows as hard as any wind I have ever seen in the chops of the Channel; long may it last.'

Dalby rang six bells as desultory firing broke out from the Greek brigs nearest the Turk oncomers: firing returned with little success. The long southerly reach of the current and consequent choppy swell from the wave crests meeting the contrary north wind, now blowing with extreme gusts, and their ships rolling in the severe swell, all made accurate firing difficult in the extreme for the Turks. Four hours passed, and the standoff remained. The gale held the Turks at bay in a way the Greek squadron could not better, and such intermittent firing as happened was more in hope than in expectation of any success. Yet, as the morning wore on, the Turks persisted, and their leading frigates slowly closed on the anchored Greeks, now barely more than half a mile separating the two fleets.

'The Greeks are now almost in range of the Turk frigates' guns, sir,' reported Mower.

'Will the Greek ships hold their position?' Simon asked.

'Brigs, Simon, they are brigs.'

'Are you making game of me, Pat?'

'Never, 'pon my word; you were doubtless misled by the bow view, and could not see that they have but two masts, not three. They cannot hold: brigs against frigates, six or nine-pound guns against twelves or eighteens. If the Turks get any closer they must slip their cables and flee. Their captains will surely become anxious in another half hour, as the Turks will be upon them,' Pat replied.

'Look, look there. The Greeks have started two brigs towards the leading Turks. Fireships perhaps?' exclaimed Pickering, pointing towards two small Greek vessels leaving the anchored squadron, slowly at first but quickly gathering speed, the gale full square behind them.

'They are headed towards the leading Turks, there, the frigate and the corvette,' said Mower. The action now was so close no glass was necessary, and all aboard *Surprise* were at her rail, had been for hours, staring hard at the Turk ships. The two little Greek brigs, both brightly aflame, were closing swiftly on the Turks who had seen the oncoming peril, and so broke away before the Greeks could attach themselves alongside. This precipitated a general abandonment of the action by the Turks, more and more of them now breaking off and wearing to run south-east, running for any shelter that might be found behind the mountains of the San Maria peninsula. On *Surprise* the crew realised the cheap victory, and were jubilant, arms and caps being waved towards the Greek ships in congratulation, a gesture wholly reciprocated until, at noon, a general torpor of fatigue settled upon them all, and the Surprises hastened below out of the fierce wind to enjoy their dinner.

Pat settled with all his officers in the great cabin. 'The wind has surely saved us this day. Mr Marston..., were you to indulge in the praying line this night, another stiff northerly would be a tolerably suitable request.'

'Our Lord doubtless hears many similar pleas, sir, in such deeply difficult times.'

'I am sorry, Michael, such a facile comment of mine. Please forgive me.'

'No apology is called for, sir. I will indeed be praying this night for the most favourable of winds on the morrow, and we may all place our trust in the benevolence of our Lord.'

'Hear, hear,' said Pat, very quietly.

'You have a greatly tired look, brother,' said Simon.

'Ne'er have the odds agin us been so high. What would I give for a seventy-four or two,' Pat sighed. 'I would be fair pleased were just a fifty-gun ship to be with us these next days; even such as the *Leopard* would serve – that leaky old tub. I pray the Greeks will not let us down when we are in the thick of it. Pardon me, Captain Zouvelekis.'

'I think you need have no fears of my countrymen fleeing, Captain O'Connor, sir. None will ever forget Chios, Kasos and Psara. All of us possessing of our liberty are determined the same will not happen to Samos.' It was a statement to which all at the table sensed that they could not adequately reply.

Friday 13th August 1824   *off Colones, Samos*

Shortly after dawn the Turks returned, coming out again from behind Cape San Maria, and tacking against the lightest of winds towards Colones, some hours passing with barely any progress being made by the Turk fleet.

'Our hoped-for strong north wind did not eventuate?' Simon remarked, emerging with Marston from below onto the quarterdeck as all the officers looked towards the enemy fleet.

'No, our Lord did not heed your prayers, Mr Marston, though it is only a trifling disappointment: his munificence ain't to be scoffed at; the wind is scarcely more than a breeze, and no Admiral could countenance any engagement without he could shift his ships. They will gain nothing this day, to be sure,' Pat replied, his words comforting in their assurance to both his surgeons.

The Greeks again stayed at anchor, firing bow guns at the oncoming Turk ships for three hours as they closed until Sakhtouri again deployed his fireships, four sent this morning, towards the nearest Turks. On seeing them the Turks again broke away, and at this juncture all the Greek fleet hoisted anchors, *Surprise* with them, and followed their retreat. More in harassment than with any intention of closing, for the Turks, with seven frigates and a seventy-four, together with several brigs and their half a dozen corvettes, remained far more formidable than the Greek fleet. In the early afternoon the Greeks hove off and returned to Colones. Some damage had been done to both fleets, and some casualties incurred, though fortunately there were few fatalities.

Pat and his officers had been invited to supper with Admiral Sakhtouri, and were graciously welcomed aboard his brig as sunset slipped into dusk.

'Captain O'Connor, welcome aboard,' from Sakhtouri personally, as they stepped onto his deck. 'Lieutenants, Captain Zouvelekis, Doctor Ferguson. Welcome gentlemen, welcome,' he enthused.

They were seated at his table, and enjoyed the very best that his cook could provide. A feast of Greek specialities, the jewel being a whole roasted lamb with plentiful garlic and rosemary, the lamb stuffed with bread and lemons, and served with steaming rice sizzled quickly in the lamb juices.

'There is nothing that eats as well as lamb; a capital dinner, sir,' Pat raised his glass to Sakhtouri. The meal wound on for several hours, many a story of the day recounted across the table to the great interest of all present until all appetites were plentifully satiated, and Pat and his officers considered of the necessity for their departure.

'Admiral, Thankee, sir, for a prodigious fine supper; I have rarely eaten as well,' pronounced Pat as they finished, all enjoying a particularly flavoursome Greek brandy.

Sakhtouri raised his glass in salute to Pat before replying, 'It is an honour to have you with us, Captain O'Connor. Samos and Greece are in your debt, sir. Your bold ruse undoubtedly saved this island. My captains still speak of it. Would that the Samiots were more enterprising. I deplore their lack of precaution. No ships have they brought to our efforts, and only a single fort fresh constructed here at Colones. They know well what happened to their neighbours of Chios, of Kasos and latterly of Psara, and do they care to help our own ships? Do they care to pay for our crews? No, they do not. Here we are; a dozen of Hydriots plus those few Psariots who escaped the Turk; Spezziots perhaps, though I know not why they are not here tonight, but not a single Samiot ship, nor any crew of this island. It is lamentable, sir. Yet here is an Englishman, an English ship, fighting to save Samos from the Turk. Why should that be? What ails these Samiots? Most have run away to the mountains. As if that will protect their homes, their families, and their livestock should the Turk land,' he lamented gloomily, adding, 'I have written to Lycurgus, the Magistrate, with my opinion of these people and their want of precaution, of their indifference. Doubtless it will change nothing,' he concluded, draining his brandy. It was a sobering statement to which the Surprises could not reply.

At ten o'clock Pat and his officers returned to *Surprise,* intent on gaining as much sleep as possible before the anticipated next day's fresh engagement began. As all slumbered fitfully, at midnight, at their anchorage off Colones, eight Spezziot brigs arrived, letting go their anchors near alongside *Surprise.* It was a very welcome addition to the combined Greek fleet thought Pat, who had been struggling but failing to sleep, and so he had decided to go on deck, to see what was afoot, his mind turning on the prospects for the morrow and the inevitable Turk return. As he looked away from the Spezziots, and about him on his quarterdeck, in the near full moonlit night, still warm, coming from the prow he could hear the gentle sound of strings and song; soft, barely more than a murmur; and he gazed forward, down over the rail in the gloaming, listening and looking, past the masts, past the galley chimney, into the shadows, to two men sitting on the deck, on the coiled ropes, one singing softly with the faintest of Scots accent. Pat, ears straining into the wind gusting towards him, could just make out a verse.

401

When freedom's flags fly, freely in the light,
We can give thanks, to those lost in the fight,
And in our hearts where they will always be,
Their memories will sail o'er this Aegean sea,
And now I can be free ...

Then the wind blew again, shaking the rigging, and Pat could hear no more of the song. 'Would that be Mower, accompanied by Maclean, perhaps?' he wondered, no longer surprised by the many and varied departures from strict tradition since the venture had begun. He stepped down and returned, tired, to his cabin.

Saturday 14ᵗʰ August 1824   *off Colones, Samos*

As dawn illuminated the eastern sky, the mountains of Cape San Maria remaining in silhouette, Pat emerged to his cold, very windswept quarterdeck to gaze south and east towards the direction of any approaching Turk fleet. He struggled to escape the tiredness that a night of little sleep had left him with. No Turk ships could he see, though one Greek brig busied about, beating back against the fierce gale. Pat shivered and looked about him, noting that the *Meltemi* wind continued to blow hard from off the island of Samos; the sea surface was very choppy, and the warmer temperature of the night lingered no longer.

'The weather remains in our favour,' he remarked to Pickering. 'The Turk will struggle again today. My barge, Tom; in an hour, if you will. I am to confer with Admiral Sakhtouri.'

After breakfast Barton and his crew rowed Pat, with Zouvelekis, Duncan and Jason accompanying him, across to Sakhtouri's brig where they hastened towards his cabin. They stared at an already crowded gathering, loud voices everywhere.

'What's afoot, Captain Zouvelekis?' asked Pat as they stood at the cabin door, Sakhtouri ignoring their arrival, engrossed in heated discussion with his prior visitors.

'It is the island leaders, sir. Lycurgus himself, with the Bishop of Samos too, Stamati and others I know not. They are here after Sakhtouri's letter of complaint,' Zouvelekis explained.

'This is no business of ours,' said Pat. 'Let us wait on deck. Perhaps you will stay and hear them out,' he added to Zouvelekis as they shuffled away from the small and crowded cabin, angry voices still reaching their ears from the continuing discussion. An hour passed, and there came a hail from a schooner coming out from the harbour, its barge tying alongside. A Samiot officer clambered aboard the brig, and engaged in a voluble exchange with one of Sakhtouri's officers before both hastened into the cabin.

'Did you grasp any of that, Mr Jason?' asked Pat.

'Khosref has been sighted, sir, off the southern cape of the island. The schooner has been sent to collect the Magistrate,' Jason replied.

The vociferous meeting in the cabin was still audible even on deck, and after a very few minutes all therein came out in some haste. Their exchanges continued as Sakhtouri hastened his visitors off his brig, the tone of their exchanges now more placatory, and great anxiety evident in their demeanour. As the last of them departed, Sakhtouri, his relief evident yet great concern plain in his face, approached Pat, who had stood aside as the party disembarked. 'Captain O'Connor, may I speak with you, sir?'

'Why of course, sir. Is there some urgent development?'

Sakhtouri spoke with some anxiety, even alarm, 'Captain O'Connor. Khosref's fleet approaches from the south-west. He has slipped south and west in the night, and comes towards the south cape of this island, Cape Colones, since the dawn. Of my hoped-for reinforcement of Admiral Miaoulis and his squadron there is still no news. He has been gone some time in the vicinity of Rhodes to find the whereabouts of the Egyptian fleet. We must fight the Turks without him, and shift out with all our ships to engage Khosref before he comes into the strait.'

Pat looked ernestly at this troubled and flustered patriot who was nominally his chief, and reflected for a brief moment, recollections of his sleepless night's deliberations coming to the fore in his thoughts before replying, 'Admiral Sakhtouri, sir, shift we must certainly not do. Whilst we are here, the Turk cannot gain the strait. This wind makes it doubly difficult for him. Yet were we to

403

leave here the same difficulty would beset us. Our prospects of beating back to block this strait would be uncertain, and the Turk might well gain the strait ere we could. No, we must stay here, anchored firm. Let Khosref waste his hours beating into this wind. We will enjoy no better prospect out there than here. And from here your fireships will remain effective for threatening his approach. That is not sure once we venture out.'

Sakhtouri was plainly taken aback by Pat's contrary advice, and he remained highly-charged and nervous after his meeting with the Samiot Primates. For a moment it seemed as if he was about to remonstrate with or even push Pat out of his way for such plain and contrary speaking, his face flushing red. Zouvelekis, having translated Pat's opinion, awaited the admiral's response. He looked highly nervous, the admiral obviously far from happy.

Then, in but a moment, Sakhtouri deflated, his mind quickly reaching an appraisal of Pat's advice, and concluding it was sound. Zouvelekis happily translated his reply, 'Captain O'Connor, I thank you, sir. Your thoughts and plainly spoken words are of the highest value to me. We will stay here and await the Turk. Come, come and take refreshment with me.'

They settled within the cabin to talk over their situation and their prospects, the newly arrived Spezziot captains crossing to come aboard to join them. Not much more than an hour had passed when a second schooner tied alongside, and another messenger arrived from the town, where news of the Turk fleet was collected from monitors atop the high peaks of the island and brought down by the fittest of runners. A great sense of urgency now enveloped the cabin, Zouvelekis rapidly translating the exchanges for Pat. 'We know that Khosref has been sighted, directly off Cape Colones. It is plain that he may be principally a diversion, for the transport ships of Scala Nova have also now been sighted. They have again begun to leave that port. Admiral Sakhtouri proposes to leave *Surprise* with the Spezziots here - to counter any approach of Khosref into the strait - whilst the Hydriots sail through the strait to attack the Turk transports coming across again. It is as well that all of us did not leave for the south-west an hour ago,' he concluded.

Sakhtouri rose, looked to Pat, and said, simply, great respect in his voice, 'Thank you, Captain O'Connor.'

Pat nodded, 'Sir, we will hasten back to *Surprise.*' Pat and Sakhtouri shook hands, and the Surprises swiftly left the admiral's brig for Pat's barge and away.

Back aboard *Surprise* the hurried departure of the Hydriots was watched by everyone. *Surprise* and just eight Spezziot brigs were all that remained to stop any approach of the mighty Turk fleet. It was really a David and Goliath situation, the likelihood of a full engagement assuredly a chilling prospect to contemplate. From the south the noise of the Turks firing on Cape Colones could plainly be heard. 'Lycurgus has stationed a division of Samiot troops on the Cape, and presumably it is they that are the target of this cannonade,' Zouvelekis commented.

'Better that than our few ships,' Pat replied, grimly.

The day warmed as it progressed, but thankfully there was no sign of Khosref approaching the strait, though the distant gunfire continued all day, the noise constant. *Surprise* sat all day at her moorings, the Spezziots near alongside, until in the late evening Sakhtouri's Hydriots returned, his squadron coming to the anchorage off Colones athwart the southern approach to the strait. Pat hastened across in his barge on Sakhtouri's signal to join him for a conference; Duncan, Simon, Marston, Zouvelekis and Jason accompanying him. On board the Hydriot flagship the mood was jubilant, the Surprises being warmly welcomed aboard by Sakhtouri himself.

'Welcome, Captain O'Connor, gentlemen; please to enter my cabin, my steward will bring refreshment directly. Please, be seated.'

'Pray tell of your day, sir,' prompted Pat.

Sakhtouri described his hurried foray to the north of the strait, 'Forty transports crossing we found, and four thousand Turk soldiers aboard them. We sank two, and captured two more. Yet they came again three hours after the first attempt. A bare few brigs in escort, and we struck them again. It was plain their heart was not in it the second time, for as we approached they turned about and fled, brigs and transports alike, and so we are returned. I doubt they will try that again without a strong escort. It is plain that Khosref must rejoin his transports, else their endeavours to land on Samos will surely be thwarted.'

'The decision is near upon us, and will be found here in the south, and in a very few days, no doubt. Admiral, my surgeons accompany me, may I offer their services? Do you have wounded?' Pat offered.

Simon and Marston left to lend a hand tending the wounded of Sakhtouri's squadron, whilst a general discussion of the prospects for the morrow continued, the Hydriot and Spezziot captains dribbling in to hear Sakhtouri's news, and to consider every possible plan for the next day, some hours of repetitive discussion of every conceivable tactic following. As the discussion petered out the admiral and his captains looked over to Pat for his opinion.

'It is sure we must stay here and await the Turk and the weather,' said Pat, wearily, the hours having passed in near tedium for him, as he could not follow much of the discussion.

As Simon and Marston returned, Sakhtouri's stewards brought in a late supper which was enjoyed by the Hydriots as something akin to a celebration, another invasion crossing plainly being defeated with significant if not yet decisive Turk losses.

As 11 p.m. approached, Pat and his officers returned to *Surprise* - Zouvelekis remaining with the admiral and his compatriots for further celebration - the Surprises desparately wishing for some hours of uninterrupted sleep, the tension of the past days and his lack of sleep reducing Pat to a state of near exhaustion, not unnoticed by his officers who felt much the same. All stood on the quarterdeck in contemplation of the day and the morrow.

'Will you not turn in, sir?' prompted Pickering, accurately assessing his captain's exhaustion, mental and physical. 'You have slept but little this past week. There is nothing to do here, sir, and the wind is plainly rising; it looks fair for a blow. I doubt any ship will haul her cable this night.'

'Yes, yes, Tom; I believe I will go below, thankee,' Pat replied, the suggestion so welcome, relief coursing through his every fibre,

Pickering's forecast according with his own. He reached the cabin and undressed in haste, near falling into his cot and pulling the blanket over him. Within moments he fell asleep yet remained cognizant of the ship's movements at her anchor; the breeze wafting in through the cabin door, left open to bring a cooling through-draught, bringing the familiar shipboard sounds and the tar smell of the deck, ever present even in his dreams.

Sunday 15th August 1824   *Colones roads*

It was the sound of the fife playing *Nancy Dawson*, the hands' noon grog about to be issued, and then Dalby's ringing of eight bells which awoke Pat, for he had slept well, and Duncan having forbidden the ringing of the bell during the Morning watch nothing had disturbed him. He threw on the bare minimum of clothing and rushed out immediately up to the quarterdeck and gazed about him. The sun was burning hot and the noon temperatures already high though cooled by a strong wind. Bright light fully illuminated the ship and Samos island; the bay approach to the strait and Cape San Maria clear in the distance, but of ships there were only the Greeks, now straining on their cables, and rolling violently in the swell, for the wind had strengthened severely and it near approached a full gale blowing.

'Guid mornin', sir,' said Duncan.

'Eight bells, Duncan. Have I slept that well?' a still only semi-awake Pat blustered to his first.

'Ah took the liberty, sir, o' nae ringin' the mornin' bells so as not to awake ye. We have kept a doubled watch o'er the bay, but agin this wind only the Lord Almighty could move,' Duncan replied, smiling.

'Is there no limit to the loss of our shipboard conventions?' retorted Pat, though he too was smiling now. 'Thankee, Duncan. I was sore pressed last night to stay awake aboard Sakhtouri's brig. Where is Simon?'

'He has crossed to one o' the Greek brigs, sir; wi' Marston, an' Jason as translator. There is a severely wounded Greek in need o' his attention. Sakhtouri sent a request fer him twae hoors ago.

Zouvelekis remains wi' Sakhtouri, he has nae yet returned. Will there be divisions or any service this mornin', sir?'

Pat took a few moments to look about him. He stared into the tops where, at each, men clung to their positions with obvious difficulty. He looked south over the bay, assessing Duncan's conviction that no ship could come north into this gale force wind, and concluded his first was correct before replying, 'No, neither divisions nor any service today, Duncan. Keep two men aloft to watch, but rest everyone else. I will take my breakfast now,' and Pat returned to the cabin, Freeman busying in with the teapot and tray within moments.

'Breakfast ready, massa,' pronounced Freeman cheerily in his customary pleasant voice; 'Soft tack, bacon an' kidneys.'

A still bleary Pat perked slightly in pleasant anticipation, saying only, 'Thankee, Freeman,' and shifted to his closet to dowse his head in water and better awaken. Pat had returned to his table when Freeman brought in his breakfast, the wind whistling loudly through the still temporary repairs to his shattered cabin windows – for neither time nor glazing had been found since the engagement with the galleys off Candia, and Mr Tizard's most diligent carpentry efforts, without proper materials, could not make good the substantial destruction of the glass in the windows and their wooden structure. Pat looked about him at the plentiful damage still so evident until his attention turned to his breakfast. The bacon smelt divine, the tea so welcome. 'Freeman, my compliments to Wilkins, if you will,' shouted Pat pleasantly to his withdrawing steward; for the first time sensing a small beginning, no more than that, of a lifting of those black feelings, a modest diminishing of his fears for his long-serving shipmates, fears which had beset him these several months past, and which had conflicted so much with the pleasure of his return to sea once again.

As the morning wore on and afternoon followed the sun's zenith there was neither any let up in the wind strength nor any sighting of Turk ships, Duncan's assessment being wholly confirmed, and so the crew sheltered below, out of the fierce wind, leaving *Surprise* swinging on her cable, the sea slapping hard on her hull as she rolled vigorously in the strong swell. It was early evening before the weary trio of Simon, Marston and Jason returned, coming directly into the cabin to report, and staying for supper. Pat was very pleased to see them, so dispensed liberal quantities of his dwindling Bordeaux to accompany the meal as he listened whilst Simon recounted their findings.

'Shocking! Shocking it is. No medical skills above a butcher's, no medicines, no place to treat any wounded save on the captain's table; blood and guts all o'er the floor, swarms o' clegs all about. A charnel house for sure. Limbs cut off and cast aside, and a bucket for them only rarely; no cleansing of wounds, and stitching that a blind man could better. Oh God, how any do survive is known only to the Almighty. No treatment at all for any wounded, captured Turk; they are simply thrown overboard. Even the unwounded Turks cower in fear for their lives.'

'Barbarians, Captain. Vile brute beasts they are. Such ingrained abomination. No claim can these people have to be good Christians, none at all. The shame of the world it is,' added Marston, taking a deep draught of his wine, Freeman refilling his glass whilst listening attentively, hovering between the table and the door.

'Sakhtouri was most economical with his list of casualties,' Simon interjected. 'Marston and I have treated more than three score of Greek wounded. Shot wounds, sword cuts, broken limbs; it has near exhausted our medical supplies, though I collect there may be one more chest below, and I have but one flask of iodine left.'

Pat was feeling immeasurably better himself, a near full day of rest, little to do, and he took all this in his stride, nodding pleasantly to Freeman to 'light along and bring fresh bottles, Freeman, if you will.' He looked towards Jason as he asked, 'Pray, Mr Jason, were you able to gauge the Greek morale, confidence, or any other measure, whilst you were about the Hydriot ships?'

Jason set down his glass, 'It is certainly not the Royal Navy, sir. Their organisation, if that it can be termed, is quite different. Each of their ships is owned by a consortium which is eager to draw pay for every day they are at sea, but does not care to risk their ship and lose that pay were their ship to be lost, and so there is a hesitancy about them, and their admiral's orders are taken as more akin to advice. It would confound any English officer, sir, and none would countenance such a regime. How they achieve anything is not far from miraculous, though it is clear that Sakhtouri's victories of these past days – for surely that is how they are seen – have much raised confidence and spirits. In truth, they have been easy victories against transports with only a few small brigs to protect them. How they will fare against warships proper if Khosref comes again must be a matter of some uncertainty,' Jason concluded.

'Thank you, Mr Jason. That may be information of the first importance if we find ourselves relying on our Greek comrades against the Turk. The wind is much down this evening, and if Khosref is ever coming back then he will be here in the morning. If he cannot join with his transports north of the strait then their invasion is doomed.'

Frigate, sails a-back   *Serres, Liber Nauticus*

Chapter Eleven

A king sat on the rocky brow
Which looks on sea-born Salamis;
And ships, by thousands, lay below,
And men in nations;---all were his!
He counted them at break of day---
And when the sun set, where were they?

Monday 16*th* August 1824   *Colones roads*

Although sleeping fitfully Pat remained conscious of much of the continuing shipboard activity, and he tossed and turned for hours, gaining precious little rest as his mind considered the military situation. The solitary one bell at the start of the Morning watch was enough to wake him, though it was immediately followed by Murphy hurtling into his cabin, thrusting his clothes at him, and gabbling in great haste. 'Mr Macleod's duty, sorr, and 'e believes you will …, er …, can 'ee come on deck, d'reckly. Well, the Turks are comin' up to us,' adding 'sorr,' as he held out Pat's boots, no sunlight yet permeating the cabin as there remained more than an hour to the dawn.

Pat immediately sensed the diminution of yesterday's gale, the lessening of the swell, and dressed hastily as Murphy departed for tea from the galley. Within moments his cabin was filled with the carpenter and his mates. 'By your leave, sir,' said Tizard, arriving in haste, though a little prematurely, Pat thought, to strip down the bulkheads before any engagement and to roll up his chequered canvas deck-cloth – the small gesture to decoration that it was; it would not do to allow it to become bloodied.

'Please proceed, Mr Tizard.' Pat's cot, chairs, sea-chest, and table were swiftly swept away to be stowed below deck.

Stepping up to his quarterdeck, it was Mower that briefed him, 'Sail sighted directly off Cape San Maria, sir, a great many of them; though since the clouds obscured the moon, little now can be seen.'

411

'Who is our watcher, Mr Mower?' asked Pat, looking about him into the still dark night sky, hoping that the moon might re-emerge.

'Young Pennington, sir.' At that moment the moon did re-emerge and shone silver on the near wave tops, a much calmer sea than the prior day, and, Pat thought, near perfect conditions for the Turk fleet to come again.

'We have no other with keener eyes,' said Pat. 'Let the galley fires be lit, hands to breakfast. Rouse up the idlers. We will clear the ship for action in half an hour. Fire the signal gun and awaken the Greeks,' he added without hesitation.

'Aye aye, sir. Mr Prosser, fire the signal gun,' Mower reiterated.

BOOM came the shattering noise; shaking all aboard and all throughout the Greek fleet from their slumbering torpor, scores of seamen quickly becoming visible, rushing about on the decks of the nearby Spezziot brigs. All about the Greek ships many were soon climbing aloft to let fall sails. Still nothing could be seen of the Turks, and Pat began to wonder if he had acted in haste, but then, in the first glimmerings of light before the dawn, off the Cape emerged the very tops of the Turk masts, sticking out above the mist still lying on the far sea surface. The keenest of young eyes could make out tops'ls too; scores of them, and Pat's doubts were rudely dispelled as *Surprise* became a scene of haste and urgency, Pat giving the order to beat to quarters, and every man rushing to his station as Dalby rang the bell incessantly.

An apprehensive hour and a half passed, the cook bringing out food to men standing by their guns, the mist burning off from the sea surface, the sun rising to just above the eastern mountains, and the wind, whilst still north-westerly, was greatly abated in comparison of the prior day, though the Greek flags flew strongly at the jack and top. Inexorably, the enemy fleet drew closer, tacking ship every twenty minutes to stay on their northerly approach to the Strait until, BOOM… BOOM, the nearest Turks were firing now, though at the very limit of their range, their shot generally falling short. Yards were braced and sheets everywhere hauled tight, and eight brigs of Spezziots and eight of Hydriots began to shift away from their moorings, the *Meltemi* wind swiftly bringing them out.

The Turks were some forty or more ships, and the Greeks plainly severely outnumbered and outgunned. The smaller of the Turk ships, brigantines, corvettes and the like, sailed in the rear, hugging the Turk coast, edging towards the entrance of the Strait, the frigates coming on towards the Greek brigs. The Turk flagship seventy-four remained on the western fringe of their fleet, and commenced firing again at the Greek shore batteries on the Colones peninsula. The Turk frigates nearest to Samos were now so close that they too could fire on the island's batteries and some did so whilst others concentrated on the Greek brigs, most of which remained at anchor as the shore batteries' longer guns now began to speak.

Surprise had hauled up her anchor and gathered way as she shifted east towards the Strait, seeking to intercept the Turks moving north and plainly visible not far off the west coast of Cape San Maria. Those Greeks that had left their moorings were in the centre of the approach to the Strait and contemplating, at a mile distance, the oncoming Turk frigates, still out of range of the smaller Greek guns. *Surprise* was sailing swiftly on a broad reach towards the easternmost Turks, nearing the effective maximum range of her own guns, as the Turk brigs sailed slowly north, their crews working hard on short tacks whilst close-hauled to maintain direction in the prevailing north-westerly wind. *Surprise* was sailing under topsails, jib and spanker alone; her courses brailed up to the customary, reduced "fighting canvas", as action loomed. Her yards were also now chained up so as to prevent any damaged ones slipping to the deck and disabling men and guns. All her boats were in tow, removing the very real prospect of them being reduced to dangerous flying splinters once action commenced.

'Mr Macleod, put the engines to work on the sails, let us get them wetted, start our water, pipe the hammocks down.'

'Aye aye, sir. Mr Prosser, pass the word fer the bosun.'

'Mr Mower, all pigs and goats to be sent below at once.'

'Aye aye, sir. Barton, pass the word for Jemmy Ducks, all animals to be shifted below.'

'Mr Macleod, our six best shots into the tops. They are to shoot

413

only at officers on the quarterdeck and anyone at the helm. Mr Mower, let us spread sand o'er the decks.'

'Aye aye, sir.'

On the quarterdeck all gazed alternately forward at the closing Turk squadron off the starboard bow and then astern to see the general melee between the main body of the Turk frigates and the Greek brigs, firing having broken out between them at no more than a half mile range.

'Should not Admiral Sakhtouri now send his fireships, sir,' asked Pickering of Pat as they watched the distance shorten inexorably between the two fleets.

'He is flying many signals from his ship and firing a gun with them,' observed Pat through his glass, 'though I see no fireships shifting out from the body of the Greeks. 'Tis a perilous task for the crews; any man captured from a fireship can be sure he will be put to death, no quarter given.'

The separation between the two fleets had closed to about a quarter mile, and the Greeks in the centre channel criss-crossed the approaching Turk frigates with all ships firing their guns. It was difficult to see many obvious hits from the distance of *Surprise's* quarterdeck, as she had come close to the Turk mainland, a bare half mile ahead, to intercept the northbound Turk brigs. Pat's crew now stood ready with all her guns run out and a dozen shot being heated in the galley.

'Look! Look there: would that be our old friend Canaris? I see his Psariot pennant flying on that fireship. There is a man to gladden your heart, a capital officer,' exclaimed Pat, 'and Sakhtouri himself is bringing his own brigantine alongside of him. What's afoot I wonder?' Ahead, the first of four Turk brigs and brigantines was closing on *Surprise;* a bare quarter mile separating them, and tense expectation prevailed amongst all aboard. Four minutes later, after Pat had given the order to come about from no more than a quarter mile from the Turk coast, to bring *Surprise* back on a south-westerly course to converge with the Greek fleet, the bow of the first Turk brig approached *Surprise's* larboard bow, the Turk firing her chasers, and no more than two hundred yards separating them.

The shots were clearly audible as they whistled over their heads. 'They fired as she pitched up,' Pat speculated. 'Note the time, Mr Pickering.'

On the quarterdeck and gun deck *Surprise's* gun crews were stripped to the waist, for not only was it hot – and about to become substantially hotter when the guns opened fire, and the very severe exertion of hauling guns of two tons out through their ports once reloaded would tax the very fittest – but the absence of clothing left nothing of dirty fabric to be carried into any wound penetrations, and so reduced the likelihood of infection. Most of the gunners had knotted their handkerchieves about their heads to soak up the anticipated sweat, so it would not obscure their vision.

'Port your helm, Mr Prosser, handsomely now,' said Pat in a matter of fact voice of complete composure, intent on bringing *Surprise* to a line from which all her larboard guns could strike the approaching Turk brig, adding, 'Gentlemen, 'tis time to join your guns. Lads,' he bellowed down to the gun deck, 'stand to your guns.' A bare minute later, as all stood ready in expectant silence, Pat shouted down to his second, 'Open fire from the bow, Mr Pickering, one gun at a time and spare her timbers,' and a moment later, 'stand by to come about, Mr Prosser, after we have fired the larboard battery. Wait on, we will fire three afore we turn.'

'Aye aye, sir,' Prosser acknowledged.

'Bow there, ready: fire from the bow,' bellowed Pickering, now on the gun deck, for'ard with his first gun team, the command to fire echoed by the gun captain, and the first gun, *Venom*, belched out its opening destruction, the eighteen-pound shot accompanied by bright flame jetting out twelve feet from its mouth, followed by bilious black smoke, swiftly carried away downwind. The second, *Dutch Sam*, fired, then the third, *Tempest*, until the firing rippled all the way down *Surprise's* larboard side to the sternmost guns, *Mendoza* and *Billy Warr*, the roar of the guns near overpowering the senses of all nearby.

'FIRE AGAIN!' shouted Pat, as loud as he could; standing at the rail over the waist, and waving his hat, as doubtless the for'ard gunners could not hear him.

'FIRE!' Pickering bellowed. The first gun had already been sponged, reloaded, rammed, and hauled out by its sweating crew, working like demons, even before the sternmost gun had fired.

'FIRE!' shouted the gun captain, and *Venom* fired its second, the broadside rippling again down the larboard side, no gun captain waiting for any command before sending their heavy ball of eighteen pounds away, accompanied by grape. The quarterdeck carronades, quicker loading, had already fired again, before any shots could be fired from the aftmost and slower loading long guns. *Surprise* shook violently with the reaction, and her officers peered through the smoke now obscuring the first Turk brig, which had closed to less than a hundred yards away. A near minute passed, and as the smoke blew away it became obvious that the Turk had been hard hit, near raked by *Surprise's* two broadsides, her larboard bow showing great damage, her foremast was down, stays and shrouds ripped away, her yards now athwart her deck, and sailors could be seen struggling amidst great swathes of canvas to cut all away. Her hull had taken several hits that could be seen, and possibly too some below her waterline, for she seemed a trifle lower in the water than Pat had previously thought. Smoke could be seen rising from amidships, the first flickering of flame becoming visible as the red hot shot started its deadly work, the reduced charges of powder ensuring that the ball did not pass right through the hull, but lodged inside so as to set the vessel afire.

'Port your helm, Mr Prosser,' ordered a grim faced Pat, his mind now settled about his deadly work. 'Fire our third,' he shouted as *Surprise* came round and the Turk came abeam, no more than fifty yards off. *Surprise's* guns opened again from her bow, and the destruction of the brig was inevitable, her main mast knocked down, her wheel simply hurled away as if by an invisible fist, her steering disabled, the grapeshot sweeping away all the crew on her quarterdeck in a hail of metal, leaving not a soul standing as she slowed to a halt, flames visibly leaping up amidships.

Pat shouted down to his second, standing on the gun deck below the boat hoists, 'Mr Pickering, we will wear ship: larboard gunners to the braces; handsomely now, for we are singularly pressed.' He stepped back to the wheel, 'Mr Macleod, helm up, hard over, come about,' shouted Pat.

'Port your helm,' commanded Duncan to Prosser, the command echoed to Barton and his mates, who heaved hard on the wheel, and *Surprise* turned quickly. The larboard gunners were hastening from their guns to the mizzen and main braces, some already hauling hard to swing the top yards.

'Head yards square,' bellowed Pat, echoed by Pickering as the larboard gunners raced forward. 'Haul, brace headyards.'

Men oblivious to their exertions hastened to brace the foremast yards as *Surprise* came round in a sweeping loop. The first Turk brig was well aflame, off *Surprise's* larboard bow again, and no danger now as the frigate settled on her easterly course to face the oncoming second Turk brig, just over two hundred yards off *Surprise's* starboard bow and struggling to make headway into the freshening north-westerly. For a moment Pat glanced back towards the body of the battle between the Greek fleet and the Turk frigates, the gap between the two fleets just a few hundred yards. A fireship, brightly aflame, and with a Greek brigantine in support, was within the leading Turk frigates, and a very severe cannonading was being meted out to both the Greeks from at least two Turks and possibly a third, the range so short that more Turks could not fire for fear of striking their compatriots. The fireship was burning fiercely all over her yards and sails and the brigantine struggling to close her to take off her crew in their boats, not daring to come near alongside. Then the smoke obscured Pat's view, and his attention returned to the second Turk brig, which was firing on *Surprise* with her bow chasers. *Surprise* was near to crossing the track of the second Turk brig, coming to a perfect position to rake her.

'FIRE from the bow,' shouted Pat, his order echoed by Duncan from the waist rail down to the gundeck.

'FIRE from the bow!' bellowed Mower, and simultaneously, 'FIRE!' shouted the for'ard gun captain.

Axeman had already fired before Mower concluded his order, the command from Pat and Duncan already heard and executed. Firing rippled down *Surprise's* starboard side, fourteen great guns

417

and three carronades spitting raking fire and shot directly into the Turk's bow and along her length. At such short range no brig could survive such fearful punishment, *Surprise's* shot travelling stem to stern, eighteen-pound shot wreaking severe damage to her structures, masts, sails and guns; splinters and thousands of canister shot tearing into her men. *Surprise's* gun crews were hastening to reload from the bow, adding grape to the already loaded shot before hauling her great guns back out ready to fire their deadly missiles, her carronades already firing again.

'Mr Macleod, we will wear ship.'

'Aye aye, sir; Mr Pickering, we will wear ship. All larbowlins, mizzen an' main braces,' Macleod shouted down to his colleague and to the men no longer in haste attending the larboard guns.

'Larbowlins to wear ship,' Pickering echoed the order.

'Port your helm, Mr Prosser,' shouted Pat. *Surprise* was hauled round again, heeling far over to larboard as she set on her new course, due south, and taking some hits from the survivors of the starboard battery of the Turk brig, though her capable guns were now few in number, their shot firing downwards as she too heeled in the wind, and being so close to *Surprise*, barely fifty yards between them, her guns could not elevate further. Several ricochets rose to strike the bulwark, more flying overhead.

'FIRE!' shouted Pat, waving his hat towards Macleod, and the starboard battery let loose again its awesome destructive power. At point blank range none could miss, and the Turk brig was smashed violently, her side stove in along much of its length, and her fighting power immediately obliterated. But now *Surprise* was under fire from the third and fourth Turk brig and brigantine, both firing from a quarter mile off, some of their shot skipping across the water and bouncing over *Surprise's* deck as well as some hits directly registering on her larboad bow. The men of the larboard battery, hastening from the braces back to their guns, had already reloaded whilst their starboard companions had destroyed the second brig, and all stood ready to fire again. Both the second and third lieutenants had come up to the waist below the hoists and awaited Pat's orders.

'Mr Mower, your lads to the braces. Port your helm... hard over, Mr Macleod; luff up and touch her. 'Tis time to return to the Greeks for us,' shouted Pat, standing next to the rail, gazing all about him in assessment of casualties and damage. *Surprise* was sailing large at a swift seven to eight knots and came round smartly, setting her course for the Greek fleet, a mile ahead. On her now south-westerly course she closed rapidly on the approaching Turk brig and brigantine. Shots were coming in from the Turk brig: both of them had tacked, and the first of the pair was now a quarter mile off *Surprise's* larboard beam, converging; the second two cables behind her. Pickering's larbowlins had enjoyed a mere ten minutes of rest, time enough only to slake fiery thirsts from the water butts standing at each gun, but they stood waiting again at their stations, ready to fire again.

'FIRE!' shouted Pat. Macleod echoed Pat's command, and the firing resumed from her larboard side, rippling again from bow to stern, the smoke billowing out and blowing downwind between the combatants, obscuring the view for all.

Round shot from the near Turk brig began to whistle about the quarterdeck, rigging being slashed and cut about the mizzen. Then came the hammer-smash of balls striking *Surprise* in her hull; blocks fell from above, splinters flew about the deck. Both the brig and brigantine pressed closer, and from the first the range had closed to a dangerous three hundred yards. *Hell's Mouth* was struck with a loud clang, pushing the gun round, snapping its restraining breechings, the gun knocking down three of its crew as it turned, the shot ricochetting across the deck and smashing out through the starboard bulwark planking, fortunately missing further victims on its way. The gun began to slowly roll backwards towards its neighbour until it slipped back towards its port with the lee lie of the deck, avoiding a destructive roll across the gun deck, men from the starboard side rushing to aid their comrades to wedge its train-tackle and tie it up. Less fortunate were the waisters standing ready forward of the quarterdeck for the next course change, half a dozen of them were struck by a shower of splinters from a round shot breaking through the bulwark, all falling to the deck.

419

'Lads,' shouted Duncan down to the starboard gunners, standing ready, 'come up an' take these men below, quickly now.'

Boswell, the master gunner standing by the aftmost carronades, who had with immense enthusiasm rejoined *Surprise*, his Royal Navy ship having paid off, shrieked in agony as his left arm at the elbow flew away, struck by a roundshot, leaving a ragged tear and a stump below his shoulder, his blood pumping out a red stream all about him as he lay knocked to the deck. Day, his companion, fell over him, unmarked but quite unconscious from the concussion effect of the shot which pressured his head and his lungs and stopped his breathing for a few moments. Wright, the firm friend of Boswell, being the adjacent gunner, had seen him fall, and gathered him up into his arms without ceremony and hastened away to the sick bay. Lewis, the spongeman serving *Delilah*, screamed as he took several grape shot into his bowels, tearing through him and leaving jagged holes, his entrails splattered against his gun, his blood running across the deck, not all soaking into the spread sand. His comrades caught him as he fell, gasping, writhing in his pain. It was plain to all that he could not live, and so to spare his agonies they threw him out the gun port and over the side, as was the custom. A score of men rushed from the starboard guns to help the injured, carrying them down to the lower deck. The Turk brig had bravely closed to less than a hundred yards through the smoke, and poured shot and grape into *Surprise*, the shot thudding into and shaking the ship, sending splinters flying as the balls penetrated, the grape pouring through the hoisted port lids and over the decks; a dozen more men went down with wounds. Mower too had been struck down. He lay quite still on the deck, blood flowing from the multiple wounds in his arms and legs. Behind the guns on the gun deck amidships, Pickering sent men from the starboard side to fill the larboard gaps. The deck was strewn with men in their agonies, limbs torn off, large splinters projecting through flesh, broken arms and legs, ears ripped away, eyes put out; blood, much blood, ran everywhere amidst thousands of splinters – the sand on the deck sodden with so much blood, yet not a man spared from the carnage let up from his task as his fellows were stripped away from beside him by the Turk fire. At this range no shot could miss from either ship.

Pat looked about him and across to the Turk brig, his gaze resting on her quarterdeck in a rare moment as the wind whipped away the smoke; thick, black, and bilious, between the two combatants. For an instant he glimpsed the Turk captain looking across: it seemed as if he was staring directly at him. Pat raised his hand and touched his hat. 'They do not lack courage,' he mused, though none could hear him. The brigantine had never gained a firing position, and appeared to be lagging far behind the brig.

'Three foot six in the well, sir,' Prosser reported to Pat. 'The carpenter is attending. Two holes below the waterline.' At that moment, the three larboard carronades fired from the quarterdeck, and Pat could hear no more of Prosser's report. Their grape shot swept the Turk quarterdeck clear, leaving not a soul standing. *Surprise's* larboard eighteen-pounders, firing shot and grape, poured their hail of metal across the Turk's deck, and it seemed the decisive moment had come; only two of the Turk guns continued to fire. Her bowsprit had been shot away, her sails, such that remained, were thoroughly shredded; many of her braces were cut. The brig fell away from the wind, no man at her helm, and then the smoke again obscured all as her guns fell silent.

In *Surprise's* own close melée little time had there been to pay attention to the rest of the battle, the intermingled Greek and Turk fleets fighting to the north-west of *Surprise*. The sound of gunfire had diminished considerably in the past half hour, and, as the great clouds of black gunsmoke which had obscured that far contest began to clear, from the quarterdeck all gazed across to the far battle with keen anticipation and not least a good measure of trepidation. Pat wiped smoke from his eyes, rubbed them vigorously and peered through his glass. After a moment he remarked to his first, 'Mr Macleod, take my glass. Will you look to our friends? I can see nothing, damn smoke in my eyes.'

'The Turks are breakin' off, sir! Look, see, they are turnin' away,' shouted Duncan, and all gazed across to the main Turk fleet. It was true, the Turks had all gone about and were sailing southwards, the Greeks beating away from them against the wind, slowly heading back towards Colones. The near Turk brig and brigantine had also broken off the action; the brigantine had closed up on the brig, and both were now steering a south-easterly course, perhaps intent on shifting towards their other two stricken compatriots for mutual assistance.

'Here, massa, water,' said Freeman, his bucket and ladle a most welcome sight to all on the quarterdeck.

Pat gulped water in haste and in the brief moment of respite gathered his thoughts. 'Mr Macleod, 'vast firing,' shouted Pat, 'House your guns.'

The guns fell silent, and *Surprise* turned about, considerable distance between herself and her adversaries quickly developing as the Turk fleet flew south with the wind full behind their sails.

'Mr Macleod, all possible hands to take casualties below. Quickly now,' shouted Pat.

'Four foot six in the well, sir; Chips has stopped one hole and is attending the second,' reported Prosser.

'Thankee, Mr Prosser, be sure to relieve the hands on the chain pumps every fifteen minutes.' Pat stepped forward as far as the waist and peered down to the gun-deck, observing men everywhere hastening to carry the wounded below. With a feeling of great shock he saw Mower, lying on his back, two of the hands crouching about him, as if in assessment of his wounds and deterred by the volume of blood, unsure how best to lift him. Pat hastened down the steps and rushed forward, Duncan behind him. Mower was still conscious, though in great pain, his clothes sodden red, his arms and legs quite limp, his breathing very shallow.

'Mr Mower... James, *James!*' Pat was shouting now, great fear overwhelming his senses. 'Oh God,' he was aghast at the expanding red pool in which Mower lay, his murmurings hardly audible. '*Oh God almighty*; stay with me now, *James*; I will take you below, you have lost a shocking amount of blood.'

'If you please, sir, stand aside, and I will carry him,' Clumsy Dalby had appeared at Pat's side.

Pat, scrabbling on his knees amidst the blood, struggling to pick up Mower, turned his head and stared, immense anxiety flooding his every fibre, 'Yes, if ye will, thankee... thankee Dalby.'

Dalby crouched down, taking up Mower easily within his grasp and stepped towards the companionway, Mower no burden at all for his huge frame and strength. Pat was profoundly grateful for the help. 'Carefully there; now, all speed, let us away below. Mason, run ahead and tell the Doctor, Mr Mower is gravely wounded, hurry now, *hurry!* Mr Macleod, you have command. I am going below to the sick bay,' he shouted. He struggled with Dalby to carry his lieutenant down the steps, descending swiftly to the lower deck where *Surprise's* casualties were laid out, more than a score of them; the number far exceeding the tiny space of the sick bay. Simon, Marston, Jason helping, and the loblolly boys too; all were immersed in their grisly task. The thick coppery stench of blood permeated the air, acrid whiffs of vinegar lingering about those men who had been treated; the greatest assaults on the senses were the moans and wails of agonised men, though subdued either voluntarily or by laudanum, everywhere loud as Pat and Dalby carried Mower as gently as they could towards the surgeons.

The unfortunate patient on the table had just died as they reached it. Simon, quickly assessing Mower's swiftly declining prospects, and seeing Pat's blood-sodden coat and breeches waved his helpers to remove the corpse. 'Put him on here, Pat; quickly now, else we may lose him too. Step away now. *Leave this place.* Marston, here if you will, we have no other patients for the next half hour.'

Pat and Dalby retreated, aghast, anxious for their comrade, but glad to leave the scene of such bloody horror. They returned to the gun-deck, and Pat thence to his quarterdeck, all the time looking about him, speaking to his men, staring at the damage all about, looking to the sails, gazing into the distance - the Turk fleet withdrawing towards the horizon. Though Pat's keen curiosity concerning his casualties was unabated, he realised he could only be a hindrance to his surgeons at that moment, and realising too his great thirst remained unquenched he returned to his cabin and gulped several pints of bumbo, swiftly brought by Freeman. Murphy arrived within moments, horrified, speechless to see his captain's state. Pat stripped from his blood-sodden vestments, Murphy dragging them from him, Pat unresisting, until within a few minutes, Murphy swabbing the still-wet blood from his legs with wet towels, he donned clean breeches and shirt.

Surprise was now sailing northbound, frequently tacking and close-hauled. The Turk fleet was gone, well beyond visible range from the deck, and the Greeks were far, far ahead as they closed on Colones. Pat returned to his quarterdeck and surveyed his ship once more. Some of the crew were busying about, sweeping and throwing debris off the deck; four men worked valiantly at the chain pumps; half a dozen more were mopping bloody patches towards the scuppers; others sat, plainly exhausted, between the guns, drinking small beer. He stepped down to the gun deck and walked its length, nodding to his gunners in passing even as his eyes registered the damage about him. *Hell's Mouth* had already been restored to its firing position, new breechings attached. He returned swiftly to the quarterdeck. There were still gaping holes in the bulwark planking and several slits and tears in the topsails; the hammock nets had been near shredded, and much torn rigging would require substantial restoration. Pickering was below, with Prosser and the carpenter, struggling still to repair the second shot breach in the hull, though the water level was no longer rising. Pat went below to see for himself. He went down the steps to the sail room where the struggle to stop the hole continued.

'Sir, the shot broke through between her starboard frames just below the wale,' reported a very wet Pickering. 'It must have happened as we turned south, a shot from that second Turk brig, she was very close and firing down her lee side.' The carpenter did not break off from his struggles, but Prosser apprised Pat of his progress, 'Mr Tizard has broken away the splinters between the frames, sir. The hole is near plugged, and he is nailing a plank o'er the wedge now; just a few more minutes.' The carpenter gave his patch a final hammer blow and turned back with a weary grin to see his anxious captain hovering at his elbow.

'Well done, Mr Tizard. A capital job, and the first hole suitably fixed too?' beamed Pat.

'Yes sir, the first was a bastard – excuse me sir – the hole was in the hold far above the deck and it was a struggle to reach it wading in five feet of water and then standing astride a salt pork barrel.'

'Well done, Chips. Get yourself away to the galley now and a bite to eat.'

Grateful that the leaks were stopped, Pat stepped up to the lower deck in hope that he might catch his surgeon's eye. He gazed upon the first of the wounded, the aftmost ones, two dozen and more, some in hammocks and others lying on the deck on blankets, unconscious and sleeping for the most part, doubtless dosed with laudanum, yet settled.

'Tell, Jim, what is the butcher's bill?' Pat enquired of Old Jim Lamb, the veteran helping carry and tend the wounded.

''Tis bad, sir, very bad: more'n a score o' wounded an' seven dead so far.'

Pat stepped slowly forward along the lower deck heading for where the surgeons were still working, towards the bow. As he passed by, midships, as far as he could take in, the casualties lying there all appeared to be treated and dressed, and a greater quietude had descended upon them, though soft moans were still audible from many. He approached the surgeons. Simon had seen Pat from his peripheral vision, and, not taking his eyes from his operating table, a swift amputation taking place, the unfortunate soul swimming between semi-consciousness and oblivion as the saw bit quickly through his leg, he shouted across, 'Not now, Pat. A half hour more and we may speak of matters.' The unfortunate's lower leg was swept away, and fell to the deck. 'Quickly Jason, tie that off.'

Pat looked over to an equally frantic Marston, working a mere three yards away from Simon, two helpers holding down his patient as very audible gasps escaped his tied mouth as his arm came off below the elbow. At his table, Simon, with Jason assisting, was now dealing with another casualty, Warden, a maintopman with a splinter wound between neck and shoulder. 'Hold firm,

Warden. We will draw this out. A moment or two is all,' said Simon. Warden, semi-conscious, agonising waves of pain washing all over his chest and head, could only nod, his tongue tied to the stick lashed across his jaw to save it from being bitten off in his agonies. The splinter was about eighteen inches long, one inch protruding from Warden's back, his upper body and shoulder with the projecting splinter overlaying the table edge. Simon and Jason both took hold of the twelve inches protruding from the front, Dalby and Wright holding Warden about his body, flat now to the table, two others firm with his knees and legs. The laudanum he had been given had near rendered Warden unconscious but not quite so. As the surgeons drew back the splinter he awoke and arched in the most acute pain in an instant, and his scream could not be held in check by the tied mouth; on it persisted for the agonising ten seconds in which the splinter was teased out, slowly, so as to allow the surgeons sight of its track and damage, blood gushing all about it, but seemingly no major vessels torn as Simon swabbed, stitched, and dressed it with speedy proficiency before shifting to the next man, lying on the nearby table. 'Jason, would you pass the saw? This cruelly shattered arm is really not worth the saving and will have to come off.'

Pat watched aghast. Though he had seen many casualties in many battles, the surgeon's work left a cold chill about him. The saw bit swiftly through the arm below the shoulder, the casualty's lower body writhing on the table, though his upper body was held firm by two of his mates, his agonies dampened by laudanum, his screams suppressed but not silenced. Within seconds the shattered arm fell to the deck, Simon drawing clear from the flesh and knotting the severed artery, folding skin flaps over the stump and pinning them with a swift stitch here and there. 'Jason, sew that up now if you please,' said Simon. He stepped away from the table, towards his captain. 'I cannot remember such a bloody day ever in any ship, Pat. How long have I been working on these men?'

'Near five hours, Simon: how is Mower?'

'He was near death when you brought him down, so much blood lost. I believe, with the blessing, Jason and I have saved his limbs; canister shot, it was, and splinters; fortunately not grape; we extracted five pieces; one in his arm, two in his legs, and two small splinters from his chest. Thankfully none struck his vital organs. Had it been grape he would by now have been over the side.

Pat was now near choking, and struggled but could not speak further.

Simon, seeing his distress, continued, 'Mower is in his cot, dressed and dosed. I will look in on him presently.'

'Come; will you take a drink with me now, in the cabin, if you may leave these men.'

'Not now, Pat, later, in an hour or two perhaps.' After a deep draught of coffee which Freeman, standing nearby, had fetched from the galley, Simon reported further, 'Seven dead, twenty-seven wounded, Pat; that is your butcher's bill. There surely would have been more dead were Marston not here to help me, Jason too. We were sore pressed and only the fleetest of attention saved three or more of these men, particularly Mower.'

'Thank you, Simon,' whispered Pat, in some small state of shock; never before had any of the ships under his command sustained so many casualties in a single engagement.

'Pray, is there still a scrap to eat on this ship, brother? The driest of biscuit would serve.'

Pat struggled to reply, his throat dry, his voice quite failing him, 'When you can be spared, Marston and Jason too, please to come up to the cabin.'

'We will remain here, Pat. I cannot spare even five minutes to visit the small room - were I minded to do so, thought I do not. I have a throat as dry as the Isles on the Sabbath, and would beg for a glass of small beer. There remain two or three men in perilous danger for the next few hours until we see their progress. Perhaps Freeman might bring us a morsel or so? I will be overjoyed to take some bread and a piece of cheese.'

'Of course, he will be here with food directly. A thousand thanks, dear friend,' whispered Pat, plainly struggling to speak. He stepped away and paced silently and very slowly along the deck to

427

the companionway, his head held down, his hand clutching his hat, obscuring his face, so that none could see his considerable distress as he passed by; his cheeks still wet as he entered the stern gallery.

Two further hours of close-hauled, hard sailing was necessary to regain Colones roads where they dropped anchor between the ships of the Hydriots and the Spezziots. A messenger swiftly arrived by boat from Sakhtouri's brig, requesting Simon's urgent attendance. Pat was rowed over for the post engagement conference, with Duncan and Simon; Jason accompanying them to translate. Marston remained on *Surprise* to tend to the wounded.

Canaris himself was aboard the brigantine, thanking its crew as the Surprises boarded, and explained the action they had engaged in. 'Doctor Ferguson, thank you for your attendance. There are fifteen wounded on this ship, one quarter of the crew, five more were killed. It was hot work out there. These men alone strived to protect my crew as we lit our fireship fuses. Three Turks were firing on us for near a quarter hour, and only thanks to their poor gunnery did we survive. When they espied the flames rising from our ship so as to engulf the magazine they turned about and fled. These wounded men have need of you, sir.'

Simon, though utterly exhausted himself after near seven hours treating *Surprise's* casualties, did not hesitate, 'Sir, my colleague Jason and I will proceed directly to attend your comrades, pray show the way.'

'Will you take a tint, Doctor? Brandy perhaps, before you begin?' asked Pat.

'I will not. Later I might look on a drop. Come, Jason, let us go downstairs. I will need your help.'

Simon and Jason hastened below to the makeshift medical bay, a scene of great dismay. The fifteen wounded were lying on the deck on bundles of blood-sodden blankets, loud groans coming from many, and the atmosphere stank with the coppery smell of blood and foul odours, flies buzzing over all. Simon looked about him briefly, to Jason nearby, and shouted, 'Hot water: as much as can be found, and quickly; vinegar too, for the wounds and to swab the deck.'

Jason translated his request to the brigantine's captain, hovering nervously at Simon's elbow. He, in turn, shouted to his men at the steps from the deck, and they hurried away.

Simon paced through his makeshift ward, looking closely at the wounds of each of his patients, striving through his own deep fatigue, his exhaustion, to concentrate on each one, trying to give each man a comforting word as he inspected them in turn, though doubtless none could understand his murmurings or his observations made to Jason. 'Splinter in the stomach ... splinter in the head ... broken femur ... splinters in upper chest and neck, no blood froth, so his lung has been spared, thank the dear, sweet Lord ... a near severed lower arm. Quickly now with this one else we may lose him with blood loss. Look he has lost much, this blanket is sodden. Tighter with that tourniquet, Jason, quickly now ... what have we here, shattered foot, that will have to come off,' and so on, as he made his inspection of all fifteen patients, his face becoming grimmer and paler as he neared the last.

Though the Royal Navy custom for medical treatment was on the basis of first come, first served, Simon had long ago adopted his own system, medical urgency prevailing over time of arrival; indeed it was his own form of triage. 'The fractures can wait until last; we will lose none of those men. The amputations must come first. Where is that hot water? Quickly now, Jason, my instruments, bandages ... ah, hot water at last. Tell them, much more will be needed; and clean blankets too. Tell them to open the gunports, let us have more light and fresh air in this place, quickly now.'

The more urgent patients, the ones that could swallow, were given laudanum to ease their sufferings. Simon passed his knife high through the flame of a small lamp several times and poured brandy over it. The shattered arm came off in a mere two minutes, the foot in five; both men held firmly down by their mates during the short operations, their mouths held firmly open with a lashed wooden dowel to save their tongues from being bitten off in their agony until the amputations were done. Simon wiped his brow on a cloth pinned to his grubby tunic. He looked to Jason with the barest of smile, the most severe cases dealt with. 'Now for the splinter cases, the fractures will be last,' he said with some little relief even as he swabbed blood from his hands. 'Jason, we can spare only the briefest of moments for those men waiting: a dose of laudanum for them, if you will, afore we extract the splinters from this man, for surely he is our severest case. My bag, quickly now, if you please.'

All evening they worked, Duncan too helping to haul wounded men to and from the table, their efforts illuminated by flickering oil lamps as they persevered long past midnight when the last man had been treated, his leg fracture splinted and bound. Simon looked about his ward, the deck had now been washed clean by Canaris's men and doused with vinegar to hide the blood smell and disinfect it, the sodden blankets removed and replaced by fresh ones from a supply sent over by Admiral Sakhtouri. 'All seem tolerably comfortable at last, Jason,' said Simon, so considerably fatigued that he could barely remain standing, but also relieved, none of his patients now in danger. 'Let us away, to *Surprise*, and pray that rascal Freeman can find us a biscuit to eat. Wilkins may yet have a morsel of leftovers, and perhaps we will share a wee dram of Ledaig. I fancy a little may linger in my trunk, which Murphy has never found.' Jason, desperate for sleep, simply nodded, his own exertions had long rendered him incapable of further words.

Back aboard *Surprise*, Pat, who had returned earlier, welcomed the returning trio to the cabin for a very late supper of soft tack and cheese, with port and bountiful hot coffee, brought hastily by Murphy and Freeman, the whisky quite forgotten. Murphy stared with barely suppressed horror at Simon's bloody clothes, somehow managing to hold his tongue. Freeman fussed about them, their exhaustion plain to see, buttering Simon's bread and pouring his coffee, until Pat sent him away. Pickering and Marston joined them.

'You look destroyed, all of you,' exclaimed Pickering to Simon and Jason, shocked to see their pitiful, soiled state, Duncan not much better.

'I am uncommonly fatigued, and long for my cot,' mumbled Jason, munching with great application on his bread and cheese, and taking great draughts of the port.

Pat recounted what he had heard from Sakhtouri after the

battle, 'Admiral Sakhtouri ordered his fireships forward, time and again, but all refused to act, their crews presumably judging it to be near certain death to sail directly into the mass of the Turk frigates, with a very doubtful prospect of being taken off and escaping into the teeth of that gale. I would not like to be one of those captains this night, Sakhtouri will have their hides. A hard flogging is the least they deserve. It was Admiral Canaris that saved the day – it was his fireship we saw from *Surprise*, reaching down to the nearest Turk frigates with only Sakhtouri's brigantine to support him, and they both took a dreadful pounding. Sakhtouri believed he was sending them all to their certain death, and that was sure were the Turks even half decent gunners. The fireship and brigantine crews were the bravest men we have seen in this war.'

'A very long day, sir,' said Duncan, very quietly, his own fatigue so evident in his voice and demeanour.

'At one time I thought it would never come to an end.'

'Time and the hour run through the roughest day – as the bard said,' remarked Pickering.

'I hope you were able to treat their wounded, Simon? Thankfully, our own excepted there were precious few elsewhere. Yet Sakhtouri claims the Greeks fired fifteen hundred ball and the Turks five thousand,' Pat remarked, adding, 'Such prodigious expenditure of powder and shot, and so few Greeks killed and wounded, 'tis amazing.'

'Will the Greeks prevail, sir?' asked Jason. Pat only stared, exhausted, and lost in his contemplation of a suitable reply.

'They have the finest of weapons – no alternative,' interjected Pickering, prompting a tired smile from his captain.

'And the wounded?' asked Pat, looking to his surgeons.

'All the Greek wounded will do well, Pat, with the blessing. I must go downstairs directly to see our own,' a deeply tired and flagging Simon replied; adding 'Pray let us hope for a sure end to this siege tomorrow.'

Pat set down his cup before replying, 'The wind is changing round to the south, which is to the Turk advantage. Khosref will

431

surely try again in the morning, and 'tis sure it will be his last shot. His troops on the cape have espied a week of failure. His attempts to bring them across have all failed with severe losses. His ships have not pressed their advantage of numbers and guns. He must know that another failure will end his prospects, and there is no purpose in waiting longer. The morning must see the end of this business. Samos will be lost or saved on the morrow, of that I have no doubt.'

On that sombre prediction, Simon and Marston left the cabin to visit the wounded, Jason with them. Pat retired to rest as best he could, yet the horror of the many casualties held sleep at bay for many hours until near the coming of dawn when exhaustion claimed him.

Tuesday 17ᵗʰ August 1824   *Colones roads*

'They are coming, sir,' remarked Pickering to Pat. On the quarterdeck all of *Surprise's* officers swept the southern approaches to the bay through their glasses. The best topmen had been aloft since before the dawn, eyes straining for the slightest glimpse of so much as a Turk corvette or brigantine. It was Khosref's full fleet approaching, and swiftly. As Pat had said the prior night, the wind now favoured the Turks, a stiff southerly speeding their approach to the bay, which would hamper the Greeks as they sought to block the Strait, for the passage of the Strait was the certain Turk objective so as to link with their troop transports in Scala Nova to the north of the Strait, and so to escort another invasion attempt.

Pat peered through his glass, studying the Turk dispositions, 'Their seventy-four and razee are approaching us directly, their frigates in the centre of their line, and the smaller brigs, brigantines and corvettes all hugging as close as they can the Turk coast again. Admiral Sakhtouri has put his Spezziots on his left wing; we are the right and the Hydriots in our centre. The Turk has the weather gauge this morning. The action will surely start swiftly. Look there. Sakhtouri has already started his fireships. It is to be hoped their captains will do their job today, for they will be of little use if the Turk passes the Strait. Mr Macleod, we will shift towards our

432

Hydriot friends. If Khosref chooses to engage with the Samos shore batteries that will serve us well. I doubt we can survive an engagement with his seventy-four.'

General firing had swiftly broken out, the Turk flagship seventy-four firing again on the shore batteries, as was the razee; all other Turk ships flying on a following wind directly towards the Strait. 'The Spezziots are heavily engaged, sir,' Pickering reported, pointing to the far left of the Greek line where the Spezziots were now intermingled with a score of Turk brigs, brigantines, and others.

Pat stared across towards them. 'Doubtless Sakhtouri spoke sharply with his captains, yesterday. They seem to have listened.'

'Look there, sir,' shouted Pickering, pointing to the middle of the battle, for it was now a general engagement as ships wheeled about in near every direction save directly to wind. 'It is the pennant of Canaris, flying again on another fireship, a Hydriot with him. Over there, near the Turk frigate: *there.*' All on the quarterdeck followed his arm, all peering through the smoke. *Surprise* approached the two Greek fireships, both of which had near succeeded in getting close enough to attach themselves to the Turk frigate.

'To your guns, gentlemen,' said Pat to Pickering and Macleod. The Turks had launched four boats to intercept the leading Greek fireship, which was fiercely ablaze, bright flames about all her sails - driven by the stiff wind, and only a score of yards away from the frigate. The Hydriots were in the process of abandoning their charge, aflame from bow to stern, but still short of the frigate, the Greeks taking to their boats and rowing with every ounce of strength they possessed; though today the wind was at least in their favour for escaping. It was Canaris's own fireship that finally attached itself alongside the Turk frigate, the fireship's flames now leaping to the Turk sails and yards, falling pitch setting small fires all about her deck as her caulking caught aflame.

Surprise herself was firing and being fired on within the general melée, her officers now concentrating on more immediate tasks as shot whistled about their heads, striking through her sails in several places, though again the Turk accuracy was woeful. On she ploughed, committed to an easterly tack, and the press of ships all about her precluding anything but the smallest of course changes, Pat and Prosser both fully engaged with their anticipation of ships passing about them and their converging approaches. Gun captains were left to fire at their own discretion, and the gunners laboured hard, both sides firing at once as *Surprise* was deeply within the mass of the Turk fleet, though the separation between *Surprise* and her enemies remained far greater than the prior day, and so casualties on *Surprise* were fortunately far less.

From his quarterdeck Pat looked about him at his men loading and firing the carronades and guns; he stepped forward and stared down into the waist, where his lieutenants, Duncan substituting for Mower, hastened up and down the gun deck, with no midshipmen to help oversee their gun crews' efforts, yet the gunners' performance was as good as ever he had seen on any ship in any engagement. The noise all about them made shouting near useless and sign language a necessity to pass any command even to the nearest man, further communication near impossible. It was difficult to follow the broad picture of events, the dense bilious smoke obscuring temporarily the view in any direction then clearing for a few moments to allow Pat a glimpse further afield to see if anything could be gleaned of the progress of the wider battle.

Three Surprises had been carried below, splinters from a Turk ball strike through the gun deck bulwark showering them as they hauled out *The Nailer* to fire again. The jibsails were reduced to near rags. The captain's barge, towed behind, had oddly received a shot and been broken in half, only the bow half still in tow. Pat looked momentarily across towards Canaris and the attached Turk frigate. The frigate blazed from stem to stern, her sails all aflame, a few men were jumping off, seeking to scramble aboard her towed boats. She was very near the shore, and as her topmast fell into the waist of the ship, sending spurts of flame soaring into the sky, scores of men could be seen leaping from her decks into the water. From her guns, still shotted, random explosions could be heard as they fired of their own accord. Suddenly, there was a huge explosion, and the frigate's hull burst asunder in a cloud of smoke and fire, simply disintegrating. Swathes of broken timber hurtled into the air amidst a vast orange sheet of flame, expanding into a glowing sphere with spars and bodies like tiny specks hurled aloft within it. As the flame subsided it was followed by thick black smoke, a huge cloud billowing up and outwith from where the frigate had last been sighted. Of the frigate herself, there was no sign left at all.

'Good God! Her magazine gone: why did they not drown it? Three hundred men killed in an instant,' whispered a shocked Pat to himself, his throat parched, and he fell into stunned silence. Several nearby Turk transports were badly damaged, such was the close press of all the ships, and parts of the debris had been hurled onto the shore of Cape San Maria, just a hundred yards or so away from where the frigate had once been, to the consternation of the watching Turk brigades there.

The explosion of the Turk frigate, audible even above the din of cannon on every ship, had brought about a shocked silence for several moments, as everyone engaged in the battle looked to see what had happened, but within minutes the general firing had resumed. Pat looked to the single ship which, by herself could win the battle, the Turk seventy-four, some three miles away and bombarding the Samiot fort, relatively newly built by Lycurgus, the Samos Primate. 'Perhaps there is a Samiot contribution after all,' mused Pat wryly, as he wiped the sweat away from his face, the day's temperatures now at their hottest and the huge clouds of powder smoke sticking to every skin surface as the wind blew the hot black particles across the deck. 'Hot work, Mr Prosser,' said Pat.

'Aye, sir; as hot as any day I ever found, and twice as busy.'

'Let her go off,' Pat bellowed, as he realised *Surprise* was nearing the Turk shore; 'Helm up!'

His command was echoed by Prosser, and, as Barton and his mates hauled down on the wheel, the Surprises hastened to pull hard on the braces and tie the yards to the new northerly course, directly for the Strait ahead, which was filled with Greeks and Turks all still firing upon each other. It was difficult to find a course which did not quickly converge with another ship, and the men at the wheel worked hard with constant small course corrections to keep her path clear. A Turk brig came near crashing into her stern, but sheered off in the last minute, steering away from her starboard side, and received three or four balls from the guns still primed. The firing now was everywhere, Turk and Greek intermingled, the endemic smoke in great clouds making it particularly difficult to distinguish friend from foe, at least until within the closest of range; only the larger Turk ships, frigates which the Greeks did not possess, being more readily identifiable in the obscured chaos. Every few minutes *Surprise* spat from her guns orange flame, black smoke and shot, canister and grape, the three broadsides within five minutes a capability long past as the sustained exertion took its toll on the strongest of gunners. FIRE! The shout reverberated again and again down the deck and about the quarterdeck. BOOM, the thud of the great guns, time after time, though few could hear anything at all at this stage, ears long pounded to temporary deafness. CRACK from the carronades, the sharper, higher-pitched sound still just audible. On several occasions Pat discerned the thud as shot struck *Surprise's* hull from afar, not penetrating; sometimes the strike produced a shower of dangerous flying splinters where it breached the gunwhale, invariably striking down two or three more of his men. Four of them worked continuously at the pumps, being relieved every twenty minutes by fresh hands as fatigue proved too much for longer spells.

The day wore on, slipping into the afternoon with no let up in the general melée. Though the Turk frigate had exploded, and the fleets had been firing on each other for many hours, neither side lacked determination to continue the fray. The powder boys of *Surprise* were flagging now, the multiple journeys to fetch powder from the magazines deep below, just above the bilges, and latterly fetching even heavy shot, which was running low on deck, had exhausted them all. In the middle of the afternoon another Greek fireship blew up a Tunisian brig, and as the sun began its slow descent towards the horizon in the late afternoon, the Greeks enjoyed a third success, the fireships blowing up a Tripolitan corvette and pursuing a frigate, which narrowly escaped.

'The fireship crews lack nothing of courage or determination today, Mr Prosser,' observed Pat, as *Surprise* slipped through the leading Turk ships and regained the Greek line. Some further hours passed with desultory firing continuing as general fatigue depleted the efforts of even the most determined of captains and crews. The sun now began to slide away into the western horizon, the diminishing light of late afternoon turning into early evening.

'The Turks are running, sir,' reported Prosser, grinning.

'So they are, Mr Prosser, so they are,' beamed Pat, amidst a dawning sense of jubilation mixed equally with relief, for it had been a hard-fought day. At no time had Pat felt assured of victory, but the Turk armada had been stopped again, and this time after near ten hours of engagement – a battle pressed determinedly by both sides - yet the Turks, for all their superiority in numbers and in gun calibres, and with the weather gauge too, had been roundly seen off with assuredly heavy casualties throughout their fleet, as well as the three ships destroyed by Greek fireships. The Greeks had lost only six burned fireships and no others, losses which were truly remarkable for such a lengthy and numerous engagement. *Surprise's* casualties were far fewer than the prior day, a near dozen wounded men, none too seriously, and Simon professed himself confident of dealing satisfactorily with them all.

As the Turks tacked south-east beyond the Cape, the Greeks let go their anchors again in Colones roads, *Surprise* anchoring near Sakhtouri's flag in the cooling dusk airs, daylight fast fading, the lights of the town twinkling brightly and reflecting on the now near still water as night approached, the wind dropping away to little more than a breeze. Pat's officers had long returned to the quarterdeck, where they stood alongside of him, everyone utterly exhausted, but blessed relief coursing through their every vein.

'Mr Macleod, we will splice the mainbrace. The lads have done well this day, and an extra tot or two is plainly deserved,' said Pat. 'My barge, Mr Pickering, if you will,' Pat asked of Pickering, still oblivious to its destruction.

'The jolly boat will have to serve, sir, as we have only half a barge since this afternoon,' Pickering replied.

'Oh, 'tis of no consequence,' said Pat, allowing nothing to dampen the rising sense of jubilation he felt within, a sentiment shared by all aboard, and all the Greeks too, as even now guns were beginning to be fired from the town in celebration, their deliverance recognised by the Samiots. It was firing that the tired men of the Greek fleet were incapable of reciprocating, as all were settling with the release of tension and the onset of deep fatigue.

Pat climbed aboard Sakhtouri's brig, and was greeted by the admiral himself, together with Admiral Canaris and a goodly number, a score or more, of Hydriot and Spezziot captains, all jubilantly grinning and chattering wildly. Sakhtouri was the first to speak, 'Well done, Captain O'Connor, well done. We did not find any moment to speak of this yesterday, but your action against the leading Turk brigs was observed by all our fleet. Your ship handling was magnificent, no less, and was the talking point of the evening.'

'Why, thank you, sir. I am very sensible of your remarks. I am sure your captains did as well. Admiral, may I congratulate you on your victory?' said Pat, offering his hand. Sakhtouri grasped it and pumped it vigorously until it pained Pat and he had to extricate it from the admiral's grasp, whence it was seized by Canaris and assaulted again, Pat enduring the painful squeeze even as he spoke, 'My compliments, sir: your fireship; that was assuredly the bravest action I have ever seen any captain undertake.'

Simon hastened below for an hour to treat the injuries of Captain Zabali, who had burned himself whilst lighting the fuses on the Hydriot fireship, attacking the Turk frigate, which Canaris had eventually exploded with his own fireship. Zouvelekis was kept busy for several hours translating the effusive thanks to Pat from all the Greek officers, thanks which they reinforced by pressing ouzo and fiery brandy into his hands and those of all his officers. Spicy foods of many varieties were brought out on to the deck, and the crew mingled with the officers until near midnight, in joyous celebration of a glorious victory, when Admiral Sakhtouri brought it to a halt with cautious words about the next day's prospects and the need to prepare for any further Turk approach, though there was now a general consensus with Pat's view that the Turks had probably had enough and would retire.

Back on *Surprise* no one felt like sleeping. The wounded were as comfortable as could be, Simon and Marston remaining below tending to them. Mower appeared to be in a stable condition, Simon more confident of his prospects than he had been the day before.

Pat sat with Duncan, Pickering, and Jason in the cabin; Zouvelekis remained onboard Sakhtouri's brig. Even as long-absent relaxation slowly seeped back into their minds, the tension of the prolonged and violent struggle fading slowly from their bodies, the adrenalin of the day ran strong still within them, and Freeman was pressed for coffee, several pots of it, as they discussed the day around Pat's table.

'I give ye joy o' yer victory, sir,' said Duncan, raising his glass, for they all clutched a well filled tumbler of brandy too.

Pat smiled at his friend and raised his own glass, sighing and looking closely at the so satisfying drink, 'Lord, how well this slips down, gentlemen. No, Duncan, it was a Greek victory: assuredly we were of help, but 'twas surely their own. All fought well today, and none hung back as they did the day before. The Greeks lacked nothing of spirit this day, and the victory will serve them well, for the battle is won, but the war continues. The Turk has been dished this day.'

'He has crossed his tiller-ropes, I dare say,' remarked Pickering, cheerfully.

'But he is not done yet. There will be more battles, of that we can be sure. I am mindful that we have yet to fight the Egyptian fleet.' Pat took a deep draught of his brandy before he spoke again. 'It is not with the first stroke that the tree falls.' He looked around his table, looking briefly to each of his officers. Even now, and despite his cautious words, the appreciation of the magnitude of their victory was still sinking in. 'Gentlemen, a toast if you will. To our Greek comrades, and let us not forget our very own; to all today on *Surprise*, to our brothers: I give you ... *our comrades and brothers.*'

'Comrades and brothers!' echoed loudly around the cabin, and their glasses were drained in one and clunked down to the table.

'Comrades and brothers,' whispered Murphy to Freeman, behind the cabin door, as he drained his own generously filled tumbler, both of them deeply pleased to hear their captain's toast.

Greek armed merchantman, mainstay of the Greek fleet   *J.J. Baugean*

ATTACK SHIPS ON FIRE
The continuing voyages of HMS SURPRISE

Chapter One

Wednesday 18th August 1824   *Colones, Samos*

The mood of the Greek gathering was strangely perplexing to all the attendees from the frigate *Surprise*. The sombre nature of their own thoughts, having lost seven of their shipmates killed and near thirty wounded in the sea battles of the immediately prior few days, contrasted starkly with the politely suppressed but still evident celebration of the local Samiot population and their Greek naval comrades in arms; Hydriots, Spezziots, and Psariots; for whom the jubilation of their sweeping and utter victory over the seaborne Turk invaders remained, burning brightly at the forefront of their thoughts. For the men of *Surprise* these happier feelings were tempered, indeed extinguished in most of them, by a deep feeling of loss, a sentiment which some could plainly not dispel and which was so visible in their grief-stricken countenances. Many other faces remained blank with a registration of shock from the climactic great battles of the recent two days, bloody battles which had undoubtedly saved Samos from sack. For most of the Surprises their emotions could be held in private check with only the greatest of difficulty; for others there were silent tears, the painful absence of their fallen comrades possessing all their thoughts, and so leaving no vestige of celebration in their troubled minds, as they stood within the gathered Greek multitude, struggling for some measure of comprehension, the scorching heat of the sun beating down upon them.

That the Turk invasion of Samos had been roundly defeated was plain to all, Khosref's fleet having departed far beyond Cape San Maria; and so the Primates of Samos, Lycurgus prominent amongst them, were holding a service of thanksgiving this day for their delivery from peril and of remembrance of the fallen.

The combined Hydriot and Spezziot naval squadrons, a few Psariot survivors amongst them, had been assisted by Captain Pat O'Connor's fifth rate, the frigate *Surprise* of 38 guns, late of Royal Navy service and presently engaged in assisting the fledgling self-declared Greek government, serving as a letter-of-marque. She was still, in secret, for such could never be revealed, *His Majesty's Hired Vessel Surprise,* and she was commissioned in her task by the British Foreign Secretary, George Canning, who was desirous of preventing the emergence of French or any other foreign influence within the nascent Greek state.

In the blistering heat of the day, with barely a breath of wind to cool the assembly and the temperature in the high eighties on the Fahrenheit scale, Pat's crew, officers and men together, only their wounded shipmates absent, stood to one side of the gathering as the remembrance service was conducted. Numerous short speeches were made, one after the other of the Samiot Primates speaking, many hundreds of onlookers present, perhaps two thousand or more, and though the words were unintelligible to the Surprises the meaning was plain to all.

Pat looked round at his men; their own natural perception of the significance of the moment and the grave weight of their burdensome thoughts preserving utter silence amongst them. His roving eyes engaged momentarily with those of several, and he nodded almost imperceptibly to each of those in turn. Clumsy Dalby, a long-serving Tenedos before the crew had switched to *Surprise* and a man who had risen inestimably in everyone's opinion after his courageous rescue of Pat's closest companion, Dr Simon Ferguson, returned his captain's nod and touched his cap.

Simon was standing alongside of Pat in silent contemplation, remembering too the death of his eminent friend, Lord Byron, many months previously.

Dalby had rescued Simon from imminent death at the hands of invading Turk berserkers on the island of Kasos, at great risk to himself and his accompanying five companions, one of whom had

2

been shot in the affray and who had been carried across the mountainous interior of the island to a small bay whence all had embarked upon *Eleanor,* a Garmouth, Geddie-built, two-masted topsail schooner which had long belonged to Pat and which served as *Surprise's* tender. Simon, however, months beforehand, had been unable to save Byron, his doctors' greatly excessive blood-letting in his fever exacerbating his decline and ultimate death; Simon's arrival at his bedside too late, and his inability to save his friend sitting ill on his mind in the subsequent months.

The Turk fleet, led by Admiral Khosref, had besieged the island of Samos for over a week, and there had been two seaborne invasions attempted from the Turk mainland port of Scala Nova on the opposite and north side of the narrow, separating strait, the Little Boghaz. The Turk warships to the south of the strait had been decoyed away from their transport charges and through the strait by the employment of a bold and risky deception of Pat's; *Surprise* presenting herself as a becalmed Greek enemy, the Turk warships pursuing her; and the Turks had thereafter been prevented from linking again with their troopships to the north by the intervention of severely bad weather with contrary winds; whilst on the more clement of days the Greek fleet, assisted by *Surprise,* had inflicted several defeats upon them, the Turks losing three ships exploded to the feared Greek *bourlotas* or fireships. The service was therefore principally one of celebration and thanksgiving for the preservation of the island, the Turks having previously sacked and burned the islands of Chios, Kasos, and Psara. In the latter two disasters, *Surprise* had also participated, though very ineffectually, she being so heavily outnumbered by the invaders and so necessarily fleeing before them.

There was a lifting of heads and a reawakening of interest in the Surprises as the next speaker came to the fore. The Psariot, Admiral Canaris it was, the hero of the recent battles, for it was Canaris aboard his own fireship who had brought the turning point of the recent battle, tying it alongside a Turk frigate which had caught fire and subsequently exploded, in plain view of all the Turk troops amassed on the mainland hillsides overlooking the strait, and who

3

had been awaiting transport across to Samos. Canaris and his men had been rescued by the Hydriot admiral, Sakhtouri, in the moments before the explosion. Sakhtouri had suffered fully one third of his crew as casualties, his brigantine near alongside Canaris's fireship, and both had been exposed to sustained firing from three Turk frigates in their approach to the target.

Captain Zouvelekis, the Kasiot who had accompanied *Surprise* as liaison officer with the Hellenic Navy since the invasion of Kasos, translated Canaris's words for Pat. The admiral spoke very slowly, his message loud to reach all of the assembled multitude, his words coming from deep within but spoken with the weariest, the most tired of voice. 'I am Canaris. I am a Psariot. My crew and I have fought to save your island this past week, and we have suffered many casualties. Many of my men have been wounded and two have died in these past days. I would ask you to remember of them, today and long in the future.' Canaris coughed to clear his throat and looked about him for several moments, gazing at the crowds of his countrymen and the Surprises at his side before he resumed, 'Georgios Tsabralis and Ioannis Mavrogiannis came with me, from Odessa, when we heard of the revolution. They came to serve their fellow Greek countrymen, and in so doing they have lost their lives; as have many others from Psara. For too long there has been bad blood between our two islands. That can no longer be ... for not a one in that place ... my home ... has survived the Turk invasion. From my own family my aunt alone escaped ... by swimming out two miles into the sea before she was rescued with a very few others. The living of Psara are now Turk slaves and will be so until their death; bereft of that freedom which we all here, and our compatriots throughout all of Greece, so strive for.'

Canaris looked up again and all about him before raising his voice, which had begun to tremble and falter as he spoke of his aunt, 'We are all of us, all here on this day, no longer Samiots, nor Psariots; we are not Hydriots or Spezziots; for we are now, all of us, *Greeks*.'

Canaris ended his speech to huge applause from the assembly, which quieted only slowly and that after several minutes of

4

exuberant and vociferous endorsement of Canaris's sentiments, as Lycurgus, the Magistrate, stepped to the fore and waved both hands in appeal for silence. 'Thank you, Admiral Canaris. We thank you and your men for your valiant struggle against the Turk tyrant. All of us, all Samiots ... all *Greeks*, thank you and your men for your sacrifice. We thank too our brothers from Hydra and from Spetzes, from Psara too.' Lycurgus turned to face the Surprises, 'We also thank our English friends. All of Greece is in your debt this day. Thank you. Thank you, from all of us.'

A great futher cheer erupted after this from the jubilant throng, continuing with great gusto, minutes passing as the Surprises gazed about them in bewildered silence; that they were the recipients of such sustained cheering registering only slowly with them.

A further hour passed by, all still standing in the blistering heat; deep fatigue the feeling common to them all, before the service came to its end and the Surprises shuffled off, back to Colones port for their return to *Surprise*; Pat taking his leave of Canaris and Sakhtouri before joining his men. Zouvelekis elected to remain with his senior naval compatriots for the remainder of the day. Pat had no immediate plans save that his own dead comrades would be buried at sea next day, as was the custom, the delay in doing so in such fierce heat only countenanced by his perceived obligation to attend the Greek service. The bodies of his men were wrapped in sailcloth and lying in the only very slightly cooler hold of the ship. He walked in silence alongside his men towards the quay, his head down, his mind deep in thought.

'Is there something troubling you, soul?' asked Simon, observing his friend closely.

'Eh? Oh, my mind is turned elsewhere; 'tis the strangest of days, Simon. Our Greek friends all in good heart but we are yet even to bury our six lads. And what are we to do with our wounded? Though the Turk be dished, we ain't seen the Egyptian fleet since we fled from Kasos, and surely they will be back; of that I have no doubt. Should we put our lads ashore, and who will care for them? Yet we cannot sail lest I put them off. 'Tis a damn pickle and no answer can I find.'

5

Simon halted on the dusty track and clutched Pat's arm, 'Pat, take heart, brother. I will tell you this – we will lose no more of those men. They will be shifted to *Eleanor*, and Marston will stay with them. Young Mr Reeve will return to Argostoli where there is no want of help in that place for them. Sinéad, Kathleen, and the bairns will tend to them with Marston. There is no doubt of that.'

'Thankee, Simon. Why I believe that would answer,' Pat murmured, very quietly, his eyes moist; his friends watching him closely and observing the deep lines of strain on his face.

Lieutenant Duncan Macleod, Pat's first lieutenant, interjected, 'Ah cannae imagine we will be long in this place wi' the damage to *Surprise* so very severe. The cabin lights are all shot oot an' we cannae properly repair the twae shot holes in her hull withoot she comes oot o' the watter. Will ye consider o' goin' hame, Pat?'

'I should like it of all things. With so many wounded we have a want of men, and to be sure *Surprise* is in need of repair and that cannot be done here. The campaign for this year will close when the Turk ships quit after the autumn. We will be home this winter; I have no doubt. Another month, I doubt it will be more, and we will haul our cable.'

Enjoy Book Two in this series:

ATTACK SHIPS ON FIRE   *Available in 2015.*

The combined Turk and Egyptian fleet returns to try again to capture Samos, resulting in the great battle of Gerontas; *HMS Surprise* is caught in the Great Tempest; the island of Sphacteria is attacked and lost, *HMS Surprise* rescues survivors, Mavrocordato escapes from the invaders at the last moment; Alexandria is attacked by fireships.

Buy Alan Lawrence's books from: www.mainsailvoyagespress.com

GLOSSARY, for pressed shipmates

Bargeman	weevil (usually in the bread and biscuit)
Blunties	Old Scots term for stupid fellows
Boggies	Irish country folk
Bombard	Mediterranean two-masted vessel, ketch
Bower	bow anchor
Breeks	Scots term for trousers or breeches
Browster wives	Scots Browster (from Brewster), ale wives
Bumbo	'pirates' drink; rum, water, sugar, and nutmeg
Burgoo	oatmeal porridge
Capperbar	theft of ship's stores
Captains' Thins	Carr's water crackers, a 'refined ship's biscuit'
Clegs	Scots term for large, biting flies
Coddle	Irish broiled sausages with leftover vegetables
Crabbit	bad tempered
Crubeens	boiled pig's feet
Dreich and Drookit	Old Scots for cold, wet, miserable weather; drenched
Etesian	strong, dry, summer, Aegean north winds
Farl	Irish soft quick bread, like soda bread
Felucca	small sailing boat, one or two sails of lateen rig
Fencibles	the Sea Fencibles, a naval 'home guard' militia
'Forty Thieves'	RN 'Vengeur' class, with construction shortcomings
Flux	inflammatory dysentery
Froward	awkward, difficult to deal with
Golden Horn	the harbour of Constantinople (Istanbul today)
Gomerel	a stupid or foolish person
The Groyne	La Coruña in north-west Spain
Hallion	a scoundrel
Hazing (and Starting)	officers would start or haze slow sailors with canes
Hoy	small (e.g. London-Margate passengers) vessel
Jollies	Royal Marines
Kedgeree	a dish of flaked fish, rice and eggs
Laidron	rascal
Laudanum	a liquid opiate, used for medicinal purposes
Lobscouse	beef stew, north German in origin
Marchpane	marzipan
Meltemi	Greek and Turkish name for the Etesian wind
Millers	shipboard rats
Mistico	similar to the Felucca sailing vessel
Scrovies	worthless, pressed men
Seventy-four / 74	a 74 gun ship, mainstay of the RN fleet
Skillygalee	watery oatmeal pastry fried in pork fat (dripping)
Solomongundy	a stew of leftover meats
Snotties	midshipmen
Stingo	strong ale
Stirabout	oatmeal porridge
Treacle-dowdy	a covered pudding of treacle and fruit
The Marshalsea	19th century London debtors' prison
Trubs	truffles
Yellow jack	Yellow fever (or flag signifying outbreak)
Yellowed	admiral with no sea command (yellow pennant)